Inherent Fate

Book Three in The Crisanta Knight Series

GEANNA CULBERTSON

BQB

Virginia

Crisanta Knight: Inherent Fate
© 2017 Geanna Culbertson. All rights reserved.

Published in the United States by BQB Publishing
(an imprint of Boutique of Quality Books Publishing Company)
www.bqbpublishing.com

978-1-945448-06-5 (p)
978-1-945448-07-2 (e)

Library of Congress Control Number: 2017939420

Book design by Robin Krauss, www.bookformatters.com
Cover concept by Geanna Culbertson
Cover design by Ellis Dixon, www.ellisdixon.com

First editor: Pearlie Tan
Second editor: Olivia Swenson

Books in The Crisanta Knight Series

Dedicated To:

This book, like everything I shall ever accomplish, is dedicated to my mom and dad. You are my heroes, my coaches, my best friends, and I am thankful for you every day for more reasons than there are words in this book.

Special Thanks To:

Terri Leidich & BQB Publishing

Of all the Inherent Fates out there that could have been my path, I am so glad each day that my choices led me to you. To be a part of the BQB family and under your guidance is an unparalleled blessing. And I have no doubt that together we are going to go very far and achieve something great.

Pearlie Tan

I know I tell you you're awesome all the time. But for the sake of consistency, I'll say it again. You're awesome, Pearlie! Thanks for pushing me to be the best writer I can be!

Olivia Swenson

Thank you for keeping me sharp and helping Book Three be the best that it can be.

Alexa Carter

Because she's awesome.

I also want to thank Gallien Culbertson, Ian Culbertson, the Fine Family, Girls on the Run Los Angeles, John Daly, Ellis Dixon, Kathie Bennett, the SMB team, Erin McCarthy, George Wissa, and everyone else out there who's supported me on this journey thus far!

Bonus Dedication

Since this is going to be an eight-book series, each book will issue a bonus dedication to individuals who have significantly impacted my life or this series in some way.

For this third book, I want to honor someone special who is gone, but never forgotten—Ana Gamboa. This woman was my aunt. She was also a beloved mother, sister, wife, friend, grandmother, and godmother who brought joy and warmth to all those around her. She was taken from us far too soon and nothing and no one can ever make that right. But we carry her with us every day and try to do goodness in her name. We remember her laughter, her kindness, and the light she brought into the world. And we promise to always carry her spirit forward.

PROLOGUE

This is a story about character.

In the enchanted realm of Book, the word "character" is commonly used to describe people. It helps classify us into groups and stereotypes. As in, "what type of character are you?" A main character? An ensemble character? A villainous character?

What is less normal in my world is placing emphasis on the other definition of the word "character." The meaning that pertains to the unique moral, mental, and emotional attitudes that make an individual something more than a group or a stereotype.

My story is about this kind of character. Or rather, the forging of it.

Unfortunately, Book is not a place where taking charge of one's character is encouraged. In fact, those in command of my realm have consistently done everything in their power to make sure my character is out of my control.

Book is controlled by several entities—the Fairy Godmothers (headed by the Godmother Supreme, Lena Lenore), the rulers and ambassadors of each kingdom, and the Author. While I have issues with all three, the Author has the greatest impact on our lives.

The Author is a prophet who lives in an off-limits part of Book called the Indexlands. By writing protagonist books that are sent to the Fairy Godmothers, she decides who in the realm is meant to be a protagonist and who is meant to be a "common" ensemble character. If you are one of the latter, you're not expected—nor allowed—to reach for the extraordinary. Meanwhile, if you're assigned to be a main character you attend one of our realm's two private schools—Lady Agnue's School for Princesses & Other Female Protagonists or Lord Channing's School for Princes & Other Young Heroes.

To some, a protagonist private school might seem like a sweet deal. But like all good things, the main character role comes with a cost. As the daughter of Cinderella, I have been paying that cost since before I could say "glass slipper."

Whether you're a hero, princess, or any other type of protagonist, as a main character you're expected to live up to your traditional archetype. For a princess, that means pretty dresses, delicate, damsel behavior, and a fate that places more emphasis on your future prince charming than your own ambitions.

Lady Agnue's and Lord Channing's hammer these roles into their students from the moment we walk through their gilded entrances. However, the brainwashing starts sooner for some than for others. According to custom, all princes and princesses are supposed to be protagonists—our protagonist books appear when we're born. Because of this, all princes and princesses start school at the age of ten. "Common protagonists" (protagonists without a royal pedigree) start school when/if their protagonist books emerge, usually in childhood or early puberty. For example, my friend Blue (the younger sister of the famous Red from *Little Red Riding Hood*) enrolled at Lady Agnue's when her book appeared at the age of twelve.

That's how the Author lets our realm know which children will be main characters. She creates actual books with people's names on them (i.e. *Hansel & Gretel*, *Snow White*, etc.). She keeps one copy for herself to continuously fill in with our stories and futures and teleports a second copy to the most high-level and powerful Fairy Godmothers, the Scribes, to share with the realm and the schools.

We have no say in what the Author will pen for our fates and are bound by her words. This always begins with a prologue prophecy.

A prologue prophecy is a summary of a protagonist's fate presented in the form of vague, rhyming lines that appear in our books, which often read like riddles. Sadly, when my prologue prophecy appeared it was not vague, and the only riddle was how I would get out of it.

My prologue prophecy dictated quite plainly that I would become a typical damsel princess who would marry Chance Darling—a prince who attended Lord Channing's and who was as handsome as he was obnoxious (very on both counts).

I was already pretty gung-ho against living a life bound by the Author's chains, but something snapped inside of me when I was told my prologue prophecy. It awoke the boldest, bravest, and arguably craziest part of my spirit that believed I did not have to accept limits just because someone more powerful said so.

I convinced my friends of the same thing. All of them except for SJ (daughter of Snow White) had already received their prologue prophecies, and while I didn't know exactly what was written for my friends, I knew none of them were happy with their fates.

And so—as the story goes—our adventure began. We all wanted to take back our lives, so we left our schools to find the Author and get her to change the fates she'd written for us.

In order to reach the Author we would have to break the powerful In and Out Spell that protected the Indexlands. This type of spell keeps people—and sometimes creatures—from crossing through the borders that the spell protects. There are four In and Out Spells in Book. The first is the powerful version that protects the Author's domain. A way stronger one encompasses all of Book, separating us from other realms. And there are two slightly weaker versions—one over Lady Agnue's, and one over the antagonist-only kingdom of Alderon.

Alderon's In and Out Spell, though, is a little different from the others. It is only half an In and Out Spell, meaning you can cross in, but you can't get out. The reason for this is that every time monsters or antagonists are captured, they are transported to Alderon to serve an indefinite sentence—ridding our realm of their evil once and for all. Or at least that's what's supposed to happen. Recently I've found some "holes" in this idea . . .

Like the others, that mighty In and Out Spell around the Indexlands was cast long ago through the combined strength of many Fairy Godmothers. As a result, Godmothers were the only ones who knew how to break it.

That's where Emma (my mother's former Fairy Godmother and my own regular godmother) came into play. Long expelled from the Fairy Godmother Agency for going against Lena Lenore's rigid rules and beliefs, Emma had been living in exile for a decade when we found her. She told us that the secret to breaking the In and Out Spell was combining three ingredients—a Quill with the Might of Twenty-Six Swords (Something Strong), the Heart of the Lost Princess (Something Pure), and a Mysterious Flower Beneath the Valley of Strife (Something One of a Kind).

To this end, we'd acquired the quill that our realm's twenty-six ambassadors used to sign their biannual treaty to fulfill our "Something Strong." Then we'd travelled to Earth to find Ashlyn—the long-lost daughter of the Little Mermaid—for our "Something Pure," which turned out to be a heart-shaped locket that held a picture of her husband and children.

Now all we had to find was "Something One of a Kind." This would be difficult, not just because of the shenanigans involved with obtaining the Mysterious Flower Beneath the Valley of Strife, but because of me. To be specific, the many entities trying to kill me.

I'd almost been destroyed so many times in the last few weeks that I'd lost count. Yes, some of these cases had been the result of run-ins with monsters, like this one dragon that had been stalking us since Century City. But the majority of my mortal peril had been at the hand of a boy called Arian.

I'd first run into Arian in Century City. It was there that he introduced himself as the head of a team of antagonists who hunted down protagonists with prologue prophecies that posed a threat to his people.

In Arian's secret bunker beneath the Capitol Building we'd discovered files on many protagonists, some of whom we knew. My friends Blue and Jason (the younger brother to Jack from *Jack & the Beanstalk*), and Daniel (the fifth member of our group) had files that labeled them each as a "possible threat." SJ, meanwhile, didn't have a file at all, whereas our friend Mark had one marked "threat neutralized," which had us very worried.

The other important folder we'd found had been labeled "Priority Elimination." There were three names in that folder. The first was Paige Tomkins—a former Fairy Godmother and friend of Emma's who'd gone missing long ago. The second was a girl named Natalie Poole. Natalie was from Earth and, along with Arian, was a recurring character in my dreams of the future.

Did I mention I have dreams of the future? Well, I do. Don't know why. But it's been happening since I was little and lately they've been getting stronger.

I'd foreseen Natalie happy during her younger years, but miserable in her teens. Recently I'd learned that this misery was the result of Arian's plotting. The antagonists aimed to open something called the Eternity Gate on Natalie's twenty-first birthday by manipulating her relationship with the boy she was destined to love, Ryan Jackson. I wish I could tell you more, but past that I had more questions than answers regarding Natalie.

Back to Arian's bunker, the last name on the "Priority Elimination" list was mine. I guess that explains why I'd nearly been killed so many times recently. Arian and his goons had been trying to off me since we left Lady Agnue's because he claimed my prologue prophecy was not what it seemed.

This was inconvenient, naturally. But the aspect that got under my skin the most was how much danger it brought to my friends. I wasn't sure what I hated more, putting them in peril or

CRISANTA KNIGHT - INHERENT FATE

the fact that I couldn't protect them despite all the advantages at my disposal.

When I was younger, Emma had imbued me with a spark of Fairy Godmother magic that was supposed to develop into a unique power. I had a trusty magic wand that was enchanted to transform into any weapon I willed it into. And I trained myself to have combat skills that would make Mulan feel self-conscious.

Alas, while I had magic, I didn't know what my power was or how to operate it, making it useless to me. My wand was awesome and versatile, but one weapon against the dozen or more belonging to the men Arian kept sending after me did not yield the best odds. And although I could fight, these skills didn't make me invincible or keep me out of harm's way.

Past all that, I think my greatest strength that had yet to make a difference in my fight against villainy was my character.

Up 'til now I'd let the greater world dictate and dampen it. Despite my desire and efforts to forge my own path, I'd allowed the world to convince me that I had no control over who I was. As a result, I'd spent a lot of time feeling insecure, denying my fears, and pushing away my friends to an extent that hindered us all.

But I was determined to change that.

Although the Author, my school, and the realm's higher-ups may have had an influence on my life, when it came to me they didn't get a vote. At the end of the day their opinions did not define me. I did.

This was a great revelation, and one I needed to have. Nevertheless, I was not at peace yet. For I was now experiencing an unexpected slew of indecisiveness in regards to one question.

How exactly *did* I define myself?

I definitely wanted to be a great hero and a great princess— that desire had burned inside of me for so long it was a wonder my heart wasn't charred—but I didn't fit with our realm's traditional definition of either archetype.

Princesses were supposed to be elegant ladies who got swept

off their feet at balls, wore glittering jewels, and embodied the softhearted, merciful air that women are conventionally expected to emulate. Meanwhile, heroes were unshakable warriors known for their fearlessness, physical strength, and lack of weakness.

I was not on board with either definition. Jewels were great, but I didn't wish to have a demure, ladylike personality that sparkled less than they did. And fighting off foes with impervious physical strength sounded awesome, but that wasn't me either. I loved combat and wanted to be strong enough to defeat my enemies. But I'd learned that ignoring weaknesses and carrying on like you were invincible was as reckless as it was idiotic.

No, as it stood, neither of those roles suited me. Which brings us to where I am now. As I prepared to face the obstacles ahead, I understood that I lacked the ability to do the one thing I'd been fighting my entire life to do. I couldn't answer the question bouncing around inside my head:

Who the heck am I?

CHAPTER 1

The Survey

"**H**it the deck!" I yelled, pushing Daniel out of the way.

Shield, I commanded my wand.

My trusty weapon expanded in the blink of an eye. Daniel and I crashed onto the purple carpet as I raised my shield to shelter us from the splattering explosion.

We'd been trapped in Aladdin's genie lamp for a few hours and had been desperately trying to figure out how to escape. Evidently the thing wasn't only for capturing genies. When the lid was open, the lamp locked onto the nearest magical creature within fifteen feet and then absorbed it (and anyone holding on to it) inside.

In this particular case the magical creature had been me and the person I'd dragged down was Daniel, who'd tried to save me.

After poking around inside, Daniel had found a journal that the genie used to catalogue his ideas for escape. Since then we'd been ardently going through one idea after another trying to bust out.

So far we'd been unsuccessful, but we were not about to give up. The genie lamp was in Arian's possession and it was only a matter of time before he arrived in Alderon and delivered me to Nadia, queen of the antagonists.

Small clouds of smoke erupted from the lamp's lid where we'd applied the explosive goop we'd concocted, but not much else happened. I coughed as Daniel and I got to our feet.

"So much for idea number 3,774," Daniel commented as he wiped dust bunnies from his leather jacket.

I transformed my shield back to its wand form and shoved it in my boot. As I straightened my dress and dusted off some purple carpet hairs, Daniel picked up the genie's journal from the coffee table and scratched an X across the page we'd been working from.

I huffed in frustration. This was getting tiresome and I was getting worried. Aside from needing to escape Arian's clutches, the longer we went without knowing what happened to SJ, Blue, and Jason, the more anxious I became.

Arian had been after me; he got Daniel as a bonus. The rest of my friends had been in the clear when I'd split from them, which was good. But not knowing where they were bothered me. It wasn't because I didn't think we could find them. We'd all been on our way to retrieve the third item on our list to break the In and Out Spell, so I had a solid idea of where they were headed. The reason I felt anxious was because I was upset about how I'd left things with them.

Over the last few weeks I'd been pushing them away, lying to them, and not trusting them. I regretted my behavior and yearned for the chance to tell them so. The thought that we might not be able to escape this lamp and they might never know that made me feel afraid. I was worried about dying, sure. But that was a fate I still believed I could avoid. The deterioration of my friendships was not. After all I'd done I wasn't sure if I could stop it.

I shook my head, refusing to let my spirits dampen. Right now I needed fire. And speaking of fire . . .

I jumped back as a few sparks erupted from the goop we'd smeared on the lamp lid.

While every escape idea we'd tried had gone up in smoke (quite literally, in this case), I was thankful we had a stash of materials to work with. We'd found an array of ingredients to use that would have made SJ (our group's resident potions genius) jump for joy.

Initially Daniel and I presumed the lamp's interior was limited to the tacky, colorful lounge we were presently in. However, thanks to the genie's journal, we located a hidden hatch in the floor, which revealed a flight of stairs that led to several more rooms. I didn't know how this lamp allowed for that structurally, but I figured magical architecture played by its own rules.

The lower chambers of the lamp featured massive white rooms full of random junk—colorful slides, a pool filled with glowing green sharks, miniature models of cities, and most importantly, a fully-stocked silver kitchen.

The countertops contained various potion-making appa-ratuses, like mortar dishes and glass beakers. Alongside the equipment was an assortment of ingredients—everything from possum urine to eggplant skins. The genie must've been in the middle of concocting some kind of escape potion when the chain of events that set him free were put in motion.

Daniel and I were grateful for this. Had this not been the case the two of us probably wouldn't have any potion-making ingredients to work with. Even though he couldn't escape, it seemed the genie's all-powerful magic had allowed him to simply poof up anything he wanted. It was the only explanation for all the stuff down there.

"Let me see the journal again," I said to Daniel.

He handed me the book. I moved under one of the lounge's luminescent floating crystal balls to have more light.

Different colored sticky notes protruded from the book corresponding to different kinds of entries. The red ones meant avoid at all costs. The blue were general observations concerning the lamp's structure. And the green sticky notes flagged haikus that the genie had written to encapsulate his feelings on that particular day. My particular feelings about them were:

Much profanity.

This hurts my eyes like onions.

Dude's got no talent.

Coming upon one of the blue sticky notes toward the middle of the book, my eyebrows shot up. Then I read the words again to be sure before looking up at Daniel.

"Hey, I think I might actually have something here," I said. "According to this, the lamp's interior was forged in the blood of something called a Stiltdegarth—a creature that has magic-cancelling and magic-reversing abilities. That explains why the genie could use his magic within the lamp but couldn't use it to get out. The lamp's walls are specifically designed to cancel out magic. Anything trapped in here can't use magic to break through."

"How does that help?" Daniel asked. "Even if you knew what your magical ability was, that just means the thing that's supposed to give you power can't do anything to aid in our escape."

"Please, Daniel. My magic doesn't give me my power. I like to think that derives from my boldness, creativity, and wit."

"Don't forget your humility."

I rolled my eyes.

"My point is that there's a note in here that says that while Stiltdegarth blood coats the *inside* of the lamp, the lamp's *outsides* are made from ordinary metal. So although these walls cancel out the force of internal magic—"

"There's nothing working to cancel out the effects of *external* magic," Daniel finished. I saw the spark of an idea flicker in his dark eyes. "So in theory . . . if someone or something used their magic on the outside they could free someone trapped within the lamp?"

"Exactly," I affirmed. "Like plan number 1,083." I pointed to the page beside the sticky note. It had a star drawn in the upper right-hand corner, which I recalled seeing on other pages. I began flipping through the book, searching for pages that were also marked with stars.

"And plan numbers 2,016, 2,310, and 2,812, and so on." I

stopped there and read from an entry beside one of the crossed-out ideas.

"It's late August. I have just finished serving a rapscallion by the name of Darralind. Between granting his wishes I attempted (yet again) to find another source of powerful magic to free me from this prison from the outside. But (yet again) I have failed. The hands of my fellow genies are tied, as they are all either trapped within their own lamps or have their magic bound to serving whomever it was that let them out. That only leaves witches and Fairy Godmothers. Most witches are locked in Alderon, but even the ones that aren't have corrupted hearts, so I doubt they'd help me. And Fairy Godmothers love order far too much to take mercy on me. They would never risk upsetting their precious fairytale norms. As a result, I must try to find another means of escape."

I looked up from the book, grinning.

"This is our way out of here," I said excitedly. "Don't you see? We just need Fairy Godmother magic."

"Knight, we went over this," Daniel interjected. "Your powers are no good here. You can't exactly throw your own magic the way a person throws their voice."

"I don't have to," I replied slyly. "And we don't need anyone else for this plan to work either. I have everything we need right here."

I picked up my satchel from one of the chrome tables in the room. The trusty old bag was still soggy, having recently been dragged through ocean currents and submerged caverns. But I was confident that the item I sought inside was still in pristine condition.

"Ah, here we go."

I met Daniel's eyes in the reflection of one of the wall's silver-and-gold mirrors. The green light of the table's candelabra made my smile look more devious than I intended and caused my green eyes to appear mystifyingly viridescent.

I presented Daniel with the envelope I'd taken from the bag. It was still in perfect condition—not a crinkle or tear in sight.

"Magic paper," I explained in response to Daniel's confused expression. "It's incapable of getting ruined."

"Sure, why not." Daniel rolled his eyes. "That still doesn't tell me how it's supposed to help us."

"Then allow me," I said as I took the envelope back from him. "Remember that night we were in Adelaide bent on breaking into Fairy Godmother Headquarters? The Godmother who was assigned to me, Debbie Nightengale, gave this to me. It's a survey to evaluate her performance. She said I wouldn't be able to lose it until I filled it out and signed it. Since she didn't give me any other instructions, it's plausible that this thing is enchanted to poof back to her when I'm finished with it. Meaning—"

"Meaning that if you sign it while we're in here, whatever Fairy Godmother magic that's supposed to poof it back to her might be able to take us with it?"

"In theory."

"Well then what are you waiting for, Knight?" Daniel grabbed a quill and passed it to me. "Sign the thing."

"All right, all right," I said.

I glanced at the envelope hesitantly.

"What's wrong?" Daniel asked.

"Nothing," I replied quickly. After looking over the rectangle of paper, I identified an overlap and carefully tried to separate the two pieces without harming the document. Alas, I started tearing the envelope.

"You're ripping it," Daniel protested, snatching it away from me.

I folded my arms defensively. "I've never been good with envelopes, okay? Princesses don't exactly get a lot of mail, and SJ's bird friends send messages for us via scroll if we need anything."

Daniel stared at me and I felt my shoulders curve in embarrassment.

"What?" I rubbed my arm sheepishly.

"Nothing," Daniel replied. "Sometimes I can't believe your life is so ridiculous."

"Well, I'm sorry we can't all be cool and collected lone wolves with leather jackets, Daniel. Being a princess has its quirks. Deal with it."

Daniel smirked at me. He reached into his jacket and removed a small pocketknife. He flipped it open and used the blade to cleanly open the envelope.

"Here," he said, handing it back to me.

"Thank you," I responded dryly.

For a moment I paused—looking at the envelope but thinking of him. Aside from some light snarkiness (which to me was like breathing), this was the longest Daniel and I had ever gone without arguing.

Our formerly tense relationship had recently reached an unexpected climax. For the first time we'd been honest with each other and let ourselves be truly vulnerable about a lot of important, personal things.

For me, that meant owning up to my fears, admitting my innermost doubts and dreams, and reaching the conclusion that I would no longer allow other people's views to define me.

For Daniel, that meant telling me the truth about his prologue prophecy. And as uncomfortable as my truths had been to face, his were way worse.

Apparently the reason he wanted the Author to rewrite his fate was because his prologue prophecy indicated he might not end up with his true love, a girl from Century City called Kai.

Worse still? His prologue suggested that while I was to be a key ally to them both, Kai might come to a very permanent end because of me.

Obviously, this made things terribly awkward between us.

So while Daniel and I were attempting to give friendship and trusting each other a shot, I knew the odds of long-term success were very low. Right now we were treading lightly and things were going fine. But I was aware of how fragile this connection was. As much as he and I had the potential to get along well, I couldn't imagine any guy who would ever truly trust the person with the potential to bring down his true love.

"Knight," Daniel said, calling me out of my space-out.

"Right," I said sheepishly.

Refocusing my attention, I opened the envelope. Inside I found a faintly glowing piece of parchment with six questions written on it. Hurriedly I filled out the questionnaire, giving Debbie five out of five stars in each category. Since this survey might be our only chance of escape, I'd say she certainly deserved them.

I reached the bottom of the form and saw the signature line. Below it—sure enough—was a short note beside an asterisk.

Fairy Godmother Headquarters thanks you for taking the time to fill out this survey. Please sign the document and it will be magically teleported to the designated Godmother. Your feedback is important to us.

"You were right," Daniel said. "It's enchanted to go back to where it came from."

I gripped the paper tightly in my left hand. This was it.

"Grab on to me," I told Daniel. "This could get rough."

He tightened the strap of his sword sheath across his shoulder then took hold of my arm. His grip was firm and warm. Even through the sleeves of my dress I could feel the roughness of his hands, callused from a combination of his hero training at Lord Channing's and also, I suspected, from his life as a working-class common before being chosen as a protagonist by the Author a few months ago.

"Here we go," I said. With a deep breath I signed my name on the document.

Oh please let this work, I thought as I dotted the many i's and crossed the many t's in my full name—Crisanta Katherine Knight.

As I added the final curl to my last name, I sort of expected there to be a delay before the magic kicked in. There wasn't. The moment I finished, the paper morphed into a new envelope. It immediately began to glow bright red and tried to free itself from my firm grasp, jerking about like a wild cat. I refused to loosen my hold. After a few seconds it stopped fighting and I felt its red glow spreading over me and Daniel.

My skin vibrated as the two of us were absorbed within the magic shell. My ears hummed. Suddenly I felt like I couldn't breathe, as if the glow was sucking the oxygen from my body like a giant flame. Then just as I thought I might pass out, everything was stripped away and replaced by a scarlet flash that blinded me before consuming us.

CHAPTER 2

My Fairy Godmother Teaches Me How to Accessorize

hen I opened my eyes I discovered that the tacky décor of the genie lamp lounge was gone. Our new setting was a sparkly punch in the face.

We must be at Fairy Godmother Headquarters. What other place would have so much glitter?

Shimmering swirls decorated the walls. Crystal light fixtures in the shape of erupting fireworks hung from above. The carpet was white and matched the desk and filing cabinets; it also seemed to sparkle, like the dust trapped within the fibers was enchanted.

Everything glistened except a black orb protruding from the wall in the upper left-hand corner of the room. It was about the size of a cereal bowl and reminded me of the lone eye of a Cyclops, complete with a tiny red pupil blinking at me in the center.

"It worked!" Daniel's voice was high in amazement.

It hit me. My face broke into a grin. We were out of the genie lamp. We were free and as far away from Arian and Nadia's reach as possible.

I let go of the envelope (still wriggling in my hand) and excitedly whirled around to face him. "We did it!" I exclaimed. I literally jumped with joy and hugged Daniel.

Hold on a sec.

Am I hugging Daniel?

Abort! Abort!

Daniel noticed the mistake at the same time and the two of us quickly pulled apart.

"Uh, good work, Knight," Daniel said gruffly as he extended his hand.

"Uh, yeah. You too," I replied self-consciously while I shook it.

"Crisa?" squeaked a timid, high-pitched voice.

I spun around. The envelope had floated into a silver tray on the desk across the room. Next to the tray was a nameplate that read: *Debbie Nightengale—Trainee*. Behind the tray I spotted red hair and big blue eyes peeking out from behind the desk.

"Debbie?"

"Crisa!" Debbie popped up from her hiding place like a piece of toast from a toaster, the confusion in her eyes replaced with delight. Her bright red ponytail bounced around her shoulders, sparkly hairpins catching the light.

The last time I'd seen my Fairy Godmother she'd been wearing a dress that looked like it was made of lightning strikes. Today her gown emulated a tsunami. It was floor-length, each ruffled layer a different shade of dark blue or gray that appeared to be rippling. The colors crashed against each other, producing fabric creases that were sparkly white and reminded me of sea foam. Watching it made me dizzy, as did the tackle hug that Debbie gave me in the next instant.

"Oh my gosh! What are you doing here?" she exclaimed. "It's so amazing to see you! Sorry about hiding." She waved at her desk. "The bright red flash freaked me out. But thanks for finally filling out the survey!" Debbie smiled as she gestured to the envelope in her inbox. When she pivoted back around she finally noticed Daniel. "Who's this?"

"Oh sorry, Debbie. This is Daniel my, uh, friend?"

I glanced at Daniel for affirmation and he shrugged his approval.

All right, I guess that's a thing.

Debbie looked Daniel up and down and scrunched her nose. "You're tall."

"Um, thank you," he replied.

"Anywho," Debbie said as she stepped back and tilted her head at me with an appraising look. "You know I'm always happy to see one of my Godkids, Crisa. But, um, regular people are kind of forbidden from setting foot on official Godmother premises. I got in major trouble six weeks ago for inadvertently contributing to you breaking in here. Like, seriously. I lost my wand privileges for a week and had to clean Pegasus stables by hand as punishment."

I cringed. "Oh, I'm sorry, Debbie. I didn't think they'd actually—"

"Relax," Debbie interrupted, her mood swinging back unexpectedly. "I'm totally over it. I'm more interested in what you're doing here now. That survey didn't exactly require hand delivery, so I assume the reason you followed it was worth risking another round of the Godmother Supreme's wrath."

Daniel shrugged. "Long story short: we were trapped in Aladdin's genie lamp."

Debbie shivered like a child thinking about getting a shot or eating broccoli without butter. "Oh, that is so not awesome. I hate those tricky, icky things. Smart thinking using the letter to escape. External magic cancelling out internal magic—classic fairytale loophole."

"Yeah, it was pretty lucky that Knight shoved your survey into that old bag that never leaves her side," Daniel added. He paused and looked over at me. "Until now that is."

"Hold on. What?"

I checked myself and discovered Daniel was right. I had forgotten to grab my satchel before signing the survey. My wand was in my boot, but its trusty carrying case was trapped somewhere far away within the lamp.

"I can't believe I left it! Now what am I supposed to carry my wand around in? The thing's barely been in my boot five minutes and I already feel a dent in my calf."

I sighed and pulled my wand from my boot. There was nothing else of particular value in the bag, but I'd had it for an eternity. It's what I'd been storing my wand in for years.

Debbie's mouth hung agape. "You have a wand," she gasped. She flicked her eyes to the black orb in the corner of the room for a moment with a touch of panic in her expression.

"Yeah, about that . . ." I responded. "It's also kind of a long story."

"And I'm also *kind of* intrigued," Debbie said. "Tell. Me. Everything."

"Deb, I don't know if I—"

"Come on," she insisted. "You've already shown it to me. You can't change that. And I promise that anything you say will stay between us; it's the Fairy Godmother–Fairy Godkid code of silence. Plus, you did trick me last time we met so you could get up here. Wouldn't you say you at least owe me this in return for all the heat I took on your behalf?"

"I thought you were totally over that?"

"I am, but that doesn't mean I shouldn't be able to cash it in as a solid you-owe-me." Debbie smiled sweetly.

Feeling unsure, I looked to Daniel. He nodded, giving me the go-ahead to do whatever I thought best. I conceded to going along with Debbie's request and telling her what she wanted to know. After all, I was giving the whole "being completely honest and trusting people" thing a shot, wasn't I?

For the next few minutes I explained to Debbie the details about our visit to Emma, her gift of my wand and the resulting mysterious magical power that accompanied it, and even the painful hand-burning episodes I suffered from when I went too long without expelling magic (i.e. Magic Build-Up).

When I finished, Debbie bit her lip.

"Hold on," she said slowly. "There's one thing I need to clarify."

"Okay, shoot."

"Are you telling me—in all seriousness—that the reason you'd been carrying around that disgusting satchel was so you could have a convenient way to transport your wand?"

"It wasn't disgusting," I muttered.

"Honey, do you see what I've got on?" Debbie pointed to her flowing, majestic dress. "Trust me, I know the difference between cute and gross. I saw that bag when the Godmother Supreme was doing her weekly briefings and she showed us images of you, and I know it was not cute."

"Hold up." I waved my arms dramatically. "What do you mean she showed you images of me? Has she been spying on me?"

"Sort of," Debbie replied like it was no big deal. "She's been looking for you ever since she found out you and your friends ditched Lady Agnue's. A princess escapes protagonist school weeks after breaking into Fairy Godmother Headquarters and you think our realm's most powerful Fairy Godmother isn't going to want to have a conversation with her?"

I opened my mouth to speak, but Debbie cut me off again. "But that's not important," she said. "What is important is the matter of that gross satchel."

Daniel shook his head. "Really? The girl just told you she has magic powers and you wanna talk about purses?"

"Ignore him." Debbie waved her hand dismissively. "This is as important as it gets. Explain yourself, Crisa. How could a princess allow herself to carry around such a hobo-esque handbag?"

"Well, it's not as though I can make my wand appear out of thin air like you can," I protested.

"I don't make my wand appear out of thin air," Debbie clarified. "I transform it from one shape to another. Look."

Debbie pulled one of the crystal hairpins from her red mane. A second later it morphed into her wand, just like I'd seen it do when we first met.

"There's no reason you shouldn't be able to do the same," Debbie continued. "All Fairy Godmother-issue wands are designed for this type of shape-shifting—that way we don't have to worry about carrying them around all the time. Here, watch. Hold up your wand."

I obeyed.

"Now concentrate on it and say *Lapellium*," Debbie instructed.

"*Lapellium*," I repeated.

My wand shrunk to the size of a sewing needle—that sparkled. It had turned into a delicate hairpin. My mouth hung open in shock.

"How did . . ."

Debbie shrugged. "Like I said, every wand is enchanted to change into an accessory—rings, bracelets, hairpins. Coco, our receptionist, even figured out a way to morph hers into acrylic nails. They look super uncomfortable, but to each her own. The bottom line is that it makes life easier for us, just as I'm sure it will make life easier for you. All you have to do is touch the wand, concentrate on it, and say *Lapellium*. You don't even have to say it out loud; just think it. And to change it back, focus your magic on the original shape of the wand and the word *Lapellius* and voilà, it'll return to normal."

I held the slender accessory in the palm of my hand, took a deep breath—imagining the shape of my wand—then thought, *Lapellius*.

Sure enough, the little piece of silver expanded in my hand until it returned to its wand state. Fascinated, I tried a second time.

Lapellium.

Once more I watched my wand shrink back to the form of a tiny hairpin. I marveled at it like a kid who'd just discovered candy.

Coolest. Thing. Ever.

I began fastening the pin in my hair above my ear where Debbie kept hers but quickly reconsidered. I didn't usually wear my hair back, and my wand felt vulnerable and out of place there. I got into so many action-packed shenanigans I figured it was a bad idea to leave it where it could fall out while I was running or something. Additionally, I didn't want anyone to identify my sparkly hair accessory for what it was. The odds of someone knowing it was a disguised wand were slim, but I wasn't willing to take the chance. I settled for clipping the wandpin to my left bra strap.

Not a very ladylike move to keep a weapon strapped to one's underwear, I know. But a girl's gotta do what a girl's gotta do.

"Thanks for the tip, Deb," I commented after securing the pin. "Who knew hairpins could be so multifunctional?"

Daniel—losing patience—punched me in the arm. "Knight, focus. We're losing time here. We should be concentrating on a way to find our friends or getting to the Valley of Strife to look for the next item on Emma's list. We need to go."

"I'm afraid you guys can't leave," Debbie responded, biting her lip. "At least not yet."

I felt a shiver in my spine and took a slight step back. "Why?"

"Like I said, the Godmother Supreme wants to have a conversation with you. And she already knows you're here." Debbie pointed at the black orb with the red blinking light in the corner of the room. "How familiar are you with the concept of security cameras?"

I thought back. Security cameras were not something I'd ever seen in our realm, but I did know what they were. When we went to Earth to find the Little Mermaid's daughter Ashlyn, we'd learned a lot about otherworldly creations from watching TV and movies.

"How long have security cameras been in Book?" Daniel asked, eyeing the thing suspiciously.

"Only about a month," Debbie replied. "The Fairy God-mothers have ways of keeping tabs on developing technology from other realms, and we incorporate what our realm's leaders deem most useful. With her love of control, the Godmother Supreme has taken to security cameras quite wholeheartedly. They were not that hard to incorporate. In a way, we've been using a more limited, magical version of this concept for ages. Think about how we project holographic images from one location to the next, like when we give real-time views of what's happening in the skies during a Twenty-Three Skidd tournament. This is just a more stationary, stable version of that. There's a camera in every office of Headquarters now. And the Godmother Supreme has them in key locations across the realm. Their number increases every day."

"Maybe she hasn't seen us yet," I said optimistically. "If she has that many cameras, the odds of her watching this room at this very moment are—"

"Debbie Nightengale . . ." We all cringed at the sound of the voice from the intercom echoing through the room. That was one type of technology in Fairy Godmother Headquarters I was familiar with.

"Please escort Miss Knight and her companion to the Management office in ten minutes. The Godmother Supreme would like a word with her. That is all."

The intercom buzzed with static as it cut off.

"I'm sorry," Debbie said. "I wish you didn't have to see that woman. She can be merciless and cruel when she wants to be, but your fate was sealed the moment you popped in."

"Should you really be badmouthing your boss with that camera right there?" Daniel said, tilting his head at the intrusive thing.

"It only does video, not audio," Debbie explained. "Our fairy engineers haven't quite found a way to cancel out the magical interference. The intercoms are able to, except for a little static. But the wiring for the cameras is more complex. So for now, while the Godmother Supreme can see everything, she can't hear us." Debbie turned to me with a slightly grim expression. "She saw your wand, Crisa. I didn't know you were going to whip it out or else I would have stopped you. Once you did, I didn't say anything because the damage was already done. The Godmother Supreme knows you have magic now, but she doesn't know you got it from Emma or any of the other details."

I groaned in frustration. "Debbie, Daniel is right. We really don't have time to waste here. A lot of important stuff is going on that you don't understand."

"My hands are tied, Crisa," she replied. "You don't want to know what would happen to me if I went against the Godmother Supreme. Lena Lenore does not take kindly to disobedience."

Debbie walked around her desk and sat down in her chair, propping her chin on her hands. "Since we at least have the privacy of our words and ten minutes, you might as well fill me in on this 'important stuff' I don't understand."

"I don't know . . ." I hedged.

"Knight, just tell her," Daniel said. "Maybe she can shed some light. What's the point of having a powerful guardian if all she can do is give you fashion advice and magic accessories?"

"You really think she could help us?"

"There's only one way to find out."

"Um, hello?" Debbie piped in. "I'm right here. Should I grab a cup of coffee while you talk about me amongst yourselves?"

I sighed. "Deb, that Fairy Godmother–Fairy Godkid code of silence thing you brought up earlier—is that a universal thing? Like it'll extend to *whatever* I tell you?"

"Totally," she replied with a shrug that made her ponytail bounce. "It's part of the oath—a Godmother has strict confidentiality with her Godkid no matter what. It's an unbreakable trust bond so that, rain or shine, I can be your go-to gal for anything without you ever having to worry about me selling you out."

"All right." I nodded. "Well then take a seat, Deb, because we're about to put that oath to good use."

Maybe it was Debbie's sincerity and willingness to help, maybe it was the whole Fairy Godmother–Fairy Godkid bond getting the better of me, or maybe it was just the fact that I'd always felt redheads were trustworthy. But, for whatever reason, I decided to tell Debbie the *whole* story about everything that had gone down since the last time we'd met. Daniel was right—if anyone was in a position to help us or clue us in on some of the stuff that was happening, it was her.

In tag-team, Daniel and I began telling our story. We opened with the part about our mission to find the Author and explained our ongoing efforts to collect the items needed to break the In and Out Spell around the Indexlands to reach her. Then we told Debbie about how our realm's ambassadors were conspiring with Lena Lenore and other Godmothers (like the Scribes—the Fairy Godmothers charged with protecting protagonist books) to rig protagonist selection.

At this part in the story I noticed Debbie eyes widen like ping-pong balls. The way her face paled and fingers clenched, I knew she wasn't one of the Godmothers on Lenore's team.

I was glad for this. I liked Debbie. She was sweet and I'd really been hoping she didn't know about the conspiracy. Knowledge of the corruption made my insides burn with injustice, and I didn't want to add her to my already long list of enemies.

I went on to tell Debbie about the holes we'd discovered in the In and Out Spell that created portals to other realms—like the one we'd used to get to Earth to find Ashlyn. Daniel followed up with a description of the antagonists that were after me, and my dreams of the future. Finally, I wrapped up the tale with an explanation of Natalie Poole.

Debbie barely blinked as Daniel and I told her of our adventures. Her eyes simply got bigger and bigger with wonder, fear, and disbelief. When we were done she uttered a single word:

"Dang."

"I know, right?" I said. "So . . . can you shed some light on any of this?"

"I wish I could, Crisa," she replied, biting the end of one of her ruby red fingernails. "But I don't know anything about those creeps that've been after you or the ambassadors' conspiracy or Natalie Poole or—"

"So to sum up, you don't know anything," Daniel interrupted, checking the clock.

This time it was my turn to punch Daniel on the arm, narrowing my eyes at him. "Don't be rude."

"It's fine, Crisa," Debbie said calmly. "But he is wrong; I do know one thing. It's about those dreams you've been having." Debbie rotated in her seat so that she was looking at me directly and her face was concealed from the camera. "Crisa, whatever you do, you can't tell anyone else about seeing the future in your dreams. Especially any of the other Godmothers."

"Why?"

Debbie bit her lip nervously. "It's . . . well, it's complicated," she replied. "I don't really know all the details. All I can say is that dreaming about the future is definitely not something you want to brag about. So please, until we know exactly what we're dealing with, just go with me on this and don't tell anyone. If the Godmother Supreme ever found out . . ." Debbie's eyes darted away nervously. "Just promise, okay? Mum's the word?"

"All right," I agreed, feeling curious. "I promise."

"Good," Debbie continued. "And as for everything else, I'm afraid the only person who might be able to give you answers is the Godmother Supreme. It sucks, I know, but she is the most well-connected person in the realm. She knows everyone and everything, so she may be your best and only bet for finding out the truth behind all this."

I rolled my eyes. "Great. I didn't exactly rub her the right way the first time we met so speaking with her a second time ought to be fun."

"Look on the bright side, Knight," Daniel said. "You rub most people the wrong way the first time you meet them. But the majority seem to get over it."

"Gee, thanks, Daniel. That helps a lot." I gave him a disdainful smile and turned back to Debbie. "I guess you should take us to her now. I want to get this over with."

"Okay," Debbie said. She shook her head. "You know, it's funny. Ordinarily I'd insist you clean yourself up a bit first—the Godmother Supreme appreciates presentation, and you guys could use all the good credit with her you can get. But despite all your misadventures, the pair of you look surprisingly put-together."

"It's the SRB," Daniel said, holding up his wrist to show Debbie the Soap on a Rope-like Bracelet that SJ had crafted for each of us. "They're made from a potion that keeps you from getting dirty or stank."

Despite the harrowing tales of danger and drama that we'd just told Debbie, it was this statement that caused her face to grow the palest. She shot to her feet. "Are you telling me that you two have been wearing those same outfits for days?"

"Well, that depends if you count the Earth-to-Book time difference," I replied. "Otherwise it's been a lot longer."

Debbie's face grew even more ghostly. "Oh no," she said, waving her arms. "No, no, no. Not on my watch."

My Fairy Godmother's tsunami dress had started to ripple aggressively, greater swells of dark gray pushing away the blue. She reached for the wandpin in her hair and transformed it. I took a step back.

"Deb, what are you—"

I didn't have time to finish the question. Debbie waved her wand. Scarlet sparks rushed out of its tip like a swarm of bees. The sparks zoomed around Daniel and me until we were enclosed within separate cocoons.

After being consumed by the purple, magic-sucking vortex that had trapped us in the genie lamp, the claustrophobic sensation of the cocoon made me tense and breathless. Thankfully, it only lasted for a few seconds. My sparkly cocoon evaporated with one mega burst. When it was gone, I looked down and discovered Debbie had magically changed my outfit.

I checked to make sure my wandpin was still where I'd placed it. I still wore black leggings, but my brown boots had morphed into a pair of dark gray boots with an inky design crawling up the sides. If I looked closely, the design seemed to fluctuate like dark clouds, pulsating around the onyx laces as if they were the eye of a storm. The laces streaked periodically with itty-bitty flashes of silver electricity like tiny lightning bolts.

The main difference in my ensemble was the dress I now wore over my leggings. It was long sleeved and a rich shade of cobalt. The material was soft and supple; its cut was A-line, and it had glittering black shoulder pads like a soldier's uniform. But it was the sleeves that made me stare.

From wrist to elbow, the underside of each sleeve had an intricate, almost unsettling pattern of miniscule crystals embedded into the fabric. It was akin to the veins that ran through my arms. Their shimmering against the backdrop of deep blue made the whole thing look like the nervous system of a night sky.

When I focused I could see the crystals change in luminescence. They went from bright to invisible and back again in tune with my heartbeat. The faster my heart pounded, the more they sparkled. When I was breathing slowly they seemed duller, like faraway fireflies.

Then I took a look at Daniel.

The first thing I noticed was that his hair had been trimmed a bit and the extra shagginess it'd developed over our adventure was gone. In addition, he looked freshly shaven and no longer had patchy stubble on his face.

In terms of what he was wearing, Debbie had left his leather jacket alone (apparently it met her qualifications for a good outfit).

But beneath it he now wore a crisp, dark gray shirt. His pants were also new, as was his belt. I wasn't very good at describing boy fashion. But if he was anyone aside from Daniel, I would've said he looked pretty h—

Nope. Can't say it. It's Daniel.

Just like I had with my wand, Daniel instinctively made sure his golden pocket watch (which held a picture of his girlfriend) was still in his pocket. Once he ascertained that it was, he crossed his arms and scowled at Debbie.

"We didn't ask you to do that. We were fine before."

Debbie twirled her wand, morphing it back into a hairpin mid-spin. "You didn't have to," she replied. "And no, you weren't. What kind of Godmother would I be if I let my Godkid run around in the same outfit for all eternity? I don't care whether you're facing magic hunters, antagonists, or mermaids—appearances matter."

Daniel looked like he was about to say something else, but I put my hand up to stop him. "It's fine, Daniel. Let it go." I turned to Debbie. "Thanks, Deb. The clothes are great. I love the weird shifting clouds," I said, gesturing to the fluctuating weather patterns on my boots. "Are all your clothes like this? Every time I see you your dresses are crazy."

"Thanks!" Debbie exclaimed. "And yeah, they are. I'm double majoring in fashion design and weather manipulation for my Fairy Godmother Training. If you want to turn off the magical effects in your dress and boots, click your heels together three times. That'll shut it down faster than cops at a Century City rave."

"*Knight,*" Daniel said with frustration in his tone, as well as a touch of hostility. I guess I could understand. First off, he was a boy, and no boy should have to spend this long talking fashion with a Fairy Godmother. It was just cruel. Moreover, the stakes were high and we had to get moving. The sooner we spoke with Lenore, the sooner we could get out of here and resume our mission.

I glanced over at the door. The promise of answers lay somewhere down the hall in the Godmother Supreme's office and I was ready to face her.

"Debbie," I said, exhaling. "Take us to the Godmother Supreme. We've stalled long enough."

"All right," my Godmother said, biting yet another nail. "One last piece of advice before you go. I realize you met the Godmother Supreme briefly before, Crisa. But we had a whole staff meeting about the subject of your break-in, and like I said, she's brought you up at several meetings since then. So proceed with caution. If there is one thing I've gleaned from all of it, it's that Lena Lenore does not like you."

I let out an amused huff. "Don't worry. That's never stopped me before."

CHAPTER 3

Stiltdegarth

aniel and I sat on a cotton candy-colored couch.

The plush seat was in the office of Joan Pricklewood, whom Debbie had introduced us to a few minutes ago. She was Lena Lenore's secretary and her office was adjacent to that of the Godmother Supreme. I didn't know what was more eccentric—this new Godmother or the area she inhabited.

Joan Pricklewood had white, wiry hair that poofed from her head like she'd been electrocuted. Her eye makeup was a flurry of contrasting colors—shadows of pink, blue, and green highlighted by sparkly silver eyeliner. Her neck was so long and goose-like that I was certain no one had ever blocked her view of a parade.

The Godmother's office was adorned with creepy troll dolls, most of which had better hairstyles than the secretary did. There was a white terrier asleep in the corner in the warmth of a red basket. I kept resisting the urge to touch the light pink walls, which looked squishy.

I rested my elbow on one of the sofa's armrests and propped my head up with my hand. Debbie was chatting with Joan at the other end of the room. I assumed the subject must've been something of particular comedic value as the two would not stop giggling. Daniel had his hands folded behind his head and was staring up at the ceiling, deep in thought.

My mind wandered to Lena Lenore. Debbie hadn't been lying

when she said the Godmother Supreme didn't like me. Granted, I didn't like her either, but I only had one magical power, which I didn't even know how to use. Lenore had the full range of Fairy Godmother magic that didn't have any restrictions that I knew of. So while I may not have been afraid of the woman, I would've been a fool to think she didn't pose a threat.

Everything I'd learned about Lena Lenore had caused me to equate her with cold guile. She'd fired my godmother Emma from the Fairy Godmother Agency then lied to keep me away from her for ten years. She was the one heading up the protagonist selection conspiracy. And she'd forced Ashlyn to choose between her true love on Earth and ever returning to Book again. Then for good measure Lenore had cursed the Lost Princess from being able to set foot in the water—despite her Little Mermaid blood—as a means to keep her from revealing the holes in our realm's outer In and Out Spell.

When I'd first met Lena Lenore, my instinct had told me that there was an unseen depth to her darkness, like an ocean's shimmering surface veiling its true power. In this case I regretted that my instinct was right. If Lenore really was the only one who held the answers Daniel and I sought—her being arguably the most powerful person in Book—I had a feeling that getting them would come at a hefty price.

A blue light lit up on Joan Pricklewood's desk accompanied by a buzzing sound. Joan straightened her posture, hustled out of the room, and returned a minute later.

"The Godmother Supreme will see you now," she said, gesturing to the door.

Daniel and I got up from the couch. As we followed Joan I elbowed him lightly.

"Hey," I whispered. "Let me do the talking when we get in there, okay?"

"Knight, when do you not do the talking?" he whispered back.

I paused. "All right, fair point."

We moved into the familiar white corridor that led to Lena Lenore's office with Debbie in tow. Joan held open the equally familiar door with the word "MANAGEMENT" printed on it. When we entered, we found the Godmother Supreme sitting in the black leather chair behind her glass desk, just like the night of our first meeting when we'd broken into Fairy Godmother Headquarters.

"Crisanta Knight," she said.

Lenore's voice sounded sweet, but it made me shiver. How one woman could pack so much subtle power into so few syllables was beyond me.

The Fairy Godmother Supreme was beautiful in an intense kind of way. Her dark skin shimmered with a (for lack of a better word) magical radiance. Her arms were relatively sculpted, making me wonder if Fairy Godmother Headquarters had a gym. Large hazel eyes—sharp and focused—seemed to see every detail.

I was glad she was seated. Adding to her intimidating persona, the forty-something woman was close to six feet tall (and that was *without* heels).

"I had a feeling it was only a matter of time before you came knocking on my door again," Lenore said as we stepped forward.

"This wasn't exactly a planned visit," I said.

"Things of an unexpected nature tend to happen around you quite often, don't they, Crisanta?" Lenore stood from her chair and walked over to us. She wore a sleeveless silk turtleneck top. It was light pink and tucked into a silver pencil skirt, the likes of which perfectly matched her light pink pumps with glittering silver straps.

I instantly knew I'd seen those heels before. They were the last things I'd seen the night in the Forbidden Forest when I'd stumbled upon the Scribes' protagonist book library. When I'd discovered the secret place, someone had struck me from behind with a bolt of magic. At the time I'd assumed it had been one of the Scribes in an effort to keep me from learning anything else about the books. Now I knew it had to have been Lenore.

"Nice shoes," I commented. "They must be comfortable if you wear them so frequently."

Lenore's eyes creased at the edges as if she were amused. Her hair was not in a bun today. Rather, it fell in dark, cascading waves around her shoulders as she looked down on me. With the boost of her pumps she easily passed six foot two. I pitied anyone who'd ever tried to give her a high five.

Lenore's hair whooshed as she abruptly pivoted on her heels and headed back across the office's silver carpet. She leaned against her desk under the shadow of the room's black chandelier. "Miss Knight, there are several things I value—order, regulation, and time. So for the sake of preserving the latter, why don't we skip to the point. Later we can discuss the matter of you breaking in here for a second time. But before I ask you my questions." I noticed her eyes and smile darken ever so slightly. "Why don't we begin with yours? Debbie told Joan that you have a few things you wish to discuss with me."

She gestured to a set of chairs against the back wall, but I stepped into the center of the room. "As a matter of fact, we do."

My brain flipped through the many things I had to ask her. With so many mysteries unsolved, I decided to ask her about one of the very first that had crossed my path when this adventure began.

"Why do the Fairy Godmothers have a file on a girl from Earth named Natalie Poole?"

My friends and I had found the folder with Natalie Poole's name on it in Arian's bunker beneath the Century City Capitol Building. But a while before that I'd found a similar folder in the Godmothers' Grand File Room when we'd broken into Headquarters.

Aside from a picture of teenage Natalie and some basic information about her background, this folder (like Arian's) contained the following information:

- *Magic Classification: Category 1, 2, & 3 priority*
- *O.T.L. Candidate: Ryan Jackson*
- *Key Destiny Interval: 21st birthday (cross-reference Eternity Gate)*

I now knew who Ryan Jackson was and that Natalie's twenty-first birthday was the antagonists' deadline for breaking her spirit and opening the Eternity Gate. But the rest remained an enigma.

I hoped maybe Lenore could shed some light on these mysteries. With a file on the girl at Headquarters, at the very least she should be able to explain Natalie's importance.

My best theory so far was that maybe Natalie had a Fairy Godmother in this building. I'd always thought that Fairy Godmothers only had Godkids in Book. But between the folder found here and the protagonist book I'd found on Natalie in the Scribes' protagonist book library, it was enough to make me think otherwise.

Lenore opened her mouth to respond, but Daniel cut her off before she could address my question, his own priorities piping in.

"And how could you let the ambassadors conspire to rig protagonist selection? Everyone in Book deserves to know who they are. What gives you the right to interfere like that?"

So much for letting me do the talking. Dude hates to keep his mouth shut almost as much as I do.

"We have a file on Natalie Poole because our Fairy Godmother Agency used to service Earth as well as Book," Lenore responded, somewhat confirming my theory. "And as to the ambassadors, they were not *conspiring*, young man; they were simply following orders."

I crossed my arms. *"Your* orders, I presume?"

Suddenly Lenore shot a look at Debbie and Joan.

"Debbie, darling, will you please escort Miss Knight's

companion to the waiting area? I would like a word with her in private."

"Um, yes, ma'am," Debbie replied with a touch of fear in her tone. She put her hand on Daniel's shoulder. "Come on, Danny. There's free candy in the lobby."

"Yeah. I've seen it," he said, shrugging her off. "No way am I leaving."

Lenore sauntered back over to her chair and repositioned herself confidently. "Leave, or I won't answer any more questions. It's that simple."

"Anything you say to me, you can say to Daniel," I asserted.

"Crisanta," Lenore sighed. "I am not going to argue with you. I have a busy schedule, so either play by my rules or leave now. The choice is yours."

I thought on the proposition. This was the closest I'd come to answers in a long time. If the only price for me getting them was being alone with Lenore for a few minutes, then I was more than willing to pay it.

"Go on," I told Daniel. "I won't be long."

Daniel shot me an incredulous look. "Knight, I don't think it's a good idea for you to be on your own here."

His concern was sweet. Irritating, but sweet. Nevertheless, I was set in my course of action. Yes, Lenore was crafty, calculating, and powerful, but I needed to hear what she had to say. I'd risked far worse in the past few weeks to cower to anyone, let alone a woman dressed like a glittery lawyer.

"Don't worry," I said to Daniel. "I'll be fine."

"I don't know."

"Daniel, seriously." I met the concern in his eyes with the certainty in mine. "I've got this. You want answers too, don't you?"

A beat passed until he conceded. "All right, fine. I'll go."

Begrudgingly, Joan, Debbie, and Daniel left the room, closing the door behind them. The confidence I had about the situation wavered when I got a look at Debbie's nervous expression before she left. She was worried, and not just a little.

When the door shut I rotated back around to face Lenore. "Okay, they're gone. Care to explain why Daniel had to leave?"

"It wasn't just him," Lenore replied. "Debbie is a newer recruit—not yet high enough in the ranks for me to ascertain the strength of her loyalty. I could not allow her to hear the details of what I am about to tell you."

"Which are?"

"The answers to your questions, Miss Knight." Lenore folded her hands together as she sat back in her chair. "You're right. The ambassadors of all the kingdoms take their orders from me, just as the Scribes do. The Author may be the one who can predict the future, but *I* am the one charged with regulating it. Protagonists are not approved to know who *or what* they are unless I say so. And if someone I feel needs to be a protagonist is not chosen by the Author, then I simply have a forged book drawn up for them."

I was surprised that Lenore was being so direct with me. I'd become so used to half-answers and riddles that part of me sort of expected the same now. I was grateful for the candid talk. At the same time, the fact that such unapologetic honesty on such a sensitive subject was coming from this powerful woman made me worried.

Yet I pressed on.

"But why?" I stammered.

"For the same reason that Fairy Godmothers no longer service Earth. *Order*. We used to cater to the people of that realm as we do the people of this one, attempt to help them reach their happily ever afters with the aid of our magical interference. But after years of struggling to keep up with the chaotic way Earth is run, we decided to withdraw.

"Natalie was an Earthling chosen as a protagonist a long time ago. But like all others on Earth, her future was too turbulent to benefit from our intervention. We decided many years back that the energy to try was not even worth it. That world is too disorderly for us to continue wasting our time there. It plays by no concrete rules, and because of that it lacks security and control. Where there is no control there is no winning against the darkness. There is just the constant, exhausting fight against it. We Godmothers were tired of taking part in it."

I blinked but stood frozen as I processed the words. Something burned inside of me like acid. It was a kind of anger I'd only felt once before—the day I'd received my prologue prophecy. While I couldn't address the cause of my anger (the Author) then, this time I had the source of my rage right in front of me. She sat there, looking unremorseful.

"So you abandoned the people of Earth?" I clarified, my voice hard and my glare even harder. "You left them to fend for themselves because you couldn't be bothered to keep trying to help them?"

Lenore shrugged. "If it's any consolation, they probably weren't worth helping. And on the off-chance that some of them were, it still wouldn't have mattered. We simply could not afford to expend energy on beings that are so perpetually lost. In this realm there are leaders who have control to shape fate in the correct image. Earth has no such regulations. Everything there is messy—people thinking that each and every one of them is special, a protagonist in his or her own right. It's as naive as it is mad. In the end that type of mindset negates any chance order has of succeeding."

"I thought Fairy Godmothers believed in happily ever afters, not order," I said, crossing my arms.

"You're young, Crisanta. You believe in fairytales because you've been taught to. Every story you were exposed to as a child was designed to give you hope and keep you blissfully unaware of how the world really works. It is a kindness that our realm's leaders, myself included, bestow upon citizens to spare them the burden of cynicism. But seeing as you're so adamant about knowing the truth, allow me to burst your bubble with it."

Lenore stood and leaned over her desk. I noticed a silver ring on her index finger. It had an elaborate ruby spiral insignia that glistened in the chandelier's light. The spiral was identical to the mark that protagonists received on their foreheads right after their prologue prophecies appeared. It also mirrored the structure of the skylights I'd seen in the Capitol Building and the Scribes' protagonist book library.

"Happily ever afters are unstable, Crisanta," Lenore said. "They can take decades of work to build, but mere seconds to destroy. And then what? Do we fall apart? I assure you that is what would happen if it weren't for the systems we've put into place to maintain order. My agency's involvement with protagonist selection has allowed us to keep a handle on this world's future, keep things running smoothly, and keep darkness at bay. It may seem harsh, but it is all for your own good and for the good of the realm."

I placed my hands on the edge of her desk. "Rationalize it all you want, Lenore," I said, my face a mere two feet from the Godmother Supreme's. "It still doesn't give you the right to decide who amongst us is worth investing in and who should be tossed aside. You shouldn't have abandoned the people of Earth, people like Natalie Poole."

Lenore scrunched up her nose. Without saying anything she went over to a bookshelf on the right side of the room and selected a dark blue book as thick as a dictionary. She opened it and spoke Natalie Poole's name. Instantly the pages began to flip on their own, emitting a flurry of red sparks like they were kicking up enchanted dust.

When the pages stopped turning, Lenore read silently for a moment before closing the book and returning it to the shelf.

"Magic Classifications, Key Destiny Intervals, the Eternity Gate," I recited aloud as Lenore made her way back to the desk. "I may not know what the words mean, but I know they're important. I know *she's* important. Antagonists are after her. They've been going to Earth to try and destroy her because they know she matters, and if she had Fairy Godmother help she wouldn't be so vulnerable. By withdrawing your support from that realm you've left her and others like her completely defenseless."

I'd been carefully watching Lenore during this statement to see if she showed any sign of surprise to the news. But there was none. She seemed unmoved.

"I've left the Earthlings to their own fate, Crisanta," Lenore replied. "If memory serves, that is exactly what you've always wanted for yourself—a life without the meddling of outside forces."

"Don't turn this on me," I said. "The Author takes our lives from us by keeping us in crates designed to be shipped to specific endpoints. You've left all the people of Earth in one large pen and turned the other cheek to the wolves that have been sneaking in. Or did you think I hadn't figured it out? You didn't even blink when I mentioned the antagonists a moment ago. You know they've been getting to Earth, don't you? They've been using the holes in the In and Out Spell just like Ashlyn did before you cursed and banished her."

The Godmother and I were locked in tense silence for a moment. I held my ground despite her intimidating glower.

Since learning that my dreams were actually visions of the future, I'd come to a lot of conclusions. This deduction was one that had been simmering in the back of my mind for some time, but it had grown clearer with each bit of new information I'd acquired from our adventure.

Natalie was not the only person on Earth I'd dreamed about over the years. She was the only recurring character in my nightmares of that realm, but I'd had plenty of other visions of people there being tormented, even killed. Now that I knew about Arian, Tara (Arian's right hand in the Natalie Poole campaign), and Nadia, the truth about their identities had also become apparent.

Nadia had ordered the elimination of protagonists that posed a threat to the antagonists, a mission she'd charged Arian with leading and underlings like Tara with carrying out.

Natalie Poole—this poor girl the Godmothers had abandoned— was one such protagonist. Since I'd found a book with her name on it in a section of the Scribes' protagonist book library marked "Other Realms," I reasoned there must've been other Earthlings with books too, just like there must've been other Earthlings with files at Fairy Godmother Headquarters. They had to be the people on Earth I'd seen tormented by Arian over the years.

Maybe they were important to the antagonists in some way. Maybe they all had Magic Classifications or Key Destiny Intervals or whatever like Natalie did, and they were paying for it like I'd seen her pay for it in countless visions.

Standing there—angry and defiant—I began to put the pieces together. I realized with horror that all these years I thought I was being subjected to surreal nightmares, I was actually witnessing the suffering of protagonists in other realms—protagonists that Lena Lenore and the like should've been protecting because *protecting protagonists was their job.*

"Did you also know there are antagonists actively trying to destroy protagonists in this realm too? Do you even care?" I spat bitterly, my spite outweighing the more sensible part of my conscience that would've advised me to hold back. "Or was your precious state of order so important that you chose to preserve appearances rather than let protagonists like me know that there were people out there hunting us down?"

Lenore's eyes flashed angrily. In the next half-second she removed the ring from her index finger and transformed it into a wand. She pointed it in my direction. Before I could move a charge of bright red energy bolted out of the tip like a surge of lightning. I shot across the room and slammed against the back wall, landing at the base in a heap. The wind was knocked out of me, and I felt my veins fizzing with a charred feeling. Lenore approached me, wand grasped firmly in hand.

"I'd heard rumors about antagonists roaming the realm, Crisanta. But to answer your question, no, until very recently I didn't know they were targeting specific protagonists. That knowledge has only come to me via the Author within the last couple of months. Since finding out, my Godmothers and I have been trying to isolate the group that poses a threat to you. We discovered their bunker beneath the Capitol Building and a couple of other hideouts in the last two weeks, but since we don't know how many more there are, we chose not to share the information out of respect for your best interest."

"Right," I coughed. "My best interest. I'm sure yours had nothing to do with it."

I tried to stand, but Lenore was faster. She waved her wand and a burst of magic rushed around my arms and slammed me into the nearest chair.

"Sit down," Lenore said sternly. "I am not through with you yet."

I was tempted to go for my wand but restrained the impulse.

"You and your friends were supposed to be at Lady Agnue's and Lord Channing's," Lenore said. "We could protect you there. Your leaving put you and your friends in the sights of people who shouldn't have been able to touch you. That choice is on your head, so don't you dare blame me for whatever's happened to you."

"How were you supposed to protect us when your In and Out Spells are *failing*?" I asked.

Lenore's expression softened ever so slightly. "The holes that have been appearing in Book's all-encompassing In and Out Spell are out of my control," she admitted reluctantly. "But the other ones in place—the ones around your school, the Indexlands, and

Alderon—all remain perfectly intact. So while the antagonists may be using the former to reach protagonists on Earth . . . I truly don't know how they've been escaping Alderon to pursue the main characters here."

The news took me by surprise. It also stirred mixed feelings inside me. For while I was relieved that the In and Out Spell around Alderon didn't have any holes, I was equally unsettled by the notion that even the Godmother Supreme had no idea how Arian and his kind were getting out.

"We will figure it out sooner or later though," the Godmother said as she made her way back to her desk. "At least the only protagonists that have been killed so far are a few of the ones whose books we destroyed. No one knew they were main characters to start with, so they won't be missed."

Boy, when this woman was direct she really didn't hold anything back. I guess when you were the person in charge of controlling others, you had the luxury of knowing there was no one who could do the same to you.

How I wished there were security cameras in this room—ones with audio that I could use to play back her horrid words for others to hear, show them the monster she really was.

I stood and approached Lenore. "How can you be so cold?"

She waved her hand dismissively and pivoted away from me. "It's not coldness; it's pragmatism. Since those people never knew they had protagonist books, they just behaved like commons. And what difference does it make if we lose a few of them in the long run?"

Fury built inside me again and I lashed out. I couldn't help it. "Those are people you're talking about, Lenore. It makes no difference what archetype they were born into. You have to warn them about the antagonists. And you have to tell all those people with protagonist books that you're hiding the truth about who they are."

"I'm not going to do that, Crisanta."

"Then I will. The moment I walk out of here I'll make sure they know. I'll make sure all of them find out."

Lenore turned on her fancy heels to face me. "You'll do no such thing, Crisanta Knight."

"Really?" I replied. "Try and stop me."

"I don't have to. You're going to stop yourself."

"And why would I do that?"

"Because if you breathe a word of what we've discussed here to the greater public—a single person outside of that little mischievous group you've been traveling with—then I can't be held responsible for what terrible, unspeakable things happen to them."

Lenore twirled her wand and pointed it at the bookshelves lining the right side of the room. Several files shook themselves free and levitated to her desk. I noticed each folder had a swirl mark on the top right corner that matched the ruby design on Lenore's ring.

Once they came to rest upon the desk, the folders opened. Shimmering bubbles the size of plates began to rise up from each one.

The orbs floated between me and Lenore and I leaned in to get a better look. Each contained the vague image of a person. As these images became clearer I recognized the faces of my parents, my brothers, and each of my friends.

"As I said," Lenore went on, "I suspected that you would be knocking on my door again. So after you discovered the Scribes' protagonist book library I began to make preparations. You were getting too close to some very private matters, and I knew you were hardly the type to stop searching for answers."

She sighed. "In retrospect maybe I should have taken you then. I'm sure Debbie told you I had been searching for you. But against my better judgment, I was convinced to let you go. A mistake I regretted almost immediately, but you left the Forbidden Forest before I could snatch you up again."

"Convinced?" I repeated. "Convinced by who?"

Who could possibly have enough power or influence to sway this woman to do anything?

Lenore waved off my question. "Anyways, the point is that I knew you would come to me in your own time, so I had a contingency set aside for the occasion."

I glanced at the images of my friends and family, making sure to keep my face blank as I turned coldly to readdress the Godmother Supreme. "So what's all this supposed to mean, Lenore?" I gestured at the floating spheres. "Are you saying that if I talk, you'll what, kill them? My friends? My family? You'll eliminate them all to keep me in line?"

"Regrettably not," she admitted. "Fairy Godmothers—like genies when they were around—are known for having all-powerful magic, but that perception is a fallacy. Our magic may be incomparably strong, but it has limits. For starters, genies could not use their abilities except under the discretion of their masters and were bound to the prison of their lamps. Godmothers cannot use their magic without the conductors that are their wands. However, the greatest restriction on our abilities, and genie abilities, is that we cannot use our magic to bring serious, direct harm to another living being.

"So—although it would be a far neater solution—I cannot kill you or any of the people you care about. But let me make one thing clear. I can still bring you to your knees. Need I remind you that my Fairy Godmother Agency is responsible for regulating all magic and happily ever afters in this realm. So I assure you, Miss Knight, while I may not employ the most conventional method for keeping people silent, if you get in my way I will find other, more creative ways to fill your friends' and family's lives with misery."

"Lenore, I swear. If you so much as even touch them—"

"There'll be no need for that so long as you keep your mouth shut, Miss Knight," Lenore stated firmly. "On that note, I'll ask you one time only—do we have an understanding?"

Once again I felt the compulsion to pull out my wand and, to quote my friend Blue, "go all Mulan on her butt." But again I restrained myself. Lenore had the deck stacked against me; there were so few cards I could hide from her. For now, I needed to resist playing this one.

With no leverage, I swallowed my temper and steadied my voice.

"Yeah, we do."

"Excellent." Lenore clapped her hands together, causing the bubbles to disappear. "You are free to be on your way."

I began to head for the exit, but when I was a foot away from the door it opened from the other side. Standing in the entryway was one of the Fairy Godfathers who had escorted my friends and I out of the building on our last visit. He was about seven feet tall and his skin was tanned and leathery. Had I been in a sassier state of mind I would've made a joke about how his stank, pickle-scented aftershave went well with the mustard stain on his white shirt.

I assumed he was here to shove me out the door. But when I tried to step past him he promptly stretched out one of his meaty hands and spun me back in the direction of the Godmother Supreme.

"Oh wait," Lenore said as she tapped the point of her wand against her free hand. "Did we forget to discuss the matter of your magic?"

Lenore waved her wand and a flurry of scarlet sparks zipped around me. The power lifted me off the ground and yanked me forward. I tried to struggle free, but the magic squeezed my limbs tightly.

Ugh. This is so degrading.

I floated to the center of the room as the Fairy Godfather stepped inside and shut the door.

"Fine, Lenore. You got me. I'm magical," I huffed. "You saw my wand from the security camera in Debbie's office. So what, you gonna threaten me about how I should keep quiet about that too?"

"I think not," Lenore replied sternly, her smile disappearing altogether. "It's as I was saying before—I control and regulate all magic. And while I am comfortable with our arrangement in regards to you keeping silent about the answers I've given you, I can't have an impertinent teenager running around the realm with Fairy Godmother magic."

Lenore twirled her wand. In a flash the sparks that were whirling around me transformed into a giant, jagged block of ice. It encased me from the floor to below my chin, leaving everything but my head completely contained. I couldn't move an inch.

"Let me go, Lenore," I snapped angrily.

Ignoring me, Lenore signaled to the Fairy Godfather. "Cederick, you brought what I requested from the supply room?"

Cederick came to Lenore's side and withdrew a small bronze box from his pocket. Lenore gestured for him set it on the desk then proceeded to unlock it with a key she retrieved from one of her drawers. I stretched out my neck to see what was inside, but the pair of them blocked my view.

That dilemma was remedied when Lenore turned around. Between her fingers she held a black piece of goo roughly the size of a small coin. Before Cederick closed the lid of the bronze box, I glimpsed a dozen or so other pieces inside.

Lenore approached me and I eyed the dark blob. At first I wasn't particularly threatened by what looked like a piece of used chewing gum. But then I noticed Lenore was holding it tightly between her fingertips to prevent it from getting loose.

Now that it was closer, I also observed that the thing had a number of extensions that emulated body parts—four tiny limbs and a fifth appendage that must've been the head because it had two flashing yellow specks for eyes.

"This is a Stiltdegarth," Lenore explained. "It is an organism native to the northern kingdom of Zeitgeist and it has the unique capability of sucking magic out of creatures—much like a leech sucks out blood. Stiltdegarths have many uses. Their blood, for instance, can serve as a magic deterrent that cancels out powers. But at Headquarters we use them to take magic out of retired Fairy Godmothers and deposit it into new ones. It's a simple process. These feisty, vicious little things suck all the power out of one Godmother, then we slit them in half and allow the magic to flow into our new appointees."

"That's disgusting." I shuddered.

"Perhaps, but as the only other known method for extracting magic is the much more violent way of the magic hunters, we consider it a pleasant alternative. Now then, please hold still."

I struggled against the block of ice. "Lenore, don't you dare—"

"This will hurt, dear," Lenore said as she reached for my face. "But do try your best not to scream when you go under. It's still working hours and I wouldn't want to disturb anyone."

She placed the black blob directly on my forehead.

"Lenore! No!"

That was the only thing I had time to shout before—with a flash of her wand—Lenore used her magic to raise the ice until the rest of me was encased.

I could still see Lenore and Cederick through the cold shield of crystal blue. Then the gooey thing Lenore placed between my eyebrows started to squirm. It immediately began to burn and sting and sear as if the creepy creature was burrowing its way through my skin into my skull.

I thought I heard myself scream, but I wasn't sure. All sounds went dead. In the next instant, everything went black.

Horrifying pain swirled in my head like a smoothie of pure torment. Visions began to flash across my mind. Chance Darling— the detestable prince who'd inspired me to come on this quest when my prologue prophecy dictated I would marry him—was dressed in silver armor and waving at me. Then he was standing next to Blue and Jason in a forest of dense vines and brambles. He held up a lantern that illuminated his striking eyes against the darkness of night.

The visions churned. Bronze animals ran this way and that against a shimmering black backdrop. A giant bronze serpent with huge fangs shot toward me. Daniel and I stood in a forest surrounded by fireflies. A glass Pegasus figurine flew around the exterior of Lady Agnue's. A red beaver floated across an empty white void.

Then I saw someone who'd only recently begun to pierce my dreamscape. I'd first heard the woman's voice in a dream I had in the Forbidden Forest. It had flooded my head several times since then, and I'd seen her full form in a dream I'd experienced on Earth.

The woman was standing across from me now. She looked to be in her mid-thirties and had light brown skin and dark curly hair. She was already halfway gone by the time I started to make out what she was saying.

"Crisa, you have to remember," she whispered faintly. "He is the key. He will give you the answer. Just remember the—"

The vision fled. The void consumed me until I was deposited into a new scene.

Jason, Daniel, Blue, and SJ sat at a long wooden table. Bookshelves were all around them; they seemed to be in a library. Blue looked a bit sunburned; her dark blonde hair was longer than usual, reaching down past her shoulders. SJ seemed tired, and her glistening black hair was in an elegant bun instead of its normal braid.

Jason and Daniel, meanwhile, looked about the same, except for the worried, reluctant look in Jason's bright blue eyes as he glanced toward Daniel.

Even in this state of dreaming, seeing them together and without me made me wonder if that was a future I would need to get used to. Daniel and I may have been on temporarily good terms, but after everything I'd done to distance myself from the others, the odds that they would forgive me were low.

That hurt. I couldn't imagine a world without them and I didn't want to. I'd known Jason and SJ since I was ten. We met the day I started at Lady Agnue's and had bonded instantly. Blue joined our crew when I was twelve, and in the four years since our introduction she'd become just as important to me.

The simple truth was that my friends not only added to my life, they added to my character. They made me a better person. SJ—always the perfect princess and unwaveringly kind—was the voice of logic and reason that helped me think things through. Blue—feisty and unyieldingly brave—reminded me to fight harder, listen to my instinct, and follow my heart. And Jason—selfless and unceasingly loyal—inspired me to do the right thing and think of others and the bigger picture.

I cared for the three of them deeply. SJ and Blue were also my roommates at Lady Agnue's. They were the people in the world I was closest to, the people I would do anything for.

"How do you know she's not already dead?" Blue asked with darkness in her eyes.

My other friends seemed startled by her question.

"What?" she said. "We have to account for all the possibilities here, especially if Daniel is thinking about doing something so crazy."

"She's not dead," Daniel asserted ardently. He turned to SJ. "You said you saw her. That the potion you invented was working."

SJ nodded. "But I do not know what portion of the future it is reflecting. The dream occurred two days ago in Camelot. With the realm-to-realm time differences, we have no way of telling what that equates to."

"That doesn't matter," Jason said, turning to Blue. "And we don't have to consider all the possibilities. Just one. We're going to find her."

Daniel turned to SJ again. "Show it to us."

"Daniel . . ." she started carefully, her gray eyes big with empathy and sadness. "It would be better if I just told you what he saw. Seeing it firsthand for yourself would just—"

"SJ," he said firmly. *"Show it to us."*

Suddenly the image cracked and a loud static filled my ears. The pain coursing through me was so intense it felt like the world might shatter. My dream was ripped apart like it was being clawed to shreds by a vengeful cat. Then everything—the pain, the noise, the visions—stopped.

When I blinked my eyes open, I saw pure white. The pain on my forehead was gone and I realized I was no longer trapped inside Lenore's ice. Still, something cold was pressing up against my face and the front of my body—something soft and powdery.

Like snow . . .

It is snow!

Aware that my limbs were no longer restrained, I sat up to discover I was in a large embankment of pristine white powder. It was everywhere—hills of it rolled into the distance, piles covered the pine trees that encircled the clearing, and a light, steady stream of the stuff fell from the sky.

What in the . . .

I rose to my feet and looked around the winter wonderland with awe and confusion. How was I here? Where was here? And what happened to the—

The Stiltdegarth!

I reached for my forehead with panic, but I discovered the malevolent, miniature animal had vanished. Just like Lenore and Cederick and everything else.

I began to search for a way out. I had not taken twenty steps forward when I collided with an unseen barrier. I stared ahead, confused. The snowy scene was laid out in front of me with the aforementioned pine trees about fifty paces ahead.

But I *had* hit something.

Hesitantly I reached out my hand. Sure enough, I felt a barrier, some kind of smooth, hard wall. The moment I made contact, the area in front of me began to shimmer. Once the disruption settled I saw a reflection of myself.

It's a mirror! I realized. *But then why hadn't I seen my reflection before?*

I withdrew my hand. The reflection vanished.

Hmm, weird.

I placed my palm on the barrier again to test the effect. The moment my fingertips touched it, my image reappeared, but only for as long as my skin kept contact.

Changing tactics, I kept my right hand against the massive looking glass as I moved alongside it—hoping this would allow me to find its endpoint. Alas, it seemed to stretch infinitely to my left and right.

I turned around and tried to find a way out through the forest on the other side of the clearing. This plan failed too. After I walked for a minute in the other direction I rammed into a second invisible wall, which also revealed itself to be a grand mirror.

How does that even make sense? I wondered as I stared at my reflection. *If both sides are mirrors and there's nothing in between them except me and the snow, then how can there be trees in the reflections?*

All of a sudden I noticed something else in the looking glass. For a second my eyes spotted the shadowy silhouette of an animal behind one of the trees.

I whirled around, but saw nothing there. That's when I heard laughter. High pitched and distant, gleeful but disconcerting—it echoed through the terrain.

I turned toward the mirror again, but the small, dark figure had vanished. The snow began to fall faster and I started to make my way back to the other side of the strange, cold enclosure. After a dozen steps . . .

Oomph!

I rammed into the first mirror again.

Wait, that can't be. The distance between the two mirrors used to be much farther.

The snow fell harder. As the last of my boot prints was buried, the laughter came again, sending goose bumps up my skin.

I squinted through the thick powder and saw the enigmatic, dark figure once more. It was peeking out from behind one of the pines. It began darting in and out of the shadows, moving too speedily for me to get a decent look at it.

The snowfall continued to thicken; the laughter continued to heighten.

Suddenly a silhouette zoomed out from behind one of the snow dunes before disappearing behind a second, closer mound. Fear began to escalate inside me. I bolted away from the mirror but only made it a few feet before crashing into the other looking glass.

I tumbled backward from the impact. Rubbing my forehead, I sat up in the snow and found myself glaring at a seated version of myself in the reflection. Despite not touching the mirror, my image was no longer vanishing. As a result I was able to get a good look at the fallen girl in the cobalt dress before me.

She looked as freaked out as I felt, perhaps more so. But her expression fell when she noticed what was behind her. The whirr of black darted from one hill of snow to the next as it drew nearer while still retaining its cover.

I scrambled to my feet and felt my shoulders press up against the first mirror. I turned on my heels and took four steps back before touching the second.

The mirrors were moving closer together. And that thing out there was getting closer too, whatever it was.

The snow was coming down so hard now that I could barely see anything in the reflection. The ongoing laughter reached a volume such that it dulled my senses, rattling inside my head and preventing me from fully focusing on the approaching threat.

I leaned against one mirror, my eyes trained on the mound of snow that the figure had just dashed behind.

"Come on, where are you?" I whispered.

The laughter stopped, the silence deafening in its wake. My hands tensed on the glass behind me. And then—

Awgh!

Something licked the back of my neck.

I whirled around and found nothing there, not even my own reflection. I put my hands to the mirror anxiously, but my image did not return even then. She was gone.

I didn't have time to worry. In the next instant my attention was drawn by the sound of a vicious shriek. I spun around to see the black creature that had been stalking me jump out of the opposite mirror—becoming three-dimensional and very, very real.

It was the Stiltdegarth, of that I was certain, though now it was much larger. The creature was roughly the size of a human adolescent with two long black legs, two thin, rubbery arms, and an elongated torso that extended into a head with a bristled top like a broom.

It screeched from a mouth filled with hundreds of dagger-like teeth.

Without hesitation, it dove at me. One arm wrapped around my neck and ensnared me in a chokehold, pressing me so hard against the mirror that I felt like I might break through it. The second arm plunged into my chest.

I screamed.

The Stiltdegarth's eyes glowed yellow as I felt its grip tighten around what must've been my heart. I thought the organ might stop beating altogether as bright bolts of energy like mutant lighting strikes began to shoot out of the creature's eyes and mouth.

The crackling power surges encircled the Stiltdegarth's arms and then streamed into me like a toxin. I heard myself scream again as they seared my body inside out, draining me of everything.

I was going to lose. This thing was going to strip me of my magic and there was nothing I could do about it, nothing at all.

No, my last remaining bit of consciousness whispered with conviction.

No.

I squinted through the snow and the light and the pain and looked the monstrous thing straight in its fanged face, raising both my arms.

"No!" I yelled.

I clamped my hands around each of the creature's arms and concentrated all my strength on expelling it from my body.

Gritting my teeth, I squeezed the arms of the Stiltdegarth harder and harder as thoughts of my friends, Emma, Natalie, and everyone and everything that had come to be important to me flooded my head. After a few seconds a bright, golden glow flowed out of my body. As it rushed out, the Stiltdegarth's lightning began to spin in the opposite direction, purging itself from my body and working its way back toward the monster.

Along with the golden energy I was emitting, the lightning poured mercilessly into the Stiltdegarth. The creature screeched and slammed me firmly against the mirror with another jolt.

My head hit the glass with a thud, but that only toughened my resolve. I fought back even harder. The surges of energy leaving my body and entering the Stiltdegarth's increased, as did the creature's piercing screams. Its eyes were starting to burn red, its teeth vibrated, and with every passing second I felt my strength returning. It was time to end this.

"LET—" I squeezed my grip so powerfully on the creature's arms that they started to fold. "ME—" I dug one of my boots into the snow and boosted the other off the mirror for support. "GO!" I pushed the creature away from me with such force that I shot backwards and crashed through the mirror.

The shards shattered around me like fragile rain. Once again everything went black, but for once I was glad. I lay there in the nothingness—happy to be free of both that place and that thing. A minute later I was drawn back to reality by the voices of Cederick and Lenore.

"I think it's dead, Godmother Supreme. And it doesn't look like it absorbed any power from her."

"What? Let me see!" Lenore snapped. "How is that even possible? We haven't had one die on us since—"

"Ugh . . ." I groaned as I opened my eyes, the room spinning.

I blinked at the floor, slowly trying to focus. I hadn't felt like this since I'd gotten my prologue prophecy. It was like half of me was still unconscious and the other half had just been thrown into the ocean and slapped around by hormonal seals.

I looked around and saw that I was in Lenore's office again. Shattered shards of ice glittered on the carpet like an explosion of frozen confetti. The block Lenore had encased me in had been destroyed.

Across the office Lenore and Cederick stared at me. A trickle of smoke rose from something on the floor. It was the Stiltdegarth. Not the giant one from that wintery death world, but the original itty-bitty one Lenore had placed on my forehead. Only now it wasn't moving. It was just lying on the carpet, much grayer than it had been before and sizzling like a tiny, burnt piece of meat.

I propped myself on my forearms. The crystal pattern on my sleeves pulsed faintly but steadily due to the slowing of my heartbeat.

"How did you do that?" Lenore asked cuttingly. "How did you keep the Stiltdegarth from draining your powers?"

I didn't respond. My head hung limply as the pounding in my skull slowed.

Frustrated, Lenore grabbed my face in her cold, smooth hand and forced me to look at her. Her pink fingernails were sharp against my cheek . . . just as sharp as I remembered.

I'd seen glimpses of this moment in a dream. Knowing that I'd caught up with another one of my visions only made me more nauseous.

"*Answer me*, Crisanta," Lenore said furiously, gripping me tighter.

"Ugh, my head," I muttered, swatting her arms weakly.

Lenore released my face. She abruptly regained her composure as if an understanding had taken hold. "Your head," she mused. She crouched down to look me in the eye.

"Crisanta, sweetheart," she said, her voice returning to its normal, slick tone. "Tell me, have you been having any strange dreams lately? Any *realistic* dreams, shall we say?"

The peculiar question snapped me out of my stupor. I didn't see what my dreams had to do with this, but Debbie had warned me about this very scenario. I heeded my Fairy Godmother's advice and feigned ignorance. After all, if this wicked woman was willing to feed me to a nightmarish, magic-sucking creature, there was no telling what more she would do if she learned anything else about me.

"What kind of question is that?" I huffed, putting on my best facade and swallowing down my feelings of weakness to look Lenore in the eye. "You just froze me in a block of ice and stuck a magic-sucker on my face, and you're asking me about my *sleeping habits*? The answer is no, Lenore. I sleep just fine. Though after this visit I doubt I'll be able to say the same."

Lenore straightened. She waved her wand once, which caused all the pieces of ice on the floor to vanish. I watched her pace steadily in front of me—thinking, calculating.

"Godmother Supreme?" Cederick said. "Uh, what do you want us to do with her, ma'am?"

"Well I don't know, Cederick," Lenore snapped. "Without the dreams it's not as though we can treat her like the others. If the Stiltdegarth didn't work, then the only other way to remove her power is by the magic hunter method: killing her and absorbing her magic."

"But you can't kill me," I interjected. Lenore and Cederick's heads turned in my direction. I confidently rose to my feet, my strength returning. "At least not with your magic," I continued. "It won't let you. You said so yourself. So unless you plan on challenging me like a normal person—which you'll have a lot less luck with, I assure you—I get to walk out of here with my magic and there's nothing you can do about it."

Lenore looked like she wanted to fry me where I stood.

"I could take your wand," she replied. "I know you have it tucked away in there." She gestured at my dress.

"That's a deal breaker," I responded firmly.

It was true I didn't really have any ground to stand on, much less the authority to make demands in this situation. But I spoke steadfastly nonetheless. I gave Lenore my best, most defiant dagger-eyed stare, clenched my fists, and stood with utter confidence.

"You want me to keep silent, Lenore? Fine. But I draw the line there. You can't have my wand or any other piece of me."

Silence hung in the air. The moment was so tense that I thought the scene might shatter like the ice I'd been encased in. But then—thankfully—Lenore nodded. "All right, Crisanta . . . I'll let you go. For today, that is."

I can't believe that worked.

And Blue says I have a lousy poker face.

I headed for the door—content to leave the stalemate with my magic and at least *some* of my dignity.

"Crisanta," Lenore added as I reached for the handle.

Spoke too soon.

I paused and took a breath, but didn't pivot around. "What, Lenore?"

She paused at first, which made me nervous. But Lenore did not fire any more magic or monsters at me. Instead, what she did extend was one final statement, or rather a promise.

"Don't think I'm finished with you yet."

She said the words simply, almost in a monotone. The weight of her threat was enough to make most people shrink. But not me.

I opened the door and stepped out, turning around to face her before closing it. "Funny. I was about to tell you the same thing."

CHAPTER 4

Faith

As I entered the lobby I was greeted by the disapproving gaze of the Fairy Godmother known as Coco La Rue.

Excellent. One more person who hates my guts.

The receptionist (whom I'd met when my friends and I had broken in here the first time) was sitting at her donut-shaped desk tapping on her holographic keyboard. I ignored the stink eye she gave me and kept moving. Daniel was waiting with Debbie next to the building directory. They rushed over the second they saw me.

"Knight, what happened?" Daniel asked.

"What did she say?" Debbie pressed.

"I'll explain later." I waved them off. "Now that we're clear of Lenore and free to get out of here, there's not a moment to waste. Daniel and I need to find the others."

"Others?" Debbie asked.

"Our friends," I clarified. "We got separated on Adelaide."

"You mean you ditched us on Adelaide," Daniel corrected.

I felt a sting of bitterness within me, but swallowed down my guilt and nodded, accepting the truth.

"Yeah. I did and I'm sorry. But at least doing so led to only you and me being captured. Last time you saw SJ, Blue, and Jason, they'd gone to collect the Pegasi we left in the Adelaide

Castle stables. They are out there somewhere right now." I turned to Debbie hopefully. "I don't suppose you could zap us to them?"

"I could if you knew where they were."

Daniel scoffed. "What good does that do us? You're a Fairy Godmother. Don't you have some sort of crystal ball or something we can use to figure that out?"

Now it was Debbie's turn to scoff. "Danny, we're Godmothers—not psychics, fortunetellers, or soothsayers."

"It's Daniel." He scowled. "So how do you suggest we find them then?"

"Maybe they'll find us," I interjected. "I know those guys, and there's no way after everything we've been through they would just call it quits and head back to school when they couldn't find us on the beach. My guess? They've probably continued on to our next destination, hoping to find us there."

Daniel raised his eyebrows. "So you think they're headed to the Cave of Mysteries?"

"That's what we decided at Ashlyn's, isn't it?"

Back on Earth, when we'd been staying with the Lost Princess, my friends and I hadn't spent a lot of time together. They were angry with me for how I'd been acting, and I was too stubborn and afraid to admit that they had every right to be. The only times when we'd really talked were when we needed to discuss aspects of our mission and the part of our journey that came next.

Emma's instructions said that the third item we had to get to break the In and Our Spell was "A Mysterious Flower Beneath the Valley of Strife." Between Blue's unparalleled expertise (and arguable obsession) with fairytale history and the knowledge Daniel and Jason brought to the table from their classes at Lord Channing's, we figured the clue had been alluding to the Cave of Mysteries.

The Cave of Mysteries was one of those delightfully un-explainable enchanted hootenannies of fairytale lore. While it

contained a myriad of magical, super powerful objects, it was most
famously known as the place where Aladdin had found his genie
lamp. This cave was located somewhere beneath an enormous
desert known as the Valley of Strife. It had to be the location of
the object we were after.

"Yeah, that's what we decided," Daniel said. "But do you really
think they'll be able to get across the Valley of Strife? We hadn't
finalized our plan yet, and it's in Alderon."

I sighed, thinking on the main obstacle that stood in our way
to finding the Cave of Mysteries. The desert it was buried under
was indeed in Alderon, which meant that an untold number
of antagonists, monsters, and dangerous circumstances stood
between us.

"How can you be so sure they'll make it?" Daniel asked.

"One, Arian was after *me*," I said, ticking off the reasons on
my fingers. "Once he caught us in the lamp he would've been on
his way back to Nadia. So that takes care of that threat. Two, the
In and Out Spell surrounding Alderon isn't an issue because it
prevents people from getting *out* of Alderon, not *in*. That's why
Aladdin had to use one of his genie wishes to escape the cave and
kingdom in the first place. And three, like I said, I know those
guys. So believe me they'll make it. I know it in the same way that
I'm sure they know we'll find a way there too, and that we'll all
find a way back to each other."

"That's a lot of faith for a girl who until recently was refusing
to trust anyone," Daniel commented—not condescendingly.

"That was never about not having faith in them," I said with
an honesty that slid out of me so easily it was surprising. "It was
about not having faith in myself. But that's over now. And I think
that I—that we—can do this. Don't you?"

Daniel's mouth curved into a small smile—reserved but
impressed. "I guess we're headed to the Cave of Mysteries then.
No going back and all in."

"No going back and all in," I agreed. I turned to Debbie.

"Deb, the Cave of Mysteries is a specific location. How close can you get us?"

"I can zap you to an area of the Valley of Strife near where the Cave of Mysteries is supposed to be located, but you'll have to get in on your own. The Cave is tricky to enter. If it wasn't then anyone could get in and take advantage of its magic knickknacks."

"I know," I said, thinking back to warnings Blue had mentioned. Then I grinned and gave Debbie a hug. "Thanks for everything, Deb. It was great to see you."

"You too, Crisa," she said, hugging me back. "Good Godkids are hard to come by and you always keep it fresh. So try not to get killed, okay? I'd hate to be reassigned."

"I'll do my best."

Static suddenly filled the area, coming from the intercom. "Attention staff . . ."

Oh, what is it now?

"All Godmothers are to report to their emergency stations immediately. We have a code ninety-seven in progress. Closing in on the red zone."

Another Fairy Godmother—short and stout with glasses and gaucho pants burst out of the side door and came rushing into the reception area. "Debbie! There you are! I saw you on the security cameras. Come on, we need all hands on deck."

"Crisa, Danny, this is my friend Sonya July. She works in Security and Surveillance, and she's my emergency buddy." Debbie turned to Sonya. "What's going on?"

"There's a dragon inbound for Headquarters," Sonya replied. "He just appeared on radar and we have about five minutes to teleport the entire compound before he collides with us."

Sonya gestured to Coco, who responded by pressing a few buttons on her holographic keyboard. A screen made of light appeared in the center of the room, projecting a real time image of what was going on outside.

Piercing the sky at top speed was a silvery dragon. He beat his wings mightily, cutting through the clouds. Despite his speed and distance, I could see the golden, glowing eyes set into his skull. They were bright and fiery like miniature suns.

Daniel and I looked at each other. It couldn't be the same dragon we'd come across twice before, could it? That creature had chased us like a hound dog out of Century City and then appeared again when we were exiting the Forbidden Forest. But the odds of it finding us a third time . . .

"All right, you two. I'm needed elsewhere so we've gotta do this fast," Debbie said. She whirled back to us and transformed her wand from its hairpin state. With a wave it began releasing a flurry of red sparks. "A couple of one-way tickets to the Cave of Mysteries coming up. BTW, I should probably mention that I can totally get you into Alderon, but the kingdom's In and Out Spell might throw me off with the specific location. Those magic force fields can really do a number on your aim."

My eyebrows shot up. "Wait. What?"

CHAPTER 5

Kidnapped by a Lobster

ne bright, scarlet flash later and Daniel and I were surrounded by oppressive sunlight.

We were standing in the sand. I couldn't see a single other living thing in the area. Everywhere we looked sand dunes rolled into the endless horizon, creating a blurry line that blended the rich cream color of the ground with the robin's-egg color of the sky.

A moderate wind caused my skirt to rustle and my hair to blow around my face. I held up a hand to shield my eyes from the sun.

So this is Alderon.

First impressions: Dry, and the air tastes like . . .

I swallowed.

Salt crackers.

"I think she missed," Daniel commented. "Your Godmother, I mean. Jason and I took a Magical Geography class this semester. This looks like what I was expecting for the Valley of Strife, but if we were near the Cave of Mysteries the sand would be a reddish color, getting more crimson the closer we got to it."

I nodded. "While we were at Ashlyn's House Blue sketched us a map of Alderon based on her fairytale history research in between watching those *Die Hard* movies she was obsessed with. I remember the Cave was by the Weser—the big river that runs through half the kingdom."

"I'm beginning to see why your Godmother is still in training then. There's not a river in sight. We're nowhere near where we're supposed to be."

"Give her a break. She said the magic of In and Out Spells can mess with aim."

I trudged up the closest dune. Daniel followed. When we reached the top I was taken aback by how big the desert was. Barren as a classroom on a Saturday, I could understand why it'd been named the Valley of Strife.

After squinting past the glare I spotted a sliver of hope. Several miles in the distance I could see the speck of a town. From here it looked like a beauty mark on the desert—a dark bulge sticking out of the otherwise smooth, beige terrain.

"Someone there might be able to point us in the direction of the river," I said.

"Think it through, Knight," Daniel responded. "We don't exactly look like villains or desert rats, no thanks to your Godmother's little makeover. The antagonists who live here are not this clean cut or fitted with fancy, magical clothes. They're going to know we don't belong. And while they don't have gilded schools like we do, they're not stupid. I'm sure even the ones born here have read fairytale books. So eventually someone will figure out we're main characters and I don't want to know what a bunch of antagonists will do to a pair of lone protagonists that were dumb enough to cross onto their turf."

"Well what would you suggest then?" I replied. "It's got to be late afternoon by now, which means the sun will be going down soon. We need to get out of this desert and I don't exactly have a flying carpet on me."

"I say we aim for the area past the town," Daniel said, pointing.

I hadn't noticed it before, but past the camouflage of distance I began to make out the outline of mountains. "Oh."

"Agreed then?"

"Agreed," I said. Then I couldn't help but smirk a bit as we descended the dune.

"What's that look for?" Daniel asked.

"Nothing," I said. "Just . . . I guess there's a first time for everything."

By the time we made it to the mountains the sun was choking the horizon.

Night was coming quickly and the temperature had started to drop. Daniel and I were running out of time to find cover. The blue sky was now streaked with gold, red, and gray. The wind had also picked up. Between that and the clouds rolling in, I began to wonder if a storm was imminent.

The two of us would have made better time if we had gone through the town. But Daniel was right; we looked like protagonists and we couldn't risk being spotted.

It was the fault of protagonists that antagonists were trapped in Alderon. Sometimes that was because a protagonist defeated an antagonist personally—like that evil witch who'd cursed Sleeping Beauty and then got defeated by the princess's prince charming, or SJ's wicked step-grandmother who'd been stopped by Snow White's dwarves and her prince charming.

On other occasions, antagonists were locked in Alderon before their evil plans got that far. Fairy Godmothers, the guards of individual kingdoms, and other forms of realm security were always keeping an eye out for potential threats. And whenever they found one—whether it was a witch, magic hunter, monster, or just your run-of-the-mill person planning to murder someone or blow something up—they were arrested and tossed in here. Then it was game over. There wasn't any known way out of Alderon, so the incarcerated would be trapped in this desolate place forever. Which meant that any children they might produce would be trapped in here too.

If I was being honest, that last part had always bothered me. If someone was wicked and got punished for it, that was their problem. They'd made a choice and had to deal with the consequences. But it wasn't fair to any future kids they might have.

I inadvertently shuddered at the notion.

While the concept of a mommy and daddy villain making a little villain may have been an odd thing to think about, it was unavoidable. It's not like the people sent here were going to live in solitary all their lives. They reproduced. It was human nature. Which meant that this kingdom was continuously filled with more and more people who didn't necessarily deserve to be here. Those children and grandchildren of antagonists had never been charged with any crimes. They were just forced to live in Alderon because of who their ancestors were.

Our realm's leaders always told us this was a necessary precaution. They insisted that antagonists had evil in their blood and that their offspring would inherit the trait. So keeping them in Alderon was a preemptive way of protecting our realm from the harm they would inevitably cause.

But our realm's leaders had also always told us that princesses were supposed to be weak, common characters couldn't be special, and only male protagonists had what it took to be heroes. Believing in my heart that they were wrong about all these assertions, I wondered if maybe they were also wrong about the people of Alderon. At least some of them.

I was not my mother. While I had inherited her last name and legacy, I forged my own path and was undoubtedly my own person. So why couldn't the same be said for the children of antagonists? If my glass slipper didn't fit, who said theirs had to?

The thought weighed on me. It was easy not to think about the antagonists when they were trapped in a contained place on the other side of the realm. But being in their kingdom—walking on their sand—made the topic about as glaring as the desert sun.

I felt vexed by the quandary. While I empathized with the

whole "people judging you because of your parents" thing, I had no proof that our realm's leaders were wrong about the antagonists. After all, dozens of them had tried to kill me since I left school to find the Author. Arian had even owned up to hunting main characters long before I came along. Plus, he had those files in the Capitol Building that marked more protagonists as possible targets.

Honestly, every experience I'd had with antagonists from Alderon affirmed what I was supposed to believe about their kind. They were vicious; they were cruel; and they threatened our realm and its people.

Like Lenore, I had no idea how they were escaping Alderon since the kingdom's In and Out Spell had no holes. My friends and I would only be able to escape if we successfully collected all the items on Emma's list and used them to break through the In and Out Spell around the Indexlands, which rimmed Alderon's southeastern border.

Daniel and I weren't being dramatic when we said "no going back and all in."

But however the antagonists were getting out, every one of them had only added to the increasing odds of our demise. Given that, maybe it was wishful thinking to believe that they had the potential to be different. I had a soft spot for people who were judged because of who their parents were, but I had also been persecuted by antagonists enough times to be unable think of them as anything but monsters.

Eventually Daniel and I arrived at the foot of the mountain range. It was a wonder that it had been so concealed by the shadows of the desert earlier. Up close it was massive. The summit was steep and far off. It would take hours of hiking to reach the halfway point. Dense woods, predominantly devoid of greenery, dotted the jagged slopes. The bark of the trees looked dangerously dry and crisp—just one match away from incinerating like a piece of decoupage paper. There was some richer foliage higher up though, causing me to believe that, despite the forsaken nature of the desert, it did rain every once in a while.

A sound like a coyote's howl pierced the still twilight. At least I hoped it was a coyote. Alderon wasn't just a place where the realm's leaders stuck antagonists; they shoved monsters in here too. And in a world where magic was prevalent and heroes were a staple, the assortment of vicious enchanted creatures in Alderon was bountiful. Ogres, dragons, six-foot-tall llamas with fangs and night vision—you name it, some hero had fought it in one of Book's forests.

You do remember how many colorful kinds of creatures tried to kill us in the Forbidden Forest, right?

I found myself looking over my shoulder at the town behind us. It was about a mile away. Although I knew we'd be at risk there, instinct still told me that journeying into unfamiliar, wild-creature infested mountains after dusk was a bad idea.

The sky grew redder. The air grew colder.

"Come on," Daniel said. "We should find some place to make camp for the night."

The two of us continued up the mountain. After a while we spotted a cave above us. My hands gripped the brim of the sharp stone as I pulled myself onto the wide rocky ledge that surrounded it like a loading platform.

The ceiling of the cave curled like a wave about to crash. Trees partially concealed the entrance from view. Some trees even grew through the cave, trunks and roots worming their way around the entrance.

After collecting some branches, Daniel and I built a small fire far enough inside that the light couldn't be detected from outside the cave. We sat there in silence as the wood crackled and burned. In the blazing red light Daniel's features looked harder. I noticed the tiredness in his eyes, the strength of his jaw, and the shadows curving alongside his face.

Realizing I was staring, I picked up a stick and began to

poke the fire. "So . . . tell me about her," I said, trying to start a conversation.

Daniel glanced at me. The reflection of the embers danced in his eyes. "About who?"

"Kai," I said. "What's she like?"

Daniel's expression was a combination of disbelief and discomfort at my having asked the question. "Knight, it's been a long day" was all he said.

He looked away from me and I let the matter drop. We'd only just agreed to give trusting each other a shot, so I supposed asking him to share personal stories over a campfire was pushing it.

In retrospect, the only reason he'd told me about Kai in the first place was to balance out what I had told him about myself. I'd revealed my innermost fears, doubts, and vulnerabilities to him and he'd felt pressured to share something with me in return. We had traded secrets as a sort of eye-for-an-eye gesture made in an attempt to restore equilibrium to our relationship.

While I was in no mood to expose myself to such a personal degree, I couldn't help but wonder if the same approach would work now.

It'd been said that an eye for an eye would make the whole world blind, but maybe this tactic was the only way Daniel and I could ever talk to each other without our natural guardedness getting in the way.

I'd always had trouble opening up to others, worrying that people would mistake any sign of weakness as confirmation of my being a damsel princess. And my doubts about who I was only added to the distance I liked to keep between me and everyone else. While I cared about and relied on SJ, Blue, and Jason more than anyone, I'd even kept them at arm's length for the same reasons.

But I didn't want to be that way anymore. I couldn't be that way anymore, especially now. Daniel and I were alone out here and we needed to rely on each other.

Unfortunately, as more time passed since our talk in the genie lamp, the more I felt my shields going back up. They weren't rising for any particular reason; it was just my way. However, I instantly recognized that this was a problem I needed to nip in the bud.

I didn't want my guard up with Daniel, at least not at the moment. On enemy terrain, antagonists after me, deep in monster-infested mountains—I needed to push away my doubts about him. Things could go very wrong for both of us if I didn't.

Which was why, in an effort to keep strengthening my reasons to trust him, I allowed myself to test this eye-for-an-eye vulnerability theory. And I hoped that being open with him would inspire him to be open with me, thus reinforcing my confidence in our partnership.

Sitting there—cold stone under my butt and the smell of burnt wood tickling my nose—I took a deep breath.

Okay, here we go. It's no big deal. Just lower the shields for a bit. Talk to him like a human being. Tell him something . . . real.

I gulped at the thought but forced myself to go through with it anyways.

"You know, when I was little I always wanted to be a great swordfighter," I began.

Daniel raised his head.

"My parents never wanted me to," I continued, stoking the fire. "I think my mom learned to accept it after a while, just like she learned to accept me, but my dad . . ." I shook my head. "Anyways, most people have always treated me like they do at Lady Agnue's—like despite my training and spirit, I could never be strong enough to accomplish those kinds of dreams. It didn't help my ego to have two older brothers who are both ridiculously skilled swordfighters. I think that's one of the reasons I didn't like you from the start. You were such a great, natural swordfighter. Meanwhile I'd been practicing for close to ten years and you defeated me without breaking a sweat."

I got the confidence to glance up at Daniel. His expression was hard to read, but I decided to finish my thought without worrying about his judgment. I put my stick down and leaned back against my hands as I blew a strand of hair out of my face. "I know I have nothing to worry about now. I've punched enough antagonists in the last few weeks to know I've got some skills of my own. And having realized that I'm relatively epic with my wand in the form of a spear, I can finally accept that sword fighting was never a natural talent for me. But things were different when we first met. I hadn't found my spear or my confidence yet, and in less than a minute you made me feel like an idiot and a weakling. I hated you for that. Now though, after everything, I guess I'm actually grateful.

"My life has been so geared toward fighting and struggling against the norm that sometimes I think it might make me persistent to a fault. Maybe if I'd accepted my lack of ability with the sword sooner I would have experimented more with other weapons and found my spear before this year. Just like maybe if I hadn't been so stubborn about protecting my image in the eyes of my friends, I wouldn't have made all those mistakes and we might still be with them now."

I sighed and shook my head. "I know what's done is done and I'm moving forward and all that. But I'm smart enough to realize that I'd probably still be on that self-destructive path if it weren't for you. So like I said, despite what our past bickering might suggest, I appreciate that you put me in my place, Daniel. In all honesty I may never stop hating you for it. But I am grateful. Whatever happens, I want you to know that."

It felt like my right hand was tingling, but I ignored it. I swallowed hard. Daniel stared at me and clenched his jaw. I could see his hands tense as they curled into fists, knuckles whitening.

It was understandable. Both of us had trouble with being vulnerable. But I hoped he would bite. I needed him to talk to me if I was going to keep my guard down around him. If I'd just revealed even more of myself for nothing, then the resulting humiliation would be like a bomb on the bridge we'd only just begun to build between us.

After a minute Daniel raised a hand to his forehead. His expression changed from uncomfortable to sad. He let out a deep breath.

"When I was chosen as a protagonist I was angry," he began slowly. "I know that might sound stupid to you, but I was happy with my life as a common. When I read my prophecy and learned about you, that feeling of anger only grew. I'm not the kind of person that takes their problems out on other people—never have been. But it was a lot to absorb at once. And I'll admit that when I first met you I took some satisfaction in making you feel, I don't know, small, I guess. I mean I was mad. I thought some selfish, prissy princess was going to destroy my life. But the more we hung out, the more I realized that I was—" Daniel stopped. "What's wrong with your hand?"

"What?"

Daniel gestured to my right hand. I brought it to the light of the fire. It was silvery and rippling and looked like melted metal. No wonder it was tingling.

"Is that still because of the watering can?" he asked, referencing our run-in with the witch in the Forbidden Forest. At the time— in exchange for our lives and some enchanted saltwater taffy we needed for our quest—we'd agreed to give up our defining characteristics of internal strength for two weeks. As part of the exchange we'd had to grasp onto a magic watering can that seared our hands and made them temporarily look like liquid metal. When the effect faded, we were supposed to receive a brand with the name of the quality that defined us. However, the watering can didn't take anything from me because I hadn't figured out my source of internal strength yet. As a result, I was left with a blurry splotch on my hand.

The witch said that if I ever figured out my special trait

the mark would morph into a temporary tattoo of the word—announcing the quality—like it had for my friends. But since our run-in, this liquid metal effect had happened several times and the blurry mark remained the same.

"Yeah," I replied to Daniel, shrugging off the phenomenon. "I'm pretty sure either it or I might be broken."

I held up my hand to show Daniel as the rippling metallic skin rescinded past my fingertips. It was almost gone. After another beat, my hand was pale and smooth again and the smudgy mark on my palm remained indiscernible. My core internal strength continued to elude me.

"See," I said. "Nothing."

"It can't be healthy for your skin to keep turning to metal," Daniel replied. "You should probably see a doctor about that."

"Right. I'll make an appointment tomorrow along with the dentist and the chiropractor. It's not like we have anything else going on."

Daniel smirked.

"What were you going to say before?" I asked, itching to know the answer to the question much more than my casual tone let on. "The more we hung out the more you realized you were . . ."

"Forget it." Daniel shrugged. "It's not important."

Like heck it's not.

"I bet I can figure it out," I said cockily, leaning back against my hands again with a twinkle of mischief in my gaze. "The more we hung out the more you realized that you were outmatched by my brilliance, humbled by my princess grace and charm, unworthy to do battle—in terms of wit or weaponry—with someone so magnificent?"

Daniel let out an amused huff. "Yeah, that's it."

Relaxing my snark, I spoke sincerely. "Daniel, come on. Tell me."

His expression turned serious and I wondered if I'd spooked him. Getting Daniel to share was like getting a wild animal to eat out of your hand—tricky, delicate work that depended so much on circumstance and timing. If either was wrong, or if you pushed too hard, it would flee from you in an instant.

"I was wrong."

My eyebrows shot up. "Sorry?"

"The more we hung out, the more I realized I was wrong about you," Daniel explained. "You weren't the person I assumed you were. You were so different from the snooty princess I had imagined. And you weren't meant to destroy my life."

"But what about your prologue prophecy?" I asked. "Doesn't it say I'm the one with the potential to ruin Kai and foil your happiness?"

"It does." Daniel nodded. "But it's like I told you in the lamp, I'm not holding that against you. For one, my prophecy—like that of most main characters—is vague. So without footnotes to explain the details I can't make assumptions about what's specifically going to happen. More importantly though, Knight, whatever *does happen*, it's my prophecy, which means it's my responsibility. I accept that and I'm committed to doing everything I can to ensure it doesn't lead to a horrible ending. And part of that means—hard as it may be for me to swallow—accepting that the very person who could destroy my happiness is possibly the best chance I have at saving it."

I hadn't noticed how dark it'd gotten. The sun had set somewhere over the mountain. The sky was a swirl of clouds tinged with bright crimson. Our small fire burned smaller as time ticked on without either of us tending to it.

"Remember how I told you my prophecy also says you're supposed to be a key ally to me and Kai?" Daniel asked. "I'm beginning to understand why. It's only because of your help that I might have a chance at rewriting my fate and changing the Author's course for my life. Every crazy choice you've made has pushed us to get here, closer than anyone's ever come to finding the Author. So like I said that day we flew to your godmother Emma's house, I was wrong to judge you off the bat and I'm sorry. But more than that—and don't turn this into a big deal—"

He shot me a pained, almost frustrated look, like it physically hurt him to say the words. "As hard as it may be to believe, the truth is I guess I'm grateful for you too."

SNAP!

The sound of a branch cracking somewhere nearby caused us both to whip our heads toward the cave's opening. I clambered to my feet and approached the mouth of the cave. Daniel was at my side a moment later. We stared into the bleak twilight before instinct kicked in. "Put the fire out," I said.

He went back to extinguish the embers. I wandered across the stone platform surrounding the cave, closer to the ledge. I stopped when I was four feet from it. There was a deep crack etched into the rock there. Definitely an avalanche hazard.

The area directly beneath the ledge was hidden from view, but I could see the vast forest at the base of the mountains. In the low light, it looked like a patch of dark fur on the back of a gravelly creature.

I pulled out my wandpin.

Lapellius.

The delicate accessory extended to its full wand form.

Dang, that was a cool trick.

My wand's soft, off-white glow shimmered against my arm, catching the light of the crystals in my sleeve. Everything was silent for a beat, eerily so. I glanced black to gauge Daniel's progress with the fire. But a distant whooshing sound, as if something was hurtling through the air, brought my attention back to the front of the cave just in time.

A large boulder came barreling toward the mouth of the cave. It approached in an arc like a Twenty-Three Skidd ball lobbed from a distance. The trajectory caused the boulder to sail over my head by about seven feet—missing me, but not by much. It did, however, come very close to killing Daniel.

I instinctively dove to the right when the boulder entered my peripheral vision. Daniel did the same, but he'd been standing under the mouth of the cave at the time. When the boulder hit, large fragments of stone rained upon him. One chunk fell on his leg, causing his knee to buckle and his body to crumple.

"Daniel!" I rushed to help him but was cut off by another boulder.

This one's arc was much lower. It plowed into the ground between Daniel and me. The impact was so powerful it knocked me over and almost caused me to tumble off the ledge.

I landed on my back. When I did I felt a crumbling vibration—the ledge was coming loose. I felt two more impacts against the rock. Unlike when the boulder crashed, these were steady and purposeful like heavy footsteps. Tilting my head to the left, I identified the cause. Firmly gripping the edge of the platform only a few feet away was a pair of enormous black claws. With haste I threw myself away from the ledge and stumbled to my feet just as the monster that owned the pincers pulled itself into view.

It was hideous—ten feet in length and shaped like a lobster crossed with a caterpillar. Its entire body was covered in black, shiny scales that resembled beetle carapaces. It had no eyes. Its domed body was smooth and only had one orifice right up front—a mouth the size of three watermelons. In that mouth were two rows of teeth so white and well aligned it made me wonder if monsters visited orthodontists.

The creature's body clung to the rock by means of at least two-dozen legs that ended in tiny grippers. The legs were long but bent. Meanwhile, the creature's two front claws were another kind of formidable. At the center of each set of pincers extended an intimidatingly sharp, pearl-colored talon.

Protruding from the creature's back were strange extremities. Like swelling vertebrae, bulbs the size of cantaloupes stuck out of the creature's spine from neck to tail. Some were translucent and looked like vacant crystal balls. Others were filled with a golden, glowing energy that churned angrily. Odder still, I thought I saw faces swirling around inside them.

The creature lunged at me. His right claw thrashed down with the needle aimed at my head. I dove out of the way, rolling to the side. The needle pierced the rock but did not break. The crack on the ledge deepened; the rocks rattled.

Spear.

I leapt to my feet and jammed the blade of my staff into the creature's side as hard as I could. It barely cracked the surface. The scaly shell was thick like an armored breastplate.

More annoyed than injured, the lobster flicked its tail to the side, smacking me to the floor. I dropped my spear. My left hand barely grabbed the ledge in time to keep me from falling down the mountain.

I desperately tried to pull myself up, but my sweaty palm slipped on the gravel and dirt. When I finally got a good enough hold to hoist myself onto the ledge I saw the lobster lean back on its hind legs and screech, revealing the only part of its body not covered in scaly armor—the high part of its chest.

When the monster finished screeching, it skittered toward Daniel, whose leg was still pinned under rocks from the avalanche.

I scrambled to my feet and grabbed my spear from where I'd dropped it, but it was too late. Swift and merciless, the lobster thrust one of its pincer needles into Daniel's chest.

"No!"

For a horrifying moment I thought Daniel was slain. But the needle that sunk into Daniel glowed brightly, as did Daniel the moment it went into him.

In the blink of an eye he dematerialized into some form of glowing energy that looked like a gas. He was absorbed into the lobster's needle. A heartbeat later one of the empty translucent orbs on the lobster's back started swirling with the same golden energy as some of the others. For no more than a second, within the energy of that newly filled orb I saw the vague outline of Daniel's face.

I was dumbfounded but focused. I was also determined, angry, and brimming with conviction. So when the creature turned to pursue me again it got more than it bargained for.

It came at me with one vicious claw after another, but I was too fast for it this time. I jumped and evaded each attack with the speed of a jackrabbit. Glancing back, I saw that Daniel had not finished putting out the fire before the attack had begun. Small chunks of kindling and firewood still blazed behind me. An idea formed inside me that was equally hot and untempered.

The lobster backed me up closer to the part of the cave that hadn't been affected by the avalanche. I picked up a grapefruit-sized piece of fallen rock and chucked it at the creature's perfect teeth.

The throw was hard and my aim was true. Enraged, the lobster opened its mouth to screech. As it did, I transformed my wand into a lacrosse sword—the weapon of choice for my favorite sport, Twenty-Three Skidd. The lacrosse sword had the staff of my spear, but the blade on top was longer and there was a basket at the other end. This basket was ordinarily intended for catching and lobbing Twenty-Three Skidd balls, but I had other plans. I spun the staff and scooped up a serving of blazing kindling from the fire. I hurled the flaming projectile into the lobster's wide-open orifice.

The wail that followed was all pain. As smoke poured from its mouth and the creature clawed at its face, it staggered back toward the crumbling ledge.

I rushed forward, slammed my spear down on the lobster's head, then channeled all my strength and fury as I used my staff like a bat to smack the side of the lobster's face. The creature was knocked on its side, landing on the ledge. Its impact was strong enough to cause the widening crack to break off completely. In an avalanche of rock, it went tumbling down the cliff.

Transforming my wand and storing it, I did not delay in going after the monster. I grabbed the new ledge with one hand, swung down, then released my grip and plummeted a few feet before my boots hit ground and I broke into a run.

I descended the mountain faster than proper safety procedures would advise. But I didn't care about being careful. The creature was toppling through the forest now, but the way it was screeching told me it was still very much alive and it was only a matter of time before it righted itself and scampered away. That was not an option, not while it had Daniel.

When the ground started to even out, the lobster crashed into a pine tree big enough to break its fall. Just as I'd predicted, the lobster was rattled, but rapidly shook off the disorientation and flipped back to its feet.

It started zipping through the woods with increased urgency. I ran faster; my heartbeat thumped louder; my breathing hastened. Reds, greens, and the darkness of shadows blurred around me as my breath got caught in my throat. I swallowed down the frigid air as my legs throbbed from the speed and the jolting friction of the bumpy terrain.

I heard the sound of rushing water. A glance to my right revealed a thin waterfall about a hundred meters over—peeking through the trees and pouring into a lake.

When I looked up a moment later I saw where the creature was heading. In the depths of the forest—somewhere in the armpit of the mountains—was a fortress. Its outer wall was composed of colossal wooden spikes. Sturdy oak bars bolstered its window frames. Upper floors featured patios covered by thick tarps that rustled about in the wind. And the entire compound's roof was paneled with giant sheets of mirrors.

The lobster whimpered and scratched at the front door of the fortress like a dog locked out of its home. The door rose steadily in response. A brilliant light exuded from within. I quickened my pace, but the lobster scurried inside and the door lowered before I could reach it.

When I arrived at the fortress I banged on the door angrily. I didn't think about where I was or who might be in there. All I cared about was getting Daniel back. No monster or villain could compare to the fire I was feeling.

I heard the sound of latches and metal chains unwinding inside. The door rose once more. The bright luminescence poured out. It was so intense in contrast to the post-sundown sky that I felt disoriented and blinded. It was like meeting the sun's younger sibling.

When my eyes refocused I saw a girl coming to meet me. Her pants were thick and dirty beige. She wore a vest made of brown fur over a flowing crème-colored shirt. Black leather gloves covered her hands and matched the weapon-wielding utility belts hanging from her waist. Her head was wrapped in a turban-style headscarf that only allowed me to see her intense, dark orange eyes.

"Your monster has my friend," I said crossly.

The girl undid her headscarf to get a better look at me. Golden, curly locks spilled down her shoulders. She huffed at my accusation and waved me forward. "Come in," she said.

She flipped a lever on the side wall and the door began to lower again. I had no choice but to hurry in after her.

My hostess continued to move swiftly down the corridors of the fortress without waiting for me. I pursued her but found it difficult. The inside of the compound was so bright it was dizzying. The primary source of radiation came from enormous panels of light that made up every inch of the ceiling. It was as if someone had stripped a star of its epidermis and cemented it here.

After a minute my eyes managed to adjust to the light. Thank goodness. This place was difficult enough to navigate without being blind. The elaborate corridors twisted and turned sharply like a maze.

In careful pursuit of the twenty-something girl who'd let me in, my boots pounded against the floors. They were wooden like the walls and were covered in animal pelts. I jumped slightly when I nearly stepped on the face of a goatskin rug. Its mouth was open and its petrified eyes were staring at me.

"Where are you going?" I called after the girl.

She didn't respond, turning down the hall and out of sight.

"Hey!" I picked up speed, getting more frustrated with every step. "Hey, blondie! I'm talking to you!"

I turned the corner but skidded to a halt to avoid ramming into the girl, who had stopped. She gave me an amused, thin smirk as she tucked a curl of hair behind her ear. "Actually, it's Goldilocks. But I get that all the time."

CHAPTER 6

Worst Tea Party Ever

itting in Goldilocks's grand dining room—so big you'd think she held regular banquets—I couldn't help but think of Madame Lisbon, my Damsels in Distress teacher. I realized that I was inadvertently sitting with the perfect posture I'd been trained to hold whenever attending a tea party. It was an uncontrollable reflex—like a dog howling at the moon or a boxer throwing a punch when someone sneak-attacks them from behind. My professor would be so proud.

Goldilocks set a plate of biscuits and a teacup on a furry coaster in front of me. She poured tea into it. I cringed—both from the smell of the hot leaf juice (which I'd always detested) and the realization that the coaster was a flattened coyote paw, dyed blue. It was gross and disturbing, but I guess it matched the rest of the room.

I shifted uncomfortably as Goldilocks went to the other side of the table and poured her own cup of tea. Animal pelts hung from the walls and covered the entire floor like a disturbing patchwork quilt. There were also giant stuffed animals everywhere—not the cute kind, but the taxidermy kind. Fully grown bears, wolves, deer, raccoons, and other woodland creatures covered every surface. While the huge ones like the bears stood upright—mouths open and teeth exposed in mid-growl—the smaller creatures were placed on tables and shelves. My eyes lingered on a pair of matching squirrel bookends before a low, muffled snore drew my attention.

The only non-dead creature in the room aside from me and Goldilocks was the lobster monster. It was lying on a plush bed the size of three mattresses by the fireplace. I guess it must've been tired from the attack. The creature was now sound asleep and looked like it was having an intense dream from the way its legs were twitching. It would have been cute if it wasn't for its orifice full of sharp teeth and the fact that it had somehow captured Daniel through its giant pincer needles.

The frown on my lips tightened as I stared at the orbs on the creature's spine. Six were filled with golden, whirring energy. They looked more ominous illuminated in the firelight. I felt my heart quicken and my throat stiffen as I focused on the orb that Daniel had been sucked into.

Please be okay, I thought as I dug my nails into the oak table.

I quickly pivoted back toward Goldilocks, knowing full well it would be a mistake to take my eyes off her for more than a moment.

While Goldilocks had initially made a name for herself by breaking into the home of three bears and becoming the world's youngest squatter, this breaking-and-entering incident was only her first account of law breaking. As she got older, her criminal activity had increased in frequency and severity to the point that she became the head of one of the most notorious crime rings in the kingdom of Coventry. There had never been confirmation of how many heists and murders she'd been behind, but the rumors were horrifying. It took years for realm security and the Fairy Godmothers to catch her. When they finally did, her offenses landed her in Alderon.

And now I'm having tea with her.

Great.

"So, protagonist," Goldilocks said menacingly. "What brings you to Alderon? Business or pleasure?"

I didn't bother wondering how she knew what I was. I figured my clothes had given me away like Daniel said.

Goldilocks's eyes gleamed like the polished, fifteen-foot-long wooden table between us. Even from a distance I could see her irises blazing.

She reached for a pile of papers and magazines beside her place setting. She pushed aside a few periodicals before picking up a newspaper, which she regarded for a moment and then tossed in my direction. The newspaper slid across the table past a couple of empty candleholders and a candelabra made from eight chipmunks whose noses protruded into lit candlewicks. The newspaper came to rest next to my teacup.

The light was so intense from the massive panels on the ceiling that it made the periodical almost impossible to read. I fixed my gaze as best I could.

The newspaper was opened to a page that said, "Wanted." Four large photographs with accompanying descriptions were printed on the page. Staring back at me were the faces of Daniel, Jason, Blue, and yours truly. I instantly thought it was strange that SJ's picture wasn't there as well. It reminded me that she was the only one of us who didn't have a folder in Arian's bunker below the Capitol Building.

I raised my eyebrows and picked up the periodical to read the copy aloud. "Crisanta Katherine Knight—princess of Midveil and seventh-year student at Lady Agnue's School for Princesses & Other Female Protagonists—is wanted by her majesty Queen Nadia of Alderon for treason against the kingdom and its citizens. The princess was last seen in Adelaide. If found, summon Arian Dark for collection. Her majesty Queen Nadia is offering five hundred gold pounds for proof of her death and one thousand gold pounds for her capture alive."

I blinked.

That's unfortunate.

I knew that Arian and Nadia were after me and that trekking

across Alderon would be dangerous. But having an obscenely large bounty on my head made things way dicier.

Jason, Blue, and Daniel had similar problems. I read that Arian and Nadia were offering three hundred gold pounds for each of their heads, and six hundred gold pounds for their capture.

One look at Goldilocks and I knew what she was thinking.

I remained calm. I'd known there was a tremendous risk when I walked in here, but rescuing Daniel outweighed it.

Wanting to stall until I had an opportunity to get his orb from the lobster monster, I settled against my high-backed chair.

"Arian's last name is *Dark*?" I huffed. "Isn't that convenient."

"So are you, Crisanta Knight," Goldilocks said as she took a bite from one of the biscuits on her plate. "I've been meaning to add another wing to my fortress. Turning you over to Nadia's henchmen will give me enough money to build four."

I crossed my arms calmly. "Let's not get ahead of ourselves. You're interested in capturing me, and I get that. I'm interested in retrieving my friend, which your lunky lobster over there seems to have absorbed into one of his back bubbles. So before we duke it out—which is where we both know this is heading—how about you tell me what happened to him."

Goldilocks reached down and removed a weapon from her belt. It looked like a miniature crossbow, but it was two-pronged (built with two arrows meant to be fired simultaneously) and had a spool of thick silver lanyard on the back that connected the arrows. She held it up casually, admiring it.

"All right," she said. "That 'lunky lobster' is a Magistrake—a kind of energy stealer. It can convert any living creature into pure, clean-burning energy that's more powerful than you can imagine. A single converted soul can fuel and light my entire compound for a month. And in Alderon—where late winter has up to fifteen hours of darkness a day—that kind of light is a precious commodity. So I trained this Magistrake to be my pet and use it to collect energy for me to use and sell."

"So the people it . . . absorbs . . ." I gulped. "Are they—"

"Dead?" Goldilocks finished. "No. They're alive. Not comfortable I imagine, but they're still in there. At least until they're used up by me or my clients."

A flurry of anger coursed through me. I was about to take out my wand, knife it up, and hurl it Blue-style at the girl across from me. But then the door opened at the other end of the room.

"Goldi, dear?" An old woman with a pleasant face and beady eyes entered. "You almost forgot. You know how important the book is to me. If she doesn't sign, my collection won't be complete."

"*Madge.*" Goldilocks rolled her eyes. "She can't stay like the others. I'm turning her over to that monster Arian."

The old woman, who was clutching a brown leather book against her crimson housecoat, approached the table. "But—"

"No buts," Goldilocks interrupted, but not without some compassion in her tone. "For one, it's good business. Five hundred gold pounds is a lot of money. For another, it's common sense. I don't want to be on Arian's bad side, let alone Nadia's. This girl's important to them both. I'm already sacrificing half the reward to feed your little fetish. Be grateful for that."

I listened to them talk. It was weird being discussed like this. Now I knew how a pig felt when a farmer bartered with a butcher over its selling price.

"Even if she isn't going to be a part of my collection, I still want her to sign the book. It's tradition," Madge argued.

"Ugh, fine." Goldilocks sighed and looked at me. "Would you mind?" She gestured at the book in Madge's arms.

Madge set the book down in front of me and flipped it open to where a quill and bookmark were waiting. I scanned the contents of the page. It was a collection of printed names followed by matching signatures and dates.

A guestbook. But why?

I looked up, dumbfounded. "I'm not sure how to respond to this," I said, speaking the honest-to-goodness truth.

"Please just sign it," Goldilocks replied, exasperated. "Madge has a thing about collecting the signatures of our guests. It's important to her. And since the woman practically raised me, it's important for me to make her happy."

I blinked, even more confused.

"Look, I'll make you a deal." Goldilocks reattached the mini crossbow to her belt and pushed her chair back from the table. She stood and strut across the room. When she reached the lobster—or Magistrake, or whatever—she swiftly removed Daniel's orb from its back with a twist and a snap that didn't seem to disturb the creature's slumber. "Sign the book and whatever happens between you and I, I'll let him go. I swear on every bear in here."

I looked around. There were at least twelve stuffed bears in the room. I wasn't sure if that was enough reason to trust her, but I did know I wanted to save Daniel and signing a stupid guestbook didn't seem like too high a price to pay.

"Fine," I said. "Give it here." I slid the book closer to me. Picking up the quill, I added my name, the date, and my signature. I paused once I was done and curiously began flipping back through the pages. The last name I saw before Madge snapped the book shut was "Billy Weaver."

The strange old woman hugged the book again and smiled at me. I'd seen a lot of unsettling things today, but the contorted look of glee in her grin was definitely in the top three.

"Here." Goldilocks tossed me Daniel's orb. I fumbled but caught it. The thing was smooth and thick like a kickball. But it was also vaguely moist and felt full like an egg. I weighed it in my hands for a beat before glancing back at Goldilocks. "How do I get him out?"

"Water," Goldilocks replied. "Just get it wet with cold water and the shell will melt. His soul will be freed and his body will rematerialize. Be careful though," she said, eyeing the way I was toying with it. "Those things are impenetrable when they're attached to the Magistrake, but once freed from its spine they're vulnerable to being broken. And if that thing cracks even a little before you get it to water then your friend's soul is kaput."

Alarmed, I set the orb on the table beside me. "I don't suppose you could get me a glass of water now, could you?" I asked icily.

"That can wait," Goldilocks said, strutting over to stand directly in front of me. "You and I have business to settle. There's still the matter of me collecting the reward on your head."

"Oh, is that all?" I scoffed, watching her carefully.

Goldilocks picked up Daniel's orb from the table.

"Hey!" I started to lunge forward, but Goldilocks held up her hand.

"Relax. I'm just putting him here." She moved to the center of the table and placed Daniel's orb in one of the empty candleholders. "He's more secure this way. Wouldn't want your friend rolling off the table and splitting in half, would we? Besides, you still need to refuel before we fight." Goldilocks gestured at the untouched tea and snacks she'd set out for me.

"I'm sorry, what?"

"I like my opponents to be at their best. It's why I only hunt fully grown creatures and why I need you to fuel up," Goldilocks explained.

"You can't be serious."

"Oh, but I am. Go on. I'll wait. It's not like you're going anywhere."

I gazed at the snacks and tea. They sat there temptingly. I noticed that Madge was sitting on the table now—legs folded and crossed like a child during story time. She rocked back and forth grinning at me and also gesturing enthusiastically at the tea, whispering something under her breath that sounded like "roll doll, roll doll, roll doll."

"You know, I'd heard stories about how menacing you were," I commented to Goldilocks. "But no one ever said anything about your demented mentor, Crazy Christine over here. What's her deal?"

"Madge is what you protagonists might call a Half-Legacy. Of course, her bloodline is of the villainous nature. Madge's older sister Lydia had an on odd fetish for taxidermy, which she combined with a nice mix of homicidal tendencies and an affinity for inn-keeping. Regrettably, the Ravelli police eventually caught her.

"Lydia and her immediate family, who knew about her exploits, were thrown into Alderon as punishment. Wolflizards killed her parents within a year. But Lydia escaped through a hole in the In and Out Spell that she was lucky enough to find.

"With Lydia gone and her parents dead, Madge was left alone in Alderon for years. She didn't see her sister again until eighteen months ago when the woman came back. Evidently Lydia had been on Earth for a while keeping up with her hobbies in a town called England but was drawing too much heat. So she decided to retire here. Unfortunately, ogres killed her a week later. Bad luck, but such is life. Anyways, Madge is kind of bonkers from her scarred childhood, but she's got her wits about her for basic stuff. And she likes to keep her sister's memory alive by carrying on the same work."

"Drink, drink," Madge said, tapping on the table to get my attention then pointing at my teacup with a wrinkly finger.

"Seriously, princess," Goldilocks said. "You best consume something or this is going to be the most anticlimactic fight since the afternoon I tackled that sheep." She gestured at a taxidermy sheep in the corner that had been converted into an umbrella holder.

My eyes fell upon the tea. Steam wafted from the cup, tempting me with its warmth. I was pretty cold, and I suddenly realized how empty my stomach was.

While I utterly disliked the taste of tea, the ravenous pit that my stomach had been reduced to felt so barren that for a second I gave in to the temptation. I picked up the cup and inhaled its heat and scent.

Almonds, I thought as the smell filled my nostrils. *It smells like almonds, but also something else, something familiar . . . Hmm. What is that? And why does it remind me of school?*

I brought the brim of the cup to my cracked lips. Then I paused. Looking up at Goldilocks—her fair skin, mean eyes, and her lush blonde hair—I was reminded of my school nemesis, Mauvrey. I recalled our first day back at school this semester when my friends and I stood outside the banquet hall exchanging spite with the evil daughter of Sleeping Beauty and her posse.

"I mean honestly, SJ," Mauvrey had said as she eyed my friend up and down. "I have always wanted to ask, did no one ever warn your mother not to take food from strangers? Any fool with half a brain knows that. It is practically rule one."

The recollection and my own instinct (suppressed by hunger and cold) turned on like a light in my head. A dozen different things clicked at once, and I put the tea down and rose from the table.

My eyes darted from the steaming beverage to the guestbook and then all the taxidermy animals. I turned to Goldilocks. "You told Madge that five hundred pounds was a lot of money. You don't intend to capture me to get the full reward. You're planning on handing me over to Arian already dead."

Madge had gotten off the table and was now standing on my right. Her previous mutterings echoed in the back of my head. "Roll doll . . ." I mused aloud. My eyes widened as my subconscious found what it needed to. *Roald Dahl.*

Another memory surfaced, this time of Blue during her "Villains of other Realms" phase two years ago. The girl was obsessed with fairytale history and she often yammered on about her latest research whenever there was someone around to listen. It could be annoying. But in moments like this, I was glad I didn't always tune her out.

She'd once told me about a villainess known as the Landlady who lured travelers into her inn, had them sign a guestbook, then poisoned and stuffed them with her taxidermy skills. A fellow on Earth called Roald Dahl had written the story. But there was a copy in the history section of our school's library because the tale was based on a woman who was said to have come from Book.

I now regarded the tea on the table anew as one last remembrance snapped into place. That wasn't almonds I'd smelled; it was cyanide, which smelled surprisingly similar. We'd learned about it in potions class last year when we were studying homemade poison.

Oh, crud. They want to kill me with tea and stuff me like a hunted animal before they turn me over to Arian!

I took a step back from Madge. A shiver passed through my body. "What happened to 'I like my opponents at their best'?" I asked Goldilocks. "What kind of a win is it if you poison me? That's such a cop out."

The conversation was a means of stalling while I formed a plan. The exit was on the other side of the room—Goldilocks's side. There was no way I'd get there before she stopped me, especially if I had to grab and carry Daniel's orb. I needed a little bit of chaos.

I grasped my wandpin from my bra strap, concealing the movement as a subtle, unconscious touching of my neck.

"We were just having a bit of fun," Goldilocks said coolly. "What's the matter, Crisanta? Don't you like games?"

"Not when people play dirty."

"I play to win. The purity of my choices has nothing to do with it."

"Good," I said. "Then you'll appreciate what I have to do next."

My eyes darted to Madge. Goldilocks reached for her belt. I grasped the old woman by the back of the neck and pulled her in front of me just as Goldilocks drew her crossbow.

Lapellius.

Knife.

"Drop it," I said, holding the knife to Madge's neck.

Goldilocks had her crossbow aimed at us. There was a slight hesitation in her eyes at first, but then her lips curved into a small smile. "You won't do it," she said. "You're a protagonist. You're not capable of it."

I glanced at Daniel's orb then back at Goldilocks. My expression narrowed. "I am a protagonist," I said. "And that means I'm capable of anything."

"Then I guess we're not so different." Goldilocks said. With that, she fired her crossbow. I pushed Madge to the right as I dove left. Dual arrows connected by silver lanyard shot out of the contraption, barely missing us both.

I dashed around the side of the table and lunged for Daniel's orb. A split-second before my fingers grazed it, Goldilocks fired again. Two more arrows shot out and my wrist was ensnared by the silver lanyard that connected them.

The arrows impaled the table behind me, pinning my hand down. Goldilocks reloaded her crossbow. I pressed down on the table with my trapped hand—using it for support—then swung up my left leg and kicked the lit chipmunk candelabra clean off the table. It landed on the pelt-covered floor.

Shield.

My shield opened up as Goldilocks fired another set of arrows. They bounced off the metal.

Knife.

I slit the lanyard trapping my hand.

The furry carpet burst into flames from the candelabra and began to spread.

Shield.

Goldilocks launched another shot. I blocked, stepped forward, and spun, releasing my shield like a discus. My aim was flawless. Spinning, the shield smacked into her head and knocked her backwards.

As she careened to the floor I dashed toward the center of the table. Without breaking stride I grabbed Daniel's orb with one hand and my shield with the other as I passed Goldilocks.

The fire had taken to the pelts faster than I'd anticipated. A third of the room was burning and smoking now. Madge had jumped back on the table and was clutching her knees close to her chest as she shouted nonsense.

I was five feet from the door when Goldilocks recovered from the hit and launched another pair of arrows. The shot ensnared my left ankle mid-step. I went tumbling to ground. It hurt, but the plush bearskin broke my fall. Daniel's orb rolled free of my grasp, thankfully not breaking.

I pulled myself up and raised my shield against two more arrows. Goldilocks ran at me—storing her crossbow and swapping it for a knife hanging at her belt. I slashed my ankle free of its entrapment with my own knife then returned my weapon to shield form to protect myself from Goldilocks's assault.

She drove her blade at my head, where it clashed powerfully against my shield. I gritted my teeth at the impact. With a quick jolt I kicked her knee. She buckled. I twisted. And then I hammered the rim of my shield into her rib cage.

She went down; I jumped up.

Grabbing Daniel's orb, I bolted out the door into the fortress's corridor system. As I rounded the corner of the first sharp turn, I heard a familiar screech—the Magistrake. I looked back and saw the creature's shadow a beat ahead of the creature itself.

"I hope you appreciate what I'm doing for you," I told Daniel's orb, which I had tucked under my arm. "If I get killed by a giant lobster or taxidermied, I'll never forgive you."

The screech came again, and with it my jokes receded. I ran down the corridor in search of the exit. Had it not been for the tight turns, the monster surely would have caught up with me. Luckily, such turns were easy for me to bank—speedy as I was—whereas a monster of that size had great difficulty. I heard loud bangs and clatterings as the Magistrake crashed into wall after wall in my pursuit.

This bought me the time I needed to reach the main door. When I did I thrust down the lever with a jerk. The chains overhead began to reel back and pull the door up. When it was halfway there I heard another screech, and this time I saw more than a shadow rounding the corner.

The Magistrake was twenty feet away. I thrust the lever in the opposite direction. The door began to lower and I made a break for it. When the door was three feet from the ground I rolled Daniel's orb beneath it then dove under myself. I toppled into the dirt outside just as the door slammed shut.

My eyes had spent so much time adjusting to the blinding light of the fortress that by comparison the forest was like a splotchy dark void. My vision was super wonky; I could barely see two steps in front of me. Fortunately, Daniel's orb still glowed with its golden energy.

Suddenly I saw his face appear inside it. I couldn't hear him, but he was mouthing a word. I picked up the orb and held it close to my face.

"What is it?" I asked.

It looked like one syllable. Maybe it started with an L.

I heard a loud crash behind me. The door to the fortress rattled. I whipped my head back to look at Daniel's face in the orb. He mouthed the word again then nodded in the direction of the forest I'd come from. At last I understood what he was saying.

"Oh, *lake!*" I exclaimed. Then my heart stopped for a beat when my ears detected the sound of chains screeching against the weight of the rising door. "Oh, crud."

I heard Goldilocks's voice echo beneath the frame of the door. "Go, boy," she told the Magistrake. "Hunt. Kill."

"Ready for a swim?" I asked Daniel as I broke into a run. I hugged his orb close to my chest, my eyes trained on the trees.

Silver sparks whirred around me for a few seconds as SJ's SRB took care of the dirt clinging to my outfit from the dive-and-roll out of the fortress. As the effect simmered away—trailing off my boots—it looked like I was producing some kind of magical backfire.

My eyes finally adjusted to the night. The mountains loomed all around. There were still touches of red in the sky, but the weather felt different—colder, harder. A storm was definitely coming. I could feel it in the atmosphere. The wind was sharp and getting harsher, beginning to whip up blades of grass and shake the trees.

I had put about fifty meters between the fortress and me, and while I couldn't see it, I could hear the waterfall. It was a reassuring sound, unlike the one I heard next.

The Magistrake had evidently grown tired of waiting. With a crash, it broke through the door and burst into the darkness, Goldilocks close behind. She fired her crossbow and I was grateful for having glanced back. The arrows surely would have ensnared my ankles had I not seen them coming. I was able to leap to the side and evade their capture.

"Ugh, what am I going to do?"

Let her catch you, my subconscious responded.

If I could slap my own internal reasoning I would have. That was a terrible idea.

Then the creature screeched again (much closer this time) and I realized something. I would never be able to outrun it. I would have to kill it, which would mean getting close enough to directly strike its upper chest. When I'd seen it reel back on its hind legs earlier, I'd noticed that the upper chest was its only weak point. My blade merely bounced off the tough shell of scales that protected the rest of its exterior.

I transformed my wand back into pin form and clutched it tightly, concealing it within my left palm. The moment I did, I found myself in a more open area of the woods. Ahead, the massive waterfall poured down, pummeling the lake and dispersing into a connecting ravine.

SCREECH!

The Magistrake's call pierced the air. I held the orb up to my face. "You wanted me to learn to ask for help?" I asked Daniel's whirring image, referencing one of the many things he'd lectured me about in the genie lamp. "Well, I could sure use some right now. So hurry up."

With that, I lobbed his orb through the air and into the lake. When it broke the surface of the water it caused an eruption of golden waves. I spun back around as Goldilocks—now riding the Magistrake—came into view. The luminescent orbs on the monster's back gave her hair a brilliant glow, even from afar.

Let her catch you, my subconscious repeated.

This time I listened. When Goldilocks fired her crossbow again I chose not to move out of the way fast enough. The arrows' silver lanyard wrapped around my ankles and pulled me to the ground.

My head hit the dirt. I regained my senses right as the Magistrake hovered over me. Its horrible mouth was open, showing too many teeth to count. A bit of the creature's drool spattered on my face. The monster drew back a pincer and I made my move. Just as it came closer I transformed my hidden wandpin.

Lapellius.

Spear.

The five-foot-long staff expanded instantly and the blade pierced straight through the Magistrake's vulnerable chest. I thrust my body to the side to evade the pincer's needle, which plowed into the ground.

The Magistrake staggered with my spear jammed well inside its body, a greenish ooze leaking down the shaft. Goldilocks toppled off its back. I sat up quickly and tried to pull the ensnarement off my ankles, but it wouldn't budge.

Goldilocks recovered and drew her knife. "I hope Arian can still identify your body after I've chopped it into a million pieces."

I instinctively reached for my wandpin but came up empty-handed. My weapon was obviously still lodged inside the Magistrake's body. I reached forward and pulled harder on my restraints.

"I'm going to enjoy this," Goldilocks said angrily. "I'm a career antagonist, but you, Crisanta Knight, are one of the most infuriating people I've ever met."

"I feel you," said a familiar voice. "But you're still not touching her."

I whipped my head around. Daniel had emerged from the river and was rushing at Goldilocks, still dripping wet. His sword clashed against her knife. She blocked, whirling around. The silver sparks of Daniel's SRB encircled them like an erratic cyclone.

Daniel pushed Goldilocks closer to the Magistrake. Their fight grew more perilous because of it. The dying creature's pincers were thrashing this way and that, adding another threat to their list of things to worry about as they slashed at one another.

Suddenly I knew what Daniel was doing. I knew because I would've done the same thing. When the moment was right, Daniel struck Goldilocks on her left side and then kicked her straight back. She stumbled as the Magistrake's claw came down.

I averted my eyes. Goldilocks screamed as the needle pierced her. Only when the sound dissipated did I turn back.

The highest sphere on the creature's vertebrae now swirled with Goldilocks's absorbed essence. Daniel stood over the monster as it collapsed with a final thud. Unlike Goldilocks, it was most certainly beyond resurrection. I'd killed it.

"You okay?" he asked as he came over to me. He kneeled down and slashed the lanyard around my feet with his sword.

"I am now," I said, rubbing my ankles. I strode over to the monster and withdrew my weapon. "What about you?" I asked as

I morphed the spear back to pin form and stored it away. "How was being dematerialized?"

"A lot like being turned into soup. I wouldn't recommend it." He nodded toward the woods. "Come on, we should probably keep moving."

"Not yet," I said. I began unscrewing the glowing orbs from the Magistrake's back, all but the one that contained Goldilocks.

"What are you doing?" he asked.

"You said you didn't recommend the experience," I replied. "I don't know who these people are, but I reckon no one deserves to be kept as a ball of golden gas." I set the fifth luminescent orb on the grass then glanced back at the orb on the Magistrake's spine that held Goldilocks. "Well, almost no one."

Together, Daniel and I launched the five orbs into the lake. "Now we can go," I said. Golden waves erupted and the surface of the water fizzled. My frown tightened. "And we should probably do it quickly. We may not know who those people are, but if they're from Alderon then they're still antagonists."

"Yeah, for all we know the Wicked Witch of the West could be in there," Daniel agreed. "And after that lobster attack, I could do without any more surprises for a while."

"Technically, the odds of the Wicked Witch of the West being in there are slim to none since she's from Oz, not Book," I corrected as we began to walk toward the woods. "But I'm with you. No more surprises would be great."

And then, naturally, we fell through a black hole that spontaneously appeared in the ground.

CHAPTER 7

Magic, Moonlight, & Self-Induced Injuries

I'm not sure I'll ever get used to feeling like a crouton in a salad spinner.

We had gone through a black wormhole once before when we went to Earth in pursuit of Ashlyn. The experience had been awful enough when we were expecting it. Falling through such a hole without warning made the experience way worse.

Daniel and I toppled through a funnel of spinning colors and churning sparks. It felt like fingers made of water and electricity were grasping at our limbs and pulsing through our nervous systems. My hair tangled around me; my body seemed to lose its molecular structure as my form blurred and merged with a luminescent chaos of purple, green, and blue. I wasn't sure what was harder to take, the nausea of the spill or the biting pain that erupted in my blood as the sparks grew brighter.

Thankfully the trip was not drawn out. After about twenty seconds of tumbling, Daniel and I plunged out of the wormhole. The landing was not soft. In fact, he and I hit the ground with such a thud that I was pretty sure I heard my spinal cord ricochet against my shoulder blades.

"Ow," I muttered, face planted in a pile of leaves.

A groan to my left indicated that Daniel felt the same sentiment.

I grunted back the shock and pulled myself together. Blinking back the fading stars in my vision, I took in the surroundings.

It was dark and quiet. As my eyes adjusted to the deep night I realized we had landed in another forest. We were standing amidst thousands of tall, slender trees. The ground was covered in their fallen leaves. Beneath them the dirt felt cold and a little moist, like it had rained recently.

When the ringing in my ears stopped, I could detect the soft babble of a nearby stream. The trees almost concealed it, but streaks of light reflected off its waters about fifteen meters away.

I tilted my head up to try and pinpoint the source of light. The moon was overhead—huge and full and smiling down like a kindly elder relative. The trees stretched toward it like they were trying to touch its face.

"Are we on Earth again?" Daniel asked as he stood, taking in the moonlight and dusting himself off.

"I'm not sure," I said. "Harry—that White Rabbit I met in the Forbidden Forest—said the holes lead to a lot of different lands. But I can find out . . ." I held up my wrist and activated the Hole Tracker that Harry had given me. The fascinating wristwatch projected a holographic map of terrain I'd never seen before.

I'd learned from fiddling with the Hole Tracker that it displayed a map of whatever realm you happened to be in. Unfortunately, the maps were pretty vague. There were no city names or borders or any other topographical markers to help you. All you had was the name of the realm at the top, a blob-like mass that generally resembled the shape of the region, and coordinates to mark where you were and where the nearest holes could be found. If you were even slightly unfamiliar with the terrain, using such a map was not helpful. The only elements that provided any aid were the aforementioned hole coordinates and the fact that the Tracker glowed brighter the closer you got to them.

At the top of this map was the label "Earth" followed by a sublabel "Germany." A small glowing sphere like a firefly noted our location on the bottom left of the map. A little black blob swirled closer to the top center.

"Yup, we're on Earth—a place called Germany. And that's where the next hole is opening up," I said, pointing to the black blob. I pressed the blob and it expanded. Coordinates and time details projected next to it that told me it would be opening in less than three hours. Not enough time for us to reach it.

I swiftly passed my index finger along the face of the Hole Tracker in a circular motion, which I'd learned from messing with it was how you scrolled through time settings.

After a moment another black blob appeared on the map, very close to the previous one. I selected it and made the coordinates and time details expand. As I did this I realized that my wrist had begun to quiver. The Hole Tracker was vibrating and the skin on my hand was burning.

"Ow," I cringed with pain as golden sparks fizzed where the injury was forming.

"Knight! What are you—"

I held up my other hand to silence him. "Relax," I said, turning off the Hole Tracker. The instant I did, the sparks rescinded but the burn remained. I grunted and swallowed the residual pain.

"I learned from Harry and Ashlyn that Book is a Wonderland," I explained. "There are quite a few of them, like Camelot or Oz or Cloud Nine. Wonderlands run on very different types of magic. They have fairies and spells and witches, whereas other realms, like Earth, don't. So when you try to use their kind of otherworldly magic here, it doesn't work. The realm rejects it. And for whatever magic emitted, there's an equal consequence." I gestured to my injured hand. "I got this burn from the Hole Tracker. I should've expected as much. The contraption must be partially built with magic because when I tried playing with it back at Ashlyn's I could only operate the thing for about thirty seconds without it overheating." I shrugged. "At least now we know where we are."

"You couldn't have thought of a better way to find out than maiming yourself?" Daniel asked, shaking his head. He tore a strip of material from the bottom of his shirt. "Here," he said, taking my hand before I could fully process what was happening. He bandaged the injured area tightly.

My legs and forearms hurt like they were also starting to bruise. This confused me until I remembered Debbie's makeover. There was magic in the inky, shape-shifting designs on my boots and my sparkling sleeves. Quickly I clicked my heels together three times. The moment I did, my boots and dress ceased their magic like Debbie said they would.

"I didn't get a good look at the coordinates of that second hole," I admitted to Daniel as I looked at my bandaged hand. "I can check it again later and write them down."

"Won't it burn you again?"

"If I leave the Tracker on for a few seconds at a time it'll be fine."

"All right. Well, how long 'til you can check?"

"Maybe a few hours."

"Fine. We can take another look tomorrow," he said. "Though we'll have to figure out a better way to track those coordinates. Even if we could use your Hole Tracker longer, that map is so vague that aside from going in the general right direction it's not going to help us much."

"At least we have time to figure it out," I replied. "While I may not have memorized the second hole's coordinates, I caught a look at the time stamp that went with them. According to the map, the hole is going to open up in twenty-eight hours and twelve minutes. So we can work on finding a way to track its coordinates in the morning."

"And finding a way out of this forest." He took out his pocket watch for a second and glanced at the time. His eyes lingered on Kai's picture inside.

I watched his expression as he did so, wondering what he was thinking. Other than when he'd revealed the truth about Kai in the genie lamp, he'd never really taken out the watch in front of me. In the past whenever I'd seen him with it he'd concealed it the moment he saw me looking. I didn't blame him. Thinking about the girl you love when the girl supposed to keep you from her is hovering nearby seems a bit weird.

I wondered if maybe he was getting comfortable enough around me to be okay with it.

"How'd you two meet?" I asked, gesturing to the watch.

The question seemed to surprise him and he suddenly realized what he was doing. Hastily he snapped the watch closed and stashed it inside his pocket.

"It's a long story. You don't want to hear it." He turned his back to me, choosing to look out at the stillness of the woods rather than my face.

"I guess it's lucky we landed on Earth," he said. "At least it means we don't have to worry about monsters or antagonists trying to kill us, for now."

I decided to pretend like I didn't notice the rapid subject change. I was too tired to get into it with him.

"That's the spirit," I said, stretching lazily as I lay down on my back. I folded my hands behind my head and gazed up at the moon. "So why don't we get some sleep and enjoy the calm? Chances are this may be the last time we'll be able to for a while."

"Losing your sense of optimism, Knight?" Daniel asked, glancing at me.

"Nope," I yawned. "Let's just say," my eyelids drooped, feeling too heavy to stay open, "I feel like I'm starting to . . . accept my role in all this." My whisper melted into another yawn. Then the pain and exhaustion finally caught up with me. Out of the corner of my eye I saw my right hand turn silvery—undergoing the magic watering can's liquid metal effect again. The sensation hurt a bit more than usual due to Earth's objection of its magical origins, but I was too exhausted to care. Sleep craved me as a captive and I was more than willing to let it take me.

CHAPTER 8

The Warning

o most people, dreams were a break from the world. My dreams were a gateway to another.

Natalie Poole (about fifteen or sixteen) was sitting on cement stairs. She was crying, or at least she had been. Bright red paint was splattered on her shirt and skin. She'd wiped most of it off her face—a wad of paper towels was crumpled beside her—but there was still some paint in her curly, maple-colored hair.

"Hey, you okay?"

Natalie looked up. She was startled, not so much by the voice, but by the boy to whom it belonged.

I'd seen him before. Long ago—the day I'd gotten my prologue prophecy—I'd had a dream where Natalie was in a school hallway. She had been the victim of a cruel prank where a balloon filled with red paint had exploded all over her. The blonde viper I now knew to be Arian's lackey Tara had been there, and so had this boy. He'd had Tara on his arm, but had been the only one in the group not to laugh at Natalie's misfortune.

He came closer to her now and sat down on the step beside her.

"I'm fine," she said, self-consciously wiping a stray tear from her eyes.

"You're Natalie, right?" the boy asked.

This took her even more by surprise. She nodded.

"I thought so," said the boy. "I'm Ryan. Ryan Jackson."

Ryan Jackson.

Natalie's One True Love.

This was my first real introduction to the other major player in Arian's game with Natalie. This was the boy Natalie was meant to be with. This was the boy Arian and Tara would use to bring her down.

Ryan extended his hand to Natalie, but she looked away from the gesture instead of returning it. She was clearly having trouble understanding what Ryan was doing there, and even more trouble composing an articulate sentence while he was in such close proximity.

I didn't blame the girl. Ryan was completely swoon-worthy. His eyes were gray-blue like the deep ocean after it had been hammered by rain. His hair was dark, curly, and so thick you just kind of wanted to touch it. And his smile was utterly genuine.

Aside from his general awe-inducing presence, I knew she was also reluctant around him because of who he was in their world. Based on the hallway scene I'd witnessed before, I'd garnered that he was some kind of popular kid, whereas she was definitely not.

Despite that, once the initial surprise of his presence lost its impact, Natalie found her voice. And it was not anywhere near as meek as I'd been expecting.

"Look, I appreciate you coming out here, but I don't need your pity," she said bluntly. "I'm sure you have better things to do than worry about the likes of some nobody. So why don't you move along. Go ahead and check off your popular kid pro bono work for the month. Then please leave me alone."

Now it was Ryan's turn to look taken aback. "I didn't come out here to show you pity. And I definitely didn't do it to pull off some kind of Good Samaritan karma. I came out here because you don't deserve what happened to you in there."

"How would you know if I deserved it or not?" Natalie replied, returning her gaze to the ground. "You don't even know me."

"How do you know my reasons for coming out here aren't sincere?" he countered. "You don't know me either."

She flicked her eyes to him. "Have you ever given me an opportunity?"

Ryan paused. He clearly wasn't used to such honest conversation. I supposed that was one of the side effects of dating a manipulative type like Tara.

"No," he finally responded. "I guess I haven't. I mean, I know we've gone to the same school for a few years, but I never really thought to, well, talk to you."

Natalie sighed. "Don't beat yourself up about it. Most people don't see that far out of their own little world. And yours and mine, they might as well be in solar systems. That's not on you, though."

"Yeah . . . but maybe it should be," Ryan said carefully.

He stared at the same pile of leaves Natalie had been focusing on and a slight silence hung between them.

"You wanna be friends?" he asked after a moment.

He might as well have asked her if she wanted to go blow up their school. She nearly fell off the step she was perched on.

Natalie raised her eyebrows skeptically. "What is this, kindergarten? If I say yes, do I have to give you my juice box in return?"

"Hey, you're the one who said I never gave you an opportunity to get to know me, or me you for that matter. Here it is. Either way you can't accuse me of not making an effort. Now if we go off to our own solar systems or whatever then it's on you."

"Well, that's just unacceptable," Natalie said, not breaking his gaze.

"What?"

"You're *Ryan Jackson*. You're the most popular kid in school—

captain of the track team, homecoming king two years running, and straight A student to boot. You're not allowed to be the one in this dynamic who extends an olive branch only to get shut down by a less noble soul."

"Then don't shut me down," Ryan said. "Come on, what do you say?"

He stood up and extended his hand to Natalie a second time. She still seemed hesitant. While her tone suggested confidence and a deep security in who she was, I detected a look of distrust in her eyes.

I could relate.

Despite her initial reluctance, Natalie took Ryan's hand. He helped her to her feet and the two stood close to one another before they faded away like ghosts dissolving from this world into the next.

The scene changed. I was in my suite at Lady Agnue's. Mauvrey was sitting on the edge of Blue's bed. Her hair fell around her in such a rich shade of gold it would've put Goldilocks to shame. She was wearing a black gown, but I couldn't quite make out the details. Unlike my vision of Natalie and Ryan, this one was a lot blurrier, like I was looking at it through a pair of glasses with smudged lenses.

"You understand how sorry I am, right?" she asked sadly, her posture and tone both reflecting a deep sense of shame.

"Don't be," my voice responded.

I (personally) hadn't said anything, so I assumed dream me was somewhere nearby but out of sight—the walk-in closet or bathroom, perhaps.

"But I am," Mauvrey responded to the voice. "Everything that has happened to you . . . I am afraid it all comes back to me."

There was a long beat of silence. Then I heard rustling coming from the door that led to the bathroom. I turned and saw a gowned shadow spill across the floor—my shadow, I presumed. But I never got the chance to confirm it. This dream vanished and a flood of new ones passed through my mind—starting slow and calm at first, but picking up speed as they went on.

From a distance I saw Chance Darling and me riding in a carriage down a mountainside. Snow fell lightly from the gray sky. Glittering clumps of white powder were caked onto the jagged edges of the rock.

The carriage was roofless so the snow sprinkled on our heads, but neither of us seemed disturbed by it. In fact, even from far away I could detect a sense of peace in dream me. She closed her eyes and leaned back so that the icy flakes grazed her face as they fell.

The vision shifted and I was transported to a lake so blue it disgraced the sky. The surface was still and glassy like crystal, but farther out there was a powerful embankment of fog so thick that it blocked all view of what lay beyond. My perspective drew closer to this area until I was consumed within the depth of the fog. It fenced me in from all sides, though I could still see the lake beneath me. My soul felt the cold kiss of the mist like a burn.

The lake now looked darker and more ominous. As the dreamscape started to fade away and my presence exited the vision, I saw part of the lake begin to ripple. A graceful, fair-skinned arm began to reach out from beneath the water, extending straight up as if it were reaching for the clouds.

Again the scene changed. It was replaced with Natalie and Ryan again. They walked through a hallway talking, but their words were muted. Natalie threw her head back in laughter. He did the same. And like a snap of awareness, a close-up of their faces triggered my dreams to accelerate, shifting through a succession of flashes.

Flash one: I was in a cluttered store. The aisle space was tight—stacked tall on either side with knickknacks of every sort from lamps to chairs to vases and other antique-looking tchotchkes. The shop was relatively dark, so the items spilled shadows everywhere. A large, floor-length mirror caught my eyes, but only for a moment.

Flash two: A woman with radiant black hair and a sparkling, long-sleeve gown sauntered past walls of thick green glass. There was a determined expression in her eyes and a glowing ball of fire in her right hand. The tight sphere of flames floated above her palm like she was producing it.

Flash three: Mauvrey and Blue were fighting, but I didn't know where or what about. The background was an onyx blur and the girls themselves were purple and shadowy like three-dimensional silhouettes. Blue stabbed at the princess with her hunting knife. Mauvrey evaded with speed. There was a ferocity in Blue's eyes that was dangerous, and a smugness in Mauvrey's that worried me even more.

I felt dizzy, almost sick watching them. I was glad when a bright flash consumed everything and transported me away. Seeing Blue and Mauvrey like that had filled me with a kind of anger, nausea, and pain that I could not describe.

I was in a white void now. Unlike every other dream I'd had in this passage of sleep, I had a physical form. I strode across the barren dreamscape by my own free will. I thought I was alone at first. But then I saw her.

The familiar, enigmatic woman with the light brown skin and dark, curly hair appeared before me. She wore a teal zip-up jacket and gray sweatpants.

I was both angry and intrigued to see her. I was tired of her coming to me in my dreams and giving me mysterious messages that were too garbled to understand. At the same time, I had to know who she was.

It was hard to tell how long I had. My moments with her never lasted, though they were getting clearer. The last time I'd dreamed of her—when I was unconscious in Lenore's office—I'd managed to hear her speak a few sentences clearly.

Now her image was the clearest I'd ever seen it. And I felt like

I had more control over what was happening. Like while I might not be able to keep her here, maybe I could hold her for a bit to get some answers.

"This is getting old," I commented with a sigh as I approached her. "Who are you? You're not like my other dreams. This doesn't feel like a slice of the future. It feels like it's happening now."

"That's because it is happening now," the woman replied. "If only inside our heads."

"*Our* heads," I responded.

I collided with a wall three feet from her. It was invisible, like a force field. It glittered gold when I touched it. I took a step away and rubbed my head. Despite being in a dream, the collision had hurt.

"You keep trying to warn me about something that I need to remember. What did you mean by that? Last time you said he was the key."

"The dragon," the woman responded, drawing nearer and stopping just before where the force field had stopped me.

"You mean the one from Century City that's been following us across Book?"

"Yes."

"Okay, what specifically do I need to remember about him?"

"I'm sorry. I'm not sure about the details, Crisa. It has something to do with the first time you touched him. Past that, all I can tell you is that when the time comes and you face Nadia, remembering him will be the only thing that can save you."

"How do you know about Nadia?" I asked, my eyebrows shooting up in alert. "And when am I supposed to face her?"

"Soon," the woman responded. "Arian is still after you. When you and Daniel escaped the lamp it gave off a signal. Arian knows you're headed to the Cave of Mysteries. He's notified all of Alderon to be on the lookout."

"Yeah, I heard," I replied, rolling my eyes and thinking of

the newspaper in Goldilocks's lair. "For a kingdom full of foiled villains, they have a ridiculously fast news cycle." I met the woman's gaze anew and noticed she was fading out, dissolving back into the void.

I harnessed whatever control I had to steady the dream and keep her in focus.

"How do you know all of this?" I asked. "How are you inside my head?"

"I see the future like you do, Crisa," she responded, her voice growing lighter with every syllable. "And it is that common bond that establishes our connection. You'll have more answers soon, but only if you survive what's coming. I can't protect you and your friends from Nadia or Arian—only you can. That is why I've been coming to you in your sleep. To warn you that it all comes down to one thing."

Her entire form was almost gone. I concentrated, trying to bring her back, but it was no use. Her body vanished. But I heard the end of her warning.

"Remember the dragon, Crisa. And follow the stream."

Her voice echoed through the empty void. The force field that had been separating us glimmered. Gingerly, I held my hand up to its boundary. My fingers extended with the intention of skimming its surface. But the moment they made contact, a powerful, abrupt burst of images jerked through my subconscious.

A beautiful sword gripped in Daniel's hand, catching the light on its blade. Jason locked in combat with Arian. A furry lavender cat with piercing green eyes lounging on a tree branch, smiling. Blue with tears in her eyes and blood on her hands. The glass Pegasus figurine on SJ's desk back at school. And then the giant bronze serpent I'd seen in previous dreams.

The serpent came crashing through my perspective, black glass raining around it. Its head was the size of a carriage; its fangs—maliciously sharp and pointed—made ice picks look like toothpicks. The creature's eyes glowed bright gold as it charged me. I braced myself for the crash, but was shocked by a much different kind of assault.

I was in a dark, confined space. The bright light of the desert flooded in with a sudden burst as a hatch door opened on the other side. An arm reached out and grabbed me by the collar. I was thrust out of the small enclosure and onto the ground outside. I grunted as my face plowed into sand.

My hands and feet were shackled. I heard murmuring voices coming from all around me. A hand gripped my shoulder.

"Knight?"

Out of instinct I jolted up, coming out swinging. Daniel barely jumped back in time to evade getting hit. "Hey!" he said. "Take it easy. I'm just waking you up."

I blinked, adjusting to real life and the cool light of morning. The ground was damp beneath me. The moon was gone and replaced with a pale coat of blueish gray. "Sorry," I muttered, my vision focusing on Daniel. "Just a reflex."

"Bad vision?" he asked.

I tensed a bit. Then I remembered that he knew all about my abilities to see the future. I'd told him and the others about them right before we left Ashlyn's to return to Adelaide.

Hmm. I guess that's gonna take some getting used to.

"Yeah," I said, releasing a deeply repressed breath. "I've been having dreams about this one woman. She's been trying to warn me about something, but I couldn't understand what until now. She says that we'll face Nadia soon and that when we do the only thing that will save us will be me remembering the dragon."

"The dragon?" Daniel repeated. "You mean the one from the capital that's been stalking us?"

"Yeah. But she says I need to remember the first time I touched him."

"When was that?" Daniel asked.

"That's the thing; I haven't. I've come close to getting barbecued by him, but I've never actually made contact."

"Weird." Daniel offered me his hand and helped me to my feet. "What else did you see? You seemed pretty torn up while you were sleeping, like you were in a lot of pain. Any more visions you want to share?"

I thought about the cell I'd just been in, the epic bronze serpent, Chance and me in that carriage . . .

"I don't want to talk about it."

"Isn't that something girls say when they actually do want to talk about it?" Daniel countered.

I shot him an annoyed look then switched my focus to our surroundings. It was at that moment that I finally took in the beauty of the forest. The same cold blue that painted the sky poked in and out of the tall, slender trees. A light mist coated the air, which my breath faded into as I exhaled the iciness. In complete contrast to everything else, the blanket of fallen leaves set the ground ablaze with autumnal grace. The earth was covered with so many warm, fiery colors it looked like a titan had spilled a giant jar of red pepper flakes.

"What time is it?" I asked Daniel.

"About six o'clock," he responded, taking a couple of steps forward.

I noticed he was limping slightly. "Those rocks fell on you pretty hard," I commented, recalling the avalanche of stone that had pinned him down when the Magistrake attacked. "I'm surprised you were able to fight as well as you did back at the lake."

He shrugged. "Had to be done. The adrenaline compensated. Hasn't the same thing happened to you?"

"Yeah, I suppose." I eyed his leg worriedly. "What about now, though? Are you sure you're okay?"

"I'm fine."

"Isn't that something boys say when they are hurt but are too proud to admit it?" I countered, smirking.

Daniel returned the comment with the same irritated expression I'd given him a beat earlier. He nodded toward the thick woods. "Any ideas on which way we should head?"

"How should I know?"

"You're the resident psychic."

I was about to protest when my ears suddenly detected a sound that they hadn't been properly paying attention to. The stream nearby was flowing gently, its waters trickling off stones as it traveled downstream.

"Follow the stream," I thought aloud. I pivoted to Daniel. "The woman in my dream also said to follow the stream. I think she meant this one."

"Knight, you don't even know who that woman is, let alone if this stream is the one she was referring to. Are you sure this is a good idea?"

My eyes traced the path of the stream all the way to where it proceeded through a curve in the earth and faded into the foreboding mist of trees. I glanced back at Daniel. "No. But let's do it anyway."

CHAPTER 9

Cake for Breakfast

nlike every other forest we'd travelled through on this journey, this one was calm, non-enchanted, and monster-less.

I couldn't help but note what great time we made when miscellaneous foes weren't trying to kill us. Following the stream through the woods for three hours was the most peaceful endeavor we'd undertaken in a while.

Daniel and I talked a little during the trek. I finally got the chance to describe to him what had transpired between Lenore and me back at Fairy Godmother Headquarters.

At one point, I reactivated my Hole Tracker to check the map and make sure we were at least headed in the right direction. Unfortunately, I had to turn it off quickly, lest it combust and take my hand along with it.

Daniel made his way around large stones on the edge of the stream. I followed, hopping from one to the next like it was a game.

"I guess I owe you a thank you," Daniel said.

His voice caught me off guard and caused me to slip, one boot submerging into the stream. Water soaked through the leather and into my sock. Silver sparks from my SRB appeared and dried my shoe and sock as I continued after Daniel. They also sent a surge of pain up my leg due to Earth's magical backlash, but I decided not to mention it.

"For what?" I asked him, ignoring the sting.

"For saving me when we were in Alderon. I could hear what you were saying when I was in that orb, and I want to let you know I appreciate what you did. You almost got killed because of me."

I shrugged. "You would've done the same for me."

As soon as I uttered the response, I scrunched up my eyebrows, struck by my own words.

That was true, wasn't it? He'd saved me several times before, but until now I'd been so blinded by my distrust and dislike of him that I hadn't properly valued the gesture. As the statement came out of me—so easily and without caveat—I appreciated how much our dynamic had changed since we'd first met. When we weren't fighting or doubting each other, things felt almost simple between us.

Part of me wished they could always be this way. At the same time I knew better. Because of who we were to each other, things could never be simple. This feeling—open, exposed, and intertwined—had an expiration date. I was doing what I could to sustain it for now. But it was a bandage on a deeper issue, one that I was not sure would hold true or protect our connection in the long term, let alone when really tested and old habits and instinct came calling.

I looked at the back of Daniel's head, trying to imagine what thoughts dwelled there during the lulls in our conversation. Did he wonder about this stuff too? Did it matter to him that our newfound peace was a result of necessity and would likely cease once our venture to the Author ended? Did he know where he drew the line when it came to protecting Kai and what he would do to keep me from standing in the way?

I shivered at the last question. It wasn't very long ago that Daniel and I had been on the magic train. When I'd fallen off the roof and plummeted toward the canyon below, he had been the one to catch me. Yet I could not forget that he'd hesitated.

The memory of his expression as he watched me fall was deeply ingrained. And the doubt inside me made me wonder if in that moment, he'd considered letting me go. After all, if I was out of the way, then so were the threats of his prologue prophecy, right?

I tried my best to bury the thought.

"You know what gets me about the antagonists?" Daniel said abruptly.

Again his voice startled me. I jumped off a large stone—my boots landing in the moist grass with a squish—and jogged up next to him.

"What?"

"If you think about it, they're braver than we are."

I was at his side now so he was able to see my face scrunch in confusion.

"Of the three core archetypes in this realm, they're the only ones not chosen by the Author," he explained. "They choose their own path whereas the rest of us—commons and protagonists—just take the lot we're assigned."

"Some choice," I huffed.

It was true that antagonists weren't appointed their roles. It's not like the Author wrote antagonist books. They were all just commons who'd decided to make evil their life's purpose.

You could break down these antagonists into three overarching types: magic hunter, wicked witch or warlock, and basic baddie. While they varied in degrees in terms of power and potential to wreak havoc, they all started as commons.

People who grew up to be magic hunters shared a genetic marker. They were born with a sixth sense that allowed them to detect magic, picking up its scent in creature and enchanted object alike. However, the gene didn't automatically affect every member of a bloodline.

For those who were carriers of the gene, the scent of magic was very tempting. Just as a person with long, strong legs might be predisposed to becoming a runner or someone skilled with animals and first aid might be inclined to being a veterinarian, the magic detection gene made you susceptible to pursuing a life as a magic hunter. Indeed, most commons afflicted by the gene decided to dedicate their lives to hunting down magic in an effort to become more powerful.

The second type of antagonist—wicked witch or warlock—was a little more dangerous. Fairy Godmothers were the only humans supposed to have magical powers, but every once in a while there was an exception. Usually that was when a magic hunter absorbed the power of his or her prey and became magical.

Having magic didn't make you evil. We trusted countless Fairy Godmothers to wield immense power and look after our realm, and they all had good intentions. (For the most part anyway. I'm not sure where I would rank Lena Lenore in that spectrum.)

But magic was a lot to handle. That's why the Fairy Godmothers didn't let just anybody join their ranks. You couldn't exactly apply to their agency. You had to be recommended by a protagonist, approved by realm and kingdom leaders, and deemed worthy by the Godmothers themselves through a rigorous selection process. Holding that much power was a huge responsibility. So you had to be strong enough and honorable enough to keep it from corrupting you.

Given that magic hunters had already embraced wickedness—you had to kill a magical creature to steal its power—by the time hunters gained their power, the evil ship had sailed. They were bad and magic only corrupted them more. Thus, they became wicked witches or warlocks.

Other forms of witches and warlocks were those commons who were extremely talented in potions (like my best friend SJ) but who decided to use that mastery to pursue evil and try to cause harm to others (not like my best friend SJ).

The last kind of antagonist—your basic baddie—was the simplest and arguably most complex branch of the archetype.

Baddies were normal commons who'd chosen a path of villainy. There was no magic detection gene, no magic powers, and no potions influencing their decision. The only thing at play was a desire to be something more fueled by a discontent with the life they currently had.

Maybe they were poor and sought riches. Maybe they were meager and sought power. Maybe they just got tired of living in a world where they were treated as second-class citizens. One way or another, they chose to make a name for themselves by pursuing antagonism. Thieves, murderers, schemers, plotters—they were simply regular people who'd grown tired of being common and elected to steal power or affluence some other way.

A good example was my step-grandmother. She was a common who was driven down a path of wickedness by the jealousy she bore toward my protagonist mother, Cinderella. Since her own two daughters weren't chosen as protagonists, my step-grandmother manipulated, psychologically abused, and tormented my mother all through her childhood so that when my mother eventually made it as a protagonist she would be subservient to the family.

However, when my father (the prince) selected my mother as his bride, my mother stood up to my step-grandmother and refused to be under her thumb any longer. This caused my step-grandmother to snap and she and her eldest daughter tried to kill my mother. Thankfully they were both caught and sent to Alderon as punishment.

Just thinking about them—even after all these years—filled me with bitterness. I'd obviously never met them; I'd never even seen a picture. But I hated the pair for all the pain they'd caused my mother. Being this defiant and snarky, I knew a thing or two about archenemies. And while my insolence may have meant I had a couple of them coming, my mother never deserved such malice. She deserved so much better than the childhood she got, and it always bothered me that there was nothing I could do or say to right any of the ways she'd been wronged.

Past this, another thing that concerned me about the situation was that people could just turn dark like that. My step-grandmother was wealthy. She had the money and lands my grandfather left her when he died. She had children; she had a life. How could her resentment for my mother be strong enough to make her throw all that away and embrace wickedness?

My grandfather had married her in the first place, so she couldn't have been all bad at the beginning. Why had she given that up? Was her jealousy really that strong? Could anyone—given the right provocation—turn dark like she had?

"Isn't that a brave thing at its core?" Daniel continued, not noticing my mental tangent. "For antagonists to decide to say to heck with the Author and the realm's division of power and seek something more than the modest lives they were born into."

"I don't know if I would describe that as bravery," I responded. "There are other ways a common can achieve a better life besides turning to villainy. Doctors, lawyers, teachers, renowned artists, all twenty-six of our kingdom ambassadors for that matter—they're all commons. They're wealthy and powerful without being protagonists. If you ask me, commons that choose to be antagonists are the opposite of brave. They're cowards taking the easy way out. They could be something more if they worked hard enough, but instead they lie and cheat and steal and put others' lives in danger as a means to gain superiority."

"Are you sure you don't just feel that way because *you're* a protagonist?" Daniel asked. "You've never had to struggle and fight like a common. You don't know what a desperate person—someone poor or pushed around—might do to feel important, let alone feed their families."

I felt an argument coming. Daniel may have been a protagonist now, but he'd been a common his entire life; I'd been a protagonist all of mine. We were bound to disagree on certain things. Still, I didn't want to lose the fragile peace between us over a squabble on antagonists. That archetype was already doing plenty to destroy us in Book. We didn't need it to chip away at us here.

I sighed, choosing my words carefully. "Daniel, I may not know what it feels like to go hungry or feel pushed aside. But I do know what it's like to fight to achieve something more than the life I've been given. That struggle has defined my whole existence and it's the fuel that's driving me now. So think what you want about antagonists and their origins, but no matter what, you have to know that this is the truth about me."

Daniel and I came out of the mossy descent. The earth leveled out as the stream picked up speed and widened into a river. The types of trees became more varied, and there was more green than orange, fewer leaves having fallen from their branches.

My carefully chosen statement seemed to have silenced Daniel on the subject—he didn't have a retort—but it did not bring silence to the surrounding forest. A loud snap burst from a section of trees nearby.

Daniel and I turned at the noise, both on guard. It was understandable given that the last time we'd heard such a sound it was followed by a giant lobster attack. True it was highly unlikely that we would run into any lobster monsters on Earth. But this was still a forest *and* it was unfamiliar terrain. Who knew what was out there?

I wanted to go for my wand but frowned when I remembered I couldn't use it. Earth's painful magic consequences would stop me before it became useful.

Daniel drew his sword and walked carefully to the area where the sound came from. I followed. We were beginning to hear more rustlings then footsteps. I peered over his shoulder as we wormed around the trees in our way.

The footsteps grew louder and were accompanied by the murmur of voices. I saw Daniel's grip tense on his sword. We rounded a particularly thick trunk. And then—

Daniel abruptly collided with a small girl holding a map. She bounced off his chest and made a startled squeak. When she looked up and saw his sword she squeaked again, louder this time.

Daniel stashed his sword in its sheath and held up his hands. "Whoa, whoa. It's okay. Sorry, we didn't mean to scare you."

The girl blinked like a confused deer. She was about five foot two. Her hair was black and short with bangs tickling her thin eyebrows. Her eyes were small and innocent. Despite her petite frame, I guessed she was about nineteen or twenty. She wore wrinkled khaki pants, a pale pink collared shirt peeking out beneath a distressed jacket, and a matching khaki sunhat with a cord that hung below her neck. There was a massive backpack on her shoulders. She clutched the straps tightly as she stared at Daniel, causing the map in her right hand to crinkle.

The girl looked us both up and down then called behind her. "Berto! Anna! Greg!"

More rustling occurred behind her. A few seconds later three other young people appeared—a girl with a perky brown ponytail, a boy with blond hair and a scruffy goatee and mustache, and another boy with warm caramel skin and glasses. They each carried gigantic backpacks and wore hiking clothes.

"Hey," the girl with the ponytail said. "What are you kids doing out here? You lost?"

Daniel and I glanced at each other. "Where exactly is *here*?" I asked.

"Oh geez, you *are* lost," the blond boy said. "This is the Black Forest. You guys need some help getting out of here? We were on our way back to town."

I looked to Daniel for confirmation. He nodded.

"Lead the way," I said.

After twenty minutes we emerged from the forest.

Blond boy and ponytail girl had introduced themselves as

Greg and Anna. They were a married couple in their late-twenties who were backpacking across Europe on their honeymoon. Meanwhile, the tiny black-haired girl (Yunru) and the boy with the glasses (Umberto, or Berto as they called him) were some travelling strays they'd joined up with along the way.

"We all met at a hostel back in Zurich," Anna explained. "We really hit it off and decided to travel together for a while."

"How do Yunru and Berto know each other?" I asked, relieved to see the town coming into view and smell freshly baked bread. My stomach growled like a troll under a bridge.

"We didn't," Berto answered. "Yunru and I both study abroad. I'm taking break from university in Spain before I transfer to college in America in the spring. She goes to university in Hong Kong and comes to Germany to do research for her college thesis."

My eyebrows crinkled. "I didn't understand half the words in that statement. What's a college?"

They all regarded me like I was an alien or an idiot—or both.

"You know, *college*," Anna repeated, as if elongating the word made its meaning clearer. "Higher education. Where people go after high school to learn about themselves and decide what they want to do with the rest of their lives, and then learn the skills they need to accomplish it."

I thought about the idea, which struck a profound chord. "Sounds cool," I said.

"You kids look about sixteen or seventeen," Greg continued. "You must have an idea of where you want to go when you finish school and what you want to be when you grow up."

Hero. Princess. Epic-worthy fairytale protagonist. Alive.

"We're kinda concentrating on the now," I responded.

Daniel and I hadn't told these people where we were from. Ashlyn had stressed that—should we ever return to Earth—we must keep the truth a secret. So when Anna asked Daniel and I what we were doing in the forest alone, I thought fast and came up with the most convincing lie we could pull out of thin air.

A long time ago Blue told me that there was a group for little kids in her village where parents enrolled their children to learn hunting, tracking, camping, and other outdoor activities. Inspired by that, I told Anna, Greg, Berto, and Yunru that Daniel and I belonged to a special school that emphasized an importance in mastery of the land. Daniel—a better liar than I realized—added that as upperclassmen we had been split into groups and sent out on assignment to navigate the forest and different areas of Germany. It was a project we needed to pass in order to graduate—proving that we could traverse the forest and then find our way back to a neutral rendezvous point.

I guess they bought it because they didn't pry any further. It helped that none of them were from Germany, I suppose. Being from other countries, they didn't question the local schooling customs.

"I get that," Greg replied to my earlier comment. "At your age you probably feel swamped. School, friends, the future—it's a lot to handle."

"Oh yeah," Daniel said, a huff of amusement in his tone. "You have no idea."

We approached a dark blue vehicle—much like the ones we'd seen when we'd stayed with Ashlyn in Bermuda. I believed they were called cars.

"Say hello to the 'G Love Mobile,'" Greg said, patting the hood of his vehicle.

I came around the side of the car and took a look at the license plate: GLVMOBL.

I opened my mouth to respond, but Daniel beat me to the punch. "It looks like it says '*Glove* Mobile,'" he said.

I chuckled.

"Don't dis the ride," Greg responded, still smiling. "Anna and I got this '98 Toyota 4Runner for a steal."

"We were planning to get something to eat at a local restaurant," Berto said to Daniel and me. "You want to come with us? Our treat."

My stomach growled again at the mere mention. This time it was loud enough for everyone to hear.

"I think that's a yes," Daniel responded.

"This is the greatest thing ever."

Along with the normal breakfast food—sausage, eggs, a giant cup of coffee—I'd also ordered a slice of the enticing cake that had been on display. The moist, lusciously dark creation was apparently a specialty of the establishment.

"It's German Chocolate Cake," Anna said. "And it's really good. Though I don't know if I've ever had it for breakfast."

Daniel gave me a sideways look as I swallowed a few forkfuls of my scrambled eggs—which I'd covered with maple syrup. Then I took a big, slow spoonful of cake. A relaxed grin spread across my face as its chocolaty richness immersed every inch of my taste buds.

"You are one of the weirdest girls I've ever met," he commented.

I swallowed and kept smiling. "I'll take that as a compliment."

It was nearly ten o'clock now. The small restaurant was about a third full—locals and tourists sitting in dark wooden chairs at rustic tables. The windows that lined the right side of the restaurant were slightly smudged. They were framed with white lace curtains that had turned beige due to time. Through them I could see the forest in the distance. It was brilliant green in the morning sunlight.

I wiped my mouth with a napkin. My Hole Tracker caught on a soft ray of light that streamed through the window beside me. It'd been a few hours since I'd last used the watch. I garnered it was about time we made use of it again.

"Hey, do any of you have a quill?" I asked our travelling escorts.

Again they gave me that confused look like I was being absolutely ridiculous.

"Um, I have a pen?" Yunru offered, reaching into her backpack and pulling out a blue writing stick.

Oh, right. On Earth they call them pens, I remembered, thinking back to the first time Ashlyn had corrected me on the subject.

"Thanks," I said, taking the writing utensil from her. I elbowed Daniel, whose chair was blocking my way. "Let me out?" Daniel scooched his chair over.

"You guys are very strange," Yunru said matter-of-factly.

Daniel noticed her eyes falling upon his sheath. "It's for safety," he replied swiftly. "Two kids wandering through the woods—you need to have something to protect yourself with, right?"

I grabbed a clean napkin from the table and moved to stand.

"Yeah, sure," Anna replied as I got up. "I mean, the sword is a little unconventional, but I get it. Our parents made us take, like, two months of self-defense classes before coming on this trip. And I've got at least three cans of mace in my backpack."

Yunru nodded as she took a sip of her tea. "I too come prepared. I have four switchblades on my person."

I left our group and made my way to the back of the restaurant. Past the area with the bathrooms was a door that led outside. I pushed it open and found my way into an alley. An orange tabby cat sat nobly beside a dumpster, licking its front paw.

"Sup." I nodded at the cat.

The cat meowed at me then scampered off.

I took a few steps away from the door. My boots crunched the weeds that poked out between the cobblestones. I scanned the area once more then activated my Hole Tracker.

The map glowed in front of me. Using the dumpster as a makeshift desk, I wrote down the coordinates of the next hole on the napkin. Once I was done I shut off the Tracker, rubbed my vaguely sore hand, and went back inside.

"And see, he was supposed to throw the fight," Greg said, in mid-conversation with Daniel when I sat down. "But he didn't. He stacked the odds against himself, then bet on himself. So when he won, he cleaned up."

"Who are we talking about?" I asked, taking another bite of cake.

"Bruce Willis," Daniel responded. "I told Greg I'd seen *Die Hard* for the first time recently and he was telling me about another movie of his we should see called *Pulp Fiction*. It came out a few years ago. We'll have to recommend it to Blue next time we're . . ." Daniel glanced at our hosts.

"Out of town," I suggested.

"Right," Daniel agreed. He noticed the napkin in my hand and gestured for me to pass it to him. I did and he glanced at the coordinates I'd written down.

"Yunru," he said, sliding the napkin to her. "We need to get to these coordinates. It's where we're supposed to meet up with the rest of our classmates. Can you look them up on your map and tell us the fastest way to get there?"

Yunru unfolded her map and picked up the napkin. "These look familiar," she thought aloud. She stared at the map. After a moment, she regarded her companions. "Just as I thought. They are headed in the same direction we are."

"How close?" Berto asked.

Yunru pointed at a spot on the map. Anna's eyebrows shot up. "That's a pretty crazy coincidence. It's almost like fate."

Ugh. My least favorite word.

"Then it is decided," Berto said, smiling pleasantly. "We will give you a ride."

My princess good manners wanted me to say something like, "We couldn't impose," but the fact was that we could and we very much needed to. We would've been idiots to turn down a free ride, especially on such unfamiliar terrain.

"Thank you," Daniel said as our hosts began to get up.

"No problem," Greg commented. "I just can't believe you guys are headed to the Weser."

Daniel and I exchanged a look. "The Weser," I repeated.

"Yup—the big, famous river on the way to Hamelin. That's where we're going," Anna said. Not noticing our surprise, she turned to her friends. "Yunru, you want to come to the restroom with me before we go?"

"Yes. I must pee," Yunru said, abruptly pushing past me.

"We'll take care of the check," Greg said. He gestured for Berto to follow and the two of them started heading toward the cashier at the front of the restaurant. "Everyone meet back at the G Love Mobile in five minutes."

When they were out of earshot I turned to Daniel. "That's bizarre. The Weser is the name of the river we were supposed to find in Alderon to lead us to the Cave of Mysteries."

"I don't think it's bizarre; I think it makes sense," Daniel replied. "When we went through the hole in the ocean off Adelaide we ended up in the ocean of Bermuda. When we fell through the hole that opened up in Alderon's forest last night, we landed in another forest here. Maybe there's a correlation between the exit and entry points of the holes, at least with respect to the Earth–Book ones." He held open the restaurant door for me. "So if we go through a hole by the Weser here—"

"There's a good chance we'll end up by the Weser in Alderon," I finished, stepping past him into the crisp air.

We approached the car. A family with two small children—probably twins—rushed past us. The little girl glanced back at me and smiled. Her blonde pigtails bounced and dimples sunk into her cheeks. The mischief in her eyes reminded me of Blue, causing my heart to pound a bit. I hoped she, Jason, and SJ were okay.

I meant what I said to Daniel. I had faith that they would make it to Alderon and the Cave of Mysteries, just like I had faith that he and I would too. So it wasn't so much where they were at the moment that caused the pang in my chest. It was where our friendship was.

As time went on, it only stung more knowing that they were out there super ticked off at me and unaware of how truly sorry I was. I'd hurt them so much at this point that I wondered if they would even be able to forgive me.

When Daniel and I arrived at the car, my train of thought shifted. Anna and Yunru were coming out of the restaurant. Greg and Berto followed behind, laughing. I looked from the car to them, then back at the car again. My eyebrows furrowed as a misgiving squawked in the back of my brain, which Daniel picked up on.

"What's wrong?" he asked.

"Nothing. I was just thinking of Mauvrey. She was the one who said that rule one in life is not to take food from strangers. Remembering that saved me from being taxidermied back at Goldilocks's house."

"So?"

"So, if that's rule one isn't rule two 'don't get in a vehicle with strangers'?"

"Oh, relax," Daniel said. "Besides, if there's one thing I know about you, it's that you enjoy breaking rules."

"You're right, you're right," I said, releasing a deep exhale as I leaned against the car. "I guess I'm just on edge."

"Nearly being killed a half dozen times will do that to you."

The rest of our party was getting closer. I could actually hear the crunch of gravel beneath their feet. Or maybe that was just my nerves.

"Not being able to use my wand here doesn't help either though," I added.

I saw the beginnings of a smirk creep up the corners of Daniel's mouth. "Don't worry, Knight. You sit back and relax. I'll protect you."

I tilted my chin in his direction and puckered my lips as if I'd sucked on something sour. "You know when you say things like that it makes it really hard for me to like you."

"Yeah," he said, his smirk fully emerging. "But you still do."

"All right!" Anna declared, clapping her hands together as she approached the car. "Who's ready for an adventure?"

We piled in. Greg got into the driver's seat next to Anna. Yunru and Berto sat in the two seats in the middle. Daniel and I plopped down in back.

Anna eyed us through the car's rearview mirror. "Seatbelts on," she called back. "Remember, kids, safety first."

Daniel and I fastened our safety restraints. When we were all buckled up, Greg turned the key. The car's engine roared to life, but not as loudly as the music that blasted from the stereo system.

A funky song with an upbeat, popping rhythm poured through the speakers. The lyrics were strange and sounded like a bunch of syllables mashed together. Best I could guess—based on the words I did understand—the song was about some dude being blue.

"What is this?" I shouted through the music.

"One of Berto's good friends is in a band called Eiffel 65!" Anna shouted from the front seat. "This is their debut album. It's super popular right now."

I was flung against the polyester seat cushions and Daniel's left shoulder as Greg jolted the wheel and we turned out of the parking lot.

Both Yunru and Berto's heads were bobbing along to the music. As I looked out the window at the small German town whizzing by, the compelling dance mix absorbed into my brain and I started to bob my head too.

Daniel raised his eyebrows at me.

"What?" I shrugged. "It's got a hot beat."

CHAPTER 10

Hann. Münden

he sun began to set as we reached our final destination.

The town of Hann. Münden was a beautiful place that reminded me of some of Book's countryside villages. Tiny streets were lined with quaint timber houses that leaned over cobblestone pathways. Panels of reds and browns were dominant in the architecture. Woodlands and fields were interspersed throughout the city, which was framed on both sides by gorgeous mountains.

Berto told us that Hann. Münden was colloquially referred to as the Three River City because it was where two rivers—the Fulda and the Werra—converged into a third, the Weser. As we drove through the town, I watched the waters of the Werra rush freely.

Greg pulled up in front of a small hotel. It was a wonderful-looking structure—beige with brown detailing. The main building had a large triangular brick roof. Window boxes spilling with red flowers underlined each window. Fragrant smells wafted from the hotel's restaurant.

Yunru told us that the coordinates we'd pointed out were only a few minutes away and that she'd show us exactly where they were on the map once we got settled in the hotel. Daniel and I were fine with that. We'd been driving all day with the exception of a couple of restroom and cake stops, and we were tired. Since the hole we sought wasn't meant to open until half past four in the morning, we were happy to take a break.

One thing we did have trouble accepting was our hosts' continual generosity. Yunru offered to share her hotel room with me, and Berto did the same for Daniel. And "offered" was putting it mildly. When they learned that Daniel and I had spent the previous night sleeping in the dirt, they flat out insisted. Our wilderness school requirements be darned—our new friends weren't going to let us camp out in the streets like a couple of hobos.

Being about ten years older than us, I guess Anna and Greg's paternal instincts were kicking in. Maybe they felt some sort of responsibility to keep us safe. And Yunru and Berto both had siblings so they were used to keeping an eye on the younger members of their families. I was grateful either way. The comfort of a hotel room certainly beat cobblestones and a pile of leaves for a pillow.

When we got to our room, Yunru put her giant backpack down and told me she was going to go check out an old local bookshop with Berto. She asked if I wanted to come, but I opted to stay put. Between the number of literary characters we'd run into recently and the Author's protagonist books that were always on my mind, I'd had more than enough of books for the time being.

Once she'd gone, I looked around the room for a bit. I took a whiff of the scented shampoos in the shower (lilac and honeysuckle). Then I opened the drawers and perused the tourist pamphlets I found inside, which informed me that the mountain ranges crowning either side of the town were the Weserbergland and East Hessian mountains. I could see the former from our hotel room window, peaks grazing the increasingly rosy sky.

There were three different complimentary newspapers laid out on the desk in the room. They were in different languages, so I picked up the only one I could understand.

The front page featured a story about the growing number of

missing persons in the area. Multiple towns in the Lower Saxony region had reported disappearances over the last two days. Eighteen children, twelve teenagers, and three adults had gone missing so far. Police had no leads yet, but locals and travelers were advised to take extra precaution when going out at night, as that was when the disappearances were taking place.

A shiver went through my spine as I thought of the missing kids. I frowned and put the newspaper back on the desk.

Like I needed any more unsettling news right now.

Picking up the remote control, I began to flip through the TV channels. Ashlyn's house had several TVs, and I found the device to be relaxing. However, both my intentions and state of tension changed the moment I sat down. The bed was too comfortable, the covers too soft. I stretched myself out on the white linens.

The remote naturally slipped from my fingers as I began to drift. I floated between reality and dreamscape. Vague images of Arian in the desert, Natalie at her school, Lenore in her office, and Lady Agnue's ballroom full of dancing couples and shimmering gowns filled my head.

The telephone on my nightstand suddenly started ringing, jarring me back to life. I rolled over and slapped the phone with my hand a couple of times before properly grabbing the receiver.

"Hello," I said through a yawn.

"*Guten Abend,* miss," a thickly-accented German voice responded. "Your companion requested a wake-up call for you to be set for ten minutes past four o'clock this coming morning. May I confirm that with you?"

"Um, yes," I answered. "That's correct."

"*Wunderbar.* Do you require anything else?"

How much time you got?

"No, I'm good. Thank you."

"*Danke,* miss."

I hung up the phone and made my way over to the window as I stretched. Geez, Daniel was on top of his game.

The sun was halfway set by then, the world soaked in orange and gold. I saw the earnest light of streetlamps beginning to glimmer below. My stomach made a rumbling noise and I moved to turn off the TV and exit the room.

I wandered the halls for a few minutes before I eventually located the hotel restaurant. It emanated warmth. The linens were clean and crisp, the wooden walls a natural caramel. Candles glinted off wine goblets. Slender vases, each holding a single sunflower, sat in the middle of every table.

The restaurant also had an outdoor seating option, so I made my way outside. I found myself on one of the cutest patios I'd ever seen. The ground was made of small black stones. Each wooden table had a white runner going down it. Each wooden chair had a bright yellow seat cushion that picked up the color of the rose bushes bordering the area. More clusters of yellow and red roses grew abundantly in arches near tall white lanterns.

Stepping further onto the patio, I gazed appreciatively at the lush green of the trees that surrounded us. I could see the mountains between the foliage, looking navy blue in the shadow of the day's fading light.

There were several couples outside, all of the romantic nature. The only table that hosted a single guest was the one at the center. Daniel sat there. He had one arm draped over the back of his chair and the other bent forward, his golden pocket watch that contained Kai's picture open in hand.

I considered going back inside the restaurant before he noticed me but shook off the notion. I walked across the patio to join him.

"Did she work at the Capitol Building with you?"

The question, and my approach, caught Daniel completely by surprise. I didn't know if it was possible for every muscle in the human body to tense at once, but all of Daniel's certainly seemed to. He shoved the watch back in his pocket as he turned to face me.

"Hey," he said.

"Hey," I said, sliding into the chair across from him. "So yes or no?"

"To what?"

"My question. You told me that you used to work at the Century City Capitol Building. Did Kai work there too?"

"No."

I started to open my mouth to ask another question, but he gestured to a nearby waitress with a round face and bangs. "Can she get a menu?" he asked.

The waitress reached inside her apron and pulled out a menu the size of an agenda book, minus the thickness. "There you go."

"Here," he said, passing it to me as the waitress walked away. "You must be hungry."

I nodded without further comment and took it from him. As soon as I accepted it, Daniel turned to look at the scenery and it was like I wasn't even there anymore.

The feeling this inspired was humbling. With one mere tilt of the head he'd managed to shut me out. Although he was two feet away, it was like he'd erased me from existence completely.

Trying not to take it personally, I focused on the flickering candle contained in the crimson glass between us.

Aside from a couple of brief exchanges when we were leaving the restaurant this morning, Daniel and I hadn't spoken one-on-one since our near-argument in the forest. Our road trip with our amicable backpacker friends had been filled with a good deal of talking, but it was with the whole group. Daniel and I had learned about movies, sports, college, and the German countryside.

For most of the day, Greg's friend's album had played on loop on the car stereo. It still echoed in the back of my head, causing me to wonder if I would ever get the "techno dance beat" (as it was called) out of my brain.

I hummed the tune faintly as I perused the menu. Then I

put it down as a thought crossed my mind. "How are we paying for this? Please tell me Anna and Greg didn't give you money. We can't keep taking advantage of their kindness."

"No. I got us some money of our own," he said.

"How?"

Daniel didn't answer. He just glanced at the couples nearby. And then I understood.

"You pickpocketed someone?" I huffed and leaned back in my chair. "I don't like it, Daniel. We shouldn't be stealing."

"*We* didn't steal. *I* did," Daniel replied, his eyes narrowed and his tone remorseless. "So don't worry. You haven't sullied your fine protagonist reputation."

My mouth tightened. There it was again—the feeling of another argument coming on. I resisted the urge to bite. My lack of response caused Daniel to shift.

"Look, I didn't take much. I doubt the guy I lifted the wallet off of even notices the cash is missing. He had tons."

"Well then I guess that makes it okay," I said sarcastically. I shook my head and sighed. "You could've gotten caught, you know. Then where would we be?"

"I wouldn't have gotten caught."

"How do you know?"

"Because I've done it too many times before." An awkward pause passed between us before he released a frustrated breath. "Before I got that job at the Capitol Building, I had to find different ways to keep from going hungry. I haven't pickpocketed in a while, but I haven't lost the skill either. I guess there are some things you never forget."

The candle flickered.

Daniel looked genuinely sorry—maybe not about what he'd done, but there was something in his expression that told me he was sorry his actions had disappointed me.

"I guess dinner's on you then," I said finally—extending the olive branch and choosing to let the matter go. "Considering my dinner last night had cyanide in it, anything here would be an improvement."

"Right." Daniel nodded. He eyed me steadily—making sure I was really going to let the previous conversation lie. Then he changed the subject. "I was actually going to ask you about that," he said. "You didn't seem surprised that Goldilocks was evil when we met her last night."

"You were?"

"Sure. I mean, I knew she'd robbed some bears once, but I didn't exactly think petty theft was enough to get you thrown into Alderon."

"That was only her first offense," I replied. "There was a whole profile about her in the *Century City Summit Review* a while back that covered all the messed up stuff she did. 'The Making of a Monster: From Little Girl to Notorious Crime Lord.' I'm surprised you missed it."

"I don't read the paper much," Daniel said.

"That's okay. I don't either," I replied with a shrug. "But SJ's obsessed with it. Unlike Alderon's surprisingly fast news cycle, since the Review only comes out twice a year she'll usually read it cover to cover multiple times and yammer on about the stories for weeks."

"Jason reads the paper a lot too," Daniel commented. "Frankly, he reads a lot in general. He likes to underplay it—guys at our school gain more credibility for their strength than their book smarts—but he's probably one of the most well-read kids in our year."

"He has that in common with Mark," I said, referring to Jason's roommate before Daniel. "Mark's oldest sister is actually an editor at the *Review*, and he is at the top of your class at Lord Channing's . . ." I hesitated and gulped. "Well, he was at the top of your class."

Another awkward beat passed.

The memory of finding Mark's "threat neutralized" folder in

Arian's bunker was burned into my mind. I could still remember the coarseness in Jason's voice and the shadow in his eyes when we found it.

"Do you think he's dead?" Daniel asked bluntly.

I cringed in horror. "How can you say that?"

"It's a fair question," Daniel said. "I know we're all hoping it's not true, but look at the facts. You haven't seen the kid all year. And if he was on Arian's radar, how long do you think he could last against the antagonists?"

"Hey, I've lasted a while. Maybe he could do the same." I scowled in frustration and discomfort. I had been so distracted by our journey and our own deadly pursuers I hadn't had much time to think about Mark. But like SJ, Jason, and Blue, I had been trying to stay positive about his status until we could find out more.

Our plan was to learn the truth about Mark from the Author. Since Mark was a protagonist, he had a protagonist book. The Author could tell us what really happened to him when we finally found her.

Daniel may have had a point, but I held on to the conviction that (a) things were not always what they seemed, (b) the phrase "threat neutralized" could be interpreted in a lot of ways, and (c) my belief system refused to accept anything else.

"Maybe he's in hiding, or actually sick like Lord Channing said," I continued. "If something really was wrong and he was . . . you know, we would have heard about it. His parents or the school or someone would have said something."

"Right. Because the leaders of our schools and realm have been so forthcoming."

"Daniel, just drop it okay. Maybe the odds aren't there, but my belief still is."

"Because you have faith in him like you do the others."

"Yes, but also because I have faith in the world. Maybe you

think that's naive or childish. But in spite of everything that's happened, I'm not ready to throw in the towel yet."

Daniel gave me an incredulous, somewhat judgmental look. I crossed my arms and sighed. "I'm not stupid, okay? I know there's darkness out there. Bad things happen all the time. But I refuse to accept that there's no way around them. Just because darkness has a high probability doesn't mean it's an *inevitability*. So Arian and the antagonists and that bunker folder aside, I genuinely think Mark is alive."

"Then you're not as jaded as I am," Daniel replied.

I was irritated and hurt but also trying to be earnest. He saw my expression. After a long moment he leaned forward in his chair with a glint of remorse in his eyes.

"I'm sorry," he said. "I shouldn't have said that about Mark. I didn't even know the guy, so I don't have the right to."

"You're entitled to your opinion," I replied with a shrug. "It's just a bit cold and dark for my taste."

"It's not darkness; its learned doubt," Daniel responded plainly. "You have your beliefs as a result of your experiences— growing up in a castle, having everything provided for you, being treated like a main character your entire life. You're someone special, not a run-of-the-mill common. And that's fine. I'm only saying that my life hasn't always been so easy, so I have trouble relating to your mentality. I'm naturally skeptical about things working out because in the real world—not your fairytale one— they often don't."

I glowered at the table.

"What?" he asked. "You have a problem with that?"

"Not with that," I said. "Just with you. How can you have faith that our friends will make it to Alderon, that you'll be able to change your fate, *and* that you can trust me not to ruin your life when you have such a cynical outlook on the world?"

"Simple," he said. "Trust comes from experience and

understanding. My experience is that the world can be un-predictable, unfair, and harsh without ever needing a reason. And no matter how hard you try to make sense of it, sometimes it is beyond understanding. But people—*individuals*—they're not like that. You guys aren't like that. I've gotten to know you all pretty well since this whole thing started and because of that understanding, and the experiences we've shared, it's easy for me to trust you. Just like it's easy for me to trust myself to get the job done where my fate is concerned."

"And you don't have any doubt about that at all . . ." I didn't intend for this to come out as a question, but the way my tone dropped off at the end caused Daniel to take notice.

"What?"

I took a deep breath and decided to come out with it, speak my thoughts into existence. My fingers traced an invisible pattern on the table runner, and I kept my eyes low rather than meeting his.

"Remember that night we were on the magic train and you saved me from falling into the canyon? Before I fell off the train, you told me to let go and that you'd catch me. I chose not to listen because I wasn't sure if I could really trust you after you made that comment to Jason about me ruining your life."

The candle's light was burning brighter. Or maybe it was getting darker. I extended my gaze and saw Daniel's hands—strong and callused from so many years of fighting.

"Is there a question in there?" he asked.

"Just one," I replied. I leaned forward, meeting his eyes. I recalled the way he looked down on me as I fell from the train into the canyon. "Given who I am to you—what your prologue prophecy says about me, and how much you love Kai—did it cross your mind for a second to let me fall?"

Daniel stared at me for a long beat. The couples and lanterns in the background blurred. For that moment, it was just me and him.

"Honestly?" he said. "Yes."

I felt my heart grow colder, but I wasn't surprised. I leaned back in my chair again, pulling away.

"You're mad," he said.

"Actually I'm not," I replied. "I appreciate you telling me the truth. And I get it. If the situation were reversed I would probably do the same thing."

"You mean you'd *think* the same thing."

"Right." I nodded slowly.

Another lull passed. Our waitress brought over a dish that looked like pork glazed in a red sauce, which I guess Daniel had ordered before I got there. It smelled amazing. Daniel didn't notice, but when the waitress placed the plate on the table she looked at me then tilted her chin toward Daniel and gave me a wink, which I didn't understand.

The fragrance and warmth of the food was enticing, but neither of us touched the dish.

"I'm not going to turn on you, Knight," Daniel eventually said, his brown eyes—hard, but fervent—looking into mine. "You know that I don't blame you for my prophecy. I'm going to fix my fate myself, just like you're going to change yours. That's why we're on this quest. I may have moments of doubt, but I don't let them control what I do. Just like I hope you don't let yours control you anymore."

I didn't say anything. I wanted to, but I didn't. He nudged the plate of food toward me then pushed his chair out from the table. "Here. You eat," he said. "I'm not hungry."

Daniel stood to go. I wanted to tell him not to. But I didn't do that either. Just before leaving he paused at my side, his tall shadow falling on me like a cloak. "I know it's a lot to ask. But I promise you, Knight, if you keep trusting me we'll finish this the way we started."

"And how's that?"

"Well, amongst other things—together."

Out of the corner of my eye, I saw his hand extend a few inches toward my shoulder—as if he was going to give me a supportive pat, or a touch of affection—but he pulled away. Instead he put some money down on the table—presumably to pay for the meal—then nodded at me before ducking back inside.

I sighed and picked up a fork, absentmindedly stabbing at the food. Once the plate had stopped steaming I took a bite. The sauce made contact with my taste buds first. Thick sugar and rich spices delighted my tongue, and I smiled as I put another forkful in my mouth.

All the patio's lanterns were glowing now. There was still more than enough natural light to see, so I figured they must've been set on timers. As I took my third bite of pork I saw Yunru and Berto coming through the restaurant. I waved and they came over to join me.

Yunru had an armful of old, weathered texts that reminded me of the Scribes' protagonist book library. For some reason it also reminded me of a book I'd seen long ago in the Capitol Building library when we were fleeing Arian's forces in Century City.

The book had been called *Shadow Guardians—Origins, Dangers, & Weaknesses*.

I didn't know why the book had caught my attention at the time, but it'd been imprinted in my memory since then. Something about it seemed important.

Yunru set her pile of books down on the table. "You missed a great adventure," she said as she sat in the chair previously occupied by Daniel. "This bookshop did not disappoint. It will be very helpful for my thesis research."

Berto grabbed a chair and sat down as well.

"Glad to hear it," I said. "What's your thesis on, anyways? You never said what kind of research it was that brought you to Germany."

I took a big bite of pork.

"Fairytale characters," Yunru replied.

I choked mid-swallow. As I coughed I made a sign to the nearest waitress—I needed water, stat.

"Are you all right?" Berto asked.

The waitress brought me water, which I chugged. When my windpipe no longer felt clogged from pork or surprise, I wiped my mouth with a napkin and cleared my throat. "Yeah. Uh, fine. Sorry. Go ahead."

Yunru gave me a puzzled look. "Yes, well, like I said, my thesis is on fairytale characters. In America, there are many television programs about people who hunt ghosts and explore other mysterious events. I believe that fairytales are based on real history, and I wish to travel the globe and discover sources of tales and magic phenomenon. At university I study film production and classic literature to prepare for a career like the television ghost hunters. Only I will call my show 'Fairytale Investigations with Yunru St. James.'"

"Your last name is St. James?"

"No, but I like the way it sounds. It will be my stage name."

"Germany is full of fairytale legend," Berto cut in. "For instance . . ." He plucked a book from Yunru's pile. The cover was mahogany-colored leather with gold flecks on the spine. He opened it on the table between us and pointed at a page. "The city of Hamelin is where the famous Pied Piper comes from. Legend says that hundreds of years ago he used his magic flute to lure children away from their homes to his lair and then drown them in the Weser."

"Berto, that is a misleading retelling," Yunru interceded. "Many of those he lured away were children, but their youth was not what caused them to hear and follow the music. People with strong hearts were the ones entranced by the Pied Piper's instrument."

Berto shook his head, unconvinced. "People with strong hearts should've been able to resist the music. That doesn't make any sense."

I took another bite of pork as I watched them argue, my eyes flicking from one college kid to the other as they bickered. They seemed to have forgotten I was there.

"It does certainly make sense," Yunru retorted, seeming peeved. "It is like with hypnosis. They say the smarter a person is, the more receptive they are to it, even though reason would suggest otherwise. The Pied Piper's music works the same way. The stronger the heart, the more susceptible to hearing and being controlled by the music."

"Then why were so many children enchanted?" Berto countered.

"Because strength of heart has nothing to do with age," Yunru responded. "It has to do with conviction of goodness—the ability to resist evil deeds and thoughts—which children are much more skilled at than adults. According to my research and understanding, the reason the fairytales only talk about children vanishing is because they were the only ones fully controlled by the Pied Piper's music. For the flute's music to completely ensnare you, you have to possess a heart that is immovably strong—otherwise known as a 'pure heart.' Without a pure heart you may still hear and even be partially controlled by the music, but like the rare adult who was hypnotized in times of lore, you can fight it off depending on what degree of strength your heart holds."

I cleared my throat, trying to end the discourse. I knew the tale of the Pied Piper well. Frankly—thanks to my Fairytale History class at school and Blue's yammering—I probably knew the tale better than Yunru and Berto did. The Pied Piper was an actual Book villain who'd been imprisoned in Alderon ages ago. He did use his music to lure people to his lair, but he only did so once a month and for three nights straight. At the end of the third night he would play a different song that caused the people to drown themselves in whatever river happened to be closest. There was never an explanation for why he did this. I guess it was just for kicks. Disturbing, but then crazy villains didn't really prioritize gentility when tending to their homicidal tendencies.

Maybe the interruption of Yunru and Berto's discussion had been a little rude, but I preferred not to talk about antagonists from the past when I had so many to deal with in the present.

"Sorry to bore you with so much darkness," Yunru said, thinking that was my problem with the conversation. "There are nice fairytales too." She selected a book from the top of the pile and flipped it to a page near the front. "This is the Sababurg Castle. It is not too far from here and is said to be the actual castle where Sleeping Beauty waited for her prince."

"I thought that was the Neuschwanstein Castle," Berto commented, sliding the book over so he could see the palatial rendering.

Yunru shook her head. "That is just the castle Disney used for inspiration."

"Who's Disney?" I asked.

"He is a famous storyteller whose company makes a lot of movies about fairytales. I guess the real castle from the legend did not live up to his vision, though." Yunru turned to a new page in the book to show me a picture of Neuschwanstein Castle, which was far grander.

"A storyteller who altered a subject into something you can't even recognize for the sake of making it look like their version of perfection." I let out a slight huff of amusement, thinking about the Author. "It's not unheard of."

"Are you familiar with Sleeping Beauty?" Yunru asked.

"You could say that."

"That's good. It is one of my favorites. Such a sweet story."

Sweet was not the adjective that came to mind considering that Sleeping Beauty's daughter was one of the most toxic people I'd ever met. I may have had run-ins with a lot of antagonists lately, but even without seeing her in weeks, I still considered Mauvrey one of my most hated rivals.

But I'll let Yunru have this one. No need to take Mauvrey's soul-dampening powers cross-dimensional.

"Yup. Sweet," I commented as I returned to eating. "You said it, Yunru."

CHAPTER 11

Confronted

After Berto, Yunru, and I had our fill of hearty German food, the pair of them had gone out for a night stroll. We'd left the restaurant just as Anna and Greg arrived to have dinner themselves.

I'd spent the next hour or so wandering around the hotel. Over the years my family and I had stayed at fancy hotels when travelling to other kingdoms on diplomatic ventures during the summer. My parents didn't leave me to my own devices very often on such trips—they knew that the longer I was alone the greater the chance I would get into mischief. But whenever I had some time to myself I loved to explore. Getting a lay of the land always gave me a great sense of peace. And being on my own gave me an even greater sense of clarity.

When I'd checked out everything of interest in the hotel— from the laundry room to the fascinating machine that produced ice—I ventured out onto the streets of Hann. Münden.

It was chilly, but the town was so beautiful at night it was well worth it. Tourists and locals carried on under the blaze of street lamps. A warm glow shone from the windows of various homes and establishments. The buildings were tall and compact, many with steep, triangular brick roofs like the hotel. They squished together on the cobblestone pathways as I worked my way through the streets.

Eventually I found my way to the riverfront. As promised, Yunru and Berto had shown me the coordinates we were looking for on the map. The wormhole back to Alderon was about a ten-minute walk from here.

Stone walls were built at the water's edge, creating a perimeter. I rubbed my arms as the cold began to seep through my skin. The river flowed on, converging from the Werra to the Weser a short distance away.

A sharp wind blew my hair back, causing my face to turn in the direction of the mountains. They were like jagged splotches of ink against the smooth complexion of the sky and the freckles of the stars. The moon wasn't full anymore, but it was still impressive. When I could no longer handle the cold I hurried back to the hotel, the silvery sphere following me, radiating ghostly light.

It was about half past nine when I trotted down the hallway carrying two bags from the hotel restaurant. Coming to the desired door, I knocked. After a second it swung inwards, Daniel waiting under its frame.

"You should really check to see who it is before answering the door," I said, entering the room.

"Right. Because an angry tourist is way up there on the list of things we have to be wary of," he responded. "Berto and Yunru showed me where we're going on the map," he continued as he came to the window to join me.

"Same," I said. "When did you see them?"

"They came back about an hour ago. Yunru went to go do some reading in your room. Then Berto and I went out for a driving lesson. I think he's in the lobby now asking the concierge about the quickest route to some castle."

"Whoa," I said. "Berto gave you a driving lesson?"

"Yup." He pointed to the desk where the keys to the Glove Mobile rested. "Greg lent us the car. When I told him I'd never driven before he and Berto both offered to give me a tutorial. Apparently it's a rite of passage for people around our age."

"How'd you do?" I asked skeptically.

"Not bad. I'm actually pretty good at it."

"I'll believe that when I see it."

Daniel noticed the doggie bags in my hands. "Really, Knight?" he said. "I know you've got a big appetite, but isn't that a bit excessive?"

"One's for you, jerk," I said, annoyed but smirking. "You skipped out on dinner so I got you something with the money you left behind." I shoved the bigger bag against his chest.

"And the other one?" He nodded at the second bag.

"None of your business."

"It's more cake isn't it?"

I laughed. I couldn't help it. It seemed Daniel couldn't either. "Just eat your food," I said. "I'm gonna find the others to say goodbye and thank you, and then head to bed. We have an early wake-up call."

I walked to the door. Daniel held it open as I stepped into the hall.

"Have you thought about what I said?" he asked.

I froze for a second. Then I slowly pivoted around. I eyed him steadily. The cake bag felt heavier in my hand, but was nothing in comparison to the weight of his question.

"I have," I said. "And I do trust you, Daniel. It's just hard not to let doubt play a part in how much. You've been there for me; I've been able to count on you since this journey began. And I know you meant what you said about believing you can change your fate and that you don't see me as an obstacle to get rid of on your way to doing that. But I also know from my own experience how rapidly doubt can replace good intentions.

"I mean, I feel no qualms about saying that I'm a smart person. I'm great at looking at the big picture and calculating best options. If I wasn't, I don't think I'd still be alive. But even so, when doubt rears its ugly head and instinct kicks in, all those qualities can go out the window. Doubt caused me to push away my friends and put myself in harm's way. And it caused you to wonder—if only for a second—if it might be easier to let me fall to my own demise from the magic train."

Daniel didn't say anything.

I sighed. "You're mad."

"No," he said. "I should've expected as much. You're incapable of letting your guard down for more than a few minutes."

Another argument was at our threshold. And this time, I regret to say that I didn't hold back.

"That's not fair," I replied.

"Oh no? Don't think I didn't know what you were doing in that cave before the Magistrake attacked—asking me about Kai, trying to get me to open up in some way so you could convince yourself not to let your shields go back up. Your trust in me is as conditional as it is fleeting."

"I didn't say it wasn't true," I countered. "I said it wasn't fair. Maybe if you weren't so guarded my doubts wouldn't have so much soil to grow in. Maintaining trust is a lot easier when it's a two-way street, Daniel. And the fact is I've asked you about Kai three times in the last twenty-four hours and you've dodged my questions at every turn. You wouldn't do that if your own doubts about me weren't causing your trust to waver."

I was clutching the cake bag so tightly that all the blood left my hand. Daniel was leaning back against the pale amber wall outside his door—arms crossed rigidly. He looked how I felt— tense, resentful, maybe a bit sad, but mainly exhausted. We were both tired of this, tired of us.

I kicked at the forest green carpet beneath my boots and sighed. "We're not very good at this are we?"

"No. We're not," he said. "So maybe we should stop forcing it."

"Meaning?"

"Meaning we can't keep worrying about the long-term doubts we have about each other. If we do, they'll drive us crazy." He uncrossed his arms and shook his head. "Look, at this moment—right here and right now—do you trust me?"

I paused for a second but nodded. "Yes," I said. "Do you trust me?"

"Yes," he replied. "So why don't we leave it at that?"

"Is that an option?"

"I think it's our only one," he said. "Bottom line: I'm sticking with my promise that you can count on me, Knight. But I don't think any number of promises is going to eliminate your doubts completely. I guess the same goes for me about you. Just because I believe in our mission and my ability to change my fate, doesn't mean all my doubts about you disappear. So instead of trying to pretend like they're not there or trying to constantly confront them, let's just let them be. We'll cross that bridge if and when the time comes. For now, let's live in the moment and trust each other one day at a time."

I stood there and thought on the notion. Daniel had laid it out pretty clearly and he was right. I swallowed my pride and the pang in my chest that wished there was another way. I knew that there wasn't, so I gave the only answer that could hope to save us.

"Okay," I said.

Daniel nodded once, finalizing our agreement, then turned to go inside his room. "I'll meet you in the hotel lobby at quarter past four," he called over his shoulder.

I took a couple of steps down the hallway. "Daniel," I said, rotating back around. He paused and looked at me. "For what it's worth . . . I hope that if a time does come when our doubts come against our trust, the trust wins and we do finish this quest together. In one piece, but also together."

CHAPTER 12

Sleepwalkers

fter tracking down Anna, Greg, and Berto to say thank you and goodbye, I made my way back to my room. Yunru was pouring over a pile of books on her bed. It reminded me of an evening at the beginning of the semester when my friends and I were in our room at Lady Agnue's.

Blue had been spread out on her purple comforter surrounded by books about fairytale history. Her dark blonde waves were tied up in a scrunchie on top of her head as her intense blue eyes scanned each page with excitement. SJ had been sitting with perfect posture at her desk, studying her potions book. Her long black hair was neatly tucked into a braid, and the gold color of her day dress matched the gold design carved into our suite's floor and ceiling.

This recollection came and went in an instant, so much like the quick flashes of the future I suffered from while I slept. My heart ached slightly. For unlike my dreams, which told of things yet to come, this passing image was of a time long gone by. It was a memory of a world that we'd left behind and people we no longer were, and that was a sad thing.

Yet as the last bits of the recollection fled, that sadness melted into something else. While I regretted the rift I'd created with my friends and was worried about all that was coming for me, I realized I was still glad for the change. I was glad to no longer be the girl in that memory.

When we'd left Lady Agnue's, I remembered feeling excited about the journey ahead despite the uncertainty and peril that came with it. I still felt that way now. The world of classes and homework and school was so small and ordinary compared to the world of today. And the girl I'd been in that bedroom all that time ago was a mere silhouette of the person I sensed myself becoming.

It was true I'd made mistakes, and I probably would continue making them. I'd been hunted and almost killed. I'd hurt people and I'd put my faith in myself through the wringer. But I knew that through it all, I had changed for the better. I felt stronger and wiser. I was accepting more about myself each day—the good qualities like my sense of fight and ability as a leader, and the less favorable ones like my fears about the future and myself. After everything that had come to pass I felt confident. It was not the hollow kind that I had felt before, but the real kind where no attack on my self-esteem or physical person could shake me to my core.

I may not have known what that translated to in terms of who I was, or what kind of hero or princess it made me, but I did know it was a start. And as I continued to fill in the pieces of myself—accepting more as I learned more—I believed that I would come out the other end as the *something* more I always hoped to be. Something stronger, something admirable, and something better than the archetype stereotypes out there ever thought I could be. I had doubts about a lot of things—Daniel, the Author, where this journey would lead—but I had no doubts about this. Not anymore.

I finished my last piece of chocolate cake as Yunru read from her texts. When the final bite of frosting had been consumed, I wished her goodnight and thanked her as well.

"Will we ever see you again?" Yunru asked.

"I hope so," I said, meaning it.

"Here," Yunru said. She scribbled a long string of numbers onto a scrap of hotel stationery and handed it to me. "This is my phone number back home in Hong Kong. If you're ever there, give me a call."

"Thank you," I said, folding the small piece of paper. "I wish I could give you one, but I don't have a phone."

"That seems impractical," Yunru commented.

I shoved the paper into my left boot for safekeeping and hugged her. "Good luck with everything, Yunru. I hope you find what you're looking for and that one day you're the world's most famous fairytale expert and TV show host."

Yunru smiled from ear to ear at the thought and hugged me. Then she headed into the bathroom. When she closed the door, an impulse came over me. I didn't know if it was a kind one or a foolish one, but I went with it anyways.

I activated my Hole Tracker, widened the perspective of the map to allow a greater area to be displayed, then flipped through the time settings. I searched for a wormhole opening on Earth sometime in the next month, far away from Germany. The holes here, after all, seemed to be connected to Alderon.

I found one meant to appear in a place called Copenhagen about six weeks from now. Quickly I scribbled down the coordinates and the time of the opening. Then I turned off the Hole Tracker—just as it started to spark—and shoved the note deep within the folds of one of Yunru's books.

I liked Yunru; she'd been kind and gracious and had treated us like family despite being strangers. It felt wrong to hold the key to her lifelong ambition and say nothing. Leaving this as a clue was a good compromise. Finding it and following it would be completely on her.

Maybe it was an irrational decision, but it felt like the right call. As I climbed into bed and drifted to sleep, I felt sure of it.

I was starting to get used to walking through the landscape of my dreams. It was like descending into the dark, musty basement of your school—familiar, but the shadows still kept you on your toes.

I floated through a sea of red, black, and blue. The black was from the general darkness of the void. Waves of blue pulsed through the backdrop like I was surrounded by water. Moving amongst it were the blurs of dozens of graceful girls in scarlet dresses.

The gowns and girls glided around me. After a minute of being dizzied by their motion, the scene shifted. I was alone in my bedroom at Lady Agnue's. Everything was still and quiet for a moment. Then a buzzing sound came from my bed. Slowly I approached it.

On my bedspread I found the source of the noise: a compact mirror. It was like the other compacts I'd dreamt about recently. The bronze shell had the words "Mark Two" engraved on it. I'd seen Arian talking to his accomplices through various Mark Two compacts in my dreams. They seemed to allow the users to communicate with one another through their looking glasses. Past that I didn't know what they were or where they came from. My only clue had been their name.

The magic mirror from *Beauty & the Beast*—which used to have the ability to spy on, but not interact with, others—had the phrase "Mark One" engraved onto its back. But I didn't know what that meant, nor if there was any way to learn the truth now that I'd destroyed the mirror in my face-off with Arian on Adelaide.

Intrigued, I picked up the buzzing compact on my bed and opened it gingerly. When I did, a woman's face filled the mirror looking back at me. It was the woman from my dreams—the woman who'd been warning me to remember the dragon.

"Are you ready?" she asked.

In a flash, everything was gone. My dream shifted. I saw Chance Darling for a moment. Then a bright explosion knocked him off his feet. Another man rushed out of the smoke toward him, cognac lapel flailing in the wind and dagger in hand.

Next I saw a vision of Big Girtha. She was Mauvrey's friend and lackey and had spent years antagonizing girls at Lady Agnue's. Given that I was Mauvrey's favorite target, I had always gotten special attention from the lumbering protagonist who was the younger sister of the famous *Hansel & Gretel* siblings.

Hence my surprise at what came next.

Big Girtha—bordering five foot ten, hands like a coal miner, and brown choppy bangs with all the femininity of a broomstick—approached dream me in a hallway of Lady Agnue's. Dream me was wearing a white peplum top over navy leggings tucked into black combat boots. Her hair was shorter and flounced around her shoulders, a style I rather liked.

Dream me didn't tense when she saw Big Girtha approaching, nor did her expression show any signs of guardedness. Most bizarre was when the two hugged.

It gave me the heebie-jeebies to witness the contact between them. I was all for breaking archetypes, but that was too out of character for me to comprehend.

After this scene came another sight that was hard to fathom— this time in a good way. I saw Mark. *Actual Mark.* The long-missing prince of Dolohaunty was walking down an elegant stone hallway with a smile on his face. Red carpet lined the floor. Tapestries hung from the walls. Two armored guards followed him.

When my perspective widened it revealed the five of us—me, Jason, Blue, Daniel, and SJ. Daniel hung back a bit, but the rest of us rushed at our friend and tackled him in a group hug.

This vision vanished, but the discovery it left was far from fleeting. It was so impactful that my entire dreamscape felt a pang as my heart registered the truth. Mark was alive. If I saw him in my dreams that meant somehow, someday, we would see him again.

Flashes fell through my perspective. A torn envelope with a logo in the top left corner that read "Metropolitan Museum of Art." A platter of nachos. The glint of the sun against the ocean. SJ letting out a scream as someone grabbed her by the neck and threw her against a gray stone wall. Black glass raining down. A round, polished oak table that was large enough to seat fifty people. Jason on some sort of street surrounded by silver knights charging him with weapons. And finally, a fluttering red flag with the insignia of a gold phoenix.

Then I turned and saw Arian.

I felt the urge to run from him and strangle him at the same time. Alas, I was unable to do either. I was not a participant in this vision, just an observer.

Arian stepped into a study of sorts. The sole doorway on the left was covered by a set of maroon curtains that fell to the cedar-paneled floor. The walls of the room were dark but glistened slightly, as if made of glass.

There were bookshelves lining the walls on two sides. Against the far back wall was a solid marble desk. It was black, as was the chandelier hanging in the center of the room. The latter reminded me of the one in Lenore's office. Then I noticed the girl sitting behind the desk.

She was young, but older than me—maybe twenty-six. Her large eyes were framed with intense eyeliner. Her black hair was pulled up in a ponytail that showed off her regal bone structure and caramel-colored skin. She wore a fitted black crop top with shimmering silver shoulder pads that matched her pointed, dangling earrings.

Something about the confidence in her posture and the commanding pout of her expression made her radiate power.

"Majesty," Arian said as he crossed the room. "We have her."

"I've heard that before, Arian," the girl said, a thin layer of annoyance in her tone. "How do you know she won't escape again?"

The sound of the voice caused a tremor of recollection inside me. There had always been three recurring characters in my dreams. Natalie Poole was one. The second was Arian. The third was a girl who I'd never seen, but whose voice had occupied the shadows of my nightmares.

I'd long wondered if I would ever be able to place that voice to a face. Now, finally, I could. From the first syllable this girl uttered the veil was lifted and I realized I'd found her. This was the girl who'd haunted my head alongside Arian for so many nights. And if Arian was calling her "Majesty," I knew this must be Nadia.

I studied her with fresh perspective.

"This time is different," Arian responded. "She is beyond the help of her friends and her magic. One way or the other, she'll give us what we want."

The girl's eyebrows rose with intrigue. "So you have your precious M.R.I. then?"

"Yes. Which means our girl will either crumble to the amount of power we force out of her after so many resurrections, or it will kill her. Either way she will be taken care of before anyone ever finds her."

The girl nodded then took a deep breath as a thought crossed her mind. She folded her hands on the desk. "Just in case, I want regular check-ins with our hunter on the inside. Her friends aren't going to give up trying to find her, and if they get too close I want you to make sure she—"

Like a gust extinguishing a candle flame, her voice was cut off by the sound of an E-flat. Faint woodwind music began to echo in the furthest corners of my mind. As it grew louder, Arian's scene faded. More flashes intercut each other like one reality tearing into the next.

A carnation with glistening red petals. A set of female hands shaking and covered in blood. The woman in the teal zip-up jacket mouthing the same sentence. The music in my head was so loud at this point that I couldn't hear what she said. But I didn't need to. The words on her lips were easy to read and always the same: "Remember the dragon."

With one high-pitched note I was shocked awake. I expected the music to stop, assuming it was a product of my nightmares, but it played on. The sound flowed in through the open window of our hotel room. I stood slowly, the soft, hypnotic lullaby compelling me to move toward it. As I made for the window I noted distantly that there was movement in the room. Yunru was out of bed and headed for the door.

"Yunru?"

She didn't respond. She simply reached for the handle of the door and turned the knob, walking into the corridor in her bare feet and lavender pajama set.

I started to call after her again, but the haunting music seemed to dampen my will. My thoughts felt fuzzy. Before I knew it, I was halfway across the room, heading for the door myself.

Suddenly the phone on the nightstand rang and my thoughts sharpened. The high-pitched sound was like a mental reset, driving away the hold of the melody.

My eyes bugged out and I dashed for the phone. "Hello?"

"*Guten morgen,* miss," a sleepy sounding man replied. "Apologies. You requested a wake-up call for ten minutes past four. Please accept our humblest apologies for the delay. I hope this does not cause you great inconvenience."

I glanced at the clock on the wall, squinting through the darkness to make out the position of the hands.

Half past four! The hole is opening now!

Daniel and I had to get to the river, but I also had Yunru to worry about. She was gone and I had no idea what had possessed her or where she was going. I slammed down the receiver, jumped into my boots, and bolted for the door. When I raced into the hallway I saw Daniel coming out of his room. His wake-up call must've been late too.

He jogged up to me. "Do you hear that?" he asked. He held up a finger and narrowed his eyes, listening. I began to hear the vague flute melody again—not as loud as before, but growing in resonance.

"Yeah, it's faint but I think it's coming from outside," I replied. "It was louder before. It pulled me out of my dreams. But that's not the only weird thing. When I woke up, Yunru was leaving the room. There's something wrong with her. It looked like she was in a trance." I hurried down the hall to the stairs. "Come on, we have to make sure she's okay."

We worked our way down the elaborate, twisting stairs of the hotel, across the bar, the library, and the lobby, then finally onto the cobblestone streets.

At first I didn't see Yunru, but then I spotted her heading along the street that led to the river. "Yunru!" I called. She didn't respond.

When we caught up to her, I was surprised by the deadness in her eyes and the bright purple color that flooded her irises and pupils. Even as we caught up to her she kept moving forward, not noticing us.

"Yunru," I repeated.

She didn't hear me. I, however, did hear something. The music.

The notes swirled around me like a thick wind, getting louder and harder to ignore. The entrancing rhythm bled into the folds of my brain. My head turned in the direction that Yunru was going and my body wanted to follow.

In my periphery, Daniel was shaking his head. The music must have been affecting him as well. He looked pained. It was hard to focus, but I put my hand on his shoulder. "You okay?"

He turned to look at me. When he did, concern streaked his expression. "Knight, your eyes."

I drew back. "What about them?"

"They're purple. Not completely like Yunru's, but it's like someone dropped food coloring in the pupils."

Behind Daniel, I saw a young boy in white-and-blue striped pajamas climb out a window. It was on the ground floor, so he easily clambered over the flower-filled window box and onto the street. He shuffled past us, pursuing the same route as Yunru. The same shade of purple also filled up his sockets.

I narrowed my eyes in thought. "Daniel, did you see that newspaper in the hotel rooms that talked about the disappearances happening recently?"

He nodded.

My gaze followed the young boy, the music still tugging at me. "I think I know what's causing them."

"Obviously," Daniel responded. "The music is luring people away. But why are these guys the only ones getting hypnotized?" He violently shook his head again. "And why does it seem to be getting louder but no one else in town can hear it?"

He was right. The music felt like it was blasting now, but we seemed to be the only two who had woken up that weren't completely hypnotized. Suddenly my left foot inadvertently took a step forward. I grunted and yanked it back. My whole body felt like a leaf caught in the tide; it couldn't help but be pulled along. Daniel clutched his head. His eyes were normal, but he was clearly being affected by the music.

Once more my body felt yanked forward; this time it was harder to resist. I took two and a half steps but grabbed Daniel's arm to steady myself before I could go any farther. Realization finally settled in.

"It's the Pied Piper," I said, digging my nails into Daniel's leather jacket. "It has to be. You and I both know he's more than a legend. He's been locked away in Alderon for years. But Germany has those wormholes opening to Alderon. I bet he's been using his magic music to draw people through."

"I thought Earth rejected Book magic."

"It must be coming from the other side of the hole—probably the same one we're headed toward. That's why Earth isn't stopping it. It's a loophole. Since the source of magic is somewhere else, there's nothing the realm can do about it. The Piper can lure people through the hole without interference."

The music's call temporarily dulled my resolve and I was jerked forward a few feet. Understanding the urgency of the problem, Daniel yanked me by the arm and pulled me closer to him.

"If that's true, then why are only some people hearing it?" he asked, eyeing a third purple-eyed sleepwalker on our left. This one was an adolescent boy with shaggy brown hair and gray sweats.

"Yunru said that the stronger a person's heart, the more likely they are to hear and be compelled by the music. That's you and me apparently. But only people with pure hearts are completely hypnotized, like those two kids and Yunru—whoa!" I lurched forward. Daniel reeled me in.

"I guess we're lucky that you're probably the first princess in history without a pure heart then," Daniel commented.

I was struck by the statement. Alas, I didn't have time to fully process it. The music was hard to tune out and I needed to focus on a way to stop it. Then it hit me.

"When you met me in the hall, you could barely hear the music, right?"

"Yeah. It was loud when it woke me up," Daniel replied, "but then the phone rang and kind of blocked it out for a minute." His eyes were bright with understanding.

"That's it then!" I exclaimed. "The same thing happened to me. The high-pitched sound must've suppressed the music's power temporarily, which means—"

"—we just need to find a continuous sound that's loud and annoying enough to cause more interference," Daniel finished. He paused and glanced back at the hotel. "I have an idea."

My feet begged to take a step. Daniel gripped me by the shoulders and maneuvered me to an empty fruit stand. "The music's not affecting me as much as it's affecting you. I'm going to risk getting something from my hotel room before that changes. Just hang on for two minutes."

I grabbed hold of the stand. "It'll take you way longer than that to get back here."

He started jogging back to the hotel. "I'll take a shortcut," he called over his shoulder. "Don't go anywhere."

I watched him dash down the street then back into the hotel. The music grew louder in my head and I found myself resisting the compulsion to plug my ears. I knew that if I let go I would be done. I was already struggling to hold on.

Whoa! Scratch that. Not holding on! Not holding on!

My hands had slipped as if they were greased with bacon fat. I staggered forward but was able to grab onto the edge of the counter. I dragged the stand a few inches along, its weight crunching in the dirt.

Come on, Daniel! Where are you?

Thankfully I saw him come out of the hotel then—but not through the door. Daniel hopped out of his hotel room window five stories up. Then he leapt onto the slanted roof of the building next to it, skidding down and repeating the process when he reached the roof of an adjacent structure. This building had several balconies. Daniel bounded from one to the next until he was ten feet above the ground. At that point he jumped. With more style and ease than I'd ever seen, he touched down, rolled, and came to his feet.

Well, he did say he would take a shortcut.

I expected him to head toward me, but much to my surprise he took off behind the hotel. I was too flabbergasted to yell at him. I dragged the stand forward another few inches.

My fingers were slipping again. The music poured through my ears like a tidal wave. And then an entirely different sound filled my skull. It was the funky song we'd been listening to in Greg's car! The techno dance beat blasted through the streets as the Glove Mobile came speeding around the corner, headlights bursting into the night. The moment it resounded in my ears it overpowered the hold of the Pied Piper's enchantment, restoring my control over my body.

Daniel jerked the car to a stop in front of me. The music continued to pump powerfully from the car's audio system, offsetting the flute's melody.

"You're brilliant!" I said as I threw open the side door and leapt into the front seat.

"You sound surprised."

Daniel yanked a lever and shoved his foot on the pedal beneath him that made us take off. Lights in various windows lit up in our wake, countless people in the village disturbed by the sound of the crazy upbeat song that filled the previously silent night.

The song also woke up the sleepwalkers as we passed them. Just like it had for me, the music blaring from the car stereo caused enough interference to cancel out the effects of the Pied Piper's music.

As we skidded into a hard left turn, the shaggy-haired boy in the gray sweats jumped out of the way of the car. I saw his eyes in the side view mirror as we drove by. They had returned to normal and he looked confused, trying to figure out where he was and what was happening.

I recognized the street we were on and pointed ahead. "Turn right!"

Daniel jerked the steering wheel. The whole vehicle shook as the tires rolled over the narrow cobblestone street. As we careened down it, I worried that the side view mirrors would get knocked off. This was the shortest way to the riverfront, but the road was barely wide enough. The worn brick walls on either side were inches away. And while he wasn't bad for only having one lesson, Daniel was hardly a professional driver.

I clutched the seat with one hand and felt grateful we'd heeded Anna's warning about seatbelt safety.

After another second, the Glove Mobile shot onto the road beside the river. A teenage girl in a nightie rubbed her eyes as we passed, looking relieved to be free from the music but also understandably shocked by the out-of-control Toyota 4Runner blaring techno music.

Daniel was hitting the forward pedal pretty hard. We sped so fast that the buildings whizzed by in a blur. About thirty seconds later we saw our target—a black hole. It swirled in front of a bridge farther down. Yunru was about to enter into its depths.

"Punch it!" I said. "She's going to fall through!"

We drove past the little boy in the pajama set, waking him up.

The cobblestones rattled beneath us. My heart pounded against my chest, contending with the bass of the song.

Daniel was doing everything he could to keep from losing control of the car while maintaining speed, but nothing could've gotten us there fast enough. Yunru was through the hole before our music was close enough to break the spell.

Daniel didn't slow down. At fifty miles an hour the car sped through the wormhole that connected Hann. Münden to Book.

Falling through a hole had been rough before, but it was nothing compared to what came next. The Toyota 4Runner tumbled through the churning colors and sparks of the dimensional connector in a violent spin. CD cases, empty soda cans, souvenir shop trinkets, and other miscellaneous items inside the car were tossed this way and that. The music made the turmoil all the more nauseating. The only thing that kept Daniel and me from breaking our necks was the restraint of the seatbelts.

Eventually we crash-landed back in the desert. The Alderon sky was dark, still encased in the red-streaked nightfall we'd left behind. Sand stretched in every direction. The only notable difference was the river we landed next to. Unlike its German counterpart, the waters of Alderon's Weser were lime green, like the blood of a mutant eel.

The car's headlights cast dual beacons on what lay ahead. Yunru was walking into a huge cave, its mouth at least a hundred feet wide. Daniel found his bearings and steered the car toward it, the wheels spitting sand. When we were thirty feet from her, Yunru ceased her zombie walk and shook herself, the music evidently having done its job. She squinted in our direction. "Daniel? Crisa?"

Daniel pushed another pedal on the floor of the car and we came to a screeching halt at the threshold of the cave. The inner walls of the cave were gouged, making pockets that were surrounded by sharp stones, reminding me of the Magistrake's tooth-rimmed orifice. There was a natural pathway that curved through the cave, passing clusters of pockets. Several larger ones featured iron bars like prison cells. Behind the bars stood nearly three dozen people.

The missing Germans!

I was relieved they all still seemed to be there, and I understood why. The Pied Piper drowned his victims on the third night of his abductions. The hotel newspaper said the disappearances had happened the last two nights. Today was number three. We were just in time to save them.

Intent on busting them out, I was about to reach for the car door handle when a large figure lumbered out of the shadows of a ground-level cave pocket. Our headlights illuminated him for all his gruesome glory. The creature looked like a hunchbacked old man crossed with a fanged beast. His eyes were huge and black and shiny like opals. He wore a feathered cap and a red peasant top over his gravely skin, which had mushroom-shaped moles growing out of it. In his hands was a large wooden pipe.

To say I was flabbergasted was an understatement. I'd always imagined the Pied Piper as a human boy. This thing was a monster.

The Pied Piper roared angrily and started to charge the car.

Daniel grabbed the lever between us and slammed down on a pedal. I assumed he was turning around to try and outrun the monster, but then he did something that made me like him even more than I ever thought possible—he drove forward.

Tires screeching and music rattling the vehicle—we slammed straight into the beast as he leapt toward us. His gruesome face smacked against the front window, cracking it, but his clawed hands gripped the hood. Daniel maneuvered the vehicle straight into the nearest wall, and the monster was thrust into the rock with the full force of the Glove Mobile.

Daniel pulled the lever again and backed up fifteen feet with a jerk. The Pied Piper fell off our hood and plopped to the ground like roadkill. After a second he groaned, starting to get back up. I smacked my hand on the area of the car beneath the front window. "Hit him again!" I yelled.

Daniel didn't hesitate. He shifted the car back into drive as the monstrous musician came to his knees. Again we plowed into him. This time he was definitely down for the count. Daniel turned off the car and we hopped out.

As we approached the monster, its body started to morph. We watched as the janky, grotesque creature transformed into a normal older man. Daniel and I stood over him. After a moment the man began to stir and lazily blinked his eyes open. He growled, his face contorted in pain. "When I change back, I will tear out your throats and sew them to my slippers."

"Pleasant image," I scoffed. "Why don't you sleep on it?" I turned to Daniel. "You wanna do the honors?"

"Nah, you do it."

I grinned down wickedly at the Pied Piper. The bottom of my boot heading toward his face was the last thing he saw before he was knocked unconscious.

The antagonist out cold from my power stomp, Daniel picked up the creature's instrument. It was long and smooth with a reddish tint, as if it was made from cherry wood. I stared at it—this beautiful, powerful instrument had been used to lure countless innocents to their demise. Without hesitating, Daniel snapped it over his knee, ensuring that no one, not even this beast once he woke up, would ever be able to use it again.

"What happened?"

Daniel and I spun around to find a slightly dazed Yunru.

"Daniel, Crisa, what's going on?"

"No time," I said, shaking my head. Daniel patted down the Pied Piped and found a key ring on his belt. I activated my Hole Tracker to verify my suspicions about how long we had left. The holographic map that popped up confirmed my fear. "That wormhole is going to close in two minutes and we need to get all these kids out of here."

Yunru looked like she wanted to ask a million questions, but we didn't have time. Daniel and I ran up to the cave cells and unlocked them, freeing the trapped Germans. The prisoners ran out in a frantic dash. "Go," Daniel told them. "Hop through the black hole outside and don't look back. It'll take you home."

The last of them dove through the hole as Daniel tossed Yunru the keys to Greg's car. He winced when he saw a sizable dent in the hood and front bumper where the Pied Piper had been sandwiched. "Aw crud," he said. "Yunru, we're really sorry about the car."

Yunru didn't respond. She was just staring at us. The black hole started to shrink. "Yunru," I said, throwing open the driver's side door. "It's time to go. You have to get back. It's now or never."

She glanced at the keys in her hand. "What if I choose never?" Her eyes pleaded with mine. "I have many questions."

"And you'll have answers," I said, grabbing her by the shoulders and quickly but gently maneuvering her toward the car. "Just not today. But we'll see each other again. Everything you need is in your books."

Yunru bit her lip but nodded and climbed into the front seat. She put her seatbelt on and powered the ignition. "I—I'll make up some story about the car for Greg," she stuttered. Then she gave a final glance back. "Thank you."

With that she turned the car back on. Its ignition roared to life, as did the stereo. Yunru slammed down on the pedal and sped toward the black hole. She, the Toyota 4Runner, and the techno music vanished within its depths mere seconds before the hole closed.

The tear in space and time sealed itself up. Daniel and I were left alone, standing side by side in the mouth of the cave.

The scarlet night sky was dotted with stars and the moon was half-concealed by clouds. By its partial glow I noticed that the sand beneath out feet seemed reddish. I knelt down and grasped a handful just to be sure. When I opened my fist, red grains fell through my fingers.

Daniel and I locked eyes.

Red sand and the Weser before us—we were in the right place. We were closing in on the Cave of Mysteries.

CHAPTER 13

Family Reunion

I t was a bit hard to calculate exactly how much time had passed since we'd left Goldilocks in Alderon. Inter-dimensional travel was a confusing thing, time-wise.

My Hole Tracker automatically adjusted to the time of whatever realm I was in. Based on what it said now and the Book-to-Earth time difference (the latter moving twenty times faster), I figured it hadn't even been an hour and a half since we'd left.

It was late evening now and the storm that had been brewing earlier was much stronger. Flurries of sand whipped around my boots and the wind blew hair into my mouth as we followed the river upstream.

Aside from the sand and the river, the third and final marker for the Cave of Mysteries was supposed to be a rock. It was one of the elements we'd discussed back on Adelaide during our short conversations about what lay ahead.

"An enchanted rock?" I remembered SJ asking Blue when she'd explained this detail in Ashlyn's living room.

"No. Just a normal rock," Blue responded in confusion. "Why does everything have to be enchanted?"

I smiled at the memory. Daniel noticed.

"What are you thinking about?" he asked.

"Our friends," I responded. "I miss them."

I heard the not-so-distant crackle of lightning. The sound was sharp and loud, a hundred times more powerful than the lightning daffodils in the Forbidden Forest that had almost killed us a while back.

Another crack echoed. Bright silver light cut jaggedly through the crimson and black sky like a dagger through an artery.

Daniel and I began to walk faster but continued talking. I finally got the chance to tell him about my vision about Mark. I was over the moon about the revelation that my friend was alive and couldn't wait to tell Jason and the others. I didn't know when, but we would be seeing Mark again and he would be fine.

The other topic we discussed was the genie lamp. Daniel was worried that Arian still had it because it meant that if we ran into him again we would be in just as much trouble as we had been on Adelaide.

I was not fond of the subject on two counts. For one, I didn't want to talk about Arian right now. I wasn't foolish; it's not like I thought I would never see him again. He was a far too persistent enemy to stay in my dust for long. But since the guy tortured my sleep as much as he did my waking life, I could use a break.

I also hated thinking about the genie lamp.

I'd grown up looking at that lamp—along with many other famous relics—in the Treasure Archives of Lady Agnue's. Those special cases at my school housed a collection of priceless fairytale artifacts, from my own mother's glass slipper to the remnants of the apple that had poisoned SJ's mom, Snow White.

While the treasures had always filled me with disdain (they were reminders of every expectation I was supposed to live up to), it was only recently that they'd begun causing me mortal peril. Sometimes it felt like the universe was determined to keep me in the clutches of my fairytale ancestors forever.

Before we left school and embarked on this journey, one of Arian's accomplices had broken into the Treasure Archives and stolen four objects: the magic mirror from Beauty & the Beast, the poisoned corset the wicked witch tried to kill Snow White with before the apple (a detail that was missing from many retellings of the story), the pea from *The Princess & the Pea*, and Aladdin's genie lamp.

I didn't know who this lackey of Arian's was, but I'd seen glimpses of her in my dreams. She always wore a purple cloak and glittering black pumps with tall silver-sequined heels. I had no idea how she'd managed to get into our school. But I intended to find out. I was determined to, just like I was determined to learn what Arian wanted with those particular relics.

Arian had said that he intended to use the lamp and the mirror on his "more important target." But I wasn't sure who he was referring to, or what he wanted with the corset and the pea. Truth was, I wasn't even sure if he had the latter. While Arian had owned up to stealing the other three items, he claimed his accomplice hadn't taken the pea. I didn't know if I believed him or not, but I guess I could add that to the list of things I needed to figure out.

Thinking about how long that list was gave me a headache. Hence why I was not fond of talking about the genie lamp. It made me too frustrated.

I was grateful when Daniel let the conversation die. I preferred to distract myself with the various oddities that we encountered along the Weser.

Every so often we came across human-shaped statues. These statues looked like they were running from something and were incredibly lifelike. We also saw lots of wildlife. Daniel and I recognized some creatures—fish in the water, snakes in the marsh alongside the bank. Others we didn't—like some weird half-rabbit, half-bullfrog things that looked like the less attractive cousins of the bunniflies in Ravelli.

I eyed one of these creatures curiously as it sat on a partially submerged sandbar in the middle of the river.

The Rabullfrog—as I decided it should be called—had a furry, grayish-brown back. Its belly was the same color, but was slimy and extended out in a bulbous lump like a fat guy who'd just dined at an all-you-can-eat buffet. The Rabullfrog's eyes were bright red and its ears were five times the size of a normal rabbit's. They draped behind the creature almost regally.

The Rabullfrog on the sandbar seemed to be looking at me. Its eyes flashed and its gut expanded further. I expected it to make a sound like "ribbit," but when it opened its mouth a very different sound came out.

"BLARD!"

Three more Rabullfrogs hopped out of the water onto the sandbar, joining their comrade. Their giant, soggy ears dragged behind them.

Trouble brewing in the sky tore my attention away. The lightning strikes were getting closer. Not only were the sounds much louder, they were more frequent.

I tilted my head toward the sky as another flash burst forth. The light caught in the reflection of Daniel's eyes. I mused for a moment how fitting it looked. His eyes always had such intensity that the sparks of the storm seemed right at home.

A cloud lit up angrily, rumbling the world. Three more cracks followed. Had I not been looking at Daniel, my travel companion would have been toast. For it was right at that second that a streak of lighting shot at the ground where he stood.

I moved faster than the violent light and dove toward Daniel, grabbing him by the jacket and pushing him out of the way. The lightning barely missed us.

A heartbeat later he and I jumped again. A second crackle struck the sand. On the third strike our worry escalated to a dangerous level.

After the first bolt of lightning touched the ground the Rabullfrogs had begun to hop back into the river. Alas, not all of them made it. Mid-hop, one Rabullfrog was struck by a lightning bolt. Instead of electrocuting him, it turned him to stone and the newly-formed Rabullfrog statue dropped lifelessly onto the sandbar.

A fourth lightning bolt suddenly did the same to one of the creatures at the threshold of the river. That Rabullfrog turned to stone as well and sunk through the tumultuous water, petrified in both senses of the word.

Daniel and I exchanged a look, but no words. We started to run.

The sky was churning sickly like it had the flu and it produced lightning strike after lightning strike as if trying to purge itself of the electricity making it sick. The other atmospherics didn't help the situation.

When you're running so fast that your heart ricochets off your uvula, oxygen is your friend. You know what isn't your friend? Sandstorms.

Wind tore up the sand, making it hard to see. The dry air made it difficult to breathe. It was becoming almost impossible to see the path ahead. There was so much sand swirling through the air that the Weser on the left was turning into a blur—everything was, except for the lightning strikes when they slit the sky and crashed down on our heels.

It was so hazy that we didn't notice that we had come to the summit of a massive dune. The sudden drop surprised us both, and we fell down the slope as an aggressive bolt of lightning impacted the ground.

I tumbled in a daze. When I got to my feet I saw something glinting in the distance. It looked like a mirror. Focusing harder, I realized there were houses nearby, tucked into a valley. Each had a roof composed of giant mirrored panels like Goldilocks's fortress. And then I understood why.

A giant crackle of lightning pummeled a house at the edge of the village. But rather than turn the mirrors and the dwelling to stone, the bolt ricocheted off a mirrored panel and shot back into the sky.

The mirrors repel the lightning!

I flicked a glance at Daniel. He'd realized the same thing.

Our previous aversion about going into town had nothing on our preoccupation with not getting turned to stone. We dashed for the safety of the houses as more lightning came down.

The nearest house had a back window that was slightly open. Not wanting to risk another second of being exposed, we made the split-second decision to go through the window rather than running around to knock on the front door.

Daniel yanked open the window fully, boosted himself up, and hopped through. I followed. Once we were both safely inside he shut the window. It was not a moment too soon. The most powerful bolt of lightning yet burst from the sky and slammed into the area behind the house where we'd been standing.

We sank to our knees and leaned against the countertop below the window, catching our breaths. The lightning continued to crackle outside, but my heart rate calmed now that we were no longer in the line of fire.

When my pulse returned to a relatively normal pace, I stood and took in the room. The shack looked humble from the outside. Inside was just as quaint. The wood floor was rough and splintered. An iron stove stood on the right, adjacent a worn oven. The ceiling was relatively low. The paint on the walls was a dark purple that reminded me of the color of the official Lady Agnue's school flag.

An archway framed in iron led to another room that was concealed from view by long curtains. I thought the curtains looked too fancy and embellished for drapery. When I narrowed in on the design I realized that they were made of scraps of ball gowns. Someone had cut up once-fancy dresses to make them. The tablecloth on the dining table was made in the same fashion.

Suddenly Daniel lurched back. I glanced in the direction he was looking. A fat gray cat had passed beneath the curtains and entered the kitchen. Its stomach dragged on the ground as it moseyed forward.

"What's wrong?" I asked.

"Nothing, I just . . . I hate cats."

The creature plopped itself down on the kitchen floor two feet from Daniel. Its stomach was spread out like a flattened beanbag chair, and it regarded me with narrow blue eyes before closing them and falling asleep.

"That's not so much a cat as it is a lumpy carpet," I commented. Then I couldn't help but release a slight laugh at the wariness in Daniel's expression.

"Shut up," he said.

"What?" I grinned. "I'm not saying anything."

"With you, that's worse."

The curtains to the kitchen were brusquely thrust aside. An older woman with a mean face stood before us. Her voluminous hair was silvery like the cat's.

"Well, well, well. What do we have here?"

This woman must've been beautiful in her younger years. Even with the wrinkles, I was struck by her elegant features and pronounced bone structure. Although she wore the housecoat of a shut-in grandma and the footwear of a farmworker, she had a powerful presence. And despite being an old lady, she demonstrated the good posture of a young protagonist under Lady Agnue's tutelage.

"Um, sorry for the intrusion," Daniel said, gesturing to the window behind us. "The storm was getting pretty bad out there and we had nowhere else to go."

The old lady nodded. "It's not wise to be wandering about outdoors when a stone storm is brewing. It would have served you right to get struck. Society has no need for ignorant children."

I suppressed a scoff. After all, such a statement didn't mean much coming from a woman who was stuck in a vast prison full of antagonists that society had kicked out.

"We were lost," I replied in half-truth.

The old lady stepped between Daniel and me and glared out the window. "Well, no matter. The storm is in its final chapter. You can go back to wherever it is you came from in a matter of minutes."

"That's a pretty fast turnaround for a storm," I commented.

The old lady tore her gaze away from the window and stared at me. Her eyes radiated coldness despite being a warm hazel. "Stone storms only last seven minutes. Everyone knows that." She leaned in closer and looked me up and down. I gripped the countertop with one hand and leaned back instinctively.

"Where exactly *did* you two say you came from?" she asked.

I narrowed my expression. "We didn't."

"Knight," Daniel said, looking over the old lady's shoulder to make eye contact with me. "She's right. Look. The storm is almost gone. Come on, we should go."

I glanced outside. The window revealed a red and navy sky with barely any clouds and no sign of lightning. The sand was also settling on the ground—the wind letting it rest at last. It was the perfect opportunity for us to leave. Unfortunately, the old woman didn't see it that way.

"Knight . . ." she repeated, swiftly coming closer to me. I took a few awkward steps back, still holding on to the kitchen countertop. The old woman pursued me until I was up against the wall. "I thought you looked familiar. Maybe not the nose; it's rather masculine. But the face . . . And the eyes, they might be green, but they're hers. There's no mistaking it."

Without breaking eye contact the old woman suddenly lunged for the knife rack on the counter. In a second she had a blade in her hand and had it halfway to my throat. My reflexes were barely fast enough. I grabbed her wrist just before the point touched my skin.

Daniel stepped in. He gripped the old woman by the back of the neck and hurled her across the room with a single sweep of his muscular arm.

"Come on," he said.

Stunned, I stood frozen for a second. Daniel yanked me through the curtained archway as the old woman tried to regain her bearings. The cat stared up at me and meowed, protesting its disturbed nap.

Daniel and I entered a living room with a sagging mustard couch, a fireplace, a desk full of parchment and withered quills, and a bookshelf. We made for the front door, but I stopped as Daniel thrust it open and dashed out. A picture frame on one of the bookshelves had caught my attention.

I picked it up. The photo featured a younger version of the old woman with three girls. The girl on the far left didn't have a face; that part of the picture had been torn off. But I did recognize one of the other two girls—the redhead. I'd seen pictures of her before.

"Daniel!"

I raced out into the night after him, slamming the door behind me. "That woman," I said, out of breath. "I think that's my mom's wicked stepmother. This redheaded woman . . ." I gestured at the frame in my hand. "She's my aunt. Well, my step-aunt anyway. Unlike my mom's eldest stepsister, she wasn't evil or banished to Alderon. I've seen pictures of her in some of my mom's old albums."

"Okay, so what?"

"*So what?* My wicked step-grandmother tortured my mom for most of her childhood and teenage years. That's the woman that my kind, wonderful mother sometimes still has nightmares about from all the mind games she endured."

"And?"

My expression darkened. "I never thought I would ever meet her face-to-face. Now that I have there's a few things I'd like to say to her, if you know what I mean."

"Oh, I know what you mean," he replied. Daniel glanced

around at the other decaying houses in the area. The glow of the lights inside poured onto the sand-covered streets. "I just think it's a bad idea."

"Don't tell me you're going to pull an SJ and tell me that violence is never the answer."

"No. Violence is always the answer. I just think we have a more pressing deadline. You don't have time for a family reunion right now."

"Two minutes," I said firmly. "Keep out of sight. I'll be right back."

"Knight—"

"Daniel, please. I wouldn't ask if it wasn't important. I always wished I could confront this woman on my mother's behalf. It's closure."

"Ugh, fine. Go. You can use your wand again, so at least this will be quick."

"I'm not planning on using my wand," I said. "I won't need it. But I promise you, this will be quick."

CHAPTER 14

Diamonds

 re-entered the house. Carefully I closed the door behind me then set the picture frame back on the shelf.

There were two other doorways in the living room—one led to the kitchen and the other led to a hallway that twisted to a different part of the house.

"Oh, Grandma, it's Crisanta," I called, easing my way to the kitchen. "I forgot to mention that I'm missing about sixteen years' worth of birthday money from you. Don't feel bad. I've got another coming up in a couple of weeks, so you can send me the back pay."

I heard a floorboard squeak and spun out of the way to dodge a knife that was hurled at me. It stuck into the wall above the fireplace mantle.

My wicked step-grandmother stepped out of the hallway on the other side of the living room. She had two more knives in her elderly—but definitely not frail—hands.

"When I heard that our queen had placed a bounty on your head I could not have been more thrilled," she said. "The only thing that would bring me more joy than seeing your mother's head cut off is knowing the agony she'd feel when her precious daughter lost hers."

"Bitter much?" I crossed my arms. "Mother's Day must be a real rough time for you, huh?"

The old woman screeched and threw another knife. I lunged to avoid it. My friend Blue was the foremost expert in combat at our school, especially where knives were concerned. She always had her trusty hunting knife and an assortment of throwing blades on her. As her training partner, I'd had plenty of practice evading them.

The curtains to the kitchen brushed against my shoulders. "There's something I've always wanted to know," I said. "You weren't always like this. You turned dark in your efforts to crush my mother. Was it really just because she was a protagonist and you and your kids weren't? Even if you were jealous, she was only a kid. How could you hate her that much?"

"Your mother was not special," the old woman said. "Simply a girl with a pretty face no lovelier than that of either of my two daughters. Her father was a protagonist, but when he died we were just another pack of commons. When your mother turned seven, I received the news. She was chosen as a protagonist. Her book had appeared. She would be off to Lady Agnue's while we were left behind in the dust. I decided I would not stand for it. Why should she have a chance to escape the life of the ordinary when my own daughters didn't? So I bribed our kingdom's ambassador to keep your mother's book a secret for a few years, giving me time to put her in her place. Thus, when she finally went off to school I had a firm enough grip on her that she would never think of herself as special."

"You manipulated and tormented her."

"I kept her from developing an ego while ensuring that she would always be obedient and would take me and my daughters with her when she rose to success. It was difficult work that required reinforcement every summer when she returned home, and through the letters I sent to her at school. But it was worth it. When she graduated she was the submissive shut-in that I'd always hoped for."

"Until she met someone who made her feel like she wasn't."

"Your father."

"My father," I agreed.

"Your mother never should have met him," the old woman growled. "He poisoned her mind against me. He had my eldest daughter and me thrown into Alderon. And we've been rotting away here ever since."

The old woman flung her final knife. I dodged it.

"Seems like the punishment was justified to me," I scoffed. "When you found out she was leaving you, you tried to kill her."

"She deserved it."

"No," I said. "She didn't. But you deserve to be in Alderon. I hope you rot away in here forever. You chose darkness over family and this is your punishment."

"Oh, Crisanta. I didn't choose darkness. It infected me like it can infect anyone; even a pretty little protagonist like you. You'd be surprised how easy it comes. It starts small, but it seeps through with the right amount of anger and hatred."

"Thanks for the ethics lesson, Grandma. Maybe I'll use it in a psychology class next semester. Lady Agnue's does offer a course called Sense, Sequins, & Sensibility. But if you're all out of creepy advice and knives, I think I'll be going."

"Just because I'm out of knives doesn't mean I'm out of options, dear."

The curtain behind me rustled and an arm brandishing a knife swung out and wrapped itself around my neck. I assumed the woman holding the knife was my oldest step-aunt. One half-glance at her blonde hair and brown eyes and I was sure of it.

"Oh good," I said, pushing back against the arm wielding the blade. "More relatives."

Utilizing a maneuver I'd practiced a hundred times with Blue, I spun with the force my step-aunt was putting into her blade and rotated her with a jolt. Her knife stabbed into the wall just before

I flung *her* into the wall. I kicked her in the stomach immediately and she was thrust back against the fireplace. She hit her head on the mantle and was knocked unconscious.

My wicked step-grandmother rushed at me. I easily evaded her attack and redirected the force of her charge, pushing her into the kitchen. I heard pots and pans clanging to the ground. Pulling one of the knives out of the wall, I pushed the curtains aside and strode in after her.

The woman was standing with her back to the countertop. There were no weapons in sight—the knife rack was empty.

"You will die here," she said. "Maybe not by my hand, but by someone else's. There's no protagonist out there who can escape the fate chosen for them."

"Let's agree to disagree," I replied. "And anyways, I hardly think you're in a position to comment on anyone's fate, given that I haven't decided what yours should be."

My wicked step-grandmother eyed the knife I twirled in my hand. "Crisanta, you're a princess. And your mother would want you to show mercy."

"You're right," I said. "I am a princess, and my mother would want me to show mercy." I stepped closer until I was barely a foot from her. I held up the knife. "But your logic is flawed in two ways. One, I'm a new kind of princess. And two, *my mother's not here.*"

With that, I punched the wicked woman in the face, knocking her out cold.

"Get that out of your system?" Daniel asked as I strode up to meet him. He stood under the eaves of a nearby building. I checked left and right to make sure we weren't being watched.

"I think so." I shook my fist, relaxing the tension in my fingers. "That woman needed to be punched."

"I don't doubt it," he commented. "I just can't believe you did it."

"You've seen me punch people before."

"Yeah, but in self-defense. I never really thought of you as the vengeful type. You must really hate her to go all dark like that."

His comment startled me and I was instantly unsettled. My step-grandmother's words about darkness echoed in the back of my mind.

"You'd be surprised how easy it comes. It starts small, but it seeps through with the right amount of anger and hatred."

I shook away her disturbing comment and readdressed Daniel. "Don't tell me you wouldn't have done the same if you ever came face-to-face with someone who'd wronged one of your parents."

Daniel didn't answer my question. He swallowed like he was holding something back, then looked away. "The river picks up over there. Let's go."

The two of us found our way back to the Weser and followed the red sand along its banks. Everything was calm for the next twenty minutes.

There was no wind, no Rabullfrogs, no monsters. By the potent light of the Weser's greenish glow Daniel and I trekked across the red desert in silence as we searched for our marker. Once again I thought back to our group's conversation regarding the subject when we were staying with Ashlyn on Earth.

"An enchanted rock?" SJ had asked Blue.

"No. Just a normal rock," Blue said, slightly irritated. "Why does everything have to be enchanted?"

"Blue, to be fair, the rock may not be enchanted, but the grave marker that's supposed to be in front of it is," Jason commented. "It's how the cave knows when to rise."

"Knight . . ."

My mind returned to the present. Daniel was pointing at an area about fifty feet away where the sand was noticeably darker. Under the shadow of night, it was the color of dried blood.

Daniel directed my attention to a small lump amidst three tall dunes. From where we stood it looked like a mole on the desert's back, but I had a feeling it was the very target we'd been searching for.

A flicker of hope sparked in my chest. I instinctively glanced around. Daniel and I had hoped that SJ, Blue, and Jason would head to the Cave of Mysteries to find us and the next object on our list to break the In and Out Spell. Perhaps it was silly to think that fate would allow our groups to arrive at the same time. Nevertheless, I felt disappointed to see no one else there.

I tried not to let it dampen my spirits. The Valley of Strife was a big place and SJ, Blue, and Jason had obviously taken a much different route than we had—Fairy Godmother zaps and inter-dimensional hole-hopping and all. Maybe Daniel and I had just beaten them here.

When he and I arrived at the rock I discovered it was bigger than it looked from far away—about three feet in height and five feet in width. Blue had been right; there was nothing remarkable about it, except for maybe the fact that it was unusually smooth. But Jason had also been right. The grave marker at the foot of the stone was clearly something special.

Away from the river, with nothing but the stars and moon to light the night, it was hard to see what was engraved on the marker. I drew out my wandpin and transformed it so that the weapon's silvery glow would offer some luminescence.

The slab of black marble was about the size of a textbook. The light of my wand revealed two images. The one on top was a gold emblem of a ram's head. Directly below it was a gold outline of a handprint.

"You want to take this one?" I asked. "There's no instructions, but the next step looks pretty self-explanatory."

"Yeah, why not." Daniel moved past me and bent down in front of the marble. He held out his hand then placed the palm on the marker—aligning it perfectly with the outline of the handprint.

The world stood still for a moment. Then the outline around Daniel's hand began to glow. Daniel stepped back. The whole of the outline was filled with gold light now, so bright we had to shield our eyes. The marble block began to descend into the sand until it was completely gone.

Silence.

"Nothing's happening," Daniel said, stating the obvious as he looked around. "Maybe we're in the wrong spot."

I opened my mouth to respond, but the ground beneath our feet started to tremble and part. The two of us jumped out of the way as a crevice began to open in the sand. To avoid falling in we dove to the side, rolling out of the way.

The ground had split and sand fell into the great crevice like a waterfall. An enormous structure began rising from beneath. It was shaped like a ram's head, horns and all, and gave off a potent, eerie glow that illuminated the area around us. The creature's eyes were radiant sapphires that sparkled with power.

We got up and I stowed my wandpin as the figure finished rising.

"Daniel, I know you're relatively new to the whole fairytale main character thing," I whispered. "But in case you haven't learned it enough times in the last few weeks, expect the unexpected. You gotta roll with the punches and have a little faith."

"Really? You're gonna lecture me about having a little faith?"

"All right, point taken."

"Who dares approach the Cave of Mysteries?" the ram's head bellowed. The voice was so loud that it shook the sand from our clothes.

Taking a deep breath, I stepped forward. "Uh, hi. Crisanta Knight, Princess of Midveil here, and Daniel, um . . ." I turned to Daniel. "Wait, what the heck is your last name?"

He brushed his hair back sheepishly. "Daniels."

I grinned. "Really? Daniel *Daniels*? Now I know there's a backstory there. Who names their kid Daniel Daniels? That's ridiculous."

Daniel glowered. "Knight, focus."

"All right, all right." I turned back to face the ram's head. "Crisanta Knight, Princess of Midveil and Daniel Daniels . . . other guy."

Daniel punched me in the arm.

"What?" I murmured with a smirk on my face. "Would you have preferred Daniel Daniels, Lord of the Two First Names?"

The ram's head roared at us again.

"Only the diamond within the tough may enter this cave!"

Neither of us was as familiar with fairytale history as Blue, but most people in Book had read at least some accounts of *Aladdin* as well as the *Arabian Nights* stories. Even if the various versions were diverse, many of them had common points. Thus, we'd somewhat expected this magic cave to present us with a proposition when we sought to enter its domain. However, my understanding was that he was supposed to say something slightly different.

"Hold on, 'the *tough*?'" I repeated, furrowing my brows. I regularly got my butt handed to me in most classes at Lady Agnue's, but I'd always done okay in Fairytale History thanks to Blue. Getting this wrong irritated me. "I thought it was—"

"I know what you thought it was!" the ram's head interrupted, rolling his giant eyes. "But it is not!"

"But the most popular versions say—"

"I was misquoted!"

"Come on, Knight," Daniel mocked. "You've gotta roll with the punches."

"Ugh, whatever." I looked at Daniel and gestured at the ram's head. "That's your cue, Daniel Daniels. Time to shine."

"What are you talking about?"

"Go and try to enter the cave," I directed.

"Are you serious? If that thing doesn't buy me as some 'diamond within the tough,' I'm history while you stand here and watch me get eaten alive."

"Daniel, why do you always have to be so difficult? Obviously I don't want you to try it because I want you to get killed. We've got to get inside to find this Mysterious Flower. The reason I think it should be you that tries to pass the ram's test is because of the two of us you're way more likely to be the special one."

He narrowed his eyes. "Nice try, Knight. I'm not buying it."

"Really, Daniel. I'm not joking." I let out a sigh as the confession came out. "I mean, if you tell anyone I said this, I'll flat out deny it. But the fact is that as a protagonist you've proven yourself to be more worthy of the title in the last few weeks than most people do in a lifetime."

Daniel studied me. "And you haven't? Knight, if anyone could pass through that cave it's you."

I rolled my eyes. "Save the obligatory return compliment, Daniel. Lady Agnue once told me that there's a difference between being a hero and being heroic. And she was right. Much as I wish it were different, I've realized over the course of this adventure that I'm no hero. I have some heroic qualities that I'm proud of, but the fact is that I've failed, hurt, and lied to too many people—myself included—to qualify as a good hero *or* a good princess. Right now I simply lack the merits to fit either role—not on everyone else's terms, but my own."

I felt my hand tingle with the magic watering can's liquid metal effect, but I ignored it, clenching my fist and drawing it behind my back.

"It's a hard truth, but I accept it. I may attract a lot of villains and put up a good fight, but I'm not as honorable as a hero or a princess should be."

"Don't sell yourself short, Knight. In my book you have all three bases covered." Daniel's tone shifted from jest to sincerity as he met my eyes. "I just wish you would accept yourself for everything that you are. Maybe if you did, you'd finally know what that protagonist title means to you, and maybe you'd see what I see."

"And what's that?"

"Someone with the potential to affect more than who she is and build something better."

This rare moment of real, unprovoked openness between us was interrupted by the sound of the massive ram's head clearing his throat.

"If you two are done, could someone get over here and enter my cave? Just because I am an eternal magic head does not mean I have all day to wait around listening to a pair of lovebirds squawk away."

Both our faces turned redder than the sand. "We're not lovebirds!" Daniel and I—equally struck by humiliation and horror—yelled in unison.

The ram's head scoffed. "Oh please. You have that whole 'will they, won't they' thing written all over you. If I had time to write protagonist fan fiction I would be shipping for you right now. Alas, I am an enchanted cave, not a couples' counselor or a fangirl. All I care about is who wishes to enter my domain. The two of you can figure out all those other diddlewatts on your own time."

"Right," I said, turning to Daniel. "How about we try going into the cave together? It'll double our chances of getting across the threshold. And if that doesn't work and we get crushed and buried alive, then neither of us will have to worry about being traumatically scarred by what that ram's head just said."

Daniel nodded. "Sounds good to me."

We turned to readdress the opinionated, presumptuous, and extremely mistaken mystical ram's head.

"We'll go in together," I announced.

"Fine by me," the ram's head replied, seeming to shrug his unseen shoulders. "I like some variety in my meals."

He cleared his throat again. "Approach then, meager mortals. *But be warned*—should you be deemed worthy enough to enter, only the object inspiring the mission that brought you here will allow you safe passage out. Claim it and it alone, or suffer the consequences."

Daniel and I expected the ram's head to lower his gigantic face to the ground so we could step inside his mouth to enter the threshold of the cave. Instead the ram rammed his head into the sand and exhaled deeply—expanding his epic nostrils until they were wide enough for us to walk through like dual entrances.

Daniel and I exchanged a glance then went inside.

The interior of the nasal cavity was vast and cylindrical. Past the entrance foyer it plunged downward in the form of a massive, zigzagging staircase. The walls were vaguely moist and carved from jagged stone; vines clung to every surface.

Daniel and I stood on the edge of the first step and stared at the seemingly endless descent. This was it. All the stories about the Cave of Mysteries agreed that once inside the cave all it would take was that first step to pass judgment.

One step and we'd either have free passage into the depths below or be this enchanted ram's midnight snack.

"It's now or never," Daniel said, preparing to go forward.

"Wait." I held up my hand to block him. "I just had a thought."

"What?"

"Well, what about SJ, Blue, and Jason? The cave was buried when we arrived. I thought at first that it was because we might've beaten them here. But what if they beat *us* here and tried to get through, only they couldn't get across the threshold and got swallowed up instead?"

Daniel thought it over for a second then answered with complete confidence. "They didn't," he said simply. "We got here first. We'll find this Mysterious Flower and probably run into them on our way back out."

"How can you be sure?" I pressed.

"Because like you I know those guys. So I know *they*, of all people, would make it through. Don't stop having faith in them,

Knight. Trust is a good look on you. Come on, enough worrying. We'll do this together."

"Together," I echoed.

"On three," he said. "One."

"Two."

"Three."

CHAPTER 15

I Make Friends with a Lawn Chair

he both of us took one step forward and waited.

There was no earth-quaking, ram's-head wrath. Other than some sand falling from the cave roof, nothing happened at all. Which meant we'd done it! The cave accepted us as worthy and was giving us passage. Unless we violated some rule while we were inside, it would remain open until we emerged with what we came for.

The tension lifted. Without hesitation Daniel and I proceeded into the heart of the mystical cave. The deeper we went, the lighter it became.

Finally, we reached the bottom.

The first room we found was nothing special—just rock walls and an insanely high ceiling. But as we went through the tunnel that led to the caverns beyond, the surroundings changed. The cave walls had a rusty red tint about them and the pathway cutting across the floor was made of tangerine crystal tile that reminded me of my favorite type of ice pop. Stalactites hung everywhere like icicles, making me feel like we were inside one giant mouth. Mountains of gold coins, a rainbow array of jewels, and other precious goodies glittered throughout the next half dozen caverns we wandered through. Dark green vines I couldn't explain wormed around the glitz like serpents trying to strangle the individual piles.

After several minutes I began to notice other less-than-beautiful things scattered amongst the treasures. There were solid gold statues of people with terrified expressions, burnt outlines of bodies on walls, and the occasional skeleton peeking out from beneath the mounds of jewels.

"Remember," I reminded Daniel as we kept moving. "Don't touch any of the treasure. You know the legends of this cave—the supposed 'Mysteries' in individual alcoves are the real prizes. Everything else is just a distraction meant to detour people from reaching their goals. The story goes that if we touch anything other than what we came for, we won't have safe passage out like the ram's head said. The cave will implode and we'll be buried."

"I got it, I got it," Daniel said, brushing me off. "Step down from the know-it-all, protagonist perch, Knight. I may be a common at heart, but I've read the stories. I'm not an idiot."

"Don't sell yourself short, Daniel Daniels. In my book, you have both bases covered."

"Hilarious." Daniel rolled his eyes. "Look, don't worry, Knight. I'll just treat this cave like I do our relationship—like it's a trap waiting to tear me a new one."

"An accident waiting to happen," I countered.

"A disaster in the making," he countered back.

"Well, good." I smirked. "At least we're on the same page."

We continued forward with great care. Daniel and I searched room after room for the Mysteries that were the cave's true trophies, believing that among them we would find the Mysterious Flower.

Unfortunately, our passage seemed to drag on for an eternity. There were so many treasure rooms, and multiple levels of them too. Many had staircases, which Daniel and I explored only to find more gigantic places where treasure dwelled. Everywhere we went there was just gold, gold, and more gold. It was enough to make Chance Darling (the grandson of King Midas) humble.

I was beginning to wonder if there was no end to these rooms of riches until we came upon a cavern filled with something quite different. Furniture.

Decorative carpets, throw rugs, and woven mats were strewn across the floor. Couches, loveseats, and futons were stacked across the room in skyscraper-high piles. Lawn chairs in an assortment of colors lined the walls. It was like a graveyard for a home furnishings emporium.

I meandered across the room until I accidentally kicked something. It was a rubber ball. It had been lying in the center of a circle of chairs that all seemed to be pointed toward it.

The rubber ball bounced off a futon and ricocheted back to me.

As mentioned, I knew not to touch anything that looked valuable in this place. Every glittery, fine object was a booby-trap waiting to set off a cataclysmic chain reaction. But this ball didn't look valuable. Moreover, I'd just kicked it and nothing bad happened. So I figured it was okay.

"Daniel, what do you make of this?" I asked, picking up the ball.

When an answer didn't come, I realized Daniel was nowhere in sight.

"Daniel?"

I looked around but couldn't see him.

"Daniel?" I called a bit louder.

Still nothing.

I whistled to see if that would get a response. A moment later, I was knocked off my feet by a robust couch cushion, which had apparently interpreted my whistle as a summons. I would have landed face-first on the ground had it not been for a pink lawn chair that suddenly swooped beneath me.

I panicked, worried that touching the furniture might set off the cave's traps, but all remained calm.

Sort of.

The lawn chair was levitating half a meter off the ground. I sat up to discover that I was encircled by dozens of other floating pieces of furniture. Futons, couches, floor mats, and carpets swooshed in front of me with unbridled excitement.

They seemed like they were waiting for something. Then a floor mat flew up close to me and nudged my hand with its corner.

The ball!

I was still holding the rubber ball I'd found. It had to be what they wanted. Just to be certain, I held it up. As suspected, the flying furniture swooshed about with even greater delight than before.

"All right." I shrugged. "Why not?"

I wound my arm back and tossed the ball across the room. "Fetch!"

Dozens of furnishings—including the chair I was sitting on—shot in the direction of the ball, bobbing and weaving with great haste.

A shaggy red easy chair won the battle for the ball and presented it to me proudly. I patted it on the seat, taking the ball to throw it again. Just as I was about to, a shadow fell across the floor in front of me.

"What are you doing?"

"Exactly what it looks like," I told Daniel. "Playing fetch with flying furniture."

"Would you stop fooling around. I think I found the caverns we're looking for."

"Killjoy."

I turned to address all of my new, magical friends. "Guys, I've gotta go."

The rugs hung limply and the cushions on the couches drooped with disappointment. Nevertheless, they protested no further and flew away. The lawn chair I was sitting on popped its recliner all the way down and I used it as a ramp to step back to the ground.

"Thanks," I told the chair as I dismounted.

The casual chair sort of bowed. Then it disappeared behind one of the mounds of futons with its other dispersed friends.

Daniel glanced around at the piles of enchanted furniture. "Flying furniture," he thought aloud. "That makes zero sense."

"I disagree," I replied. "I've read a bunch of versions of *Arabian Nights*, as well as specific stories about *Aladdin*. One thing I always wanted to know is what's the deal with magic carpets. I mean, they're such random objects but plenty of folktales have them. A girl's gotta wonder where they keep coming from. This place is the answer. The Cave of Mysteries literally has a flying furniture department."

"I take it back," Daniel said. "This makes about as much sense as anything else on this adventure."

I followed Daniel into an adjacent cavern. This place glowed brighter than all the other rooms we'd been in thus far. That was because a pool of lava churned on the far side of the room. The magma gurgled and the rich yellow and orange light flickered off the rock walls.

Although there were many tunnels converging into this cavern on the left side, the only route on the right was a single, narrow pathway crossing the lava. On the other side of the pool the path continued up a stone staircase until it reached a small alcove. The alcove was carved into the wall and had ragged vines concealing what lay within. I guessed it must've been where one of the cave's great Mysteries was hidden, possibly the elusive flower we sought.

Daniel and I approached the lava walkway. It was bordered by robust columns constructed of gigantic rubies. These columns were three feet high, allowing us to easily take a look at the contents they held.

On top of each column was a wide-mouthed carved wooden

bowl filled to the brim with luminous copper coins. The identical bowls were each marked with an explanatory placard.

"Wishing Coins," I read aloud as I examined the label of the first bowl, careful not to touch it or anything else. Unlike the ball and the furniture, these riches had booby-trap written all over them. "Every coin tossed into a well is a guaranteed wish come true."

"Why would anyone have gone on looking for a genie lamp or any of the other famous treasures in this place if they found these?" Daniel said. "I mean, a genie can provide three wishes; a bowl of wishing coins can be cashed in for dozens."

"I think that's the point," I responded. "Logically no one would go on looking for a genie lamp or any other magical knickknack when they found these. It's the perfect final booby-trap. A test of whether or not you can focus on the one wish that made you strong enough to come this far rather than give in to the greedy possibility of having many others."

"A quality over quantity test," Daniel summarized.

"Exactly. What we really want is up there." I gestured at the alcove.

Together, Daniel and I carefully made our way across the lava then climbed the staircase. I pushed the vine curtains aside, allowing us to step through.

We were now in a tiny pocket of a room. In the center was a display pedestal. This one was not fancy or bejeweled; it was made of stone. And it did not offer a bowl of enticing, wish-granting coins. In fact, it offered nothing at all.

Despite there being no treasure here, there was a beam of light streaming onto the perch through an itty-bitty hole in the ceiling. That, and the placard at the base of the column, made it clear that there had been something of great importance here at some point in the cave's history.

"The Wondrous Lost Lamp of Vanatu," Daniel read, "grants

owners three wishes upon release of the immortal genie kept inside. Item: One of Eleven."

"I can't believe it. This is where he found it," I marveled. "This is where Aladdin found the lamp."

"Seems like," Daniel agreed. "But that's old news, Knight. Come on, we've gotta keep looking. I bet there are other caverns just like this that still have their treasures. And if we're lucky that flower will be in one of them."

"You're right," I said firmly. "Let's move on."

CHAPTER 16

The Test

aniel's prediction was right; there were many more caverns just like the one that originally held Aladdin's genie lamp.

Each was identical in layout—the lava, the wishing coins, the staircase. All that was different was the actual item inside the draped-off alcoves and the accompanying placard. Some items we discovered included rose-colored glasses that allowed one to see a person's true intent, a golden lyre whose musical chords produced waves with hypnotic capabilities, and a wax candle that froze time when it was lit.

These items were extremely tempting—any one of them had endless uses for us. But Daniel and I resisted from touching them, keeping in mind the advice of the ram's head to only claim the object we'd come for.

Unfortunately, finding that object was proving difficult. Each mysterious cavern had a myriad of other tunnels leading into it. As a result, we wandered in and out of interconnected treasure rooms without any direction. It was like endless shiny déjà vu.

Between the Therewolves' underground complex, the labyrinth within Adelaide's cliffs, and this Cave of Mysteries, I acquiesced that "confusing tunnel systems" was a solid theme for the last few weeks of adventure.

Daniel and I entered the sixth cavern. We proceeded across the lava lake, up the stairs, and pushed away the vines, stepping into the small cubby that housed this cavern's treasure. When we did, we stopped.

It was a flower.

An actual flower!

The gorgeous thing resting on the pedestal looked like a carnation frozen in full-bloom. Its petals were scarlet and the stem was olive green. The only elements that made it distinctly different than a normal carnation were the delicate golden leaves attached to the stem like peels of sunshine. Its beautiful radiance outshone much of the other pretentious contents in the cave.

"The Carnation of Duality," I read from the placard. "The petals are capable of strengthening magic and the leaves are designed to weaken it."

Emma's instructions had said to locate a "Mysterious Flower Beneath the Valley of Strife." If this pretty carnation was not enough to convince us it was what we sought, the description of its powers on the placard certainly did. After all, we were trying to construct a potion to break the In and Out Spell—one of the most impervious spells in existence. What better way to do that than by utilizing an ingredient specifically designed to weaken magic?

"Looks like we found our Something One of a Kind," Daniel said.

"Yup," I agreed. "Now here's hoping nothing freaks out when we touch it."

Rather than letting my nerves delay the inevitable, I reached out and picked up the flower. Once the carnation was in my hand, Daniel and I froze as we waited for something to go horribly wrong. To our relief, everything in the cave remained still. The ram's head had been right; the cave would let us take what we came for.

I slipped the flower into my left boot for safekeeping. Then, assuming that our passage out was assured, Daniel and I headed down the stairs and began our journey back to the entrance of the cave.

After making our way through various treasure caverns, we reached the magic furniture gallery. This time nothing stirred when we passed.

I guess they only move when it suits them, or when someone whistles and lets them know it's time to play, I thought to myself.

We continued along the winding path through half a dozen more glittering caverns. As we neared the opening that would lead us to the next room, a shiver went up my spine. I held my hand up in front of Daniel, signaling him to stop.

I glanced around suspiciously. The large mounds of gold and a rainbow array of jewels twinkled innocently from floor to peak just as they had in all the other rooms. But something felt amiss.

When a few more seconds passed without additional cause for alarm, I convinced myself I was just being paranoid. We'd been attacked so many times in the last few weeks that it was understandable. Then again, paranoia was rooted in instinct acquired from real experience. And as such, I probably should have heeded mine a bit longer.

As I turned the corner, I spotted Arian. My dark-haired, heroically-built hunter was at the other end of the cavern with a dozen men behind him.

I didn't know how Arian had made it down here with his men. Maybe the cave thought his mission to come after me made him worthy? I doubted it. More likely since the cave was bound to give Daniel and me passage unless we violated a rule, it would stay open even if more people entered after us.

Just seeing the antagonist caused me to hesitate. Each time we'd crossed paths I'd faced him without fear or cowardice. But the more times we fought the more I realized that maybe I should be afraid of him. It was as much luck as it was skill that had allowed me to escape his grasp before. And the last time we'd met he'd won. I'd come at him with my best plans and he'd still sucked me inside the lamp.

The lamp.

One of Arian's lackeys was holding the bag I'd seen back on Adelaide—the same bag he'd pulled the genie lamp out of.

Arian's intense black eyes locked with mine and I knew there was no time to waste figuring out how he'd found me again. If I didn't get out of range, he was going to suck me inside that lamp. And this time there would be no escape.

"Run?" Daniel asked under his breath.

"Yep," I answered.

He and I turned on our heels and took off back through the cave.

"Go!" I heard Arian yell after us. "She has to be within fifteen feet!"

Daniel and I skidded across the gold-lined floor, barely staying on our feet as we maneuvered the tight corners. Eventually we entered the magic furniture gallery again and dashed past the collection of enchanted objects. When we made it to the cavern that once held the genie lamp we arbitrarily headed through the tunnel that lead toward the cavern with the golden lyre. I drew my wandpin as we ran.

Lapellius.

The weapon morphed in my hand as we searched for another route to the exit. Alas, when we reached the fifth cavern that guarded one of the cave's Mysteries, we stopped in our tracks. Arian's men poured in from the other connecting tunnels like rats into a sewer intersection, leaving Daniel and me with nowhere to go.

Out of desperation we raced down the pathway across the lava lake and up the stone staircase. Daniel drew his sword and observed the dozen men approaching us from below.

Arian entered through the center tunnel. His helpers maintained their positions at the foot of the boiling lava pool, awaiting his orders. When he saw Daniel and I trapped at the top of the stairwell, he smiled.

"Honestly, Knight. I swear each time we go through this you just get more pathetic."

"Yet I keep managing to outsmart you," I called defiantly. "So maybe it's time you reevaluated your confidence."

One of Arian's henchmen brought forth the dreaded bag and my enemy removed the genie lamp from inside. Its chrome shell glistened in the glare of the lava like the flash of a memory. He started moving across the pathway that led to the staircase.

"I wouldn't if I were you," Daniel threatened, holding up his sword.

"Stupid hero," Arian said snidely. "I don't have to fight you. I barely have to climb a handful of these stairs and my work will be done. My advice to you is to step away from the princess."

Arian continued making his way closer. "We've done our research and know all about you, Daniels. Every little detail of who you were, who you are, and who the Author has predicted you're going to be. So in the spirit of pity, I'm going to make you an offer. Right now my employer's interests lie in Crisanta Knight. So if you don't attempt to fight us, I see no reason why we can't let you go."

"You've got to be kidding," Daniel scoffed.

"Surprisingly no," Arian replied, "My people have a soft spot for commons, and I am genuinely offering you a way out. All you have to do is take it."

"And why would I do that?"

"Because you want Crisanta Knight out of the way as much as I do. Come on, Daniels, you know what she's done to your life—what she's going to do to your life. You can pretend to be her friend for a while. But we both know what you really want. And this is your opportunity to take it.

"Think about it. Why throw away everything for her when you could change your fate right here? Forget the Author. With Crisanta Knight out of the way you'll have nothing to fear. You'll be free to go on living your life exactly how you want to—never having to worry about the likes of some volatile, uncontrollable princess potentially screwing it up."

Arian stopped and gestured upward, as if throwing the ball in our court. I glanced over and saw that Daniel had lowered his sword slightly. He was still glaring at Arian and that expression was hardening. However, when I looked closer I saw that it wasn't a look of anger or concentration; it was *reflection*.

Daniel was thinking. I didn't know if he was seriously considering what Arian said, but I didn't wait to find out.

"Daniel," I whispered cautiously. "Take the deal."

He whipped his head toward me. "What?"

"You heard me. While I'm not that keen on being shoved into a lamp again, and I'm not sure how I'll get out a second time, I do know one thing for certain. You need to go."

"Are you out of your mind?"

"No. Honestly, for the first time in a long time this isn't my pride or my stubbornness talking. I'm thinking clearly and you should too. You stay here and they kill you. You go into that lamp again and you get delivered to the psycho queen who wants my head and the head of anyone in her way. And I'm sorry, but I'm not letting either happen. I don't want you to die. And I especially don't want you to die for me. So take Arian's offer, for your own good and for Kai's. Get out of here, find our friends, and don't look back."

He stared at me, dumbfounded. "You're serious?"

I nodded.

"Well then you're even crazier than I thought. There's no way I'd ever ditch you, Knight, especially not to save myself. As hard as it is for you to believe, I meant what I said earlier—we're finishing this together."

I didn't have time to reply.

"Suit yourself," Arian scoffed as he stepped toward us.

My eyes darted back and forth, searching for an idea. There weren't many resources within my reach. The only other things here were those columns with the bowls of wishing coin booby-traps and . . .

Wait, that's it!

"After all this time you get that there's a method to my madness, right?" I asked Daniel under my breath.

"Yeah."

"Good. Hold on to that thought."

Boomerang.

I hurled my transformed wand down into the cavern. It flew over Arian's head, knocked one of the bowls of wishing coins off its pedestal, and then ricocheted back to my hand.

Wand.

Arian looked at me, amused. "I hope that wasn't for me."

"No," I said with a grin, remembering the last time he'd said that to me—in Century City, right before I buried him beneath an avalanche of fruit. "But this is."

By disturbing the bowl of wishing coins I'd set off one of the booby-traps. Now the entire cave and everyone in it were doomed. Affirmation of this came a moment later when a menacing roar pierced the atmosphere and everything began to shake.

My enemy glanced at his feet where the wishing coins had spilled. The tiny pieces of metal melted into goop then combusted into flames. A thunderous shockwave hit the cavern and threw Arian to the ground. He dropped the lamp and barely avoided rolling into the lava. The quake triggered a ripple effect of more tremors and the cavern started to implode. Stalactites fell like daggers. Lava spewed from the pool and from cracks opening up in the floor. Everything shook with the wrath of a violent beast.

"What did you do?" Daniel asked as he and I clung on to the edges of our alcove.

"What Bruce Willis did in *Pulp Fiction*," I replied. "Stacked the odds against me, then bet on myself."

I raised my fingers to my lips and whistled as loud as possible. If Daniel didn't think I was crazy before, he definitely must've thought so now. And maybe I was ordinarily. But not today. Moments after the whistle, dozens of flying pieces of furniture shot out of the adjacent tunnels into the room and came straight toward me.

"Get on!" I shouted to Daniel.

He dove onto a tan loveseat while I leapt onto a lawn chair. It was the pink one from before, and it was all too happy to be of service.

"Dive!" I yelled.

The lawn chair was so excited to be included in the game that it practically whinnied. On my command it swooped downwards— avoiding the rocks that fell around us.

Lacrosse sword.

My wand transformed. I swung the basket down and scooped up the genie lamp that Arian had dropped.

I gave the chair a little kick like I would a Pegasus. "Now go, go, go!"

Daniel and I zoomed over the heads of Arian's scrambling men and fled through the tunnels. Everything whizzed by in a fiery, dusty blur as we evaded spontaneous spouts of fire, crumbling chunks of cavern, and the massive explosions that erupted each time rocks dropped into the lava.

Molten ooze was everywhere. By now all the treasure in the treasure rooms had dissipated into it, adding a shimmering gold tint to the tidal waves of lava that pursued us.

Splashes of gold lava seared the ends of my dress like acid, but I paid them no attention. I had other problems. Some of Arian's lackeys had managed to hitch rides on their own pieces of furniture. Instead of concentrating on surfing out of here before they were killed, they were continuing to come after me.

Really? Like they don't have bigger things to worry about? The cave is collapsing! Perspective, people!

With my spear, I blocked a futon rider who tried to attack me from the side then parried another man who attempted to stab me from behind with his sword.

Daniel glanced over his shoulder and saw what was happening.

He turned back his loveseat and drew his sword. Together we fended off the attackers for a beat, but we were both so distracted that neither of us noticed the oncoming fork in the path. Without instructions to do otherwise, Daniel's loveseat took him down the tunnel to the right whereas my lawn chair skidded through a narrow crevice on the left.

I emerged into another disintegrating cavern. I'd left most of my assailants in the previous room, but I still had one enemy to contend with.

Somehow Arian and his own lawn chair had caught up with me. He was now hot on my tail. I ordered my lawn chair to turn as he bee-lined toward me. His sword shined maliciously in his hand.

"Don't you ever give up?" he shouted, trying to get closer while dodging the falling debris and lava bursts.

"I could ask you the same thing!" I yelled back.

Tightening my grip on the chair, I spiraled upwards through a thin opening. Arian followed. I had been holding the lamp, but it was slipping from my fingers. I couldn't hold onto it and the chair with one hand. And I needed to keep my spear on guard so long as I was being chased by my sword-wielding foe. Something had to give.

We leveled out in another treasure room consumed almost entirely by lava.

"Might as well hand over the lamp, Knight!" Arian shouted over the quaking. "You're going to drop it and I'm going to be there waiting! We both know how this ends!"

I eyed the lamp.

"You're right, Arian! I do know how this ends . . . Right here! In the same exact place it started!"

Wand.

I held my wand between my teeth. Using my free hand, I chucked the lamp as hard as I could into the distance. It somersaulted through the air before dropping into the thrashing yellow and orange sea, setting off an explosion that made the entire room resound with rage.

Arian couldn't believe it.

"What have you done?" he shouted as his chair darted to avoid the collapsing ceiling. "That lamp—"

I grabbed the wand from my teeth as my chair bobbed and weaved.

"That lamp went back to where it came from!" I called. "Now I suggest you do the same! Because without it and the magic mirror, you won't be catching me again!"

Arian signaled his chair to fly toward me. I gave my chair a terse jolt with my foot. "Up!"

Spear.

My lawn chair shot straight to the ceiling and I jabbed the edge of my spear into an enormous stalactite that was primed to fall. The impact knocked it loose. As the stalactite plummeted, I dove out of the way and headed for the slight opening at the front of the cavern.

The stalactite plunged into the lava. Arian had been so concentrated on pursuing me that he didn't react in time to avoid the devastation that came next. While my chair escaped through the narrow exit, his swerved sideways to evade the eruptions the stalactite caused.

By the time he managed to gain control of his chair I'd already made it through the fissure, which was immediately sealed off behind me by an avalanche of falling rock.

Good luck following me through that, Arian.

Lapellium.

With Arian taken care of, I clipped my wandpin back to my bra strap and held onto the chair with both hands for the rest of the ride.

I didn't know how much time we had before the entire cave came crashing down. Worse still, I had no idea where Daniel was.

I tried not to think of all the colorful and violent explanations for what might have happened to him since we'd been separated.

My lawn chair and I entered the remains of a cavern. After a brief survey, I could see only one tunnel that was still open. We flew toward it as fast as possible. Just before reaching it, the cave roared and released a shower of sharp stones.

I leapt to the back of my chair as a stalactite slammed onto the front. It created a seesaw effect and I was shot forward into the air. My hands grasped the edge of the tunnel we'd been headed for. Several more stalactites took down the chair and it plunged into the lava.

I knew the chair would be fine. The Cave of Mysteries was enchanted. Everything in here would reform the next time it rose out of the desert, which—according to legend—was ten years after the last time it'd been sealed shut. I, however, would not reform if I fell into that pool.

My muscles groaned as I pulled myself onto the ledge of the tunnel.

The inside of the passage was dark and barely four feet wide. I couldn't see how far it stretched, but as it was my only available route, I ran into it without hesitating. The entire thing shook, knocking me against the walls like a croquet ball in a drainage pipe. The thick dust and heat slowed me down with each passing step. I turned a corner and crashed into something hard.

Oh geez, please don't be a dead end.

"Knight?"

"Daniel?" I squinted through the darkness. Joy and relief swept over me in a wave stronger than the lava. "You're alive!"

"I wouldn't be much of hero is I wasn't." I knew he was smirking, even if I couldn't see his face.

A powerful explosion somewhere close produced an extra large cloud of dust that caused us to cough. "What happened to your couch?" I asked between wheezes.

"Caught on fire. Had to jump. Come on, we've got to get out of here!"

We ran faster as more dust filled our lungs like slow-acting toxin. I was beginning to think we might not make it when the tunnel abruptly opened up. The roof was barely ten feet above our heads. And across the way . . . a miracle.

We'd found the exit! Seven feet from the ledge where we stood was the entrance we'd originally come through. Or what was left of it anyways.

The foyer-esque platform still stood. But past that all that remained of the ram's nasal cavity were three dangling stairs and a few vines that clung to the jagged rock walls beneath them. Everything else was in its final stages of disintegration. A giant pool of lava was filling the cavern fifty feet below.

Without a moment to lose, Daniel backed up and jumped across the gap between us and the exit. He bridged the distance easily and landed in a crouched position near the stairs. I took several steps back and prepared to do the same. Taking a deep breath, I raced toward the ledge, expecting to cross over the divide just as easily.

But of course, I didn't.

The instant I pushed off the edge, the whole room shook from an explosion. The ill-timed disturbance not only caused the level of lava to rise, it threw off my trajectory—thrusting me away from the intended landing platform.

I fell through the air. I managed to grab hold of one of the vines drooping beneath the stairs. My hands slipped, causing me to slide down several feet. Thankfully I was able to tighten my grip and keep myself from sinking any lower.

I hung there for a second—dangling above the rising molten pool that boiled and hissed below. With all the strength I had left, I proceeded to pull myself up the vine, arm over arm. It wasn't easy. As the cave grumbled the vine swung me around like a pendulum.

Daniel leaned out over the ledge and stretched his hand so that it was within reach.

"Knight, give me your hand!"

I glanced at it, then the lava, then back at him.

In that moment of hesitation the vine snapped beneath my weight.

"Knight!"

I clawed at the wall and was able to clutch onto one of the protruding rocks. I hung on, feet scrabbling furiously until they found a foothold that could bear my weight. The cavern's vicious trembles increased as I climbed the wall using only cracks and bits of jutting out rock.

There were no longer any intervals between the cave's rumblings—it was one constant roar and shake. More and more pieces of ceiling fell loose, splashing into the angry lava below.

At one point I looked up and saw the tip of a single giant stalactite wobbling above me, still attached to the roof, but not for long. With each vibration it came closer to coming down.

I was running out of strength and the rock wall was crumbling beneath my fingers, but I struggled on until I made it back to where I'd been before the vine snapped. Daniel's hand was still outstretched, offering his help. Instead of accepting it, I kept going. I'd already made it this far; scaling a few extra feet on my own was well within my capabilities. At least that's what I thought until one of my handholds broke loose and for an unbalanced moment I swung out from the wall, holding on by a toe and a hand.

The lava surged and bubbled beneath me, much closer now. I pulled myself back against the wall and dug my fingers into a crevice in order to keep from falling. A loud cracking noise echoed through the cave, and I glanced up. Like a loose tooth attached only by a sliver of gum tissue, the large stalactite was barely hanging on.

Daniel, noticing the same thing, called down to me with renewed urgency. "Knight, just give me your hand!"

I bit my lip but didn't answer. Instead my eyes darted around for another option while my heart pounded furiously. This was the moment. I had to decide whether I trusted Daniel as much as I trusted myself. I had to make a choice. Could I give up control and surrender to faith that he would come through?

"Daniel, I—"

"Crisa."

I froze. This was the first time he'd ever used my first name. The shock, and the calm steadiness in his tone—despite the chaos around us—caused me to look up at him.

"Forget the future. Forget fate. Right here, right now—do you trust me?"

I looked into his eyes. They were stern but gentle, reassuring yet antagonizing, unyielding and yet so willing to bend for me. And then I knew. I knew like a baby bird knew it could fly when it perched on the edge of its nest. My heart swelled with fire like the lava beneath us.

I could trust him. Not just right here, not just right now. All the time, completely. Every part of me—head and heart—was suddenly cleansed by the truth. I could trust him. I would trust him. I *did* trust him.

With a rapid thrust I boosted myself up as far as I could on the wall and reached out for Daniel. My fingers were about to touch his when my foothold crumbled from the pressure. I started to scream, but Daniel grabbed my hand just in time and heaved me onto the landing.

"Thanks," I panted.

"You're welcome," he replied. "Now move!"

We ran to the exit right as the last stalactite shook free. While I didn't see it come down, the tidal wave of lava it caused consumed everything behind us like a malevolent belch. Daniel and I slid out of the ram's nostrils just before they descended beneath the roiling red sand. By the time we reached the bottom of the dune in a sandy heap, everything was calm. The Cave of Mysteries was gone and we were alone.

Daniel and I lay on the sand, trying to take a normal breath.

"That was . . ." I panted, then coughed up some sand.

"Yeah. It was," Daniel responded.

I checked the inside of my boot to make sure our prize was still with me. The magical flower remained tucked safely inside, undamaged despite the tight quarters with my calf. Relief flooded through my body before the shock began to sink in.

For a long minute, Daniel and I lay there staring up at the night. The stars glowed brightly. The reddish tint to the sky made the moon look pinkish but did not diminish its shine. As horrid as the Valley of Strife had been, in that moment everything seemed beautiful.

Once I caught my breath I sat up, as did Daniel. He wiped his forehead with the back of his hand, and I saw slight traces of blood from a fresh gash near the crown of his hairline.

"Hey, are you—"

"I'm fine."

"But you—"

"Knight."

"All right, all right." I held up my hands in response to his glower. "Changing the subject . . . Daniel, I want to say that I'm . . . Well, what you did in there, I just—"

"Yeah, you're welcome."

I raised my eyebrows. "Someone's feeling a bit presumptuous. Who says I was about to thank you?"

"Weren't you?"

"Um, no," I lied.

But all Daniel had to do was look at me and the truth escaped through the smile in the corners of my eyes.

He laughed and rose to his feet. "No, I guess you weren't," he said, playing along. "You already did that in the cave and getting one thank you out of you per millennia is an accomplishment. There's no way you could ever do it again. You're not capable of it."

I jumped to my feet, accepting the challenge. "Oh really? Well then, how's this: Thank you, Daniel. Thank you oh so very much for saving my life, helping me when I needed you, and proving that I could trust you. I truly, deeply, and *oh so sincerely* appreciate it."

He smirked. "You'll do anything to prove me wrong, won't you?"

"Maybe." I smirked back. "Or maybe I really mean it."

A beat passed between us.

"So you got the flower?" Daniel asked abruptly.

"Yup." I nodded. "But I wouldn't celebrate yet. We have to find the others and I have no idea how. I don't think it's wise for us to sit around here anymore. If Arian knew where we were, so might some of Nadia's other henchmen. We can't just wait to see if our friends show up."

"Maybe we won't have to," Daniel said, pointing to the top of a nearby dune.

Four silhouettes were framed against the moonlight. My first thought was of our missing friends. But then I did the math.

Blue, SJ, and Jason—that's three. Who is the fourth?

I squinted through the distance, the darkness, and the wishful thinking.

"Aw, come on!" I groaned when discovery set in. "How did they still make it out? And before us too? Like that's fair."

"It's time to go, princess," Arian, with three men at his side, called from atop the dune.

"Not likely," I snapped in response. "In fact, you know what, Arian? Get over here. You have no magic mirror, no lamp, and no army. All you have is a sword, three guards, and a persistency that borders on psychotic. So please, come down and try to take me. I'd love nothing more than to tear you a new one."

"Tempting offer." Arian shrugged. "But I grow tired of chasing you, Crisanta Knight. So for a change of pace this time you're going to come to me."

"And why would she do that?" Daniel interjected as he drew his sword.

Arian gestured to one of his remaining men. "Because, hero, I have this."

The lackey vanished behind the dune then returned moments later with something in his hand. He passed it to Arian, who tossed it down to me.

The fabric tumbled through the air then fell into my grasp. It was a cloak . . . a *blue* cloak. I narrowed my eyes as hatred and worry twisted within me. Arian had Blue.

"Where is she?" I growled.

"I think you mean where are *they*?" Arian corrected. "Turn yourself in, Knight. Or all three of your little protagonist friends will be slaughtered before sunrise."

Daniel leaned in close to me. "When this is over, if you don't want to kill him yourself, I'd be more than happy to do it for you."

"Noted," I replied. I tilted my head toward him. "You sure you're up for this, Daniel? It's not too late to abandon ship."

Daniel put his sword back in its sheath. "I think you already know the answer to that. Besides, they're my friends too. And we're not going anywhere without them."

I nodded in agreement.

"So what's it going to be, princess?" Arian called down. "Nadia grows impatient."

I looked straight into his shadowed eyes.

"We wouldn't want to keep the queen waiting, would we?"

CHAPTER 17

Antagonizing Antagonists: Part 1

ased on size alone, I figured my current transport had been intended to hold a goat. The ripe smell and the few animal hairs I discovered on the floor only confirmed the theory.

As the carriage rolled along the sands of the Valley of Strife, I found myself wondering what had happened to him—the goat that was this crate's previous passenger. Probably the same thing that was going to happen to me: slaughtered and then forgotten.

Great. Something to look forward to.

Fidgeting in my prison keep, my thoughts drifted to Daniel. His designated form of incarceration was likely no better than mine, but I couldn't know for certain. He had been shoved into a different crate on a separate carriage.

The opening at the rear of my crate had been bolted closed from the outside. My sole source of light and connection with the outer world was a small barred window behind me. It faced the passenger cabin of the carriage. The only thing I could see through the barred window was the back of Arian's head.

Talk about a room without a view.

The ride across the desert was taking forever. I didn't know how far away Nadia was located, but if she was the queen of Alderon, I figured we were headed for the kingdom's capital. It was called Valor, if I remembered correctly.

And yes, I did appreciate the irony of that.

Between the wait, the cage, and the shackles on my hands, I was growing restless with the whole situation. My wand—still disguised—remained hidden beneath my shirt. But I wasn't about to try and escape until Daniel and I found our friends, otherwise there wouldn't have been a point to surrendering in the first place.

Might as well try to make good use of the ride. And given my current options, that means irritating Arian as much as possible and maybe gathering some information from him.

"I'm not sure if you realize this, Arian, but running from you can be a bit rough on the calves," I said as I shifted to a position where I could better see his face. "If you had my friends, you could've just opened with that and saved us both a lot of cardio."

Arian gave me a bored glance. "Capturing you in the lamp was preferable because I thought we could better contain your magic that way. Luckily your ineptitude extends to that part of your life as well. You may have magic, but you have no idea how to use it, do you?"

I didn't respond.

Arian huffed, amused, so I decided to wipe the smirk from his face.

"Changing the subject," I said. "Tell me something, Arian. I've been wondering . . . is shameless, barely competent, evil henchman like a day job for you? Or is it more of a full-time career?"

This time he didn't respond.

"And how exactly did you get into this line of work?" I continued. "I mean, did you aspire to be the right hand man of a ruthless leader when you were a child? Or maybe you attended a special trade school for it like us princesses do. I bet that's it, isn't it? Hmm, I wonder what your curriculum must be like.

'Immorality 101'? 'Introductions to Arrogance and Arson'? Oh, I've got one! 'Quit While You're Ahead: A Beginner's Guide to Knowing When You're Beaten.'"

"Do you ever shut up?" Arian scowled.

Bingo. Bait accepted.

"That's not really my thing," I went on obnoxiously. "So as I was saying, do you enjoy this profession? Does it have a lot of advancement opportunities? And how good are the benefits? I've been thinking about changing character archetypes myself, so I'd love to know—is villainy really its own reward? Or do you have dental?"

"The rewards will come when my job is done," Arian said flatly.

"Well I guess that's soon given that you've already got me."

Arian turned to look at me. His face was separated from my own by a mere six inches. Staring into his dark eyes at that proximity, I felt colder than when I'd been in that Stiltdegarth's wintery death world at Fairy Godmother Headquarters.

"You're not the job, princess," Arian responded. "Like I told you in the Forbidden Forest, you're just a side issue that needed taking care of."

"Still, it's gotta be pretty annoying having to chase someone all across the realm like that. You must be glad it's almost over."

"I wish. Compared to the hunt to come, capturing you was barely a warm-up."

"That's a bit of an exaggeration." I pretended to be insulted. "I made you work to catch me. You've had to follow me through, like, five kingdoms and a ton of magical, unpredictable settings."

"That was child's play. The Wonderlands are nothing but magical, unpredictable settings. Tracking down Paige Tomkins will be close to impossible, especially *now*," Arian complained before he realized he was telling me more than he should.

I raised my eyebrows. "You mean because I destroyed the magic mirror?"

Everything had been happening so fast that I hadn't had the

time to properly think about the information I'd acquired about Arian and his mission. Now, with nowhere to go and nothing else to do, I finally started to process what it all meant.

I'd known since the bunker in Century City that Arian's band of antagonists wanted to eliminate the ex-Fairy Godmother called Paige Tomkins. She had been a friend of my godmother Emma and had been missing for some time. But it wasn't until right then that I put two and two together.

Targeting Paige was why Arian's purple-hooded accomplice from my dreams had broken into the Treasure Archives at Lady Agnue's. Arian had told me that they hadn't originally meant to use the magic mirror from *Beauty & the Beast* nor Aladdin's genie lamp on me; they were tools for capturing their "more important target." And if that were Paige, I understood why.

As I'd mentioned to Daniel, I'd learned from Harry the White Rabbit that the Wonderlands consisted of a lot of realms—Oz, Neverland, Limbo, and countless more. If Arian and his boss Nadia were targeting Paige and she was hiding somewhere in the Wonderlands, then locating her really would be close to impossible without the use of a magical aid like the mirror. Which meant that when I had shattered it on Adelaide I'd not only slowed them in their pursuit of me, I'd seriously hindered their hunt for her too.

I'd also inadvertently helped protect Paige by getting rid of the genie lamp. Paige was a Fairy Godmother, which meant she was full of magic. That's why Arian wanted the lamp in the first place. It was specifically designed to contain magical creatures. If he found her, he could just as easily trap her like he had me. But now that I'd thrown it in the lava, Arian could no longer capture the missing Godmother in this way. He would have to contain Paige by some other means.

"The loss of the mirror was a setback," Arian admitted after a long pause. "But we'll still find our target regardless of what you've done. You certainly couldn't hide forever, and neither can she."

"Maybe, but I'm guessing you're gonna have a heck of a time catching her without that lamp, aren't you?" I asked in an attempt to confirm my theory.

He narrowed his eyes and glared at me, suddenly realizing that he may have told me too much. "I didn't need it to catch you in the end."

"Maybe not." I shrugged. "But keeping me in your grip . . . that's a different story."

Arian studied my poker face through the bars of the window. The crescent scar I'd given him at the capital was hardening around his eye. A smirk appeared on his lips.

"Such a brave little princess," he mocked. "Here you are facing imminent doom and still you make-believe like you have a chance. I have to say, the lengths you'll go to fool yourself and others really is remarkable."

I was not even remotely perturbed by his comment. Instead, I smiled. "You'd like to think so, wouldn't you, Arian?" I said calmly. "You'd like to think that this is all some act for my benefit. Well, I have news for you. This 'little princess' isn't pretending to be brave; she's just being honest. I'm not beaten yet. Put me in your tiny cage, clamp on your giant shackles, do whatever else you've gotta do to make yourself feel better. But deep down, you and I both know I'm not so easy to contain."

"That kind of overconfidence can get a person killed, you know," Arian scoffed.

"Then it's a good thing I'm already headed that way."

Arian shook his head in an amused manner that made me both annoyed and nervous. "You know what, Knight," he said. "I'm glad you've got so much spirit. In fact, I hope you hold on to it."

"Oh yeah, and why's that?" I asked.

"Because believe me, you'll need it when you find out what's really coming for you."

CHAPTER 18

Antagonizing Antagonists: Part 2

 didn't mean to fall asleep. It's not exactly a good idea to lose focus when the dude who's been trying to kill you is only separated from your face by a few inches of metal. But sleep came nonetheless. Well past midnight, my crate was pitch black and I was incredibly tired. I drifted into dreamland without even realizing.

Lena Lenore's silhouette appeared. After a moment her features sharpened, as did the setting around her. The Godmother Supreme was sitting in her office and was dressed in a fitted, silvery pantsuit. Her flowing dark hair was partially pulled up in a half ponytail and her lipstick looked freshly applied.

She leaned back in her chair. In her right hand was one of those compact mirrors with "Mark Two" engraved on the back. Her compact was bright silver; its sheen (like that of her outfit) created a glare. Lenore had the compact open toward her, so I couldn't see whom she was talking to. But I did get a name.

"Liza," Lenore said. "I know she has Pure Magic. I'm not a fool. I just need you to confirm it so I can deal with her properly."

"Are you planning on dealing with her the same way you dealt with me?" the woman at the other end of the compact asked. The voice sounded kind of familiar but was warbled by static. I wasn't sure if that was the compact's fault or mine for not getting better dream reception.

"Don't be ridiculous," Lenore responded. "You are an exception."

"She could be too."

"Please, you've met her. Defiant, headstrong, disrespectful—that girl's heart was meant to turn dark even without the extra push. I will not humor her, or you, by pretending otherwise."

"Well, you're going to have to for the time being," Liza responded. "Because I'm not going to give you the confirmation you're looking for. And without solid proof, you'll have to leave her alone."

Lenore's face sunk into an irritated glower. "Liza . . ."

"Save your threats, Lena," Liza interrupted. "You need me. And there's nothing more you could possibly take away from me that wouldn't backfire on you."

Lenore released a deep, frustrated breath. The sound was so bitter I imagined it would cause flowers to wilt.

"Fine," the Godmother Supreme responded. "Protect her if you want. It is only a matter of time before I have the proof I need. Then she goes to Alderon like the rest of them."

There was a pause.

"Lena," Liza said after a moment. Her voice was gentler, calmer, but still earnest. "You can't do that. I told you what I've seen of her future. I read you her prologue prophecy. Sending her to Alderon won't solve anything; it'll only push her closer to the less desirable of her two Inherent Fates. I know you don't want to believe it, but I think for all our sakes it would be wiser to bet *on her* than against her."

Lenore tucked a loose strand of hair behind her ear and looked seriously at the mirror. "Liza," she said. "I don't bet on wildcards."

A sudden bump in the road jarred me awake. I rubbed my eyes as I came to my senses. Tiny streams of light entered through hairline cracks in the crate. It was morning. I shuffled around awkwardly and managed to activate my Hole Tracker. The map I brought up did not display any holes in the area or any other useful information. I only knew we were on the far southeast side of Alderon.

The carriage came to an abrupt stop. I hit my head on the side of the crate and quickly turned off my Hole Tracker. Outside I heard voices and the clattering of footsteps. The door of my cage snapped open.

After riding in the confined darkness for so long, the sunlight burned my pupils. An arm abruptly reached out of the brightness and grabbed me by the collar. In one terse movement, I was yanked out of the crate and thrust onto the sand.

I coughed from the sudden impact. Dry air hit my face and the warmth of the sun beat against my hair. The brightness overpowered my senses. I shuddered at the familiarity. This was the last of the visions I'd had the night Daniel and I spent in Germany's Black Forest.

Déjà vu.

Or, I guess, Dreamjà vu.

I felt a large hand on my shoulder. It pulled me to my feet. I staggered and rammed into the crate behind me as the guards snickered at my disorientation.

The world was starting to come into focus. It took me a few more stiff blinks, but soon I was able to make out the surroundings. Once I did, I was nothing short of amazed.

Valor, Alderon's capital, was unlike any city I'd ever seen. The buildings were constructed of gleaming copper, dried tar, and glass. Stained glass to be exact. It was dark at its core, but I could see mutations of gold, black, crimson, and opaque silver depending on which way the light hit it. The palace, constructed of the same materials, loomed before me in all its grandeur.

Such a castle had no precedent—its graceful malevolence was unparalleled. Each tower was sharpened to perfection, but the turrets were twisted like towels being wrung out to dry. The main door and balconies were the same rich copper color that edged the other buildings in the vicinity. The angle of the sun reflecting off the door made the entire front gleam, highlighting the colors in the stained glass.

Honestly, had the city not been my designated point of execution, I would have liked to marvel at it a bit longer—the unique architecture demonstrated such an extraordinary equilibrium between hardened intimidation and complex beauty.

Alas, sightseeing was not in the cards. I was shoved forward by another guard. Like all the others patrolling the area, he wore a black uniform with dragon-scale sleeves and a red insignia shaped like a phoenix on the chest plate. It was the same insignia embroidered on the flags waving from the castle's towers and hanging above the grand door. These flags were deep red and the phoenixes a livid gold.

At that point I noticed two things. Other guards were maneuvering my former prison transport next to the palace where a row of carriages was parked. They were empty, but several had mighty black stallions attached to them, ready for a quick departure.

The other thing that got my attention was Daniel. He was getting out of his own prison crate. His escorts began steering him toward me. Relieved to know he was safe, my eyes drifted over the citizens of Alderon. There were many of them, this being the capital of the kingdom and all. Their faces were angry, their were eyes cold, and even their posture was crone-like.

I didn't know if it was something in the water, but everyone appeared to be afflicted by some kind of viral discontent. More unsettling was the fact that all their negative energy seemed to be converging solely on me. People (antagonists, as it were) had stopped in their tracks at the sight of my shackled person. They booed and hissed and stared daggers as the guards pushed me past them.

Nice welcoming party. I guess they all saw Arian's little newspaper post.

The antagonists looked like they wanted to kill me. And I understood why. Protagonists were their enemies, but being trapped in this forsaken kingdom kept them from ever acting out any form of revenge. And here Daniel and I were on their turf, two main characters that they could finally channel all their animosity toward.

In hindsight, it was surprising that at least one of them didn't try to murder us on sight. The way they glared at us like a pair of defenseless minnows passing through a school of sharks certainly suggested that they wanted to.

"Any thoughts on a plan yet, Knight?"

I turned my head and found Daniel on my right. He and his escorts had caught up with me and mine. His hands were shackled and his sword had been taken from him. We entered the palace's foyer side by side.

"Plenty of thoughts," I whispered. "But I wouldn't exactly say any of them are plan-based. At least not—"

"No talking," one of the guards snapped.

I rolled my eyes—a gesture that Daniel mimicked. Without calling further attention to myself I studied the palatial surroundings, memorizing every bit of the layout for tactical advantage.

The interior of the palace featured bold tapestries, dozens of suits of armor, incredibly high ceilings, and the unstable glow of flickering chandeliers.

You know, the usual.

But beyond that, I noticed there was an additional thematic layer to the décor that was quite unique. I wasn't sure whether it was more disturbing, distasteful, or morbid. However, deciding which adjective best suited the circumstance was not important. All three applied.

While it was pretty commonplace to have one's palace

decorated with tapestries, statues, and other fine artwork, the ones in this place were of a dark nature. The pictures woven into the tapestries, for instance, depicted grotesque scenes of witches, monsters, and dark knights violently assassinating their prey. Meanwhile, display pedestals featured miniaturized models of various demon species, including ogres, Magistrakes, and other creatures I didn't recognize.

The base of each onyx candelabra was crooked like the nose of a hag. The suits of armor appeared to have aged bloodstains on them. The most benign decorations were the life-size bronze animal statues that lined every corridor like a petrified zoo.

While these animal statues were grand, what really caught my attention was an elusive, connecting metalwork structure twisted near the ceiling of every room. It was the most ambitious piece of metalwork I'd ever seen—a singular, giant working of bronze jutting in and out of the highest part of the hallways. It was smooth and rounded and wide as a redwood tree, sort of like a really big water pipe. The creation was constructed in a way that made it look like it was writhing through the innards of the palace.

My eyes kept shooting back to it, trailing the tube of bronze through the walls as we made our way through the compound. I was fascinated by its magnitude and curious about what it actually was and where it ended. As we emerged through a grand archway I finally discovered its end—or rather, its beginning.

I gazed up at the face of an enormous metal serpent protruding over the door. The monster's head was as massive as a carriage. Constructed from the brightest bronze, it was offset by the deep red tapestries that hung from the wall on either side of the entry.

I gulped as I recognized its awful face.

The serpent from my dreams.

It was exactly as I remembered it, all but the eyes. They'd been gold in my dreams. These were black and scarlet, shining like burnt stars.

I couldn't help but pause as I looked up at the creature's

gleaming fangs. They hovered above our heads in the frame of the doorway—smoother and more polished than the stalactites at the Cave of Mysteries, but just as sharp.

When I tore my attention away from the bronze creature, I realized that we'd entered a throne room. It contained an elaborate arched ceiling reminiscent of a cathedral. The room featured red flags emblazoned with phoenix insignias, cedar floors, countless guards, and . . . my friends.

My eyes widened with relief.

Blue, SJ, and Jason stood in the center of the ballroom. With the different worlds Daniel and I had passed through—and the Earth-to-Book time difference—it felt like I hadn't seen them in ages. But in truth, it had barely been a day.

Had it really only been yesterday morning that we'd been separated on Adelaide? Good grief, how's that possible when it feels like I've turned through so many chapters?

Blue's dark blonde hair was messy around her face. She wasn't wearing her cloak, which made her look incomplete. Jason's intense blue eyes were stern and fiery with defiance. The sheath across his back that normally held his axe had been taken from him. SJ's long black hair was still perfectly braided and her outfit (like that of the others) remained crisp and clean due to her SRB. However, she looked more frazzled than I'd ever seen her. The expression on her face was irritated, confused, and anxious.

Seeing them filled me with gladness. But it also caused my stomach to flip. Because while I may have been excited to see them, I knew that the way I'd left things on Adelaide meant they probably felt no such glee in looking at me.

I could see it in their eyes.

They probably still cared for me. We'd been through too much together for our friendship to be gone completely. And they also had bigger things to worry about—being in the heart of antagonist country and all. But I detected anger in their expressions. And I knew I deserved it.

The guards led Daniel and me to where our shackled friends stood.

"What are you doing here?" SJ asked tersely.

"What do you think?" I responded. "Saving you guys."

SJ glanced at the dozens of guards that had brought us in and then at the meaty handcuffs restraining us.

"It's a work in progress," Daniel admitted.

"Yeah, yeah, whatever," Blue interceded. "The point is you shouldn't have come. How was it not obvious that this was a trap?"

"Of course it was obvious. We're not stupid," I replied. "But whether it's a trap or not doesn't matter. There's no way we were going to abandon you guys."

"Aw, isn't that sweet," someone cooed.

A tall girl in her mid-twenties had suddenly appeared at the head of the room through a curtained-off door next to the throne. She was strong and slender, confident and poised.

She nodded at us pleasantly enough as she seated herself upon the throne, draping herself across it like a cat on a couch. Her smiling eyes were trained on us, causing me to notice their hypnotic nature. They were big like a caricature's, the irises black as night and even more pronounced by her dark eyeliner. The girl's midnight hair was pulled back in a flowing ponytail that allowed her long neck to be prominently displayed. She wore flattering bronze armor that complimented her light brown skin.

Overall I'd have said she was pretty. At least in the way Venus Flytraps are pretty. But in my eyes the most notable thing about her was that I recognized her from her recurring role as a character in my nightmares. This was Nadia.

Arian entered the throne room via the same entrance Nadia had used. He positioned himself at her side like a loyal retriever. She clapped her hands together as if she was a schoolteacher trying to get her class's attention.

"So then," she said merrily. "Which one of you is Crisanta Knight?"

I hesitated. I hadn't yet decided on an appropriate course of action. When I failed to immediately acknowledge myself, Arian nodded to one of the guards behind us and he shoved me forward.

He and one other guard came up behind me, invading my personal space. I glared at them then back at Arian. Then I met the gaze of the girl on the throne.

"Hmm, not what I would have imagined." She sounded a little disappointed. "But, well, what ever is? I'm not going to lie though, Arian, I had sort of hoped she'd be a bit less . . . ordinary."

Hey!

"She doesn't look like much, Majesty," Arian agreed. "But I assure you she's capable. I wouldn't have insulted you with her presence if she wasn't."

Well, okay, that's better . . . I think.

Nadia raised her eyebrows at Arian. "We shall see," she mused. She turned her attention back to me and sat up straighter on her throne. "I suppose introductions are in order, aren't they?"

"Not really," I said. "You're Nadia. The chick who's had Arian killing protagonists and chasing me across the realm like a hound on a foxhunt."

"Informally, yes," Nadia affirmed. "But formally is another matter. For example, if we are to discuss things with proper respect, I would say that you are Crisanta Katherine Knight, the volatile princess who's been causing a ruckus all over the realm and throwing our plans off charter for the last two months. Meanwhile I am Nadia Vitalli-Suratt, leader of New Ever After and crowned queen of the great state of Alderon."

I blinked—a beat of silence settling between us before I realized it was my turn to talk.

"Am I supposed to be impressed?" I asked.

Nadia shrugged. "Not necessarily. Titles are meaningless in the end. But I did expect some sense of decorum. You are a princess, aren't you?"

I shrugged. "Depends who you ask."

"Regardless of that and your lack of civility, I am still delighted to welcome you to my kingdom, Crisanta Knight," Nadia said. "We don't receive many visitors here, and I've truly been looking forward to meeting you."

"I'll bet."

"Not that this little exchange isn't fascinating and everything," an irritated Blue suddenly interrupted. "But aside from the meet and greet, why exactly *are* we here?"

"I'm glad you asked," Nadia replied as she casually stepped down from her throne. She made her way across the room, coming to a stop a few feet in front of our group.

"While eventually I might need Arian to kill the three of you," she nodded at Blue, Daniel, and Jason, "the lot of you are here now because of this one." Nadia gestured to me. "And she is here because of one thing."

"Care to expand on that?" I asked.

"I could . . ." Nadia lingered. "Although the explanation can be summed up in a single word: *antagonist*."

"Yeah, I got that."

"No, I don't think you do," Nadia responded with a glint in her eye. "At least not in the proper sense of the term as it applies to our situation. You see, Crisanta, *I* am not the antagonist here. You are."

"What are you talking about?" I scoffed.

"I am talking about looking at people for who they truly are in the grand scheme of things. You, for example, were chosen at birth to be a protagonist by our realm's higher powers. But the question remains why? You are just another princess—a sad excuse for one based on what I've been told. And there is nothing extraordinary about you in the slightest aside from a claim to royalty and a unique set of self-destructive tendencies. Despite that, the world has decided that *you* of all people are allowed to be special. That you—unlike the rest of us trapped in this strife-ridden kingdom like rats in a cage— are allowed to live a life of riches, spoils, and greatness.

"Well I have news for you, Crisanta Knight. You have been living a lie. Until now you might've been able to hide from it with your precocious boarding schools, your regulated kingdoms, and the Author's ego-inflating words. But they can't protect you from the truth here. And the truth is that *I* am the protagonist of our shared story. I am the person fighting for what's right and just—the one who will finally bring justice to the deserving people of this realm. While *you*, my overly entitled princess, are the adversary—the antagonist designed to keep me from achieving my goals."

I was struck by Nadia's analysis. I couldn't believe the nerve of her, calling me an antagonist when she'd sent her henchman to kill me and my friends. It was an absolutely ridiculous accusation.

Still, remnants of my conversation with Daniel regarding the antagonists being braver than us—as well as my own earlier reflections on Alderon—poked at my subconscious, allowing bits of Nadia's words to seep under my skin.

The queen paced around me like a lioness encircling prey. I followed her with my eyes, tempted to make a run at her with my bare hands. Though I knew that the armed guards standing behind me would swiftly chop off my fingers before I got anywhere near her.

"And what goals are those exactly?" I asked.

"In a word?"

"If you can spare it," I mocked.

"As a matter of fact, I can," she said calmly. "I'll even do one better and give you four."

Nadia held up her hand and counted off the words with four fingers. "Kill. The. Main. Characters."

I was speechless.

"You can't be serious?" Jason blurted.

"Oh, but I am," Nadia assured him. "For countless generations the citizens of Alderon have been tossed aside and disregarded like garbage—all of us lumped into a giant stereotype of villainy and locked in here without hope of escape, retribution, or any kind of life for our descendants outside of the one you've forced upon us. Well, no more. My people have had enough of it and enough of you main characters. Which is why we've decided to wipe the realm of your kind—the over-privileged, cliché-dependent, so-called protagonists of our land. You and your leaders have plagued our realm like a sickness. And like any disease, you must be expunged completely if the rest of us are to thrive."

The throne room was silent for a solid beat.

And then I laughed.

It was an abrupt, condescending scoff that echoed across the chamber and caused everyone to look at me—some with fear, some with confusion and shock. I shook my head, giving Nadia a disdainful smirk.

"Great diatribe, Nadia. Really. You make insanity sound *super* noble. But aside from the high-and-mighty attitude, let's face it— you're no better than all the other villains out there. Go ahead and pretend all you want that you're some big savior fighting for fairness, but nothing about a plan involving mass genocide equals heroic justice. You're no protagonist; you're just another power-hungry maniac masquerading as some sort of enlightened humanitarian. You couldn't be a more stereotypical antagonist if you tried."

Nadia sighed like an adult tired of the antics of a stubborn toddler. "So typical," she said. "Just the type of response I'd expect from a weak, irrelevant relic of fairytales past who herself is masquerading as some sort of awe-inspiring hero."

"Is that supposed to be an insult?" I tried to take a step forward but was firmly stopped by one of the guards.

I thrust his paw off my shoulder. "Come on, Nadia," I continued. "We both know not even you really believe that's who I am. Otherwise you wouldn't have had Arian work so hard to get me here."

Nadia shook her head in amusement. "Silly princess. This isn't about who you are. It never was. This is about who you have the

GEANNA CULBERTSON
241

potential to *become*. Oh, I stand by everything I've said about the 'you' that stands before me now. But that is not the girl anyone here cares about. Now the girl your prologue prophecy describes, that is an entirely different story, if you'll pardon the pun."

"Ugh, this again. Look, it's like I told your lapdog over there." I nodded to Arian. "The prophecy the Scribes sent me is as lame as they come. So unless you provide me with a little more to go on, I really don't know what you're talking about."

"And it's like I told you, Knight," Arian interrupted brusquely as he stepped toward the center of the throne room, "your prologue—"

Nadia glared at Arian, silencing him. "Your prologue prophecy," she said, resuming control of the conversation, "or at least the version you are familiar with, is just another lie—a pretense put on a shelf to distract people from what's real."

"Meaning?" Blue asked.

"Meaning that there is too much at stake with our plans for this realm, and the others, to allow for even the slightest problem," Nadia responded. "This is why we've recruited one of the Scribes to monitor protagonist books and look for prologue prophecies that might be of interest to my antagonists. Whenever my Scribe finds a prophecy that describes a person who will pose a threat to our mission, we can swiftly take care of it, and them. The ambassadors of the realm manipulate protagonist selection for their own reasons; we're simply doing the same. Without anyone being the wiser, my Scribe can confiscate an original book and prophecy and have a fake one drawn up to replace it so no one will think twice about that main character. This buys my people time to eliminate them without raising any red flags."

"So your Scribe replaced Crisa's prologue prophecy?" Jason clarified. "Her real one made her out to be a formidable protagonist and you wanted to keep her in the dark so you could get the jump on her?"

Nadia sighed again and sashayed back to her throne, settling in her seat. "Yes. As hard as it may be to believe looking at her *now*, it is the truth," she conceded. "But it is also a bit more interesting than that. For unlike so many of the other protagonists we've had to preemptively silence, your situation, Crisanta, bears much greater weight and, ergo, required a bit more precision.

"As my plans and forces gain momentum, the Author has prophesized that there will be one person with the power to oppose us. One person alone who will possess the ability to stop our mission and prevent my people's rise to power. You."

"*Me?*" I repeated in shock.

"*Her?*" I heard one or more of my friends gasp from behind.

Thanks, guys. Love the confidence.

"Yes," Nadia affirmed. "You, Crisanta Knight—princess of Midveil and last in your class at Lady Agnue's School for Princesses & Other Female Protagonists—are foretold to stand in my way. Which means that I cannot allow you to remain standing."

The information hit me like a tidal wave. I'd never felt so many conflicting things at once.

I was happy that I'd finally gotten confirmation that the putrid prophecy I'd come to know was not my fate. I was kind of flattered that there was actually someone out there—crazy, villainous tyrant or not—who actually believed I was a threat. I was fairly freaked out that being seen as this threat had earned me the label of "Public Enemy Number One" to the people of Alderon. And I was indescribably, unequivocally speechless to learn that I was prophesized to be the sole person responsible for stopping them.

It was a lot to take in.

"So why the big show then?" Daniel asked, breaking the silence with a very reasonable question. "Why not just kill her now, kill all of us now? If she's so dangerous to you then why go through the trouble of the whole prisoner routine when you could've gotten rid of us the second we got here?"

"I swear, does no one appreciate proper showmanship anymore?" Nadia asked Arian rhetorically. She huffed in annoyance. "Look, Daniel. It is Daniel, isn't it? I am trying to mount a rebellion here. So why kill you all in seclusion when I could rally my fellow Alderonians by executing our main enemy and a handful of you bonus protagonists in front of a live audience? It's free publicity for the cause, morale for the troops, and all in all just a smart leadership strategy for a young, up-and-coming warlord such as myself. I mean, nothing unites people like a common enemy. Wouldn't you agree, Crisanta?"

I glanced around at my friends, whose faces shared the same newfound simmering hatred for the wicked girl on the throne. Then I glared at Nadia—all too certain of my answer.

"Agreed," I said.

The queen turned her attention to Arian. "Escort the lot of them to the dungeon."

He nodded and approached us as the guards began to maneuver my friends and I toward the door. Despite the shackles and number of guards (which already seemed like overkill), Arian drew his sword.

"What's wrong?" I huffed, impertinence outweighing whatever fear or common sense should've colored my speech. "Afraid I'll make you look bad in front of your boss by escaping again?"

"Not quite," Arian sneered.

He raised his blade. The last thing I saw was the pommel headed straight for my head.

Aw, crud.

CHAPTER 19

My Best Friend is a Thief . . . Yay!

rian's blunt strike to the side of my head knocked me out. In the brief unconscious spell I fell through a funnel of vision flashes.

First came a shot of a stadium full of people dressed in powder blue and silver—my kingdom's colors. They were eating junk food and cheering loudly, no doubt for some type of sporting event.

Next I saw SJ's glass Pegasus figurine from our room back at Lady Agnue's. It was swiftly flying across the grounds.

Finally there was the woman. That mysterious woman with her teal zip-up and ambiguous whispering. She looked me in the eye, repeating her message: "Remember the dragon." Then I woke up.

I was in a dungeon cell with SJ, Blue, Jason, and Daniel. Nadia had put us here to await the hour of our public execution—high noon.

I wasn't sure what was worse: waking up in the prison of the person who had literally been trying to kill me, or waking up in a prison with three people who figuratively looked like they wanted to kill me.

Daniel and I were the only ones on good terms now. I hadn't seen the rest of my friends since Adelaide and I knew I had some explaining to do.

"So, what's going on?" I asked, sitting up on the cold stone and rubbing my head.

"Well, I've filled the others in on the main plot points of our adventures," Daniel said. "Everything from Goldilocks, Germany, and the Pied Piper, to retrieving the final item from the Cave of Mysteries."

I looked over at Daniel thankfully.

"SJ, Blue, and Jason told me where they've been," Daniel said. He tilted his head toward my friends. "Guys, care to recap?"

My friends begrudgingly obliged.

After failing to find Daniel and me on Adelaide's shores, they had, in fact, decided to head to the Valley of Strife. As I'd predicted, they'd believed that Daniel and I would make our way to the Cave of Mysteries in the hope of reuniting with us and attaining our final object to break the In and Out Spell.

Not knowing Arian's exact position on the beach meant that being in the air could put them at risk for being spotted. So— unaware that Daniel and I had been captured—they'd chosen to leave our Pegasi behind in the stables of Adelaide Castle. As an alternative means of transportation, they'd "borrowed" regular horses from the stable and used them get to the magic train. From there they'd taken the train as close to the Alderon border as possible before remounting their steeds and crossing into the kingdom.

It had been a treacherous endeavor in more ways than one. For starters, SJ was terrified of horses. But she'd swallowed her fear and kept up with Blue and Jason. Past that, they'd discovered a variety of monsters waiting inside Alderon's In and Out Spell border.

It was a good thing my friends were so skilled—Blue with her knives, Jason with his axe, and SJ with the marble-sized portable potions she'd invented and fired via slingshot. Had they been any less capable they probably would've been killed no fewer than six times.

Unfortunately—skilled as they were—they only made it halfway across the Valley of Strife before their good luck ran out. They ran into a group of antagonists who'd seen Arian's "Wanted" ad. These antagonists had several powerful witches in their ranks and my friends never stood a chance. They were easily captured and delivered to Arian.

"Did you tell the others about Mark?" I asked Daniel when they'd finished.

He hadn't.

When I explained that I'd seen Mark in one of my visions, SJ, Blue, and Jason looked utterly relieved. While there were still questions about why he was gone and what the deal was with his file in Arian's bunker, the confirmation that he was alive and that we would be reunited in the future made the others relax a little. For a moment, their anger dissipated. Sadly, that moment came and went. The revelation was a good distraction, but it by no means made them forget the grudge they bore toward me. I still owed a pretty hearty explanation.

But—much as I had been longing to make things right with them—I simply couldn't do it in that moment. I knew the confrontation was coming. I could feel it like an approaching avalanche. But I was still trying to absorb everything Nadia had told us. There was a lot to process and we didn't have much time left before her forces came to take us to our execution. My number one priority was finding a way out.

My friends had managed to free themselves from their shackles by the time I woke up—utilizing the very lock-picking skills that'd helped save us from the Therewolves back in the Forbidden Forest. My shackles were off too, so I figured one of my friends had taken them off while I was unconscious.

Aside from being shackle-free we were pretty stuck. The

underground cell had no windows and the front wall was completely sealed off with the exception of a napkin-sized porthole in the door.

While everyone else's weapons had been confiscated upon incarceration, my wandpin was still tucked in its hiding place. The antagonists hadn't found it, or at least they hadn't known it was a weapon. I was grateful to have the sparkly thing on me, just as I was grateful that the flower from the Cave of Mysteries remained shoved tightly in my boot.

Alas, neither helped me in this situation. Which was surprising, for I could usually rely on my wand to get me out of most predicaments. But no matter what weapon I morphed it into, it barely made a scratch on the cell door.

I found this frustrating. My wand was unbreakable, and its magical sharpness and strength made it able to cut through just about anything. This was the first time I'd encountered such a problem and I really couldn't understand why. I placed my hand on the deep black stone of the iron-lined door. The moment I did, I was overcome with dizziness. My thoughts warbled like there was static in my brain. I felt faint, as if I'd just run a marathon.

I quickly removed my palm from the stone. The moment I did, clarity returned.

Although common sense told me to give up, I decided to transform my wand into an axe and take a few more swings at the door. Common sense was not really a luxury I could afford right now.

"Crisa?" said Blue, trying to get my attention after my sixth swing.

I ignored her and kept hacking away at the door. "Ugh! Why! Won't! You! Open!"

"Crisa," Blue repeated.

"I'm a little busy, Blue," I replied.

She shrugged. "That's fine. I've just got an actual way for us to get out of here. But that's not important. You keep doin' what you're doin' and let me know when you've got a sec."

"Wait, what?" Jason said.

I stopped and turned around. "One more time?"

SJ, who'd been leaning against the wall up 'til now, put her fingers to her temple to try and suppress a headache. "Blue, what are you talking about?"

Blue grinned, full of self-satisfaction. "I'm talking about this!"

She reached into her boot and pulled out a small green speck with her index finger and her thumb. It glowed with a bright green hue like the butt of a seasick firefly. We all moved in to take a closer look.

"Blue. That's a pea," Daniel said.

"Correction," she practically sang with pride. "It's a *magic* pea. The missing one from the Treasure Archives at Lady Agnue's to be exact."

SJ looked like she was going to have stroke. "*You* stole it?"

"Blue, really?" Jason commented.

"Of course not," Blue responded. "I'm mischievous, not a delinquent."

"Then why do you have it?" I asked, morphing my axe into a wand again.

"I thought it was stolen along with the corset, the lamp, and the mirror."

"Do you remember that morning after the break-in at school when everyone was being herded back to class?" Blue asked.

I thought back to the morning in question. All the students at Lady Agnue's had gathered in the hall of the Treasure Archives, astounded by the shattered cases and stolen artifacts. After a few minutes our teachers began corralling us away from the scene, but I remembered Blue ducking into the crowd and disappearing for a moment before rejoining us.

"I was checking out the damage when I saw it lying on the

floor by the cases," Blue explained. "People thought it was stolen, but it must've fallen to the ground when the other items were taken. It was just too small for anybody to notice. So I picked it up. I figured I'd hold on to it for a little while to study and then put it back when I was done. You know how nuts I am about fairytale history and the objects in those cases. So I figured, what would be the harm? It's not every day that we actually get to experiment with famous magical stuff like this, and since people already thought it was stolen I knew no one would care."

"Blue, that was unethical," SJ chastised. "You should have turned it in to Lady Agnue the moment you found it."

"Well, in a second you're going to be glad I didn't because we're going to use it to get out of here."

"Blue," I repeated for emphasis. "It's a pea. Magic or not, I doubt it's going to help us against stone and iron."

"Shows how much you know.," Blue scowled. "Look, I realize that most people don't care about old fairytale junk, but I actually do the reading assignments at school and I can contribute more to this situation than a useless weapon and a sarcastic comment."

"Blue, I never said—"

"Forget it," she cut me off. "Look, here's what I'm getting at. Everybody knows that this magic pea from *The Princess & the Pea* is famous for giving the female protagonist in the story mega injuries while she was sleeping even though the thing was buried beneath, like, a hundred mattresses, right?"

We nodded.

"Okay, well no one ever bothered to ask how. They just wrote it off as magic and never figured out exactly what kind. But not me. This pea—like every other magical object—has a very specific function. And in the pea's case it's propagating energy disturbances. While it may not look like much, this itty bitty veggie is enchanted to send out powerful shock waves when it hears trigger words and then turn back into an ordinary pea when it hears a stop command."

SJ's mouth dropped open like a surprised goldfish. "I cannot . . . I mean that is just . . ."

"Total genius? Yeah, I know. And you thought being brilliant was your specialty." Blue smiled smugly. "I brought it on our quest because I thought it might come in handy at some point. Right now, I think it's just what the doctor ordered."

"Why haven't you used it before?" Jason asked.

"For starters the pea has some restrictions. It takes eight hours to recharge. Aside from that, the Adelaide tunnel system and Therewolf lair were both structurally unstable. Using the pea there could've buried us all. Here though it should work fine."

"That's great, Blue," I said, "but why the heck did you let me hack away at the door for so long if you had this up your sleeve, I mean down your boot?"

"For one, you looked like you had a decent amount of rage built up, so I thought I'd let you channel it out a bit. And second and more importantly, there are a few issues between us that need to be addressed before we can get out of here."

I grimaced, feeling the weight of everything that I wanted to tell them. Why was confronting archenemies so much easier than confronting friends?

"Is this really the time and the place?" I asked, the stress rising inside me. "We're trapped in a dungeon."

"Which is exactly why it is the perfect time and place," Blue countered. "You run from us and the truth everywhere else, Crisa. And I'm tired of it. There's nowhere for you to run here so you're going to talk to us whether you want to or not."

I turned to SJ. "Will you reason with her please?"

"No, I do not think I will," SJ said. "Blue is right. We are all tired of your behavior and will not stand for it any longer. You tricked us in Adelaide, Crisa. When we were at Ashlyn's you did not tell us your whole plan. You only opened up to us partially so that we would forgive and believe you. You told us what we wanted to hear and did the exact same thing you have been doing for weeks—you pushed us away. You did not trust us. And you got captured as a result. Well, now is where we draw the line. You either give us one impressive explanation or we end this here."

"End what here?" I was almost too afraid to ask.

"Our friendship," Blue replied. "We've given you multiple chances to make amends and you keep lying and pushing us away. And like SJ said, we're tired of it. If you don't want to trust us—if all those years of friendship mean nothing to you and you'd rather be in this alone—then just end things. We can agree to work to escape this castle together, but once we get out of Alderon we can go our separate ways if that's what you want."

"Of course that's not what I want!" I exclaimed, horrified at the idea. "But it's just . . . those people out there are trying to kill us. I know I owe you guys an explanation, but can't it wait?"

"No," Jason said bluntly. "It can't."

I looked to Daniel. "A little help please?"

He shrugged. "Sorry, Knight. They're right. The only reason you and I aren't at each other's throats the way we used to be is because I got you to be honest with me in the genie lamp. Evidently the only way to get anything out of you is to trap you in enclosed spaces."

I resisted the urge to bang my head against the wall. "Fine. I give. Go ahead," I said. "What do you guys want from me?"

Jason crossed his arms. "That's just it, Crisa. All we want is you."

"Um, hello? I'm right here."

"No, the *old* you," he clarified. "The you who doesn't push us away. The you who doesn't obsessively keep things to herself and lie to us. You've been acting weird for weeks now. We've all been cutting you a fair amount of slack, but Adelaide was the last straw.

We gave you a second chance and you still kept us in the dark and went ahead and did whatever you wanted."

"Seriously, what is up with that?" Blue interjected angrily. "I mean what is so hard about letting us in? We're your friends, Crisa, and you've been treating us like strangers—acting like a . . . like a . . . ugh, I don't even know the right words." She threw her hands in the air in frustration and stomped to the other side of the cell.

I exhaled deeply and morphed my wand back to pin form, stashing it away. The avalanche hit. The truth flooded every part of my soul and all thoughts of Nadia and the antagonists were washed away. Everything I'd been feeling—everything I'd wanted to tell my friends since my conversation with Daniel in the genie lamp—was finally ready to flow free.

"That's fine, Blue," I said. "Because I do know the right words. I've been acting like a proud, stubborn, insecure jerk and . . . I'm sorry."

"It's a bit of a long explanation," I continued. "But the short version is that I was scared. I never wanted to admit it to you guys. Heck, I never wanted to admit it to myself. But it's the truth. Not trusting you was never about you; it was about me. It was about me being deeply, indescribably afraid of what you might think of me if I conceded that I needed you."

"Why would you be afraid of that?" SJ asked.

"You guys know how the rest of the world sees me—as a weak princess, a damsel incapable of being a hero. The last thing I wanted to do was give you a reason to agree with that perspective. And asking for help—admitting that I needed it—felt like showing weakness. So I pushed you away. Even if I knew it was stupid and dangerous and reckless, I just couldn't risk you guys thinking of me the way everyone else does. It hurt too much, the idea that there'd be no one left to see me as something other than an inept protagonist who can't exhibit any admirable character traits."

I raised my right hand—the hand with the blurred watering can mark on it. "I mean look at this. Not even that stupid watering can thought I had a single strength worth taking. This blur is just a constant reminder of how bleak and up in the air my chances are of becoming any of the things I want to be . . ."

I let out a sigh with a shake of my head. The memory of the pain these thoughts once caused me was soreness in the back of my neck, like an old injury you still felt on a rainy day.

"Since our journey began I have been so riddled with doubts like this," I confessed. "And every day those doubts grew around me to the point that I felt I would be swallowed whole. Believing that I could still change the way you saw me was my only lifeline. It was the sole saving grace keeping me going. So . . . I needed to hold onto it with everything I had."

I looked at each of my friends. SJ and Jason seemed to soften, but Blue remained stiff and resentful.

"Crisa, that just isn't a good enough reason to forgive and forget everything you've done," she said. "You've deceived us *repeatedly*. Back at Ashlyn's I looked you in the eyes and gave you a second chance and you threw it in my face. Since we started this mission you've misled us about how much you knew at every turn, you've come up with plans designed to trick us into going along with them, and—"

"And you have almost gotten yourself killed!" SJ chimed in crossly. "Repeatedly!"

I wrung my hands anxiously. "I didn't though. Doesn't that count for something?"

"Crisa, of course it counts for something. But that isn't the point," Jason replied. "We've been friends for years. Do you have any idea what it's like to watch someone you care about continuously come close to death like that?"

"Is that an actual question?" I was surprised by the anger in my tone. But I realized it wasn't anger; it was frustration. "How do you think I feel whenever I have nightmares about the future?

You think it's easy for me to hear and see all that stuff—all those people and things that are going to put you guys in harm's way? It's not. That night before we went to Adelaide I had a dream that Arian gave his men orders to kill you if you stood in the way of him getting to me. And that's hardly the first time I've envisioned something dark. Every time I shut my eyes I worry over what fresh horrors the night will bring. The only good thing that can possibly come of the nightmares is that I sometimes get a heads-up about what's coming for us and I can use that information to protect you, like I did on Adelaide. And I *have to protect you.* Not because I think you guys can't take care of yourselves, but because I care too much about you to risk anything else. I realize lying wasn't the best way to go about it, but I had to do whatever I could to keep you safe." I clenched my fists. While I regretted a lot of things I'd done over the last few weeks, I didn't regret this motive behind many of the choices I'd made. "That's just what friends do," I said.

Blue stepped forward. Her arms were still crossed, but her scowl had faded. Her eyes shone with fire, but they were no longer looking at me with rage or resentment.

"It is what friends do, Crisa," she replied. "And you have to give us a chance to do the same. We're not going to judge you for asking for help or relying on us or admitting that you're not strong enough to do everything on your own. Because it's like you said—we're friends. Being there for one another is part of the package. It's a two-way street that's definitely not something to be ashamed of. And you seriously have got to start learning to accept that."

"Yeah, I know. And . . . and I do. I get it now. Even if I don't always need someone to save or protect me, it's still nice to know that there are people out there who care enough about me to keep trying. Having friends in your life who want to help you is something to be grateful for, not ashamed of. And I'm done letting my insecurities control me or convince me otherwise."

Blue, SJ, and Jason stared at me in surprise.

"And what—dare I ask—inspired this revelation?" SJ asked.

"It pains me to admit it," I sighed, "but Daniel and I sort of had a talk." I gestured to Daniel, who was leaning against the prison wall with his arms crossed, watching the scene unfold like it was private theatre.

"You had a talk with Daniel that ended in self-growth, not murderous impulses?" Blue asked, dumbfounded.

"I couldn't believe it either." Daniel shrugged. "By the way, Knight, your hand is doing that liquid metal thing again."

"What?" I looked down and saw he was right. I was so in the moment that I hadn't noticed my hand envelop in the magic watering can's liquid metal effect. When the phenomenon dissipated a second later the blurry brand remained. And yet, for a second it looked different. The mark on my palm fluxed like a word was trying to form. It shrank and pulsed and I really thought this might be it. But then it stopped. I squeezed my fist shut and rolled my eyes.

"Still nothing?" SJ asked.

"No," I said. "But it doesn't matter. Maybe I'll never know what my defining personal strength is and the mark will remain blurry forever. But I'm not going to let that, or anything else, keep me blurry too. My head and heart are clear now and I know what I want. And that's *this*." I gestured at the group of us. "Our friendship. It's something special and I've taken it for granted for way too long. And I'm sorry, guys. I'm so, so sorry. While I don't expect you to trust me again any time soon, I am going to work hard every day to earn your trust back. I just need to know if you'll let me. Can you guys give this supposed protagonist a *second*, second chance—a chance to prove she's not an antagonist like Nadia thinks?"

My friends exchanged a look and my heart quickened as I let their judgment pass.

I'd made a good pitch, and I truly was sorry for keeping

things from them and committed to mending my ways. But I'd also taken screwing up to epic new levels, hurting all three of them in the process. So maybe a heartfelt apology wasn't enough.

What if the damage I've incited can't be undone? I wondered as worry sunk in.

What if they don't forgive me? What if they can't forgive me?

But then SJ smiled and said the four greatest words I'd heard in a very long time.

"*Second*, second chance granted."

My eyes lit up. "Really?"

"Yes, really. But you must let us in from now on, Crisa," SJ said. "Sincerely, we have to trust one another no matter the circumstance."

"I will. I promise," I assured her.

"And no more lies either," Blue added. "Shenanigans, tomfoolery, malarkey—you know I'm fine with all three. But deception—no dice. Got it?"

"I got it."

"Good." Jason nodded. He put his hand on my shoulder. "Because we've got you."

"Yeah." I smiled. "I know."

I turned and hugged him. Blue and SJ joined in.

For the first time in weeks it felt like we were *us* again. The air was clear; the tension was gone; the deceit, duplicity, and pretext melted away. It was just my friends and me. And that was all I needed.

"So then," SJ said as we pulled away. "Blue, care to enlighten us on the specifics of this ingenious, pea-based plan of yours?"

"Gladly," she said, unleashing another grin. "So here's the deal. While there are a lot of versions of *The Princess & the Pea*, the gist is that a prince was looking for a wife, but he was a mama's boy and his mom had absurdly high standards for every princess he chose. The girl her precious son married had to be the most perfect lady—delicate and dainty as can be. So along comes this common female protagonist that he falls in love with. She's not even a princess, so there's zero shot his mom's gonna go for it. But the prince asks a Fairy Godmother for help. She gives him an enchanted pea. The prince introduces the girl to his mother and claims that despite not being a princess she is the most delicate creature in all the land, and therefore worthy to be his wife. To prove it, he bets his mother that a pea buried beneath a bunch of mattresses can bruise the girl. He and the girl plant the enchanted pea under the mattresses and sure enough, in the morning she is bruised like a two-month-old cantaloupe. They repeat the test several times with the same result. And the rest is history."

"Yeah, yeah," Daniel said. "I read the story for a homework assignment at the beginning of the semester. What you haven't told us is how the pea works."

"Right." Blue nodded. "So basically there are two things you need to know. First off, the energy this thing creates is silent. Second, its force will be concentrated solely on the first thing it touches once activated—like the mattresses the protagonist slept on in the story. So all I have to do is fire the pea at the wall while I say the trigger words and it should create enough of a shock wave to destroy the front wall of the cell. Once we're out, Crisa can use her wand to slice through the lock on the storage room at the beginning of the hall."

Jason pivoted to me. "That's where they shoved our weapons before putting us in this cell," he explained.

"I'm impressed, Blue," I commented. "That's a solid plan."

"Hey, just because you're usually our designated leader in these situations doesn't mean a scrappy girl like myself can't contribute."

"Definitely," I agreed. "Especially now. Because after we've gotten our stuff we'll need one heck of a plan to get out of here and it's going to take all of us to get it done." I turned to the boys.

"Daniel said you both took a Magical Geography course at Lord Channing's. How well did you do?"

"Easiest A ever," Jason responded.

"Great. So Alderon is next to the Indexlands where the Author lives. That much I know. But how far is the border from where we are now?"

"Not far actually," Jason replied. "Valor is maybe three miles from the border. Why, are we gonna make a run for it?"

"I don't see how we have any other choice. We don't have a lot of resources so we can't afford an elaborate kind of play here. SJ, do you still have all the portable potions you brewed at Ashlyn's?"

"I have plenty of explosion, slime, and ice potions. They are in the storage room along with my slingshot and our weapons."

I thought about how useful SJ's portable potions had been in our previous fights. The marble-sized creations may have looked cute and harmless, but they held huge amounts of power. The red portable potions emitted fiery explosions. The jade ones produced giant blobs of super sticky slime on impact. And the silver potions temporarily froze things solid.

While this was great in terms of a fighting advantage, we'd never faced a threat like this before. There were hundreds of antagonists out there. If we had any shot of escaping the palace, we needed something extra.

"What about that *other* potion you made?"

SJ's face paled.

Prior to leaving Ashlyn's, SJ had used a combination of ingredients to brew a very experimental and extremely powerful portable potion. She was planning to destroy it because she'd decided it was too dangerous, but I had stopped her when I found out, believing that it might come in handy on our journey.

"Crisa, you know I have not tested it," SJ replied. "I created the potion from memory. If my calculations were even slightly off, the results could be—"

"Cataclysmic. I know. But you also said that if it did work it would produce an intense temporary earthquake. And right now that's our best option for when we get upstairs and the guards eventually outnumber us."

"I'm with Crisa," Jason said. "If we get into trouble, SJ, you need to fire first and have regrets later."

"Agreed," said Blue.

"What she said," Daniel added.

SJ exhaled a sigh and reluctantly nodded. "All right, fine. I will do it."

Jason put his hand on her shoulder. "Don't worry. We'll back you up. And we have our new weapons too, remember?"

"What new weapons?" I asked.

Blue grinned deviously. "What, Miss Magical? You think you're the only one who gets to level-up on this journey?"

She, Jason, and Blue went on to explain that while they were on the magic train the three of them had saved the life of a Fairy Godmother. Since the recent attack on our magic train ride to Adelaide, Fairy Godmothers had been randomly checking in on the transports to make sure they were safe. Unfortunately, this Godmother—Lucille as she was called—happened to pop up on a magic train where there were several magic hunters.

They got the jump on her when she was inspecting the cargo hold. Luckily, my friends intervened. They'd spotted the hunters standing on the platform at Adelaide station and after what happened the last time, they elected to keep tabs on the hunters throughout the ride. As a result, they'd been there when Lucille was attacked.

My friends subdued the hunters before they could kill the Godmother and take her magic. As a reward, Lucille had granted each of them a special gift. Blue's utility belt, which normally held her throwing knives, was now charmed to replenish the knives as they were thrown. She would never have to worry about running out mid-battle again. Jason's axe was enchanted to produce a small force field whenever he gripped the handle and thought of the word "protect." This energy barrier would project from the blade and create a temporary shield around him. And SJ's gift . . . Well, SJ's gift was a little more complicated.

My friend carried around her portable potions in a sack that she attached to her belt. However, we'd been through so many attacks on this adventure that she'd run out midway. Thankfully she'd been able to re-brew more ammo at Ashlyn's. But the risk of running out of potions was an ongoing obstacle. So she'd requested that the Fairy Godmother enchant her sack to remedy the situation.

If she reached in right now she would still find all the portable potions she'd recently made. But inside the sack also existed a tiny, contained wormhole that SJ could activate by thinking of the word "compress."

Once activated, SJ could reach into the sack and pull out any object so long as: (a) it existed (b) it could fit through the mouth of the sack, and (c) she knew exactly where it was. She couldn't just reach inside and yank out a miscellaneous taco or a random knife from the kitchen at Lady Agnue's, but if she remembered the exact location of something, say, a quill on her desk, she could pull that out with no problem.

At the moment it wasn't a terribly useful enchantment, but it held endless possibilities for the future. For example, she could make hundreds of portable potions ahead of time, keep them hidden in a specific location, then call on them when necessary. She would never have to worry about running out of ammo again. Assuming that we survived our current predicament, that is.

"That sounds awesome, man," Daniel said when Jason finished detailing the new abilities of his axe.

"More importantly, it's handy," Blue added. "With what's upstairs waiting for us we can use all the advantages we can get. Now as to our plan . . ." Blue pivoted toward me.

"Right," I said. "So we're going to make a run at the main

entrance. One, it's the only route out of this place we know. Two, no one will be expecting an escape via the castle's front door. And three, in front of the castle is where the guards parked the carriages. We just need to make it to them and then get to the border."

"You do realize that there are hordes of guards roaming the halls, a small army in the foyer, and a large number of miscellaneous antagonists outside the castle who would not mind eliminating us themselves," SJ said.

I shrugged. "Hey, given that the alternative is public execution, I'm willing to give it a go if you are. So what do you say, oh great and logical one?"

"This plan is about as sane as any of the other plans you have come up with recently," she replied.

I raised my eyebrows. "Is that a good thing or a bad thing?"

"As usual, I think it is a bit of both. Ergo, I am in. I cannot speak for the rest of you, though." SJ gestured to the others.

"So you want me to take on impossible odds while armed with nothing but a few weapons, gumption, and a half-baked, unorthodox plan?" Blue asked. "*Of course* I'm in. This is an endeavor worthy of Bruce Willis himself. And if it's good enough for Bruce, it's good enough for me."

"Not the words I would've chosen," Jason commented. "But yeah, definitely in. Daniel?"

"Knight already knows I'm on her side. Let's get this done."

Despite the bleakness of the situation, I felt a warmth in my heart at my friends' words.

"All right then, now that's settled," Blue continued, "I've about had my fill of this place. So, if you're ready . . . ."

"Do it." I nodded.

Blue grinned. "Aye, aye, captain."

The five of us stepped back so that we were as far away from the front wall as possible. Blue removed the rubber band she'd been wearing on her wrist since our escape from the lair of the

Therewolves *(thank Book she hadn't taken it off)*. She used the band to fire the magic pea as she called out its trigger words:

"Good night!"

BANG!

CRASH!!!

KS!@D**H%3#$FH@!!!!!!!

The pea shot forward and unleashed a string of enormously powerful shock waves at the front wall of our cell. When the dust cleared and we saw the gaping hole it'd created, Blue called out the pea's stop command:

"Good morning!"

Instantly the enchanted pulses ceased and Blue went to retrieve the little green thing from the wreckage.

"That's why no one caught on to the pea's enchantment," Blue explained as we helped her search the rubble for it. "Its magic only activated when the prince's mother left her alone each evening after saying, you know, the first thing. And then the enchantment was shut off when she re-entered the room the next day and said the second thing."

"All right, that's it. I'm definitely doing the reading assignments from now on," I commented as we continued poking through the debris.

"Blue, I think I found it," Jason said. "But . . ."

We dashed over. Jason had picked up the pea from the chunks of iron and stone, but it wasn't in good shape. The once bright green color was flickering and it was no longer perfectly round and smooth. It was flat and smushed like a tiny pancake. After flickering a few more times it abruptly turned to dust.

"What happened?" Blue exclaimed.

"It's your pea. You don't know?" Daniel asked.

"Once you say the stop command it's supposed to return to its normal form and begin recharging," she explained. "There's no reason that wall should've destroyed it."

I bent down and touched a portion of the crumbled wall. Instantly that weird dizziness and brain static I'd felt before returned. "There's something about this stone," I said, removing my hand. "My wand should be able to hack through anything. Whatever this stuff is made of, it's powerful. It must've been too much for the pea to take."

"I'm sorry, Blue," Jason commented thoughtfully, knowing that she would be upset about losing the pea. She had a deep love and respect for fairytale history and its related relics.

"Same, but we need to move on," Daniel replied. "Anyway it's hardly the first magical relic we've destroyed."

"Exactly," I said. "The pea went down in the name of saving us, just like the magic mirror and Aladdin's genie lamp."

Blue and SJ turned on me in unison, their faces shocked and dismayed. "You destroyed the genie lamp?"

"Not the time," Daniel said, herding us forward. "Designed to be silent or not, someone upstairs definitely felt that pea's explosion. We'll have company in a minute and we need to get out."

We followed his lead and began our dash down the corridor. As we ran, SJ glanced at me. "When this is over we need to have a serious talk about your affinity for destruction."

"Noted," I said.

CHAPTER 20

Remembering the Dragon

 e hurried to the storage room where our weapons
had been stowed. The door was made of regular
steel and locked with regular bolts. I transformed
my wand back to an axe and easily hacked my way
through.

Once the door was removed we dashed inside. SJ found her
slingshot and sack of portable potions. Blue located her trusty
hunting knife and her newly enchanted utility belt with throwing
knives. The boys grabbed their sheaths and weapons—Daniel's
sword and Jason's upgraded axe. As an added bonus we found
Blue's cloak, which my friend happily put back on.

Thinking we had everything, I started to make my way out into
the hall. But SJ didn't follow. She was still desperately searching
around the storage room.

"What's wrong?" I asked.

"When Arian and his men captured us, they took the quill
from the Century City Summit and Ashlyn's locket. They took
your Hole Tracker too." She gestured to my wrist.

My eyebrows shot up as I discovered she was right. So much
was happening that I hadn't even noticed it was gone. Now that I
did, I was even more ticked off at Nadia.

"They must know the worth of those items," SJ continued.
"I thought they would be in here with the rest of our things, but
they are not."

"They could be anywhere in this place," Blue moaned. "Where do we even start looking?"

"Maybe we should split up—try to cover more ground," Jason suggested.

"No," I said firmly. "We're stronger together. No matter what happens, we stay as a team."

The others stared at me for a second. I didn't blame them. After all the stunts I'd pulled I'd practically become the poster child for going it alone. But no more. I'd made my mistakes and had meant it when I said I was going to learn from them.

"She's right," Daniel said, looking as surprised as the others. "Our chances of getting out of here are a whole lot better as a group."

"Then what should we do?" Jason asked.

"We're not leaving without those items. If we don't get them then we'll have come all this way for nothing," Blue said.

"Agreed," I replied. "Plus, without them we'll be stuck in Alderon. They're our only means for breaking the In and Out Spell and escaping this kingdom."

"Where should we start looking?"

"I think we should head toward the throne room," I said. "I have a feeling that the curtained area next to Nadia's throne leads to her royal study. I've had a vision about it and I'd put money that's where she's keeping our stuff."

"What makes you think that?" SJ asked.

"You saw the big fuss she made about getting me here; the girl likes trophies. She probably has our things sitting on a shelf in her study right now like commemorative souvenirs."

"It's as good a guess as any," Daniel replied.

"That's the spirit," I said. "Now let's move, they'll be coming for us soon."

Wand in hand and friends by my side, we bolted up the stairs. We had to climb several flights to escape the forlorn underground prison. On our way up we ran into a few guards who'd felt the pea's disturbance and were coming to check on us. They didn't waylay my team for long. A few guards were no match for our combined skill.

The hallway at the top of the stairs was empty so we moved swiftly in the direction of the throne room, knowing that our safe passage could be compromised at any moment.

That moment took place right as we rounded the corner.

Aw, dang.

All it took was one guard to see us, sound an alarm, and throw the scene into chaos.

When he spotted us he placed his palm against something that looked like a half crystal ball lodged in the wall. In an instant its color went from translucent white to bright red. The light shot through the black glass walls like a streak of lightning and ignited the ceiling in the same shade. A low-pitched siren began to sound.

We made a break for it—taking out the guard then pushing aside a handful of others who entered the corridor.

A blur of black glass walls and life-size animal statues rushed past us as we moved forward. This evade-and-outrun approach could only last for so long. Guards began to pour in from everywhere. Before we were halfway to the throne room we got cut off. This left us with one violent, but arguably more fun option. Fight.

Spear.

I blocked the first man with a thrust of my spear and continued the momentum to jab the bottom of the staff into a second attacker's abdomen. I quarter-turned and reversed the process— blocking a third guard and jabbing the first man.

My friends dealt with their own serving of antagonists.

SJ's attack was two-fold. She fired portable potions at the attackers who got too close—stopping them in their paths by encasing them in either ice or slime. Then whenever she had a clean wide shot she cleared a path for us—releasing explosion potions to blast back attackers and create an opening for our group to forge ahead.

Daniel moved alongside SJ, defending her from attackers as she fired. He fought swiftly and with more skill than any of his opponents had been trained to handle. One after another he disarmed and knocked out guards in their way.

At the rear of our pack Jason and Blue protected us from guards who were coming up from behind. Him with his trusty axe and she with her equally trusty hunting knife and throwing knives, they worked in perfect synchronicity. Their dual-powered defense was so in tune that it looked like they were moving with one brain and one instinct.

A couple of throwing knives sank into a pair of attackers' calves beside me. I glanced over at Blue as Jason shielded himself from two attackers with his axe's shimmering force field. Their assault bounced off of it. He lowered the shield and thwacked his elbow into one guard's temple while kicking the other in the spine. He lunged to finish them both while Blue slid underneath the sword of an attacker, rolled to her feet, and slashed at two more. She popped up and nailed one man with a right hook and thrust the other back with the heel of her hand—sending him staggering into a couple of soldiers right behind him.

As SJ's explosion potions lit up my peripherals I noted that we were doing well. Despite the onslaught, we had managed to migrate through three more sections of the palace. I knew not to get cocky though. Like ants on a carcass, the number of guards kept multiplying, and it wouldn't be long before they threatened to consume us completely. All we could do was keep fighting and hope we made it to the throne room before then.

And duck and turn and bam!

I flipped my staff and struck one attacker in the head then double jabbed him in the solar plexus. I swung around to block a second guard. With another flip and downward thrust I struck him high then quickly flipped the staff to strike him low.

An ice potion erupted a few feet away—encasing four men in a block of frost. Three knives thrown in perfect sequence took out a trio of archers trying to get a shot at us. Daniel kicked an attacker so hard that it sounded like the man's bones shattered when he hit the wall. Jason slammed the side of his axe into one man's head, jutted the handle upward to nail him in the jaw, then blasted three more men back with his energy shield.

In spite of our best efforts, the number of guards kept increasing. As we continued forward, the intersecting hallways allowed them to converge from all angles. The combination of these factors was slowly drawing us away from one another so that we were fending for ourselves rather than fighting as a unit.

At that moment, the five of us were spread out in a large intersection with a grand staircase that led up to other floors. Too many guards to count were streaming down and heading straight for us. I glanced at my friends. Our time was up.

"SJ!" I called.

She looked over.

"Now!" I pointed at the staircase.

She understood what I was saying, as did the others. We all worked to clear her a shot. Daniel forcefully knocked back three guards who were closing in on them. Blue fired so many throwing knives in such quick succession it looked like she had four arms. Jason slashed and smacked anyone who tried to get too close to any of them.

Unseen by the others, a guard escaped their assault and rushed at SJ from the right.

Shield.

Like I had with Goldilocks, I flung my shield like a discus. Just as the guard raised his broadsword to bring it down on SJ, the hard metal rammed into his head and knocked him out.

SJ was clear to take the shot. She snatched out the indigo-colored portable potion that would either save us or bury us, pulled back on her slingshot, and fired.

The potion smashed into the staircase among the twenty or so guards that had been rushing down it. When the orb impacted, it felt like the world seizured. Five powerful shockwaves slowly rippled through the palace. A giant crack formed on the staircase amidst a cloud of indigo smoke. The fissure widened as the pulses continued, ripping the area apart and swallowing countless guards into its depths as it expanded.

Portions of wall came crashing to the floor. Sections of ceiling imploded. Every person in the vicinity was knocked off his or her feet and thrust to the ground by the magnitude of the earthquake's energy.

Like the others, I rolled over and covered my head, shielding myself from the black glass that rained down.

When the pulses stopped, my head still rang. Thankfully I had been knocked about so many times during this adventure that my recovery was getting faster. I jumped to my feet and dashed amongst the shattered glass, bronze, and stone to retrieve my wand—still in its shield form.

If you counted the guards that had been coming down the stairs, we'd previously had about forty men to worry about. With many having fallen through the chasm in the floor and others downed from being hit by debris, only a third remained. But they were already starting to get to their feet.

I grasped my shield with one hand and extended the other to a nearby SJ to help her up. Blue, Jason, and Daniel quickly joined us and we made a run for it.

It was a decent head start, but the guards were not far behind. And soon enough we were cut off by a fresh insurgence that came from the hallways ahead. Between the two factions there was no way to sugarcoat it. The odds were not in our favor.

Once again we were pushed apart—the circle of our defenses forced to widen in order to evade being overwhelmed.

One of SJ's ice potions exploded on my left, encasing two guards. Jason swung his axe at an opponent and Blue came around back and punched that same attacker in the head. A slime potion erupted on my right and trapped four guards where they stood. Daniel rushed past SJ and clashed his sword with one man before breaking the guy's jaw with a thrust of his elbow.

My friends were moving with as much speed and strength as before, but there was a definite change in tension. Our confidence and purpose was overshadowed by desperation. We were outnumbered and losing control. At this rate it wouldn't be long before we were just losing in general.

Shield.

I blocked a sword at my left and began to pivot to block another on my right, but didn't get around in time. I was slashed on my upper arm.

Spear.

I blocked high and low, and side to side, then back and forth, and—

Awgh!

While I'd been parrying my attacker's sword he'd swung around his other arm and nailed me in the head with a right hook.

I tumbled back from the force of the punch. He came at me. I raised my spear just in time to avoid the strike. Our weapons collided. I jutted out my leg and kicked him in the shin. He was thrown off balance. I leapt up and hammered his face with my fist. Then I spun around to back-kick a second attacker and smash a third one in the skull with my staff.

Geez, how many guys was that?

It feels like I've been fighting for . . .

Yikes!

I ducked to avoid another hook punch.

Shield.

Block. Thrust. Block.

Sword.

Parry. Strike. Strike. Parry.

Spear.

Swing. Thrust. Block. Thrust. Jolt.

Awgh!

I'd been punched in the face again by one of the guards. This time was worse. His hand had been covered in a metallic gauntlet. It left me with a pretty substantial cut on my cheek.

I staggered a few feet and tripped over some fallen debris. I backed up against one of the life-size animal statues that lined the hallway. This one was a dragon—a fairly big and kind of familiar-looking dragon.

Light streamed in from a gaping hole in the ceiling that had been created by SJ's earthquake potion. The gleam reflected off the bronze statue. The way it hit the metal creature, it kind of reminded me of . . .

Oh no.

There were eight guards steadily coming toward me.

I glanced around.

Jason and Blue were fighting back-to-back with a group of attackers the size of my own. Daniel was almost out of options—about to be cornered against a large bear statue directly to his right. And SJ . . . SJ had been pushed to the ground!

I wanted to go to her. I wanted to go to the others as well. But I was in no more a position to help them than they were to help me. We were trapped. We were all trapped and I didn't know how we were going to escape this time.

Wait, where is that shadow coming from?

An enormous, oddly shaped shadow spilled across the floor. My eyes darted to the ceiling.

What in the . . .

I hit the floor and covered my face. Glass didn't just rain this time; it poured. Five seconds later a large thud, which sounded like an earthquake in its own right, impacted the ground beside me. I slowly picked myself off the ground and looked up.

The gaping hole in the ceiling had been replaced by an entire lack of ceiling.

A weighty snort against my face drew my attention.

Crouching before me was a dragon, panting heavily. He had created the great hole in the ceiling when he'd forcefully crashed through it. It was the same dragon that had been chasing my friends and me across the realm over the last few weeks. And I knew this time there would be no outrunning him.

I stood rapidly and instinctively tried to back up, but was stopped by the dragon statue behind me. I was cornered with nowhere to go.

Talk about being stuck between a rock and a hot place.

I gazed over the state of the massive hall.

Statues had been tipped over, glass covered the floor, and dozens of people were on the ground. They'd all been taken down by the crash. So far, I was the only one who'd managed to regain my senses and get back up.

Lucky me. I get to be super aware of what's going on when this thing eats me.

That's when I noticed something. The silver-scaled dragon was blinking at me curiously. He'd extended his neck so that his face was barely two feet from my own, but he didn't look like he wanted to eat me or set me on fire. He just stared at me like he was waiting for something.

The first time I'd gotten near this dragon was when I was flying through the sky over Book's capital. At the time I had been splitting my focus between maneuvering my Pegasus and working my lacrosse sword. The second time I'd seen him had been in the outskirts of the Forbidden Forest when we were evading Arian, his men, and their cannonball launchers. Finally, the last time the dragon came near us was yesterday at Fairy Godmother Headquarters. When the creature had been inbound for the building, I'd only gotten a quick glance at him through the Godmothers' shimmering hologram screen.

This was the first time I was close enough to get a good look at the dragon. Between that and being pressed up against the bronze dragon statue, I realized something.

This live dragon bore a striking resemblance to that stone dragon statue we'd come across in the Capitol Building—the one that guarded the passageway to Arian's bunker.

It was uncanny. Not only was the face identical, the dragon's approximate length and height were the same too.

There were only two notable differences between the dragons. One, that dragon had been composed of gray rock whereas this one had glistening silver scales on the outside and flesh and blood on the inside. Two, the eyes were wrong. The pair on the statue at the Capitol Building had been pure black stone. This live dragon's eyes were a rich shade of glowing gold that felt weirdly familiar.

"Crisa, remember the dragon."

The phrase the woman in my dreams had been communicating came to the forefront of my mind.

"It has something to do with the first time you touched him," the woman had said. "When the time comes and you face Nadia, remembering him will be the only thing that can save you."

But I'd never touched this dragon. The only dragon I'd technically ever touched was . . .

I gasped.

The dragon statue at the Capitol Building.

I stared into this dragon's eyes and a ludicrous idea popped into my head. It was so crazy that I hesitated before allowing myself to fully process it. *Those eyes . . .*

What was it about them? It was like I had seen them before. And not just on this dragon, but following me everywhere like a dream or a ghost or . . . a memory.

That's when it hit me.

A flash of recollections crashed down like a tidal wave.

The seagull that had attacked Mauvrey the night of the ball in Adelaide Castle, the rock monster in the Therewolves' lair that had saved me from the troupe's evil director, the killer tree outside the Forbidden Forest that assaulted Arian's men, even those vine blossoms growing outside our bedroom at Lady Agnue's with their bright, glistening stamen. They all had exhibited some form of these golden, glowing eyes.

But what did that mean? What was the connection? In retrospect, all those creatures had appeared when I'd needed them to, as if by command. And in the minutes before they'd sprung up I'd just been . . .

I glanced down to where my hand rested on the face of the bronze dragon statue.

I'd been touching them.

The understanding came at me like a slap in the face as I recalled touching the dragon statue in the Capitol Building, the vines on our balcony, the stone seagull in Adelaide Castle, the rocky interior of the Therewolves' lair, and the tree I'd hidden behind when Arian was chasing me through the forest.

The sudden appearance of those creatures had not been mere coincidence. The same went for other occasions in years past when unexplained magical creatures crossed my path. They hadn't been coming to life on their own; I had been *giving it* to them.

Prior to touching those objects I'd sometimes experienced one of those weird hand-burning episodes that I recently learned were cases of Magic Build-Up—the phenomenon that occurred when power built up inside me until it erupted. This explained why the episodes stopped so suddenly each time. I had been releasing the excess magic into whatever I'd been touching.

And during all those other run-ins with magical creatures I must've unknowingly been using my magic too, just without the Magic Build-Up provocation.

Holy bananas! I know what my power is!

It's . . . Life

My watering can mark started to tingle, but I had bigger things going on that demanded my concentration.

I looked at the dragon for all that he was for the very first time. "I remember you," I said slowly. "I remember the first time I touched you and I know what you are."

I started to reach my hand toward him, but was distracted by the realization that a fresh wave of troops was storming the halls and headed for us. The guards that had been taken down by the arrival of the dragon were also getting up. Some were faster than others. And some were making a move on a knocked-out Daniel!

My attention shifted from the dragon and I bolted for the other side of the hall. I pushed past several guards and swung my spear to smash others out of the way, making it to Daniel in time to step between him and the guard that intended to end him.

Angrily, I blocked the guard's strike, roundhouse-kicked his ribs, then brought my staff down on his neck. To finish, I spun around and pushed him off his feet.

I saw that Daniel and the others were coming to. But that didn't change the fact that we were outnumbered. I glanced at the dragon—who was still eyeing me, unsure of what to do. I dashed to the hefty bear statue directly behind Daniel and placed my hand on the creature's face.

Please let this work.

I closed my eyes and concentrated.

Wake up, I thought. *Wake up and defend us.*

I opened my eyes to see my hand flicker with an aura of golden light. The mystical color transferred into the bear and filled his eyes with an iridescent shade of liquid gold.

The creature blinked as the rest of his body turned animate. Then he looked to his left and his right before hurtling himself toward the nearest battalion of guards.

It worked!

My reasoning had been sound. As I raced over to Daniel I reflected on the general wording of everything I had been thinking when my hands had given life to so many creatures before.

"Come on, flower! Live, darn you! Live!" I'd shouted overdramatically as I humored SJ when she discovered the flowers on our balcony were dead. The result—the next morning the flowers were emanating more life than any plant I'd ever seen.

"Ugh, come on. Get up, get going, and go get Mauvrey," I'd grunted as I clutched the seagull fountain at Adelaide Castle on my way to pursue my teenage nemesis.

"Just pull yourself together and go crush some Therewolves," I'd urged myself as I gripped the rock of the Therewolf tunnel and prepared to rejoin the fight.

"Just go and kick his butt—him and all his annoying friends. You can do it. Just get up from the ground and go," I'd thought fervently outside the Forbidden Forest as I clutched the tree I was hiding behind to garner the courage to face Arian.

And finally, "Come on, come on! Let's go!" That's what I had been thinking when I'd laid my hand on the dragon statue back at the Capitol Building.

My power was giving life. Whatever I thought or commanded when I was using the ability was the very order that my creations felt obliged to follow. Like this dragon. Because of my wording, he'd thought he was supposed to come with me. That's why he'd been following me across the realm.

It all made perfect sense. Not only that, it felt right. Emma said that when I figured out my magical power I would just know. Well, I knew. The assertion burned in my heart and gut with such fervor it was like I'd swallowed the sun.

My friends and the rest of the guards had gotten up by that point and were all surprised by the full-sized bronze bear that had joined the fight. Daniel glanced at me as if to ask a question, but I didn't wait for it. I simply went to the next statue in the lineup—a lion—and put my palm on his head too.

Protect my friends; stop the guards.

My hand tingled as the glow I produced passed to the statue. The lion stretched to life and began obeying my orders like the bear.

This was too good to be true. The creatures I gave life to automatically regarded whatever I'd been thinking at the time of their inception to be their command and purpose. Which made me wonder if they would listen to me after the fact as well.

Feeling threatened, the dragon in the center of the chaos started to lash out. He swiped his massive tail and claws at the guards who were trying to contain him. I figured it was only a matter of time before he set this whole place ablaze. Which I wouldn't have minded so much if my friends and I weren't stuck in here.

While the four of them continued to fight, I repeated my magical life-giving process on three more bronze animals then raced back to the dragon, trying to put myself in his line of sight. I returned my weapon to a wand and hurriedly shoved it in my boot. Then I waved my arms to get his attention.

"Hey!" I shouted.

He turned. His immense nostrils were inches from my face. I stared straight into his gaze and raised my hand steadily. It glowed like his eyes as I purposefully concentrated on my magic. "Whoa, boy. Whoa."

I saw the dragon's mouth open slightly, allowing me to get a glimpse of the many sharp teeth inside. I remained calm and continued to move my hand closer to the dragon's face until my fingers touched his scales.

"You can save us," I said. "Please, no fire," I commanded. The energy around my hand pulsed. "Just protect my friends. Keep the guards away from us."

The dragon paused and blinked at me. I worried for a second that I'd been wrong. Maybe my command over these things was a one-off. But then the dragon rammed his head into two guards who were rushing at me. He followed up with a snort and a flick of his tail, which swept away four guards charging Blue.

Yes!

With the dragon on our team, I redrew my wand and rushed to join Daniel and SJ.

Shield.

Block. Thrust.

Spear.

Jab. Swing. Smack.

"What the heck is going on?" Daniel asked as he slashed and struck his own set of opponents.

"Short version: I have magic and it's time I used it!" I slammed my staff into one guard's head then kicked out his knee. "These things—the statues, the dragon—they listen to me!"

"If they listen to you . . ." SJ fired a slime potion to her left and an ice potion to her right. "Then let the rest of them help us while you make a run for the throne room."

Roundhouse. Elbow. Block.

"No way, no splitting-up," I called over to her. "I'm not ditching you guys again!"

"Crisa," SJ began, "this is not ditching, it is—"

Daniel pushed SJ out of the way to stop an attacker from slicing her in half. She spun around angrily with an ice potion in hand.

Instead of using her slingshot to release the orb's power, she crushed it in her fist—causing the lower half of her arm to become consumed in a shell of ice. She punched her would-be slaughterer in the face and shattered both his jaw and her makeshift ice gauntlet on impact.

Awesome.

"As I was saying," she continued, "it is not ditching because this time we know why you are going and that you will come back for us. So go! Take Daniel for backup and find our In and Out Spell ingredients while you have the chance!"

I nodded at SJ and transformed my spear back into a wandpin. There was another bear statue a few feet over. I awakened him with orders to take us to the palace throne room.

I hopped onto the bear's back. Daniel knocked one last guard off his feet, stored his sword in its sheath, and jumped on behind me.

"Go," I commanded the bear.

And he did just that.

CHAPTER 21

Power

With Daniel and I hanging onto his fur, the bronze-colored bear plowed past countless guards and bounded down the halls until we reached the throne room.

The majority of the guards were involved in the main battle so there weren't many in the room when we entered. Daniel and I dismounted as the few soldiers who were inside charged us.

I put my hand to the bear's head coolly.

"Defend," I said.

Gold energy lit up my hand. Without a second thought the bear took off toward the men.

I heard their yells but did not break stride as Daniel and I marched to Nadia's throne on the other side of the room.

I pushed away the maroon curtains to her study and discovered it was also empty . . . except for Arian. He looked at me in utter surprise. I spotted our quill, locket, and my Hole Tracker on a shelf beyond Nadia's black marble desk.

"Get the stuff," I told Daniel. He nodded.

Arian drew his sword and started toward me. "You just don't know when to quit, do you?"

I didn't flinch. I casually placed my hand on the bookshelf to my left and summoned my magic. "Protect," I commanded.

The bookshelf jerked to life. It ripped itself from the wall, flipped on its side, and rammed its way across the room—blocking Arian from getting anywhere near me.

This was the first time I'd ever seen Arian look genuinely, completely fazed. "How did you—"

"It's like you said, Arian," I interrupted. "I have magic. A lot of magic, it turns out. But you know what I don't have a lot of anymore? *Patience.* So before my friends and I get out of here I want you to tell me something."

"What?"

"The one thing I was never able to figure out. How can you and your men get out of Alderon to come after me and the other protagonists you've been hunting? The In and Out Spell over this land is still intact. If it wasn't, Nadia wouldn't be sitting here while you knock main characters off her list one at a time. She would have made her move on the rest of the realm a long time ago. So tell me, how do you escape?"

Arian didn't respond.

Ugh, I don't have time for this.

I knew that if I had any hope of permanently stopping these people, or protecting the other protagonists they'd taken an interest in, I had to know. Otherwise what was to stop Arian from coming after us again?

I put my hands on the maroon curtains hanging in the doorframe and willed them to obey me. Tearing themselves free of their hooks, they flew over to Arian and violently wrapped around his arms, yanked him off the floor, and hung him a few feet off the ground like a tortured scarecrow.

"I thought I told you I was low on patience," I said. "So talk."

He refused, remaining silent.

"Fine." I looked to the curtains. "Pull."

Without my having to touch them, the curtains obeyed and began pulling Arian's arms in opposite directions, stretching him out like a rag doll until . . .

"All right, all right!" he eventually croaked.

I raised my hands, which hadn't stopped glowing. Despite the fact that I hadn't spoken an order, the curtains seemed to read my mind and corresponding gesture. They stopped stretching Arian.

"Well?" I said.

Arian gritted his teeth as he met my gaze. "Every soul in here is trapped with no option for escape, unless . . ."

"Unless what?"

"Unless they surrender their soul. It's a simple loophole. One that may not apply to the all-powerful In and Out Spells around the whole of Book or even the Indexlands, but that can certainly get past the weaker versions that encase Alderon and your school."

"I don't understand."

"It's not that complicated, Knight," Arian sneered. "The In and Out Spell around Alderon has magic designed to prevent living things from crossing its borders. And the way the spell can detect living things—humans or even higher-functioning monsters and magical creatures like you—is by their souls. *Soulless* forms of energy face no such limitation."

"So, what, you're telling me that in order to cross Alderon's barrier you surrendered your soul?" I asked. "If that's the case, then how are you even alive?"

Arian hesitated.

I tightened my fists and the curtains responded by giving Arian a forceful yank. He grimaced and responded through gritted teeth.

"Shadow Guardians."

"Yeah, I'm gonna need a little more than that."

"Shadows are not just the castings of darkness we leave in our wake, Knight. They're a species—energy creatures from another realm. If you surrender your soul to them they can inhabit your body like a vessel in its place. The people who undergo this exchange are called Shadow Guardians. Only about one in every hundred people is compatible for the process though, so very few of us can leave Alderon and carry out Nadia's work. My team of hunters and I can only take on so much. That's why my sole focus for years has been recruiting commons on the outside and leading the hunt for priority protagonists like you."

"You may want to request a reassignment then, because it doesn't look like that's your forte," I replied. "Keep biting off more than you can chew like that and you're gonna get yourself killed."

Arian laughed.

"What's so funny?"

"You are; you and your baseless threats. See, here's the advantage that you don't get about me, princess. Unlike you, death is not something I worry about."

"Because you're some big, bad antagonist—yeah, yeah, I get it."

"No, because hosting a Shadow already comes with that cost. You don't just give up your soul. Every minute one inhabits you it gradually drains your body of its life force until there is nothing left."

"So by hosting that thing inside you, you're basically dying?" I shook my head. "You know what, Arian, on second thought my advice is to forget the reassignment and just quit. Unless you want to waste the rest of your limited lifespan on more vain attempts to capture me."

"Don't worry," he scoffed. "I'll be fine. It's only a year until the Eternity Gate opens, and when it does, I assure you each and every one of us Shadow Guardians will be stronger than you can even imagine."

"The Eternity Gate," I repeated. I'd heard and seen that phrase far too many times before—in Natalie's file from Godmother HQ, her documents in Arian's bunker, multiple dreams—but I still had no idea what it meant. Now I had a chance to find out.

"What is it?" I asked earnestly. "What is the Eternity Gate?"

Arian glared at me, refusing to answer.

"Tell me!" I barked.

He still did not speak.

Filled with frustration, I raised my glowing hands and jerked them apart—causing the enchanted curtains to recommence wringing Arian's arms. Even so, my enemy continued to resist.

"Arian!" I shouted as I drew my hands further apart. They started to glow even brighter. He writhed in pain as the curtains yanked harder and harder, threatening to tear him in half.

"What is the Eternity Gate?" I growled.

Vicious, ardent emotion pulsed through me. I couldn't recall ever having felt like this before—so full of anger and vengeance and power. It emanated from me like heat off the sun. For a moment I thought the intense feelings might burn me out completely. But then I felt something else, something gentle anchoring me.

"Knight."

I turned to discover Daniel standing behind me, his hand on my shoulder.

As if I'd been in a trance, I suddenly shook my head and blinked, lowering my hands. The glow of the curtains, as well as my own, faded. Arian dropped to the ground behind the bookshelf and I took a wobbly step to the side.

"The others," Daniel spoke steadily. "We need to get to them. I've got what we came for."

I looked back at Arian. Part of me wanted to get away from him and the person inside me that had taken over and almost ripped him in half. Yet . . . a small part of me wanted to stay and let that person go even further.

"Yeah, okay," I said, willing away the vengeful feelings.

Daniel and I made for the door.

"You can't escape," Arian called after me. "Even if you make it out of here, there's no changing that your card's been punched. One way or another, Crisanta Knight, your end is coming."

I met his gaze. "Try and hurt me or my friends again, Arian, and I can promise you the exact same thing."

With a touch to the bookshelf on my right I trapped him inside Nadia's study, ordering the thing to seal the door behind us.

Daniel and I rushed back into the throne room. The circumstances were way worse than they'd been a minute ago.

The moment we emerged, we were ambushed. The number of soldiers had tripled and a group of attackers had gotten past the bear and was rushing toward us. Adding to the problem, through the entrance of the throne room I could see another dozen men heading down the hall. Some were archers who were already taking aim.

Lapellius.

Shield.

My wand spiraled out and protected my chest from an arrow. The guards began to attack. Daniel and I clashed and ducked and spun and jabbed. They drove us closer to the wall. Another three escaped the bear's defenses. I barely evaded a sword swinging toward my head.

The bear wasn't enough to protect us from this. And he wasn't enough to get us past the oncoming surge blocking our way back to our friends either. I needed something . . .

I spotted the large serpent head above the main door.

Bigger.

I think I actually smiled. For once I was not only glad to see one of my nightmares evolve into reality, I was happy to help it complete the transformation.

I concentrated on the serpent's head but couldn't hold the focus. An attacker's sword slashed at my arm.

Awgh!

I cringed at the cut and kicked my attacker. Two more soldiers rushed in before I could block them. Each one grabbed an arm and slammed me against the wall.

Pinned there, I felt rage and power flood through my body. I shot my eyes to the serpent on the other side of the room and called on my magic with every fiber of my being.

Free yourself. Stop the guards. Give us a ride out of here. NOW.

A blinding, golden light burst out of me. Across the room the serpent's formerly black-and-red eyes began to glow gold. With unimaginable force he pulled himself from the wall and started following my commands. His body wormed out of the castle's infrastructure—jerking violently and causing large cracks to form throughout the compound.

In mere seconds, enough of him was loose to attack. Using his body like a battering ram, he swatted away the surge of guards surrounding Daniel and me before going after the others. When the coast was clear, he lowered his head to Daniel—who climbed on without question—then came for me.

Wandpin stored, I gladly hopped on. He took us through the halls, slithering with incredible speed, his thick torso knocking aside anyone who opposed us. We made it back to the battle in no time at all. The rest of my friends were still holding strong.

I pressed my hands into the creature's scaly body and commanded him to sweep away the remaining guards in the room. He slammed them against the wall. Daniel and I slid off his back and joined the others.

"We got the stuff," Daniel told them. "Knight, what's our play out of here?"

My dragon bounded over, knocking over a handful of guards that had entered from a side hall.

"*He's our way out of here*," I said, gesturing to the creature. "Everybody on."

The five us climbed onto the dragon's back and prepared for lift-off.

"Crisanta Knight!"

I looked down the hall and saw Nadia approaching with more soldiers—many of whom had crossbows aimed at us and at the animal statues I'd turned into my personal army.

Again I felt the urge to confront her as I had Arian—to dismount the dragon and do everything in my power to rip her apart here and now. As the angry emotions flowed through me, the magic in my hands started to glow more fervently, surging through my fingers and palms like furious electricity. But I gritted my teeth and resisted the impulse.

No, I told myself. *Now is not the time.*

I had to be smart. Priority one was getting my friends and I to safety while we still had the chance.

Double-checking that everyone was on board, I kicked the dragon's side with the heel of my boot and held on tightly, pouring my glow into him. "Go!" I commanded. The dragon roared and shot us through the hole in the ceiling.

The sky we broke into was bright and the desert wind was dry and sharp. Air rushed against my face and shocked me as much as the understanding that came with it. We were free. I couldn't believe it. We'd actually made it. Not only that, but in the process I'd learned the truth about Nadia and Arian, gained a pet dragon, and realized how to use my magical powers.

Pretty productive for one afternoon, if I do say so myself.

I glanced back at Alderon's citadel.

From high above, the city of Valor looked dark. Hundreds of shadows and small black specks stood under the height and hearth of the palace.

I felt an odd tinge of foreboding wash over me as we flew away. Our escape should have filled me with utter relief, but watching the city then, any swell of victory or finality felt displaced. I knew that whatever triumph had occurred here was not an ending.

It was only a beginning.

CHAPTER 22

Dreams Come True

ravelling by dragon was way more awesome than travelling by flying carriage.

Obviously with a carriage you got actual seats for comfort, doors to prevent you from falling, and walls to keep the icy air from freezing you like a popsicle. And yet, even with all that, travelling by dragon was still a million times better . . . and super fast.

Using Jason and Daniel's navigational skills, we reached the border between Alderon and the Indexlands in no time. We felt fairly comfortable with the safe distance we'd created between ourselves and Nadia's army. Even so, we couldn't afford to dillydally. It might take the army a while to catch up with us, but I had no doubt that they would unless we got past the In and Out Spell. It was our only way out of here. There was no Plan B.

I used my magic to will the dragon to land near where Alderon's sandy desert melted into the lush forests of the Indexlands. The five of us slid off his back. He trotted a slight ways away then flopped down and closed his eyes—evidently tired of flying, fighting, and my commands.

I was overwhelmed with exhaustion too. As I stood there, I felt like a kitchen sponge that had been wrung out to dry. I was completely zapped of energy.

My friends—who looked slightly shaken but remained surprisingly calm—turned to me for answers.

"I take it you figured out your power," Jason commented.

I nodded, smiling slightly as I took a deep breath. "I can give life to things. I'm not sure exactly how it works yet. Sometimes it works without me touching the object; other times I have to touch it. I do know that whatever I enchant is compelled to follow me and my instructions. Like Lucky here." I gestured to the dragon. "That's why the poor guy's been following us since Century City. He used to be the stone dragon statue in the Capitol Building. But when I touched him to close Arian's bunker I was thinking something like, 'Come on, let's go'. Those orders brought him to life, so he couldn't help but stalk us. He thought I wanted him to come with me."

"Lucky?" Blue repeated.

"Yeah, that's what I've decided to call him." I shrugged.

"Crisa, you are not keeping this creature," SJ said.

"Hang on," Blue interceded. "Having a pet dragon sounds pretty boss to me. Plus, look at how handy he is. He just helped us escape Nadia's castle; we might as well embrace the situation. I do have a few issues with the name though, Crisa. I think a good dragon name should be a little more butch than Lucky. You know, like Brutillius or Eradell. Or Chuck."

"Lucky is an excellent name because it was pretty darn lucky he showed up when he did," I countered. "And we can discuss the specifics of adopting a dragon later, SJ. Right now we need to get out of Alderon and into the Indexlands or Nadia and her crazy army are going to find us."

"We know, we know," Blue said. "All right, Daniel, give SJ the quill and the locket. Crisa, you've still got the flower, right?"

"Yeah." I reached into my boot and pulled it out from where I'd stashed it since the Cave of Mysteries. Instead of handing over the entire carnation to SJ, I grabbed the blossom and ripped off the petals before giving her the stem.

"The instructions at the Cave of Mysteries said that the petals were for strengthening magic and the leaves on the stem were for weakening it," I explained as I shoved the petals back in my boot. "Seems like the latter's what you need if you're trying to weaken the In and Out Spell. We can save the rest for later. You know, just in case."

Daniel handed me my Hole Tracker and turned over the other ingredients to our potions expert. "So now what?" he asked. "I mean I know you're good at this stuff, SJ, but we don't exactly have a lab for you to concoct something."

"A lab is not necessary," SJ replied as she crouched down on the sand. "When it comes to these types of multi-item, curse-breaking potions you do not need fancy equipment or specialty brewing supplies. All you need to do is combine the ingredients together in the most logical way and then ignite a bonding spark."

As we watched her silently concentrate on the three objects, I couldn't help but marvel at what we'd done. We had travelled across the realm, and even crossed worlds to secure the items on Emma's list.

After a minute SJ decided how to approach the puzzle. She picked up the quill and ripped off a piece of its feathered tip.

"Something Strong," she recited aloud.

She opened Ashlyn's locket to reveal the small picture of the Lost Princess and her family. "Something Pure."

She placed the feather over the picture and then carefully picked up the stem of the enchanted carnation. "And Something One of a Kind."

SJ plucked off the leaves and laid them over the picture too. Then she closed the locket with the leaves and feathering both clamped inside.

"Now all we need is a bonding spark," she said as she stood up. "Some kind of contained burst of fire. I am all out of explosion potions, so something else will have to do the trick."

"Leave that to me," I said confidently. "Everyone back up."

I slowly approached the newly named Lucky. As I drew closer he opened his golden eyes and lifted his head, watching me. I raised my hand with the intention of calling my magic, but the moment I attempted to harness it, pain pulsed through my body. I grunted and took a step back, lowering my hand.

"You okay?" Jason asked.

"Yeah, fine," I said.

I tried again, but I couldn't generate the golden light around my fingers. The dizziness and pain I felt from trying intensified.

"Maybe you're out?" Blue suggested. "That was your first time purposefully using magic. And you did use a lot. It could need some time to reboot."

She was probably right. I may not have understood the specifics of how my powers worked yet, but I knew I felt exhausted. I guess I didn't have enough strength at the moment, which meant I would not be able to force my will onto Lucky.

Then I glanced over at him and wondered if I needed to.

Dragons couldn't really smile, but it looked like he was. My magic may have brought him to life and gotten him to follow me, but it seemed that the creature genuinely liked me. Maybe I didn't need my powers to get him to listen to me.

I raised my hands—not to activate my magical glow, but to show him I meant no harm. "Hey bud," I said, moving closer. "Can you breathe a little fire onto that necklace for me?" I titled my chin toward the locket in the sand. "Nothing big, just a small puff?"

Lucky and I locked eyes for a beat. I kept my breathing steady. He did the same.

After a beat, he snorted. Then he got up from his cozy spot on the sand and squared off with me. He puffed out his chest and spread his wings to their full extent. They were massive, and their magnitude cast me in shadow.

I remembered how scary it had been to face off against him

in the skies over Century City. I remembered how the fire he'd released when he got angry had almost toasted an entire battalion of the city's soldiers. And I remembered how many times I'd made mistakes on this journey.

I wondered if this was one of them.

I had no idea if bringing Lucky to life was enough to earn long-term obedience without the reinforcement of my powers. If I was wrong there were a million ways he could kill me. I could get smoked by his fire, squashed by his clawed feet, or even suffocated in the armpit of his massive wing.

But I held my ground nonetheless. I may not have been an ace with woodland creatures like SJ, or have had regular training at school for facing off with beasts and monsters like Jason and Daniel, but I knew enough about both to understand that holding my ground was key. If my confidence wavered in the slightest, the dragon would sense my doubt. I could see it in his eyes. There was a fondness and warmth for me there, but there was also the spark of a wild, powerful creature that did not relinquish control easily.

"Come on, boy. What do you say?"

Another beat passed.

Lucky tucked in his wings and inched closer to where the locket rested. His silvery belly turned slightly orange like his innards were heating up. Then he opened his mouth and coughed up a small fireball that roasted the sand around the necklace. I exhaled with relief.

Lucky rotated and extended his neck until his face was beside me. I hesitated—unsure of what he wanted—then carefully pet him on the snout. He huffed with delight and wagged his tail, making my friends duck abruptly to avoid getting body slammed.

"Good boy," I said. "Nice dragon."

I pet him a few more times, which he seemed to like.

Blue tilted her chin toward SJ. "We're keeping him."

The fire dissipated relatively quickly and the sand around the ingredients had transformed into chunks of black glass. At the center of the shards was the locket. It had turned a luminous shade of purple and was glowing brightly.

SJ walked over to the necklace and gingerly touched it with her finger. When she'd confirmed it was not going to burn her, she picked it up and placed it around her neck. "All right," she declared. "I suppose it is time to see if this was all worth it."

SJ moved closer to where the sand melted into the grass of the forest and the Indexlands began. She picked up a small stone and threw it to locate the exact border of the In and Out Spell. Such spells remained invisible to the naked eye unless disturbed by something or someone trying to cross it.

The air flashed pink and purple about three feet in front of her. The stone landed on the ground on the other side of the force field (it was not a living being after all, so it could go through), but the magic of the In and Out Spell still snapped and sparked angrily at its passing.

I remembered the time back at Lady Agnue's when my finger barely grazed our In and Out Spell. The shock it gave me had been substantial but was only a taste of what we would receive if we full on attempted to cross such a spell. The all-powerful energy in this thing was deadly and would electrocute anyone who tried.

SJ turned to us. "If this works, it will change us permanently," she said. "When you break a curse or a spell, that same curse or spell can never affect you again. It is like chickenpox. Once you overcome the virus it does not leave you, but it remains inactive in your system and you become immune to the illness."

Blue frowned in puzzlement.

"What I am saying is that we will not be limited by the barriers of In and Out Spells anymore," SJ explained. "If the necklace works, it will alter our physiology. We will always possess the ability to cross such spells, even without wearing the necklace."

"*All* the In and Out Spells?" Daniel asked in disbelief.

"Those that are of equal or lesser value," SJ elaborated. "So this one, and the spells around Alderon and Lady Agnue's. The spell around all of Book is much more powerful. And we will not be immune to any new ones created either."

"Still, that's pretty awesome," Blue said.

"It is if it works," SJ replied. "And on that note . . ."

SJ stepped toward the boundary of the spell.

"Wait!" I rushed over to her. "Do we all have to wear the necklace when we cross the spell?"

SJ shook her head. "The power of the necklace will project to anyone that the wearer is touching, like a chain reaction."

"Then I'm going with you." I took her hand. "We've come too far together for you to do this by yourself."

"Crisa, if this does not work the spell will kill us both."

"No, it will kill us three," Blue said as she took SJ's other hand.

"Make that four," Jason said as he moved next to Blue and took her hand in his. "Crisa's right. We started this as a team and one way or another that's how we're finishing it."

Daniel came up beside me and took my hand in his. He didn't meet my eyes. "Five," he said.

I sucked in the awkwardness and warmth of his touch as SJ let out a deep breath. "All right. On my mark then. One. Two . . ."

Please let this work. Please let this work.

"Three."

I held my breath as we all took a giant step forward. Energy washed over my face. It felt like silk sheets being pulled across my body and a light rain beating against my skin. My insides vibrated. And then . . .

I opened my eyes and we were on the other side of the In and Out Spell. There was no backlash from the force field—no shock, no surge, nothing. The locket around SJ's neck glowed even more fiercely for a moment and the area of the spell we'd passed through lit up brilliantly, flickering at the disturbance. But the five of us were fine.

Elation surged inside me.

We'd done the impossible! We had broken through the In and Out Spell around the Indexlands! Joy and triumph flooded through my friends and me. We rejoiced—relieved, excited, and amazed. A myriad of high-fives and hugs were exchanged.

"Oh, Crisa," Blue said after a second. "What about Lucky?" She gestured at my dragon, who was still on the other side of the spell. He began to approach the force field curiously.

"Crud. He'll get zapped. SJ—"

"Here." She rapidly removed the locket and tossed it to me.

I placed it around my neck and dashed across the spell. I placed my hand on Lucky's neck just before his nose touched the force field. The locket glowed more brightly again as its powers transferred to him as well.

I let out a sigh of relief. Thank goodness. I just got this dragon. I didn't want him getting barbequed on our first day together. That would qualify me as the worst pet owner ever.

I gave the locket back to SJ and looked toward the depths of the Indexlands that awaited us.

"Well," Jason said, gesturing to the forest. "Onward I guess . . ."

Unlike our previous experiences journeying through forests in Book, this one was relatively safe and uneventful.

It reminded me of walking through the Black Forest in Germany. There were no fire-breathing chipmunks, log monsters, or lightning flowers. There were just trees and deer and other normal stuff like that. Most notably, not once did anyone or anything try to annihilate us. Talk about a change of pace.

The downside, though, was that we were proceeding without a single idea of where to go. We didn't have a clue where the Author lived. All we could do was push past tree after tree in directionless search.

Daniel and I were at the back of the group with Lucky picking up the rear, trying his best to squish through the trees without causing too much damage. The others were pretty far ahead, so I garnered the courage to ask Daniel about something that'd been bothering me since we left Valor. Given all we'd accomplished today, it wasn't a big deal. But it was gnawing at my mind, and he was the only person I could talk to about it.

"Daniel," I said slowly, fiddling with my Hole Tracker.

"Yeah?"

"Back at the palace when we were in Nadia's study with Arian . . . Something happened to me. I just . . . I don't know. It was like I lost control for a minute. All that anger I had kind of took over. I almost used my magic to rip him in half with those curtains."

"Does it matter?" Daniel asked. "You didn't actually do it."

"But part of me felt like I wanted to," I asserted. "And I very well might have if you hadn't intervened."

Daniel stopped and looked me in the eyes. "Knight, relax. You wouldn't have done it."

"How do you know?"

"Because I know you. So seriously, stop worrying about it. You weren't yourself."

"Yeah," I admitted, "but that's what worries me."

"Guys!" Jason called from ahead. "Come check this out!"

Daniel, Lucky, and I picked up our pace and joined the others. Our friends were standing in a large clearing, staring upward.

At the center of the clearing was an epic tree that was so mighty in width and height it would give most buildings a run for their money. What was more intriguing, however, was the beautiful mansion at the top of the tree. It was perched there like a birdhouse, the branches of the tree woven around its exterior to keep it in place.

I didn't know what to say. And I continued to not know what to say a second later when a golden flash of light erupted in front of us.

While I may not have had words for the occasion, the woman who suddenly appeared before us certainly did.

"It's about time," she said.

My eyes widened to the size of saucers.

The woman looked about thirty-five. She had skin the color of brown sugar. Her eyes were dark, but warm, and her fluffy hair curled around her shoulders. She wore a teal zip-up jacket and a pair of loose gray sweatpants.

I was totally against fainting or any other kind of damsel-esque behavior. But if there was ever a time to pass out from shock, it would've been right then and there. This was the woman from my dreams.

"The dragon has to stay down here, I'm afraid," she told us as she stepped closer. "I don't exactly have a front door he can fit through."

Before explaining any further, she closed her eyes and clenched her fists—causing a golden aura to envelop us.

"Wait, hold on a sec," Blue started to say.

But she was cut off. Another flash of light consumed our group. An instant later we found ourselves staring down at the clearing from five hundred feet above. We were standing on the front porch of the tree mansion.

I looked down at Lucky, who seemed upset to have been left behind. He roared when he saw me and I waved to assure him we were all right. "It's okay, boy. We're fine. Just wait there."

He roared again but flopped down for a rest. I turned back to face our hostess. "You're . . ."

"Elizabeth Henley Lenore," the woman said, extending her hand in welcome. "But you kids probably know me as the Author."

CHAPTER 23

Liza

kay, this is weird.

The Author is making us tea and coffee in her tree mansion while the five of us sit in her living room. I'm not sure there's anything I could've done to prepare myself for this moment.

The living room was huge and filled with an assortment of leather couches, knickknacks, paintings, and wildlife. Across from me was a huge aviary. Despite the fact that its door was open, the colorful birds did not fly away. They flitted about happily inside.

Staring at me from the opposite end of the room were three black cats perched on shelves set into alcoves in the wall. Every other section of the mansion's wall space was covered in hundreds of beautiful oil paintings. These were not paintings of fruits or flowers. Aside from a few landscapes, most were of people. I wasn't sure why, but the paintings made me feel a bit uncomfortable.

I saw one where a dashing, dark-haired man with curly locks and mischief in his eyes was arguing with a woman with long black hair. Focusing on her regal features and pale skin, I realized I'd seen her in one of my dreams. She had been surrounded by green glass and had a ball of fire levitating in her hand. Here, though, there was no fire. But the background was a pale shade of green, leading me to believe the settings were the same.

The painting next to it was of a boy. He was about twelve or thirteen and had blond hair. He sat high in a tree and stared out at the ocean. It was night, and the moon's glow cast a mystical light on his fair hair.

Beside that painting was a vivid rendering of a gorge. The colors were rich reds and oranges, but there was a black streak across the sky that looked like a crack had formed in the heavens.

I looked around and continued admiring the works of art. There was a blonde woman in a pink dress wearing a golden tiara; a ballroom full of girls in gorgeous red gowns; a curly haired brunette lying face down in the snow surrounded by men in black uniform; and . . .

Natalie Poole.

I stood from the couch, drawn to the painting like a ghost, my boots pressing delicately into the periwinkle carpet.

Natalie's image was life-size, and she looked about eighteen. She was holding hands with Ryan Jackson—a sunset creating a glare of light between them. There was love there that was undeniable.

I could tell by the style of artwork that the same artist who'd painted this had drawn the sketch of Natalie in the file from Fairy Godmother Headquarters and Arian's bunker.

"Who are they?" Jason asked as my friends came to stand beside me.

"Natalie Poole and Ryan Jackson."

"The girl you've been dreaming about and the guy she's supposed to fall in with?" Jason clarified.

"Yeah." I nodded. "I—"

I stopped.

In an adjacent hallway, I saw another painting. A painting of me.

My friends and I moved wordlessly toward the hall. It was lined with as many paintings as the living room. This first one was of me in the Capitol Building, gazing up at the blue sapphire chandelier I'd discovered there. The paint representation of me stared up at the enchanting light fixture with as much awe as real me stared at her image now.

The next painting showed Blue and I in the banquet hall of Lady Agnue's. We were eating waffles and talking about something excitedly. My hair was much shorter, about shoulder-length.

Following that came a painting of Daniel and I in a forest. We were fighting a dozen men whose earthy garb led me to believe they were magic hunters.

The five of us turned the corner and my heart almost stopped. We had entered a huge studio. There were tables full of paints and watercolors and pastel chalk. Half-finished paintings stood on easels throughout the space while blank canvases were stacked in the corner like mountains.

The shocking part, however, was that adorning the studio's three-hundred-foot walls were a good number of renderings featuring me as the subject.

The moment we'd rounded the corner I'd seen my face looking down on me. It was a familiar scene—me falling through the sky in armor, terror in my eyes, Pegasi darting about in the background. It looked like the day Blue and I had gone undercover and entered the boys-only Twenty-Three Skidd tournament in Adelaide—the day I'd gotten my prologue prophecy.

I recognized other familiar scenes. Daniel and me furniture-surfing through lava tidal waves in the Cave of Mysteries; Lenore and me arguing in her office; Jason and Blue sitting in a crimson booth on the magic train, lecturing me. The list went on.

Only about half these paintings contained familiar scenes, though. The others were of experiences we'd yet to live.

I stared at a watercolor of me standing in a small boat with Daniel. The vessel was simple wood and was surrounded on all sides by foreboding mist.

The clinking of dishes made us all spin around.

"Let's adjourn back in the living room, shall we?" the Author said, nodding back the way we'd come. Her hands held a tray of steaming cups. "There's not really a lot of sitting room in here."

We began to follow the mysterious woman. I noticed Daniel pause. His eyes were locked on an unfinished piece of art. When I approached the easel I recognized both girls in the rendering. The first was Kai. Her face had been imprinted in my mind since Daniel had shown me her picture in his pocket watch.

The other girl in the picture was me.

We weren't doing anything of interest—just standing there facing each other. But there was some sort of haze in the background that looked like weird clouds with faces. The image caused me to shiver.

"Guys?" Blue called from the hall.

We turned to follow her. Daniel flicked his eyes to me as we walked. "Not a word," he murmured.

My friends and I sat down on the same couches and chairs as before.

"You're surprised, aren't you?" the Author said as she joined us, placing herself on a leather armchair.

"Um . . ." Blue bit her lip. "That's one word for it."

"Confused would be another," Jason added.

"Ooh, I'm changing my answer," Blue declared. "I'm going with confused too."

"I think we'll all go with confused," I responded on behalf of the group, half-joking but also with seriousness in my tone.

"I don't blame you," the Author said. "I imagine they don't tell you much about me out there, do they?"

"Beyond the whole 'she chooses protagonists, writes their futures, and then ships their stories off to the rest of the realm' thing—no, they don't," Daniel said.

The Author sighed. "That sounds about right. None of it's true, I grant you, but it is more or less what I expected."

Our mouths dropped open.

"Sorry . . . What do you mean, none of it's true?" Jason asked.

"My sister is going to want to kill me for telling you all this," the Author mused. "But she is the one who put me in this position, so the fault lies with her. Plus, I am not on board with her agenda. And since she won't listen to me, speaking with you kids might be my only hope of influencing what's to come."

"Again, not following," Blue said. "Starting with the whole 'my sister' thing."

"Yes, well, as I said, my name is Elizabeth Lenore—Liza if you like. My 'Author' title is an invention of my sister, *Lena* Lenore."

I practically choked on the biscuit I'd bitten into.

"Yes, uh, lovely woman," I said clearing my throat as I tried to recover from the awkwardness.

"You've met her?" Liza asked.

"Yes."

"Then we both know you're lying."

I couldn't help but smirk a bit. "I take it yours is not an amicable sibling relationship?"

"Considering that she locked me in this forest over a century ago, I am going to say no," Liza replied.

"Wait, wait, wait," Blue interrupted again. "You keep saying all these things that don't make any sense, Miss Author . . ."

"Liza."

"Okay, *Liza*. What in the name of Book are you talking about?"

Our hostess sighed. "Since it seems that all anyone out there knows about me is those books and that 'Author' title, how about I answer your questions by telling you a story. Does that sound good?"

We all nodded.

"Fantastic," Liza said. She leaned back in her chair and crossed her legs. She looked relaxed but there was eagerness in her tone that suggested she'd been dying to tell this story for a long time.

"Our tale begins many years ago with two sisters reporting for their first day of training at the Fairy Godmother Academy. They are your average, fresh-faced recruits—spirited and youthful with anxiety aflutter in their stomachs. The future looks bright as they enter the magic transfer chamber. It is there that they are imbued with the powers of retired Fairy Godmothers, and receive the corresponding wands. But alas, that is where the world alters for the younger sister in a way that can never be reversed.

"At first everything seems fine. But as the weeks go by and training progresses, the younger sister begins to experience strange dreams. Most are fuzzy at first, and she writes them off as nothing. However, as her magic training intensifies, so do her dreams. And stranger still, she soon begins having dreams about people she knows. Not people she knows directly, but visions of people whose faces she's seen in files at Fairy Godmother Headquarters. Visions of Fairy Godkids from all across the realm."

I shifted in my seat.

"The younger sister keeps quiet—not wanting to admit the strangeness of the phenomenon or burden her older sister, who has received a big promotion within the Fairy Godmother Agency. However, as the years go by the younger sister begins to realize that the strange dreams are not just nocturnal imaginings; they are visions of the future. She validates this time and again by finding the Fairy Godkids whom the visions are about and keeping an eye on them."

I gulped and realized that my hands were gripping the armrests of the chair I was sitting in. I had only recently gone through the same discovery that my dreams were visions of the future. I tried not to let this similarity unsettle me as Liza continued.

"Fascinated by her new ability," our hostess went on, "the younger sister finally decides to try and make more sense of it. She begins writing down her dreams in journals like stories. And when she has multiple visions of the same people, she develops outlines for these stories like plot points so as to better keep track of them. The problem is that she is not quite sure in what order the events in her visions are going to take place.

"However, after some reflection, she ascertains something crucial—the times when her dreams are the strongest and most detailed correlate with the amount of training and wish granting she performs in her daily Godmother duties. In other words, the more magic she uses, the more dreams she has and the clearer they become. In some cases, if she uses enough power in a short period of time she can even navigate her way through her dreams while she sleeps."

The blood left my hands completely. They were white from clutching the armrests so hard.

I thought back to recent months when I'd slept without dreams of the future. The dreams had vanished completely during my two weeks trapped in the Therewolf prison in the Forbidden Forest. I'd had no dreams for a majority of our stay at Adelaide Castle during our class field trip earlier in the semester. And before that I'd experienced a customary spell of dreamlessness in the summer before returning to Lady Agnue's.

Now I understood why.

Ashlyn had explained that Magic Build-Up occurred when I went too long without using my powers. Since I didn't experience Magic Build-Up all the time, we figured that my wand was what was keeping me in check.

Despite being enchanted to turn into whatever weapon I willed it into, wands only responded to the magic touch of a specific Fairy Godmother (which I had courtesy of Emma). So, although it was an extremely small amount, every time I used my wand I used a tiny bit of magic.

Therein lay the answer.

I hadn't gotten a chance to use my wand much during our stay in Adelaide, it was hard to get practice in over the summer under the watchful eyes of my parents, and my wand had been confiscated during our Therewolf incarceration. At the close of all those episodes, I experienced Magic Build-Up.

Complete understanding washed over me.

No wand = No magic usage.

No magic usage = No dreams and inevitable Magic Build-Up.

Magic Build-Up = Dreams return with a vengeance.

Based on this revelation I also knew why my dreams had been getting so much clearer lately. With all the antagonist attacks we'd been dealing with, I'd been using my wand more frequently. And more magic led to increased vision strength and clarity.

"It is an amazing discovery—"

My attention snapped back to Liza as she kept telling her story.

"—and over the next few years the younger sister pushes her magic more and more—intensifying her training in an effort to fortify her foresight. As the power of her magic rises, so does the power of her dreams and her ability to make sense of them. Eventually she succeeds in learning how to completely navigate through her visions, ascertain where they fit in with real timelines, and channel them deeply enough to draw specific details—names, locations, dates, and so on. And then . . . one night the younger sister experiences something new. She does not dream of people or places; she dreams of words. They appear in her head in the form of cryptic, rhyming lines detailing fates for people in the realm. They are prophecies."

My friends and I exchanged a glance.

"With this additional power the younger sister concludes the information she is gathering has grown too vast to be kept within simple journals and logbooks. She starts charting out the lives of her dream subjects across her walls and ceilings—turning her entire apartment at Fairy Godmother Headquarters into a giant map of the events she's foreseen in her head."

Liza reached over to a small table beside her seat. It had a remote with two buttons on it. She pressed a button and the room rumbled. A second set of overlapping walls descended from the ceiling. These new walls appeared to be giant whiteboards. They were covered with timelines and scribbles of names, dates, places, and other labels in different colors.

Once the walls settled, the room stopped shaking and a table holding a basket of whiteboard markers emerged from the floor. Liza rose to her feet. Behind her, I spotted a timeline in red labeled: Chance Darling.

A lot of Liza's writing was too messy to make sense of, but I did pick up a few keywords written around Chance's timeline: "Magic Hunters," "Daphne & Cereus," "Twenty-Three Skidd Arena," "James," "Wonderland," and "Crisanta Knight."

My name was written at the beginning of the timeline, again in the middle, and toward the end. Looking at it made me gulp.

Liza didn't address this, though. She seemed to have picked a spot on the whiteboard at random to illustrate her point, gesturing at it widely.

"With her dreams growing so powerful and plentiful, the younger sister has to know more; she has to figure out what's meant to happen to these people. But that, unfortunately, is her downfall. One night the older sister—the great and powerful Lena Lenore—has terrific news. The Agency's current Godmother Supreme is retiring and after many years of arduous, committed service, the older sister has been selected to fill the boss's shoes. Unable to contain her excitement, the older sister bursts into the younger sister's apartment and sees everything."

Liza glanced at the whiteboard behind her. For the first time since she began her story I saw sadness and regret in her expression. She looked at her own writing and seemed to forget we were there for a moment. Eventually she sighed and sat down on the armrest of her chair.

"Lena listens to the explanations of her younger sister and is dismayed. And then she tells the younger sister why."

Liza shot me a quick glance. It was fast and subtle, but I didn't miss the guilt in it.

"There is secret sickness in Book that only people in higher-up positions like the Godmothers, ambassadors, and kingdom rulers know about. It is a rare mutation—a disorder of the mind and body called Pure Magic Disease. And for those afflicted, the normal rules of magic do not apply.

"As the younger sister already knows, magic in our realm is easily removed and transferred between people and objects. What she doesn't know is that in unique cases magic can bond with a person differently. Instead of it being something that the holder carries and can shed like a coat, it fuses to them and weaves into their DNA. When this happens, two things result. The magic will manifest in the form of a single, incredibly potent ability that does not need a wand to work. And the magic will slowly but surely corrupt the person hosting it.

"The power of Pure Magic is too strong for humans to keep in check for very long, you see. As time goes by it amplifies the host's anger, aggression, and malice. In turn, no matter how strong the initial will or purity of the host, the power eventually drives them to darkness.

"The younger sister learns that this illness is responsible for creating many of our realm's witches and warlocks. It is another hidden truth that the higher-ups in Book have tried to keep in the shadows. Many of these evil, powerful people locked up in Alderon were once Fairy Godmothers and Fairy Godfathers. They contracted Pure Magic Disease when they were imbued with their powers and their hearts and minds turned dark as a result of the affliction."

Liza slid fully back into her chair. "At that point, the younger sister wonders why her older sister is telling her this. And then the older sister reveals that the strongest sign of Pure Magic Disease is the ability to see the future through dreams. Somehow, the nature of Pure Magic allows those carrying it to connect to other powerful fields of magic."

I felt the eyes of my friends fall on me, but I couldn't meet their collective gaze.

"The strongest, most complex type of magic in Book is the grand In and Out Spell covering the entire realm," Liza continued. "Sufferers of Pure Magic Disease are able to bond with it and see all that it sees—every significant event that will ever come to pass beneath it.

"Terrified, the younger sister allows herself to be taken to the magic transfer chamber with the hope that maybe her gift of foresight is just a fluke. Maybe her magic can be removed and she does not have the sickness. But her hope is in vain. When the Stiltdegarth—the standard creature used for magic removal—is attached to the younger sister, it fails to drain her magic completely. It sucks out the set of Fairy Godmother powers she'd been officially imbued with years earlier, but it cannot extract the magic from her body entirely. And when the process is over and the Stiltdegarth has burned out, the younger sister is still left with a single power, which is fused to her blood like the older sister dreaded. It is confirmed. The young sister has Pure Magic Disease."

It felt like I'd been struck by lightning. The familiarity of my own situation with everything Liza had described made me want to throw up. But her story was not over. I remained still as a statue as she continued her tale.

"The higher-ups in the Godmother Agency think that it is only a matter of time before the younger sister succumbs to the disease and will need to be banished to Alderon like the others who've come before her. But the older sister insists that they don't exile her until the darkness has effectively taken over and permanently changed her. The realm's higher-ups agree to wait. Unfortunately for them, the wait proves much longer than anticipated.

"Weeks, months, and years go by without the younger sister turning—causing the higher-ups to become anxious. The girl should have succumbed to the disease's dark side effects, but she remains herself. In fact, the only thing that has changed is her tolerance for being kept in Fairy Godmother Headquarters like a prisoner under house arrest. Which is why, having discovered that her Pure Magic manifested in the power of teleportation, the younger sister tries to escape again and again. Alas, her attempts always end in vain. No matter how fast or far she can travel . . ."

Liza suddenly raised her hands. They flashed gold like her eyes and she was enveloped in the same aura of light that she'd first appeared in. When the flash vanished, so did she. Then another flash occurred on the opposite side of the room and she materialized again. Liza repeated the trick three more times—disappearing and reappearing in different parts of the room to make her point.

When she teleported back into her chair I saw a slight look of satisfaction in her eyes. She was proud of what she could do. Despite the seriousness of her story, I could see she enjoyed showing off her magic.

I kind of understood. I had never felt as powerful as when I'd unleashed the full force of my magic in Nadia's palace. It felt good to be able to do something extraordinary.

"Anyways," Liza said, as she pushed a curl of hair out of her face. "Despite her ability to teleport, the younger sister can never elude her older sister's team of Special Forces Fairy Godmothers for long. She is always inevitably caught.

"The realm's leaders reason that something has to be done about this. The afflicted girl—" Liza pointed her thumbs at herself, "has to be controlled in some way. But how? Cue the big idea . . ."

Liza got up from her seat again and picked a purple whiteboard marker out of the basket. She strode over to an area of whiteboard with some space on it and wrote in capital letters:

THE AUTHOR.

"In the two years since finding out about the younger sister's powers," Liza said, facing us, "the Godmothers have been able to secure an unprecedented number of happily ever afters for citizens across the realm—using the girl's visions to anticipate, prepare, and steer important people toward their designated fates.

"The spike in performance is also due to the fact that the Godmothers no longer look after everyone. Since the younger sister's visions are connected to the In and Out Spell around the realm, the Godmothers now only consider the people she dreams about—and royal children, of course, given their future leadership roles—to be valuable.

"This system makes the Godmothers' lives much easier. Fewer Godkids equals better results. It is a quality over quantity adjustment. Before, the Godmothers used to spend their lives running around trying to create happily ever afters everywhere—never knowing which people they invested in were worth the time, effort, and magic. But no longer.

"Given this, the older sister, who is now Godmother Supreme, proposes the following notion: why not make writing the future stories the younger sister's full-time work? This would streamline the realm's regulatory systems permanently. Going forward, the Godmothers could officially only focus on looking after those people in the realm whom the younger sister foresees as important.

"Brilliant. Inspired. Revolutionary. At least that's what all the higher-ups think of the idea. The only problem with the plan is the younger sister herself. She must be hidden and the details of her identity kept a secret. Otherwise people might try to seek her out and influence what has or has not been written about them."

Liza crossed her arms. "The younger sister obviously refuses to agree to being locked away forever. And she thinks her powers of teleportation would counteract any normal type of enchantment used to secure her.

"So the Godmother Supreme comes up with a plan. If no

normal type of enchantment can keep the younger sister safe from herself or others, what about something even more potent that has proven successful at preventing even Pure Magic witches from crossing borders for generations? An In and Out Spell.

"What if they simply block off a portion of the realm and isolate the younger sister? She would not be able to teleport through it, and since the enchantment is not designed to keep *objects* from crossing its lines, she can still teleport her future stories to the outside world for the Godmothers and the rest of the realm to use.

"All of the higher-ups agree to the plan, and in the blink of an eye it is enacted. Everything changes. The younger sister is locked away to serve as an alienated, eternal soothsayer. A new In and Out Spell goes up. And with a few perception filter enchantments, a lot of memory-wipe magic, and an influx of purposefully generated urban legend, Book's modern way of life is born. The people the younger sister dreams about are 'chosen' as protagonists and everyone else is deemed common.

"Behind the scenes a Fairy Godmother is assigned to each protagonist at some point. But these days the Godmothers just get the name of a protagonist, not the details of the visions like they did in the beginning. The Godmother Supreme worried that if the Godmothers of today knew about the way her younger sister's visions worked then they would learn the truth. And the more people who knew about the younger sister, the greater chance there'd be of that truth spreading to the rest of the realm."

Liza capped her marker. "Well, that's everything. The end, as it were," she said as she sat back down. Then she bit her lip.

"Oh wait—just to add a little epilogue to this tale—a few years after this prison sentence begins, both sisters are enchanted with powerful anti-aging spells so the younger sister can continue her work for all eternity while the Godmother Supreme keeps an eye on her and keeps her in line. As an extra bonus the younger sister's anti-aging spell is also tied to the In and Out Spell around the Indexlands. The very force field designed to keep her prisoner is what keeps her alive, thus providing extra incentive to not go looking for a way out."

Liza exhaled deeply and stretched, clearly wiped from such a long narrative. "Well, that's the story," she sighed, "of how my dreams became 'Protagonist Books,' I became 'The Author,' and everyone in the realm came to live in a world where they are kept in the dark about the true origins of both. I'm sure you have questions."

The room fell silent. There were so many questions swirling around my head it was hard to decide where to start. It was like being under attack by a cyclone of crows and having to defend yourself with a bow and arrow—how do you know which bird to take a shot at first?

"But . . . the Author and her books have been around forever," SJ thought aloud. "No one remembers a time before them. I know you mentioned that the Godmothers utilized perception filters and memory-wipe magic to create your myth, but what does that mean in terms of your age? How long have you been here?"

Liza shrugged. "About a century and a half."

We all went bug-eyed.

"It's not as bad as it sounds," Liza replied somewhat wistfully.

"*It sounds like a century and a half,*" Blue repeated. "If you've been trapped here all this time, how are you not, like, lonely-hermit crazy? You seem perfectly fine."

"I wouldn't describe my situation as 'fine,'" Liza said, a look of irritation crossing her face. She took a deep breath and re-centered. "I have simply made peace with it. I was defiant and angry for the first decade. Then that turned into depression over the second and third decades. But that's the thing about realizing you're going to live forever; you eventually get that you might as well live to the best of your ability. So I do my work for the realm—keeping busy figuring out dreams, putting together timelines, and slowly but surely piecing together the stories for each of my protagonist books. Then in my downtime I entertain myself. I love to paint; I've mastered twelve different instruments; I'm excellent at crafting; I can speak sixteen languages, knit, sew, cook, bake, build weapons out of just about anything I find in the forest, and thanks to so much working out I am probably in better physical shape than many heroes at Lord Channing's." She shot a glance at Jason. "What can you bench, like 205?"

Jason stuttered, caught off guard. Liza waved her hand dismissively before he could answer and turned back to Blue.

"And to answer your question about why I'm not 'lonely-hermit crazy,' Lena keeps in contact with me and I get some regular visitors. My sister has a team of extremely loyal Godmothers in her agency who are aware of my situation. They are the ones who helped Lena cast the In and Out Spell around my land in the first place, so they are actually the only ones who can pass through it. Well, until the five of you anyways. Those Godmothers are also under the same anti-aging spell as Lena, so they can dedicate themselves to the cause eternally."

"Are those the Scribes?" Jason asked.

"Good guess, but no," Liza replied. "Lena doesn't like to trust any one person with too much power, so she keeps her loyal followers in separate categories. The realm ambassadors that once knew about my situation are long dead. The ones today don't know the truth. And since they work directly with the Scribes on the protagonist book selection process, Lena has chosen to keep the Scribes in the dark about me as well. For all they know, I'm just a mysterious prophet who controls our realm.

"The five Godmothers that Lena has trusted with my secret are normal Godmothers. They pay me visits to deliver food and fresh supplies because, while I can teleport myself and teleport objects to other places, I can't teleport anything to me. I guess I'm glad for this flaw. The regular deliveries allow me a little human contact. Talking with those Godmothers—well, three Godmothers and two Godfathers—is a way to catch up on news of the outside world. It also keeps me grounded and not crazy." Liza shook her head, as if reflecting on her century-old relationships. "I've grown fond of a couple of them, but the others are just tolerable. Though I suppose I can't be too picky about the company I keep considering the five of you are the only other people I've seen since being put in here."

"Why the Forbidden Forest?" Daniel asked abruptly. "You said you can teleport objects out of here. Why do you send your protagonist books there?"

"My prison's In and Out Spell is so strong that—powerful as I am—I even have trouble teleporting objects through. That's why I can't just randomly send out a note for help. I can only teleport things to where there is an *extremely* high concentration of magic, like the Forbidden Forest. In addition to the magical creatures there, the Forbidden Forest has a lot of magical surges due to the holes leading to the Wonderlands." Liza paused. She turned to me. "You've met Harry the White Rabbit, right? I had a dream about the two of you that should've already come to pass. Did he tell you about the holes in the spell?"

I nodded.

"Right, well, since my Pure Magic allows me to connect with other forms of magic, those holes act like lightning rods for me to hone in on. So that's where it is easiest for me to send the books, and where it's easiest to send random stuff to keep my magic sharp. Like I said, the strength and clarity of my dreams is tied to how much magic I output. Teleporting stuff out of here takes a lot more power, so I do that when I feel like giving my visions an extra boost."

I thought about the field where I'd discovered the Scribes' protagonist book library in the Forbidden Forest. It had been littered with random junk—quills, baskets, artwork, candles. Now I knew why.

"I won't be sending anything else to the Forbidden Forest though," Liza said. "I recently sensed a disturbance in the magic field there. Afterwards, Lena ordered me to start teleporting my books to another place where Wonderland holes constantly appear, the Dolohaunty Mountains. I'm not supposed to use the Forbidden Forest as my drop zone anymore."

"Oh, uh, sorry," I said, rubbing my arm sheepishly. "I think that reason was me. I sort of found the Scribes' protagonist book library."

"Really? Well done!"

"Um, thank you?"

"Hey, Liza," Jason interjected. "What about our prologue pangs? The seizure pains that supposedly correspond with the intensity of our fates, and those spiral marks we receive right after we get our prophecies. If you're stuck in here, how does that work?"

"Those aren't my doing," Liza replied. "The spiral marks were my sister's idea. She felt they added a little drama to the situation and made the Author seem intimidating and powerful. That's why the marks don't appear at the exact same time as the pangs. There is a slight, few minute delay. The pangs occur when I have visions of your prophecies. I write them down and immediately tell Lena. Then she uses her magic to make the marks appear. That spiral mark is the same insignia that she and her followers— the Scribes, the other elite Godmothers, and the ambassadors— use to notate their allegiance to the same beliefs about upholding order and control."

I nodded again. I had seen the spiral mark in the Capitol Building library, the Scribes' protagonist book library, and on Lenore's ring. I'd already realized the same thing.

"And the pangs?" Daniel asked curiously.

"That I can't completely explain," Liza replied. "My best guess is that those pangs you protagonists experience when I receive your prophecies have something to do with the intrusiveness of the phenomenon. Maybe using my magic to glimpse into your futures so invasively causes you to physically react to it. I don't know. Lena may not like things she can't control, but as the pangs only add reverence to the mystique of the Author, she just kind of goes with it."

"Hold on," Blue raised her hands. "Hold on. Hold on. Hold on."

"Blue, what is it?" Jason asked.

"I'm sorry," she said, turning to Liza. "I know there's a lot of other stuff you told us that we should be freaking out about. But there's one thing I can't get over. How could your sister imprison you here? I have a sister, and while our relationship may not have as dark a history as yours, there is a lot of contention between us. But I would never do anything like that to her. How could Lenore leave you trapped *forever*?"

"Simple," Liza said. "I'm an outlier—I'm different. Every part of Book relies on classifying people into groups. It's the way the higher-ups like it—the Godmothers, the twenty-six ambassadors, the protagonist schools they built to further my legend—and it's the way my sister likes it too. They think it keeps the realm from falling into chaos like so many of the other worlds. Which is a fine theory until someone doesn't fit into any of their categories. Then you are a threat—an anomaly that they don't know how to classify or control. And when that happens . . . well, you end up like me."

Liza sighed again. "It's not ideal, but at least it's better than turning into a psychotic, bloodthirsty witch. While I may be trapped in the Indexlands forever, I am still grateful for my fate. I've been able to do the impossible and remain myself all these years despite my sickness, and that is an unparalleled blessing. In the past, victims of Pure Magic Disease always turn. There is no cure or antidote. At the end of the day there is just one truth—Pure Magic corrupts and destroys anyone who carries it."

I met Liza's gaze. Her face was tinged with sadness. But from the way she looked at me, I could tell the sentiment was not a reflection of her fate this time, but my own.

"You mean like how it's going to destroy me," I said bluntly.

I'd been silent on the matter this whole time, allowing Liza to continue talking while I absorbed one truth after the next. But now the understanding burned inside me with too much heat to keep in. It flowed out of me with the same power as a Magic Build-Up episode—intense and mercilessly painful.

"What?" I said, addressing the dismay in my friends' expressions. "You were all thinking it. I saw your faces when she was talking about her dreams of the future. Why not face facts? I have Pure Magic Disease."

"We cannot be certain of that," SJ tried to assure me. "There could be many explanations for your dreams. Moreover, you may have one very strong magical power, but that does not mean that it is fused to you and cannot be removed."

"But that's just it," I pressed, rising from my chair as desperation rose inside me. "When Daniel and I were at Fairy Godmother Headquarters, Lenore tried to take my magic away. She put one of those Stiltdegarth things on my head and the freaky creature took its best shot at sucking me dry, but in the end it couldn't do it. After it died trying, Lenore asked me if I'd been having any strange dreams. I lied of course, but don't you see? She must've realized that I have the disease and was trying to verify it."

"She's right," Liza told the others solemnly. "I foresaw the signs a while back. Though I didn't tell my sister, I've had enough dreams to confirm it. Crisa has Pure Magic. It's been dormant for a while because she's only ever used her magic unknowingly when operating that wand of hers. But once she's learned about her power—which I suspect she has, based on my visions—and starts to utilize it for real, there is no going back."

I sunk back in my chair—the weight of the revelation heavy on my shoulders like fat vultures.

"So what happens now?" I asked bleakly. "How long do I have before I . . . *change*?"

"I'm sorry, Crisa," Liza said, seeming like she genuinely meant it. "But I don't know how or when the Pure Magic's corruption will start to affect you. It affects everyone differently, and could take anything from days to years to fully develop. But if it offers any solace at all, I think there's a chance you might be able to beat it."

I lifted my head in avid attention. A flare of hope streaked through me like an electric shock. "What do you mean?"

"As the first person who was able to fight against Pure Magic Disease and keep it from taking me over, I've shown that it can be done," Liza explained. "Furthermore, your prologue prophecy seems to suggest that you could go either way."

"My prologue prophecy?" I repeated, as if in a daze.

It was the whole reason I'd begun this quest. But after everything my friends and I had been through, and all that I'd just learned from Liza, the matter seemed so small. Still, I knew it was anything but. It was why Arian had been hunting me all this time. It was why Nadia had taken such an interest in me.

"What it boils down to is this, Crisa," Liza continued. "By next year's end your new friend Nadia is going to launch a full scale invasion of the realm. I have foreseen it. I do not have many of the details, but I know that she will have all her dominos lined up by then to succeed. And she *will* succeed, Crisa, unless you stop her. That's what the prophecy I had about you foretold. When all is said and done, you will either play the key role in helping Nadia achieve her mission, or you will be what ultimately stops her from doing so. I believe this eventuality is linked to whether or not your Pure Magic turns you dark. So you see—silver lining. Based on your prophecy, I would say there's a fifty-fifty chance you won't be corrupted."

I closed my eyes and let out a deep breath. It was a small hope, but it was hope nonetheless. It flickered meekly inside my chest.

On the day I'd received my prologue prophecy and decided to find the Author to change it—all I'd had was a small hope too. And that hope had been rooted solely in the belief that I could do it. I wanted to believe in myself the same way now, but it was difficult.

"Do you think she can do it?" SJ asked Liza after a pause. "Do you think she can fight the Pure Magic Disease?"

"I'm afraid I don't know," Liza admitted. "I can see pieces of the future, but I can't read minds or hearts. That is the great fiction about what I am and what I write. The Godmothers and ambassadors have made it so that everyone assumes my visions and prophecies influence the will of others, but the truth is quite the opposite. All people affect their own fates; they choose who they want to be. What I see is nothing more than a reflection of that—reactions to their actions, if you will."

Liza stood up.

"On that note, I think two things are in order. One, we better divvy up so that I might speak with you all privately. I've seen enough of most of your futures to know why each of you has really come here."

"And two?" Blue asked.

Liza crossed her arms. "Before that, I need to explain to you the concept of Inherent Fate. I have a feeling it's going to change everything for you."

CHAPTER 24

Enough Exposition to Last a Lifetime

s dusk fell over the Indexlands, Liza altered our perspectives on the world and the control we had over our fates.

We'd always believed that the stories the Author wrote influenced our choices, but on this day we learned the truth—it was actually the other way around. Our choices were always our own; the visions Liza wrote in our books were just glimpses of the choices we were eventually going to make. Despite what our schools, the Godmothers, and everyone else had always insisted, she wasn't *creating* our futures. This whole time her job had been cataloguing them. Telling us otherwise was simply a way for the realm's leaders to control us and convince us that we couldn't be anything more than what they wanted.

As for our prologue prophecies, while they vaguely summarized our fates, they were vague for a reason. All of Liza's prophecies were completely accurate and destined to come true unless we unexpectedly died due to third party intervention—like Arian trying to kill me before my prophecy became reality. However, the prophecies' lines were riddled with double meanings and shrouded with possibilities for eventual outcomes. This was because of a concept she referred to as "Inherent Fate."

After so many years of observing people and their paths, Liza and the Godmothers came to understand that each individual has a number of destinies he or she can achieve. These outcomes may be very different in nature, but they are all based on that person's unique inherent character—his or her heart, mind, personality, and beliefs. What determines which fate a person ends up with is their choices.

Liza used my own mother's fairytale as an example. Cinderella was strong hearted but also a timid soul conditioned for obedience. The night of my princely father's ball she had two choices: not go to the ball or go to the ball. She chose the latter. When her wicked stepmother tried to stop her, she could have given up or kept fighting. Again she chose the latter. When the clock struck midnight she could have left like her Godmother advised or chosen to stay at the ball in spite of it. She chose the former. When she lost her glass slipper on the stairs of the palace she could've dashed back to get it or kept running. Obviously, she chose the latter.

If any one of these choices had been different her fairytale would've resulted in a different fate and her life would've had a different outcome. Maybe not a bad one, but a dissimilar one nonetheless. She could've stayed under the thumb of her wicked stepmother forever. She could've eventually moved out of the horrible woman's house and forged a fresh start somewhere else—maybe even in another kingdom—and pursued some sort of career (she mentioned to me once that she had dreams of being an ice dancer when she was younger). She could've even met and married someone else.

The point Liza was trying to make was that fate can only take us so far. The rest is up to us. We decide the specifics of our own destinies by following what our hearts and minds prompt us to do when we're faced with choices.

Hence the vagueness in Liza's prologue prophecies. Because our choices could lead to different Inherent Fates, our prophecies could be interpreted in multiple ways. They might not be what we expected at all. The futures we'd been "assigned" were far more changeable than we realized.

Take my friends for example. Until now they'd been focusing on single interpretations of their prologue prophecies. If they read more deeply into the cryptic lines—as Liza suggested—they would see that their fates had many other possibilities that their choices might lead them to.

In other words, our destinies might be written, but the Inherent Fates we ended up with were up to us.

This wasn't the most assuring idea and definitely hadn't been what we'd been expecting, but it did inspire hope that there was another way. After all, if our Inherent Fates mirrored our choices, I had faith that we would choose the right ones.

My head reeled from the revelation. Lo and behold, we'd been the masters of our destinies the entire time. We just hadn't known it because we'd always been told we had no control over our lives.

I didn't know if I should be more happy or ticked off by this twist. The notion was churning in my mind as I tried to process everything. I felt like an unsettled ocean trying to regain calm after a storm.

As I waited for my turn with Liza, I imagined the discovery was also messing with my friends' brains. I was sure they were all full of questions about their specific prologue prophecies. Well, all except SJ since she hadn't gotten her prologue prophecy yet. But Blue, Daniel, and Jason definitely would be.

Of my friends, Jason's was the only prologue prophecy I'd never known anything about. I knew he wanted to change it; he'd come on this quest with us after all. But I'd never pried for details. I wondered if he would share some now that the pressure of singular outcomes with our prophecies was off the table.

Before she left to speak to each of us individually, we had given Liza a recap of the various adventures that led us here and the various characters—Arian, Ashlyn, Nadia, etc.—we'd run into along the way. Since she'd bestowed so much information on us, it was the least we could do to offer her the same in return.

As it turned out, she already knew a lot of it. Like me, she could see the future in her dreams, but after a century and a half of practice her powers were like a million times stronger. She probably had an incredible amount of control over navigating her dreamscape and must've witnessed an obscene number of images every night. My visions had only become more vivid in the last few weeks and I already felt overwhelmed. I couldn't imagine seeing so much over so many years like she had. It was a wonder her brain hadn't cracked in half.

Liza explained that she had timelines and paintings and storyboards cataloguing what she saw for all her protagonists. Contrary to what we'd always believed, our prologue prophecies were not the first things that Liza glimpsed of our futures. Her visions didn't appear in chronological order, which is why she needed such elaborate means to keep track of them. When she received her very first vision about a person she let the Scribes know. That's when the Scribes told us we had a book, designating us as protagonists. But it wasn't until Liza received the corresponding prologue prophecy that she would pen it down in an actual book, which she would then send to the Scribes to share with the schools and the protagonist. From there as her visions came and went, Liza filled in the blanks.

In order to keep up with so many characters and story lines, Liza had seven tree mansions across her forest prison. Each was huge, multi-leveled, and contained full living quarters so that she could vary her routine as she worked.

My friends and I wandered about the original tree mansion she'd brought us to while she took each of us to another location to discuss our private matters. I was in the grand art studio by myself when Liza appeared in a flash.

I'd been staring at a rough sketch on one of Liza's easels. The drawing was half-finished, but it featured Chance Darling. He was riding on the back of a dragon, which looked like Lucky, with me sitting behind him.

"You ready?" Liza asked.

With another flash Liza released the golden aura of her magic and teleported us away. When the light receded, I was standing in a library.

The library was much more welcoming than the one that belonged to the Scribes in the Forbidden Forest. The walls were warmly colored, the floors were blonde wood, and twinkling lights illuminated everything.

When the weird aftershock of teleportation subsided, I noticed that the shelf on my right held an electric red book that I'd seen before. The name "Natalie Poole" was engraved on the spine. I picked it up and looked at it as if it were made of gold.

"I saw this book in a section of the Scribes' protagonist book library marked 'Other Realms,'" I told Liza. "I guess this means you've dreamed about her too?"

Liza sighed. "Natalie Poole. 'A girl of good but fragile of fate.'"

I frowned in confusion.

"It's a line from the prophecy that came to me about her," Liza explained. "She is very special."

"She's in trouble is what she is," I asserted. "Or at least she's going to be. You know how we told you about that bunker we found beneath the Capitol Building—the one where Arian and his men were keeping track of protagonists they need to eliminate? She had a file there. Just like she had a file at Fairy Godmother Headquarters. Nadia has Natalie at the top of her hit list, so Arian and this girl named Tara are trying to destroy her."

"It seems like you've figured out a lot," Liza commented.

"Maybe so," I shrugged, "but one thing I can't understand is why. What makes Natalie so special, Liza? How are we able to dream about her when she's not even a part of this realm?"

"I told you that people with Pure Magic are able to see the future because of the way their spirits connect with the magic pulsing through our realm. But the same goes for other realms too. Earth may not have magic in the traditional sense like Book does, but that does not mean the realm doesn't host other kinds of magic."

"What do you mean, *other* kinds?"

"Crisa, magic is not simply limited to spells and curses and fancy abilities that Book and the other Wonderlands are known for. The root of magic is power—the kind that is strong beyond compare and potent enough to affect change. Every realm has its own form of it. Earth, for example, has as much good magic and dark magic as Book does, but it is generated from actions and experiences so it takes the form of emotional energy. We call that aura magic—the kind of magic that you can't see or touch but can feel around you nonetheless. Dark magic on Earth is created through acts of evil, and it manifests in the form of hatred, revenge, heartbreak, and malice."

"And good magic?"

"Good magic on Earth is the result of true love, self-acceptance, and hope. These forms of good magic—like the forms of dark magic—are all connected to some kind of complete, unwavering belief. The three core belief systems are belief in another person, belief in one's self, and belief in the world at large. Before the Godmothers abandoned Earth, they referred to these core belief systems as the three magic classification categories."

A light bulb went off in my head. I remembered one specific line in Natalie's Poole's file that I had never been able to figure out: "Magic Classification: Category 1, 2, & 3 priority." Based on what Liza was telling me, that meant all three aspects of Natalie's core belief systems were important to her destiny, making her Earth magic potential off the charts.

Liza didn't notice my eyes glaze over as I thought on this. "So you see," she said, "that is why we are able to dream about Natalie. Her life and her future will be characterized by high levels of Earth magic and that is what we are tapping into. It's the same reason why there is a whole section in the Scribes' protagonist book library, and my own, for books about people in other realms. While those visions are a lot fewer compared to the protagonists I've foreseen in our realm, they still exist and I am able to see them just as clearly as the others."

An embittered look crossed Liza's face. "Of course it's not like the higher-ups will ever acknowledge any of that. It would throw off their precious system. So instead, what do they do? They pretend like they don't exist, just like they do with any books I write for people who don't fit in with their stupid protagonist quotas."

I raised my eyebrows. "You know about that, huh?"

"I didn't before; a couple of your friends told me during our individual chats. I really can't believe it. Like it's not bad enough that Lena and her ambassadors think the characters I dream about are the only important people in the realm worth investing in; now they're limiting how many of them there can be too? It's ridiculous and insulting. And I hate that Lena didn't tell me." Liza firmly banged her fist on the railing of the library walkway. "She and I are going to have words about this, I assure you."

Liza took a deep breath and composed herself. "Though I guess I understand," she said, leaning against the railing and looking out at her sea of books forlornly. "And I definitely should've seen it coming. Lena and the rest of the higher-ups love order. They love tradition and continuity and keeping people in boxes. When I started writing protagonist books for a few children in Alderon, I knew Lena would never accept it. Allow the descendants of antagonists to be protagonists? It would unravel our realm's entire belief system that everyone in Alderon deserves to be there, and that people don't change."

"But people do change," I said. I hadn't meant to interrupt, but the comment slid out of me matter-of-factly.

Liza turned her head and looked at me. A small smile crossed her lips. "Indeed," she said. "But you know as well as I do that most people in Book don't believe that. And the higher-ups encourage that form of thinking. It's why they've been forging protagonist books and prophecies for princes and princesses I don't dream about. Which I was aware of."

"And you're okay with that?" I asked.

"No. But again, I get it. Princes and princesses are seen as leaders in our realm; they have important roles to play in our future with or without my visions, particularly those who are next in line for their thrones. But based on the way we assign worth in our land, no one would ever bow to a leader who isn't a protagonist. A common king or queen would never be taken seriously, and that could lead to kingdom instability, rebellions, rulers being overthrown, and many other consequences. So while I don't approve of it ethically, I can understand. I do feel bad for all those poor protagonists that the higher-ups are pretending don't exist, though."

"What will you do?" I asked.

"I am going to talk—well, *yell*—at Lena about this. But I doubt she will listen to me. She hardly ever does. And she knows there's not much I can do to protest. My magic has grown very powerful over the years and the dreams even plague me during the day. Sometimes I'll just be going about my business and I'll black out and fall into them without meaning to. Getting them out through my books and paintings offers such relief; it clears my head and soothes my subconscious, so I can't really stop. And even if I could, Lena has other ways of making me cooperate."

A shadow passed over Liza's face and I was tempted to probe the matter further, but she kept talking.

"Still, even if the Scribes and the ambassadors and Lena throw out certain protagonist books, I'm not going to stop sending them. Just because the people who control the world have given up on what's right and wrong for the sake of ease and order doesn't mean I have to."

Liza shook her head like I so often did whenever unpleasant

thoughts consumed me. "Anyway, getting back on topic. If Nadia is targeting Natalie, then it is because one of her henchmen found the Scribes' copy of Natalie's book. Lena and I have actually suspected for some time that one of the Scribes might be taking bribes from antagonists, which is not unheard of considering the questionable morality that allows them to help the ambassadors forge and destroy books in the first place. But until now we didn't have proof. Discovering that antagonist bunker beneath the Capitol Building finally gave Lena the authority to interrogate the Scribes." The shadow crossed Liza's face again. "I'm sure one of them will break soon."

An unspoken thought passed between us. I knew what it was like to be questioned by Lena Lenore, and it wasn't fun.

After a beat, Liza sighed once more and gestured for me to hand her the book I was holding. "While I have only dreamed of Natalie a couple of times, I did have a vision of her prologue prophecy a while back," Liza explained. "And to answer your original question, that is what makes her so special." Liza opened Natalie's book and turned to the first page. Then she began to read:

"A girl of good but fragile of fate,
Her unnatural path forged by a queen's hate.
Able to be broken until her 21st year,
The Birthday and Destiny Interval her Guardian feared.
True love taken and magic stands still,
From the heart shaken by the reaper's martyr will.
Three heroes and a savior trapped—their worlds forsaken,
The only escape—The Sorrowing Old Man awakened.
New titans shall rise as old ways fall,
A struggle in Time to decide it all.
Three worlds in Eternity where judgment awaits,
Vulnerable to the girl who can open its Gate."

Liza closed the book. "Now do you see?"

The words swirled in my head. Some made sense but others didn't.

"The Eternity Gate . . ." I thought out loud. "Liza, what is it? That's what Natalie's prologue prophecy is referring to at the end, isn't it—the Eternity Gate? I saw it referenced in her file, and Arian has mentioned it a few times too."

Liza walked over to the shelves behind me and slid Natalie's book back into place.

"Personally, I don't believe that's what the prophecy is referring to, Crisa. The Eternity Gate is nothing but legend. People believe in its existence the way others might believe in religion—solely based on faith. Which means that no one, no matter how desperate, is likely to ever find it."

"I wouldn't be so sure," I challenged. "After all, the Author was always just a legend, but my friends and I were just desperate enough to find you."

"Crisa, I don't think—"

"Liza, please," I said. "I need to know. You of all people should understand why."

Liza seemed reluctant, but after a moment she conceded.

"All right, Crisa," she said. "But recognize this. When I was a girl, the elders used to tell us the story of the Eternity Gate. That was over a century and a half ago. Since then its existence has been forgotten and suppressed. So my understanding of the Eternity Gate is a mixture of folklore and gossip that could very well be based on nothing. Understand?"

I nodded.

"Okay then," she said, swallowing her better judgment. "The story goes that there is a mysterious place outside the realms, not just Book or Earth but *all of them*. It exists somewhere between time and space and is responsible for maintaining balance within the universe. This place is called 'Eternity,' and its immortal protectors regulate every realm by making sure no singular world's good-to-dark-magic ratio throws off the equilibrium of the rest.

"You never have to worry about good magic getting out of control. There simply isn't enough of it, and it takes a long time to build. But dark magic grows and spreads quickly. So if one world's dark magic ever exceeded the allowed limit, it would threaten to consume everything like a virus—not just that realm, but the others too.

"As such, if the dark magic of any one world ever crosses that tipping point, the protectors of Eternity re-evaluate the world's place in the universe. They decide whether or not it is worth saving. And they do this by means of a judgment period, during which they observe the world and its populace. If in that time the people of the world prove that their capacity for good can outweigh their capacity for darkness, the protectors will return the realm to its magic equilibrium. But if during this period the people of the realm exhibit more darkness than good, the protectors will respond by tossing the realm into the void and eliminating it, cleansing the universe of its impurity forever.

"In order to make this judgment and see a world in raw and clear context, the protectors must open their 'Eternity Gate,' the gate that separates them from us. When they do, there is supposed to be a massive fluctuation in every realm's magical state, like a powerful energy surge that causes all existing forms of normal magic to power down for as long as the gate is open."

"Like hitting a big reset button," I said.

"Exactly," Liza affirmed. "*That* is why I imagine Nadia and her people are so adamant about ruining Natalie's life. If they believe she has the ability to open the Eternity Gate, then they have to turn her three core belief systems to darkness. If they succeed, based on her prophecy, this would theoretically cause her to produce enough dark magic to throw off Earth's magic equilibrium. Then the Eternity Gate would open and the power surge would temporarily shut off all normal magic in our realm."

"Like the In and Out Spell around Alderon," I gasped, making the connection. "All the antagonists, the monsters—Nadia's entire kingdom would be free to invade Book."

"And the people charged with protecting us from them— the Fairy Godmothers—would be powerless to stop them," Liza added. "People with Pure Magic—like you, me, and the dark- hearted witches and warlocks of Alderon—will not be affected. Our magic is bonded to us and can't be removed. But everyone else with normal magic like the Godmothers will temporarily lose their powers." Liza stopped and tried to write off the seriousness of her statement with a casual shrug. "But again, Crisa, this is just theoretical."

"Liza, with all due respect, how can you possibly believe that?"

"I believe that because I have spent countless decades seeing incredible things in my head from multiple worlds, and I have never seen anything that would lead me to believe Eternity is real. It is simply an old tale."

"Liza, everything about Book is based on old tales. My entire life my friends and I have been taught that we are reflections of the classic fairytales that came before us. And while I've never believed we should limit ourselves to their precedent, I know that it's an important part of our origins. With everything that the antagonists have done and are willing to do, as well everything you've told me, I have to believe Eternity is real. For goodness' sake, your own prophecy references it."

"*Supposedly* references it," Liza corrected. "For all we know, that prophecy could mean something entirely different. I already explained to you that my prophecies may have multiple interpretations."

"Nadia's actions *don't* have multiple interpretations, and neither do her plans," I countered. "The antagonists are acting under the assumption that the Eternity Gate is real and Natalie is going to open it. Which means it would be foolish for us to proceed without believing the same thing. You've been isolated in the Indexlands a long time, but I've seen what the antagonists are capable of—not just in my head, but firsthand. So I know with certainty that something is happening and that we need to do something about it."

I paced across the library floor, frustrated. "I just wish there was some way for me to warn Natalie. If I could, then maybe it wouldn't matter what the antagonists are planning because she could be one step ahead."

Liza bit her lip. There was a torn expression on her face. "Actually," she replied softly, "there might be a way."

I perked up. "Really? What is it?"

"You're able to dream about Natalie because your Pure Magic is honing in on her magic potential on Earth, right? Well, using that same rationale, you can train yourself to send telepathic messages to others who are as powerfully linked to the realm's magic as you are. I've done it a few times myself, but only recently have I really been putting effort into it."

"The dreams where I saw and heard you . . ."

She nodded. "It took a lot of power and training, but a while back I was able to teach myself to communicate with certain people through their dreams. I haven't done it in a long time. Typically only people with Pure Magic can connect to the realm's magic that way, so my options for who to contact have been pretty limited. But theoretically, if Natalie is powerful enough, it might be possible to reach her when she is asleep. When we are dreaming, our minds are most connected to the magic field."

"That's awesome!" I exclaimed.

"Yes and no. It worked when I tried to reach you. It definitely got easier the more magic you used because you were emanating greater power for me to hone in on. But that hasn't always been the case. When I first tried to send dream messages, the amount of strength and control it required almost burned me out several times."

"What do you mean, *burned you out*?"

"Despite the potential of our powers, Crisa, we all have limits. For us, Magic Exhaustion and Magic Burn Out are two of the greatest. The former occurs when we use a lot of magic over a short period of time. We exhaust our abilities temporarily and they typically take about twenty-fours to reboot."

So Blue was right. I couldn't use my magic on Lucky earlier because I was recharging.

"Magic Burn Out, however, has a more permanent consequence. If you use more magic that you are capable of, then the power can literally burn out your system and you die."

"Well, that's not great." I rolled my eyes.

"No, it's not. It's been almost a century since the last time I nearly succumbed to Magic Burn Out. The stronger I've become over the years, the more I am capable of. But even if that weren't the case, and I'd faced that risk when trying to contact you, I still would have done it. I dreamed that eventually Arian would capture you and take you back to Nadia, and that when he did your only hope for escape would be your magic. But I wasn't sure if you would figure out your power in time. So since I'd foreseen that a realization of your powers was linked to touching a dragon from your past, I did my best to warn you, even if I didn't know the specifics."

"I really appreciate what you did, Liza, but if you were able to communicate with me through your dreams, that means you can do the same with Natalie, right?" I asked.

"Unfortunately I don't think I can," Liza replied. "I was able to do it with you because we both have Pure Magic and I have visions about you all the time, which strengthens our link. But my connection with Natalie isn't anywhere near as strong. I've only dreamed about her a couple of times. But your friends SJ and Blue told me that you've been dreaming about Natalie for years. So I believe *you* would have the best chance, if not the only chance, of successfully reaching her."

"Then show me how," I said earnestly. "You can teach me to channel my magic the way you did yours so I can communicate with her."

Liza looked down at the books on the lower level of the library. "The thing is, I don't know if I should," she said slowly. "It's not just about Magic Burn Out. You could theoretically become strong enough to send dream messages without that being a risk, but it would take years of slow and steady practice. If I help you push yourself to reach that amount of power in the short time we have left before Natalie is supposed to open the Eternity Gate, it will require you to channel a lot of magic without holding back."

"So?"

"So I had a vision a few nights ago of your time in Valor—the confrontation, the escape, and what happened in Nadia's study."

"What are you getting at?"

"I saw what you did to Arian, Crisa," Liza said. "I know what you *wanted* to do to Arian."

I flicked my eyes to the floor, a weird combination of shame and sternness simmering in my stomach. "Maybe it was necessary," I said. "Maybe he deserved it."

"Maybe. Or maybe that was the Pure Magic talking," Liza countered. "You used extremely high doses of magic only minutes before confronting Arian. You pushed yourself too hard, too fast, and the power inside you began to flow without restraint. Because of that, even if it was just for a moment, you lost control. The Pure Magic consumed you and your actions because that's how it works. It's a sleeping monster that stirs every time you use your powers. The more free rein you give it, the more it takes over and the harder it becomes to control. If you push your magic enough, Crisa, you could lose control of it permanently. Then forget your fifty-fifty chance; the disease *will* corrupt you."

"But Natalie—"

"Natalie is just one piece of the puzzle," Liza interrupted. "You can't focus solely on her well-being when there are other important factors at play. I have a lot of visions, Crisa, about a lot of people. So I'm forced to see the big picture. And what I'm telling you is that it's in the realm's best interest—*and* yours—not to pursue this. It is too risky to push your magic that hard."

"But didn't you say you were willing to risk the same thing with me? You said using that much power is dangerous and taxing—even for someone as adept at it as you. But you still put yourself through the threat of Magic Burn Out to reach me. And you saved me because of it."

An awkward beat passed between us.

"Crisa," Liza finally sighed. "I'm not going to force you to do anything or keep you from doing what you want; that's not who I am. All I ask is that you think about it. You've got time. So give the matter some serious thought, okay?"

"Yeah, okay," I conceded. Then I tilted my head in confusion. "What do you mean I've got time?"

"Well, Natalie hasn't been born yet so even if you could get a message to her right now, there'd be no one to receive it."

My eyebrows shot up. "Natalie hasn't been born?"

I remembered Arian saying something about her not existing yet, but I'd never really understood what he'd meant. I just figured he'd been messing with me, as he so often did.

"Liza, that doesn't make any sense," I said. "I mean, you showed me her book and her prophecy."

"Relax, Crisa," Liza said calmly. "We see the future, right? Well, your visions of Natalie are just a really long-distance view. According to my inter-dimensional timelines, right now it is autumn in the Earth year 1999. And according to the few visions I've had of Natalie, she will be born in the next few weeks, at the start of winter 2000. So if all these great events surrounding her are meant to happen on her twenty-first birthday like my prophecy indicates, then with the Earth-to-Book time difference, that means her Key Destiny Interval will take place . . ." she furrowed her brow as she did a brief calculation in her head, "a little over a year from now."

"Key Destiny Interval?" I repeated, weary from so much information but alert enough to remember the phrase from Natalie's file.

"It's a term the Godmothers used to use to describe the pivotal moment when a person on Earth either heads down a path where their belief systems ultimately lead to good magic or dark magic."

I put my fingers to my temples and closed my eyes, grimacing.

"What are you doing?" Liza asked.

"Just something SJ does when she's stressed. I think I'm having a brain seizure. This is way too much for one day, or one lifetime."

"Don't have a meltdown yet," Liza said. "I have one more thing to show you, and this is something I know you'll want to be at full attention for."

I lifted my head slowly. "What is it?"

Liza meandered to a nearby shelf and came back with a book.

It looked just like the one Lady Agnue had presented me with when I'd received my prologue prophecy. It was forest green with my name etched into the front cover in shimmering gold letters. The only difference between this copy and the one I'd been presented with before was the understanding that the previous one had been a fake—forged by the antagonists to keep me in the dark about my true fate.

This copy was real. This was my actual book with my *real* prologue prophecy inside. All I had to do was look.

CHAPTER 25

My Choice

t was early evening when we arrived in the kingdom of Adelaide. The sky was tinged black and blue like a bruised eye, and we rode Lucky the remainder of the way to the royal castle—arriving there as the first stars showed themselves.

Our mission to find the Author was complete. Our quest was over and we knew that it was time to return to our lives—time to go back to school and deal with all the new understandings, responsibilities, and revelations we'd acquired. But we had one last stop to make before that.

When Ashlyn gifted us her locket back on Earth, she only asked one thing in return—that once we were done we return to Adelaide to find her mother (the former Little Mermaid and the present Queen of Adelaide), give her Ashlyn's (now enchanted) locket, and tell her the truth about what happened to her "Lost Princess" daughter.

True to our word, we were on our way there now—intent on finally giving the royal family closure about their long-missing child.

How did we reach Adelaide so quickly, you might be wondering?

In a word: teleportation.

Liza had been able to teleport us pretty close to our desired destination. With the waters off the coast of Adelaide being highly prone to holes in the In and Out Spell, it provided enough of a magic beacon for Liza to hone in on. However, because we'd been on the other side of the realm, and had the interference of the Indexlands' In and Out Spell to contend with—messing with Liza's aim—the exact drop zone had been difficult for her to gauge. As a result, the five of us and Lucky had been zapped about sixty miles off Adelaide's coast.

It was actually a pretty sweet ride from there. I was starting to get the hang of steering Lucky without magic. He had some ridges on the back of his neck that he seemed to respond to directionally—it allowed me to let him know whether I wanted him to go left, right, faster, slower, or stop.

While I steered Lucky, my friends were seated comfortably behind me. Liza hadn't been kidding when she said she was excellent at crafting. She'd fashioned an awesome temporary saddle out of willow branches in less than half an hour, which allowed everyone to sit comfortably on Lucky's back. Fortunately, Lucky didn't seem to mind the accessory.

My only regret now was that Liza hadn't been able to come with us.

We felt bad leaving her behind, but there was nothing we could do. I'd hoped that she could use Ashlyn's locket to break through the In and Out Spell like we had, but with Liza's anti-aging spell tied to it, she could never leave. If she ever stepped outside the barrier she would fall victim to the extra years she'd been alive—all 150 of them—and would pretty much turn to dust on the spot.

It was a really sad, twisted clause, but she asked us not to worry about her. I didn't know if it was pride, strength, or denial, but she refused to accept any of our pity.

On the dragon ride to Adelaide Castle, my friends and I finally spoke about all we'd been through. First came discussion and reflection on everything Liza had told us about her origins, the Godmothers, her sister, Pure Magic, the true nature of protagonist books, and so on. Then we shared what happened during our solo meetings with her.

Daniel and Blue's recaps took the shortest amount of time. Their whole interest in finding the Author had been rooted in a desire to have her alter their prologue prophecies so they could achieve different fates than the ones she'd prescribed. However, once Liza explained the concept of Inherent Fate, my friends realized she could not help them. Our prophecies did not mirror her wishes for our futures; they were predictions of how our futures would turn out based on our choices. And those predictions could have many interpretations, including some that might not be so obvious.

I knew perfectly well how much Daniel and Blue were dreading the futures Liza had foreseen—Blue having to marry Jason, and Daniel not ending up with Kai. Discovering that Liza did not have the power to change them, and that the interpretations they'd been concentrating on might not even be their true fates, was a hard truth to swallow.

At the same time, it was a liberating one. The forms in which their prophecies came to fruition would be on them and them alone. And that was what we'd wanted in the first place, wasn't it?

I could tell my friends were still digesting the notion. They weren't upset, but they weren't necessarily happy about it either. It was just a lot to take in.

We'd spent our whole lives believing we were restricted. And we'd been attributing the constraints on our lives and futures to someone else. Realizing the Author couldn't control our destinies changed things completely. However life played out, we knew it would be totally on us. Our fates were our responsibility, and we had to own up to them. We had to grow up and accept that there would be no one to blame for our problems. Going forward, the only people accountable for those futures was us.

From the look on his face, Jason was feeling the same way as Daniel and Blue about his conversation with Liza. While I still did not know what his prologue prophecy said, I could tell he felt humbled, surprised, kind of disappointed, but also relieved about being in charge of his own destiny.

In addition to discussing his prologue prophecy, Jason had been the one to ask Liza about Mark's well-being.

It seemed like a lifetime ago that we'd found our old friend's file in Arian's bunker at the Capitol Building. Thanks to my dream we knew he was okay, and we would be seeing him again, but we still had a lot of questions. Why had he left school? And if he wasn't dead, what did his "threat neutralized" file mean?

Unfortunately, while Mark did have a book in Liza's library, its contents were predominantly blank. He didn't even have a prologue prophecy yet. Liza had only ever had one vision of the boy. She foresaw it coming to fruition about a year from now. Like mine, it involved the five of us reuniting with him.

Liza had envisioned us visiting Mark at his home in the Dolohaunty Mountains. She'd gleaned from her dream that Mark really had been sick since the start of the semester, but with an illness that his parents didn't want to make public. Evidently it was bad and he was not receiving visitors. But he would recover by next fall and the five of us would journey to his home where he would become an integral part of our mission.

It was comforting to know. Having confirmation of his current state—and that he would be okay—set our minds at ease. And since there was nothing in his book that would make Arian or Nadia consider him a threat, we hoped he was safe from their protagonist hunters.

The revelation did confuse us though. For if Mark didn't even have a prologue prophecy, why had the antagonists taken an interest in him?

The topic definitely required further investigation, but for now we simply couldn't come up with a plausible theory as to what was going on.

When Jason finished recapping what he'd discussed with Liza,

I finally explained what transpired during my talk with her, going into detail about everything I'd learned about Natalie, Eternity, and Earth magic. After that came the matter of my prologue prophecy.

Until now we'd all respected one another's privacy in terms of prologue prophecies. However, as mine was the cause of so much that had happened to us, my friends asked me outright what it said.

It was a fair question, and I would have gladly divulged the details as I was no longer in the business of hiding things from them. But the fact was that I couldn't tell them anything. Not because I didn't trust them or didn't want to let them in, but because I simply didn't know.

When Liza had offered me my book—my prologue prophecy right behind the cover—I hesitated. And then after a moment of careful thought, I handed the book back to her.

"What do you mean you didn't look?" Blue exclaimed, her mouth agape.

I calmly recounted the moment of my enlightenment. "Look, I know my prophecy is important and that there is a lot riding on it. But I also know that if what Liza said about Inherent Fate is true, then what good would there be in looking?"

"You would have clarity, and maybe feel at peace knowing some of the details," Jason suggested.

I shook my head. "No, I'd have the opposite. If I've learned anything about prophecies, it's that hearing them brings nothing but endless questions, doubts, and anxiety. So if knowing mine would truly make no difference in the events about to unfold, why invite these insecurities in? You guys may find it shocking, but I think it was the right choice. I'll come to know what the future holds on my own terms when the time is right. When Liza handed me my book, I simply decided to give myself the very gift I always thought someone else had to bestow upon me. I decided to live my life just for me."

My friends had nothing more to say. I didn't know if that was a reflection of my own sureness while I spoke or their surprise. But I was grateful they let the matter lie. It had been my choice and there was no changing it. All they could do was support it.

Once I finished sharing, the only person left was SJ. She'd been extremely quiet throughout our retellings, which I'd mistaken for avid listening. When it was her turn to talk, I discovered that the reason for her silence had been something quite different. Embarrassment.

SJ didn't have a protagonist book.

Like, at all.

We'd all known that she was the only person in our group who had yet to receive a prologue prophecy. Her determination to reach the Author had been inspired by a wish to preemptively keep anything undesirable from being decided about her fate. But we'd always assumed she had a protagonist book.

I mean she was SJ. She was at the top of our class at Lady Agnue's. She was the world's most perfect princess, heir to the throne of her kingdom, and daughter of Snow White. How could she not have one?

Yes, we'd learned that the ambassadors had been forging books for royals who didn't have them. And Liza had informed us that being royal had nothing to do with the people she dreamed about—she simply dreamed about people who were special in some way. Their selection was random and she couldn't control that process in the slightest. But for SJ not to have a book, for Liza to inform her that there were no visions of her future, no prophecies foreseeing any sort of larger importance to her life, no inkling at all that she was destined to be special, that was *unfathomable*.

The rest of us tried to console SJ. Daniel asserted that just because she didn't have a book now didn't mean she wouldn't eventually get one. After all, his had only shown up a few months ago and his prologue prophecy appeared along with it. Meanwhile, to ease my friend's mind I proposed the following notion:

Who said Liza's word was law?

Just because our new Author friend hadn't had visions of SJ doing anything mega important didn't imply it wasn't going to happen. I had the same abilities as Liza and I'd had visions of SJ along with the rest of our group, so that had to count for something. And even if it didn't, that did not automatically mean SJ wasn't supposed to do something awesome. The inarguable truth was that she was awesome, so her eventually *doing* something awesome was a no-brainer.

Maybe Liza's predictions weren't something to live and die by. Maybe SJ didn't need to have one of Liza's books to become a protagonist of her own story. Maybe being herself was enough.

After we talked about it a lot, SJ insisted she was fine and requested that we drop the subject. Respecting her wishes, we fell into silent contemplation for the rest of the journey.

Our eventual arrival at Adelaide Castle was not particularly welcomed. The guards outside freaked the geek out when Lucky landed at their front gate. My friends and I were barely able to stop them from attacking.

Once we'd calmed everybody down and explained why we were there, we were hesitantly granted admittance. Leaving Lucky outside, we entered the throne room with great delicacy, ready to fulfill our promise to Ashlyn.

The king, queen, and their young, auburn-haired daughter Onicka received us—intrigued, but confused as to why we'd come. When SJ presented them with Ashlyn's locket and proceeded to tell the story we'd come to deliver, both these sentiments were replaced with astonishment.

The three royals sat motionlessly through the retelling. When the story was complete, the silence persisted until the queen abruptly rose from her throne and excused herself from the room. The king and Onicka swiftly pursued her.

Following the curt exit, the five of us stood there and waited, not sure what to do. Our job was done and our promise had been fulfilled, but leaving didn't feel right—not like this, anyway. Thankfully, after fifteen minutes had passed, one of the castle guards signaled for us to come with him.

He led us to a room a slight way down the hall. We entered and found the queen gazing out a balcony that overlooked the sea. When the door clicked shut behind the guard, the queen turned around.

The brightness of the rising moon cast her face in shadow. But the light danced upon the glistening fabric of her one-sleeved mint and white gown, causing it to shimmer like the very ocean behind her.

She gestured for us to sit and we obeyed.

I squished onto the plush, powder blue fabric of the couch between Jason and SJ. The queen walked over gracefully and sat down on the chair opposite us. She rested her soft-skinned hands on the golden armrests as she crossed her ankles to the side in the shape of a fishtail.

The coral tiara woven into her auburn updo captured my attention. It was sharp but whimsical. Small diamonds glinted on it like a myriad of tiny undersea bubbles. Its minty green color contrasted the scarlet tendrils of her hair.

My gaze drifted to the accessory around her neck. She was wearing Ashlyn's locket. I shifted in my seat as I waited for her to speak. Eventually she exhaled and gave us a small smile. "Thank you," she said.

"Um, you're welcome," Blue responded on our group's behalf.

"How are you doing, Your Majesty?" Jason felt the need to ask. "With all of this, I mean?"

"I am at peace," the queen sighed. "Finally at peace."

"You're not angry with her?" Blue asked. "At Ashlyn, for leaving the way that she did? You forgive her?"

"Of course I do," the queen responded. "How could I not when I was willing to do more or less the same thing when I left my family, my whole people, in the name of true love? It was the price of my happiness, as my daughter's leaving was the price of hers. Much as I miss her, I could never be angry with her for making that choice. Everyone deserves a chance to find true happiness. The costs are just different from person to person."

SJ nodded. "Ashlyn said something fairly similar."

"I am not surprised." The queen sighed again. "As demonstrated, she is very much her mother's daughter." Her eyes turned slightly glassy and she took a deep breath to rein in her emotions.

"As I was saying," she continued after a moment, "I want to thank you all for delivering my daughter's message and her necklace to my family. You have finally given us closure and set us free from the terrible veil of mourning we have been under. And to see my daughter so happy with her family, to see my grandchildren in this picture inside the locket . . . Words cannot express the gratitude you deserve."

"It was the least we could do," I replied. "Your daughter was very kind to us."

"Nevertheless," the queen continued, "I stand by what I said about you deserving my thanks. And since no words can sufficiently convey it, I would like to offer you something in return—a favor."

"What kind of favor?" Daniel asked.

"Whatever kind you like," the queen responded. "On behalf of my family and my kingdom, I grant you one favor to be fulfilled with our full royal allegiance. Whatever it may be, whenever you desire it in the future—my husband and I have agreed that we will grant it to you. All you have to do is ask."

"Wow, thanks," Blue said. She looked at us and shrugged. "I'm thinking talking dolphins. How about you guys?"

"Blue . . ." SJ narrowed her eyes. "I think this is the kind of reward we should save for a rainy day."

Blue leaned back against the couch and blew a wave of blonde hair out of her face. "Fine. Sue me for trying to have a little fun."

SJ shook her head disapprovingly then readdressed the

queen. "Thank you, Your Majesty, but you may want to rethink that kindness. Truthfully, my friends and I borrowed a few horses from your stable yesterday without permission. We meant to bring them back, but they were lost on our journey."

Blue shrugged and looked at the queen. "Witches and monsters, what're you gonna do?"

"Given that," SJ continued, "we understand if you would like to take back your offer of a favor. We hardly deserve it for the thievery."

The queen blinked and then huffed in amusement. She smiled warmly at SJ. "Dear, you are a princess. How many horses does your family own?"

"I do not know. A few dozen perhaps."

"My family—like most royal families—is no different. So given that you crossed worlds and various dangers in order to bring me closure to my daughter's mystery and restore my life's peace, I think we can forgive you for a few missing steeds. My offer of a favor still stands, and always will."

"Thank you, Your Majesty," Jason responded. "That's more than we deserve."

"You are welcome," the queen replied. "Now, would you children like anything to eat before you depart, or perhaps you would like to stay the night?"

"Again, thank you," Jason said. "But we've been gone a while, and . . ." He paused and looked at the rest of us to see if we were thinking the same thing.

I nodded. "I think it's time we go home."

"All right then." The queen stood from her chair. We followed her lead and began to rise as well. But before I could get up, she was standing in front of me.

"Crisanta, dear, would you mind if I had a word with you in private before you leave?"

I glanced at my friends in confusion but agreed.

"This will not take long," the queen told the others. "Crisanta will meet you in the main foyer in a matter of minutes."

I followed her iridescent pumps into the hall one click after another, wondering how hard it must've been adjusting from a fish tail to high heels. I'd been human my entire life and I still couldn't move with that much grace.

CHAPTER 26

The Death of Crisanta Knight

he queen led me to a secluded balcony with a single glass table and a set of iron chairs facing the placid waters. My royal escort sat in one chair and I placed myself in the other.

"Crisanta," she began, "when you and your friends described the events that transpired when meeting my daughter, you mentioned you learned she was gifted with a special magical ability."

"Yeah. Healing," I replied. "She told us that all Mer people, or people of Mer descent, are born with a magical power."

"That is correct," the queen affirmed. "Mine, for example, is empathy."

I raised my eyebrows. "Does that count? I mean, no disrespect, but that seems like more of a personality trait than a superpower."

"Normally that would be true," the queen admitted. "But my ability is a bit more developed than that. It allows me to read hearts the way others with psychic abilities might read minds. It lets me feel everything that a person is feeling—like an open window to the soul of another."

"Uh-huh," I said slowly. "So, the reason you wanted to talk me is . . ."

"I can feel the conflict inside of you. It has always been there, but it has grown quite complex in the last few weeks. Your friends, like most people, all have their worries and troubles. But you, my dear, have been at war with yourself for quite some time. I can sense that this internal conflict came very close to tearing you apart, but recently it has begun to work itself out."

I blinked, taken aback by the frank analysis.

"You and your friends did something very special for me today," the queen went on. "So I would like to try and help you find the same kind of peace you have given me by assisting with your internal progress."

I leaned my head back against the chair and exhaled deeply. Ashlyn's enchanted locket glowed vaguely purple against the queen's neck from its new In and Out Spell-breaking ability. We hadn't mentioned this ability to the queen. That was another story. I shifted my eyes to the glass table, which reflected the moon.

"I appreciate the gesture, Your Majesty," I replied. "But I'm afraid fixing me isn't that simple."

"Because you think you cannot accept who you are?"

"Not exactly," I responded. "I used to think that I was defined by other people's opinions of me. And I let myself get lost in them. But then . . ."

"Something changed," the queen stated, finishing my sentence.

I nodded. "Daniel—the kid out there with the brown hair and the know-it-all face—he helped me realize that the only person who gets to choose who I am is me."

"And you think he is right?"

"I do. I just . . ." I sighed and stared out at the waters, which were now the same shade of dark blue as the queen's eyes. "I feel like knowing who I am, *accepting* who I am, isn't enough. I've come to accept a lot about myself in recent weeks—good things, bad things, incredible things, terrible things. I've gotten to a point where I genuinely think I've accepted everything I am and everything I'm not. Yet something still feels like it's missing.

"I thought that when I finally knew who I was I would feel better inside—stronger, more confident. I thought that I'd undergo some big, liberating epiphany. But I haven't and I think it's because . . . I don't entirely like who I am. There are aspects that I'm proud of. But overall I feel like it's not enough. While I may be heroic, I'm not the hero I wish I were. And while I may be princessy, I'm not the admirable princess I wish I were either. I'm just Crisanta Knight. And I don't know if it's my pride or my shame talking, but I'm not satisfied with who that girl is, with who I am. Somehow . . . I don't know. Somehow, I hoped I could be more."

The queen nodded with understanding. Then, much to my surprise, she took my hand. "Crisanta, sweetheart, did you ever stop to consider that maybe the reason you feel so conflicted is because you have been asking yourself the wrong question?"

I pulled my hand away gingerly. Touchy-feely was not really my scene, but I didn't want to offend the queen either. "I don't understand," I said.

"The question 'who am I?' seems to be the great question that drives many of us," the queen said thoughtfully. "It is certainly what underlies the thematic elements of most stories, so please do not mistake what I am about to tell you as an implication that it is a worthless inquiry. But the truth is, I do not believe the question matters as much as people think. The simple reason for this is that the answer changes all the time.

"Who you are as a person is always in flux; it is not a constant because every day we are changing just like the world around us—we are growing and learning and adapting and becoming something new. Thus, trying to find a finite definition for who you are is irrelevant because who you are today could very well be different from the person you will become next week or next month or next year. Knowing this, I believe that there is a far better question people should ask themselves in life. And that is, 'Who do I want to be?'

"It is the answer to this question that defines us more than anything else, because this is what defines our choices. And that is what a person is truly molded by in the end. *Their choices*. Each path that they do or do not decide to take, big and small. For there is so much about this great world that is out of our control, but our choices—those are ours alone. And in deciding who you want be, you are giving your choices a sense of direction—a sense of purpose that will drive you and influence your destiny.

"So my advice to you, Crisanta, is to move on from accepting who you are. That is an important part of total self-acceptance, but it is not the only part. The other side of that coin is deciding and accepting who you want to be. Even if you are not that girl right now, in actively accepting that you want to be her, your choices will reflect that, and every day you will become more like her as a result.

"To summarize, my dear girl, if *this* Crisanta Knight is not enough for you," the queen gestured at my general person, "then simply stop being her. Let that girl go and accept who you want to be instead. Because if you feel like you could be something more, then you have a responsibility to yourself to see that you become just that. And once you accept this, I promise you, you will finally feel whole."

I spent a great deal of the night reflecting on the queen's advice.

After we'd said our goodbyes to the royal family, my friends and I retrieved our Pegasi from the castle stables where we'd stashed them upon embarking on our search for Ashlyn on Earth. It felt like an eternity since we'd left them there, but in reality (and due to the Earth-to-Book time difference) it'd only been a couple of days. When we asked the queen about the Pegasi before leaving the castle, she'd informed us that the staff had found the creatures and had been taking care of them.

I was grateful for that—glad we could return to school with the steeds. We'd already lost two Pegasi and a carriage on this adventure. With all the trouble we were going to be in when we returned, losing more of the schools' property wouldn't improve our situation.

On our way back to school Daniel and Jason rode on individual steeds while SJ paired with Blue on the third Pegasus (my favorite, Sadie). SJ was never a fan of horses, but somehow an enchanted horse seemed like a less scary transport option than a fire-breathing dragon.

I rode back on Lucky alone. The air got progressively colder as the skies became darker. And yet, the more I thought on the queen's words, the brighter my heart and mind burned. Enlightenment was building inside me, priming for its dawn.

We arrived back at Lady Agnue's a few hours before sunrise. All six of us (including Lucky) passed through the In and Out Spell around the campus effortlessly. We were no longer hindered by such things. And since our school's simpler version of the spell was never designed to keep animals from passing through, the Pegasi fazed through with just as much ease.

We didn't have much time for goodbyes. While Lucky's landing was not particularly loud, his size drew the attention of every guard on duty. Within seconds of touching down in the practice fields, guards began to rush toward us.

"Good luck," Jason said as he quickly hugged each of us. "I hope Lady Agnue doesn't roast you."

I smirked. "Considering the amount of firepower we brought back, I hardly think she has anything on us." Lucky snorted, as if he agreed.

Daniel wasn't a hugger, but SJ hugged him anyways. Blue punched him amicably in the arm. "See you boys at the next ball, I guess."

"Assuming we are not placed under house arrest for the rest of the school year," SJ said, nodding at the guards headed for us.

The Pegasi belonged to Lord Channing's, so Daniel and Jason hopped back on their steeds. Jason rapidly tied a rope to the saddle of the third Pegasus so it would follow them. It was best if the boys weren't here when the guards arrived. Which meant they had about thirty seconds to lift off.

Looking up at Daniel on his Pegasus in the shadow of the moon, I felt my heart beat slower. I couldn't tell you why. I just felt its rhythm change in my chest. Since the beginning Daniel and my relationship had been full of fiery emotions, but the energy between us finally felt at peace. We'd changed. We were friends now. Of all the incredible things to come out of this journey, that was one of the twists I was most grateful for.

"You were right," I said.

"I'm right a lot," he said. "You'll have to be more specific."

I shook my head and smiled at him. "We were able to finish this story together."

"Time to go, man," Jason said to Daniel. He kicked his Pegasus's side. Pairs of brilliant, holographic wings sprouted from the creature's back, as well as the back of the second steed.

"Come on, Knight," Daniel replied with mischief in his eyes. "Who says this story is finished?"

He gave his own Pegasus a kick. The pure black steed's eyes blazed silver and matching wings sprouted from his back. Jason and Daniel shot into the sky with a gust of wind moments before the guards reached us.

After forty minutes, thirty guards, and two warnings for the guards not to provoke my pet dragon, my friends and I were standing in our headmistress's office while Lucky was being babysat by school security.

I'd never seen Lady Agnue in her pajamas before. And this was no exception.

The woman had somehow managed to make herself look headmistress-ready at four o' clock in the morning with barely half an hour's notice of our arrival. Her brown hair was twisted into a bun. Her flowing, dark green dress was offset by her pale expression and sharp features.

Our headmistress glared at us from behind her desk. As she sat there—the light from the moon shining in from the grand window behind her high-backed chair—I noted the fascinating contradiction of her vicious eyes. How they could be such a warm shade of copper yet still seem so cold was a marvel.

The four of us had been at it for about twenty minutes now. On our return journey to school my friends and I had agreed that we'd share our most notable revelations with our headmasters when they inevitably took us in for questioning.

There were certain aspects of the journey we were going to keep to ourselves. Finding Ashlyn was the private business of the Adelaide royal family. My magic was my business. The holes in the In and Out Spell were too precious a revelation to divulge. We didn't have proof of the ambassadors' book-related deception and Lena Lenore had forced us into silence about them anyways.

But apart from that we wanted to communicate the truth. From Shadow Guardians to antagonist plots to the real story of the Author, we felt we owed it to the other protagonists at school to share the information we'd discovered and warn them about what was coming. They needed to know what kind of threats we were dealing with. Moreover, we felt they deserved to understand that they weren't bound to the Author's words and it was their own choices that would inspire their fates, not the other way around.

We thought that our headmasters would agree and that they'd understand the importance of accepting this information and sharing it with the students.

We thought wrong.

This confrontation was turning out to be nothing like we'd expected. For starters, we'd been surprised to learn that Lady Agnue hadn't told our parents we were missing. For all our families knew, we'd never left school. It seemed the headmistress wanted to save face. Having three girls (two of them princesses) find a way to escape school and get past the In and Out Spell hardly made it look like she had things under control.

The second realization that stunned us was how obstinate she was being about our revelations. I hoped the initiative was going better with the boys over at Lord Channing's, because our attempts to reason with Lady Agnue so far had been in vain. I didn't know if it was because she was stubborn or stupid, but the woman would not listen.

"Lady Agnue, you're not hearing us," Blue interrupted for about the twelfth time. "The Author isn't what you think she is!"

Once again the headmistress dismissed the claim with a wave of her hand as if it were nothing. "Children," she began through thinly veiled contempt, "I do not know what you intended to accomplish with these wild stories of yours. But if they are merely a ploy to lessen your punishment, then let me stop you right there."

"Headmistress, these are not stories; they are truths," SJ insisted.

"They are nonsense is what they are," Lady Agnue responded. "I mean, antagonist rebellions, and Shadow Guardians, and finding the Author? Complete lies—that is what I say."

"But we did find her," I argued back. "We're telling you the truth, Lady Agnue. The antagonists are not going away; they're coming for us—*all of us*. What's more, there are kids at this school that are high on their hit list and if you don't tell them and their parents and the teachers and everyone else about what's happening, then—"

"Then what?" the headmistress interjected. "The three of you will try to get people to listen to your deranged, rambling theories?"

"Maybe we will," I said firmly.

"And what, Miss Knight, makes you think that anyone will believe you?"

"Absolutely nothing," I replied calmly. "But you know what? That doesn't matter. Because even if everyone thinks we're crazy, they won't be able to un-hear what we tell them. It'll be out there—the what-ifs simmering in the back of their minds. What if the Author doesn't control us? What if In and Out Spells aren't impenetrable? What if we are not safe from Alderon and its antagonists? And what if all these protagonists' deranged, rambling theories are more than just theories; what if they're true?"

My eyes locked with our headmistress's defiantly as I crossed my arms over my chest.

"We encountered a lot of different types of people in our time away from school, Lady Agnue. Godmothers, ambassadors, villains, century-old legends—you name it. And you know what all those people had in common with one another? You know what they all have in common with *you*? They taught us the power of an idea—about how it can spread and grow and take people over. Maybe not at first, but with enough time and encouragement, it can change them. It can restructure and shift the way they look at the world until one day they go along with the notion completely, forgetting the old ways and choosing to believe in something new.

"Think about it, Lady Agnue. The tradition and order you love so much is slowly, progressively disappearing. Do you honestly think it matters whether or not anyone believes us at first? Or is it really just a matter of time?"

Lady Agnue glared at me steadily. Then without breaking eye contact she gestured to the door. "SJ, Blue . . . get out."

"What? No way!" Blue protested.

"That was not a request."

"Neither is our insistence on staying," SJ countered. "We are not going anywhere."

Lady Agnue turned to my friends. "Fine then," she said. "I was just going to give you both a month of detention in the school's prison towers, but since you continue to behave disobediently I am increasing it to two."

Blue put her hands on her hips. "Right, like that's going to make us change our minds about—"

"Make that three," Lady Agnue said.

"We are not leaving," SJ asserted. "You cannot—"

"Four," Lady Agnue interrupted again.

"Guys," I interceded. "It's all right. Go. I'll be out of here in a minute."

Blue stomped her foot in frustration. "Crisa—"

"Five," Lady Agnue went on.

"Guys." I looked at them earnestly.

"Ugh, fine," Blue moaned.

I gave them a nod of reassurance and the two of them stormed out of the room, leaving me alone with our headmistress.

"Crisanta Knight."

I pivoted back to the woman I once considered intimidating. She leaned back in her plush, high-backed chair and addressed me anew.

"I cannot begin to describe the levels of reproachable behavior you have achieved these last few months."

"That's not going to stop you from trying though. Is it?" I sassed.

"Miss Knight! This is hardly the time for your smart mouth."

Agree to disagree.

"Fine, fine," I sighed. "Go on. Get it out of your system, Lady Agnue."

"I have half a mind to suspend you, or expel you, or put in a request that *you* be transferred to Alderon. For goodness' sake, you are the most terrible, irresponsible, inappropriate, unruly . . ."

I yawned as I waited for the list of derogatory adjectives to end—a response that my headmistress clearly did not appreciate.

"Miss Knight, are you listening to me?"

"Honestly? No," I replied flatly. "I'm not, Lady Agnue. I'm done wasting my time listening to you or Mauvrey or anyone else around here who thinks they know more about me than I do."

"You insolent girl. I have seen princesses and common protagonists and Legacies pass through these halls for years. And all that time has not gone by without my intuition learning to call a kettle black when I see it. So believe me when I say, Crisanta Knight, that you are nothing but a weak, delusional, little girl who is as much a failure at being a princess as she is at being a hero, and is too incompetent to ever be anything else of value either."

"You're wrong," I said unfazed.

"Excuse me?"

"You heard me. I said you're wrong. I'm not weak. I'm not delusional. And I'm not some incompetent failure either. Oh believe me, you almost had me convinced for a while there. But I've changed since you last saw me, Lady Agnue. And because of that, I can say with complete certainty that I am not any of those things at all. You know what I am, though? I'm smart. And I'm strong. And I'm persistent and resourceful and capable of a lot more than you think. So go ahead, hand down your punishment. Do your worst. But I'm not apologizing or backing down on this, not to you or anybody else ever again."

"Well, look at the brave, tiny princess," Lady Agnue sneered. "She goes on one quest and suddenly she is not afraid of anything."

"Wrong again, headmistress. I'm afraid of a lot of things. And I'll admit that so far the main thing I've been afraid of is being defined by what you, and everyone else around here thinks of me. But that's okay. I accept that. I'm just not going to let that fear dictate what I do anymore. Just like I'm no longer going to let you—or the rest of the world—dictate my character."

"Because you are so sure of who you are?" Lady Agnue asked, rolling her eyes.

"Partially," I admitted. "But also because I know who I *want to be*—someone as true of heart as they are clear of mind, someone as kind as they are strong, and someone who exemplifies all the qualities of a great princess *and* a great hero."

"How many times must I tell you, Miss Knight? You cannot—"

"Don't even start, Lady Agnue," I said. "I can be anything I want. I know I can because—despite what you believe—people are capable of being more than one dimensional. We are not designed to fit into a perfect singular slot like a round peg in a round hole. We're much more complex than these stereotypes you keep trying to shove us into. I've seen it with my own eyes. When we were in the Forbidden Forest, my friends were under the influence of a magic watering can and there were these Therewolves and . . . well, that's another story. The point is that a person can be unkind but still be a good friend. They can be selfish but also loyal. They can be brave even when they are full of fear. And they can even be trustworthy when so much of them is cloaked in mystery."

"So is that what you are claiming, Miss Knight?" Lady Agnue said, standing slowly from her desk. "That you are one of these great contradictions—this mighty hero-princess as you so described?"

"No," I responded, watching her steadily as she moved around her desk. "At least not yet anyways. The truth is that the Crisanta Knight I've been up 'til now hasn't come close to being the admirable, powerful person I'm describing. She's been lost, letting her life be defined by everyone else in the world—friends, enemies, the Author. But that ends now." I stood my ground firmly. "That Crisanta Knight is dead. Her limitations no longer shape me or my decisions; the only thing that does is the worthy hero-princess I want to be. My choices are a reflection of her from hereon out—not anything or anyone else. Least of all . . . *you*."

My clenched fist tingled with the familiar sensation of the magic watering can's liquid metal effect. I squeezed it tighter and subtly moved it behind my back so Lady Agnue wouldn't see.

"Well . . ." the headmistress mused after a moment, leaning against her desk. "Quite the speech, Miss Knight. Really. It demonstrates a great deal of personal growth and self-acceptance, the likes of which you should be proud of."

"Pride isn't relevant here," I said, unmoved. "What is important is whether or not you're going to listen to my friends and me about everything we've just told you."

"I am afraid the answer to that is still a firm no," she replied.

"Then you know what I have to do—what we have to do," I countered.

"I know what you want to do, Crisanta Knight," she said calmly, her copper eyes sparkling with the kind of bloodlust that a coyote might display toward a deer. "But that does not mean you are going to do it. In fact, you and your friends—both here and at Lord Channing's—are not going to tell anyone what you have just finished describing to me."

"And why not?"

"Because I was not being overly dramatic when I said I might send out a request to have you transferred to Alderon. Tell me, Miss Knight, if you actually believe all those stories you have told me, how long do you think a protagonist like yourself would last in such a place?"

I scoffed. "You don't have the power to send anyone to Alderon. It's not your call. And even if it was, no one would ever let you get away with it."

"That may be true," Lady Agnue conceded. "But it is the call of a good friend of mine. Perhaps you know her; her name is Lena Lenore."

"Nice try. Lenore doesn't have that kind of authority either. If she did, she would've already sent me to Alderon herself."

"Right again," Lady Agnue said. "But the only reason she has not is because she has yet to find a justification for doing so."

"And what, now she has?" I asked, still not taking her seriously.

"No, but she will as soon as I tell her you have Pure Magic Disease."

My heart stopped. I didn't know how Lady Agnue knew about the sickness, much less that I had it, but I wasn't about to give her the satisfaction of seeing me squirm. I kept my expression neutral, swallowing down any emotion that might give me away. "I don't know what you're talking about," I replied carefully.

"Oh, I think you do. I think you know all too well what I am talking about and what would happen to you if anyone else found out."

I held my tongue.

"No back-sass?" Lady Agnue commented. "My, that is a first. I assume you are aware that if the Godmothers or any of the other realm leaders became aware of your Pure Magic they would have all the just cause necessary to lock you away forever. The greater population of the realm might not be aware of the illness for the time being, but for the right reasons I am sure the ambassadors would tell them. And once they do, there would be no place for you to hide. After all, none of the citizens of Book would want someone who could turn into a vengeful, powerful witch at any moment running about freely. Our leaders would insist that you be imprisoned within Alderon and no one would protest."

"Alderon's In and Out Spell has no effect on me and my friends anymore. We already explained that to you."

"Yes, but Lena Lenore has command over an entire agency of powerful Fairy Godmothers," Lady Agnue replied. "I am sure we could find some sort of magical enchantment that would counteract your new ability—keep you in Alderon until you either turn into the villain your disease is priming you for or your antagonist friends silence you themselves."

I tried to keep my tone even. "Your word is not enough to convince anyone I have Pure Magic."

"Perhaps not," Lady Agnue admitted. "But as you said, an idea is a formidable thing. And more than that, I have proof."

My eyebrows shot up. "What proof?"

"As you may already know, there are two symptoms that diagnose Pure Magic Disease—the inability to remove one's magic and dreams of the future. Prior to your return this evening, Lena

Lenore also paid me a visit. She told me about your magic and that she witnessed the first of the two symptoms when you killed a Stiltdegarth in her office. But she cannot make a case against you unless she has evidence of the second symptom as well. So she reached out to me to see if I might have something. And the thing of it is . . . *I do.* I may not have told her about it, but I possess proof of your sleep-induced abilities, Crisanta. I simply thought I would keep it to myself so that I might use it as leverage."

Now it was my turn to glare. "You're bluffing," I accused.

"I assure you, I am not," the headmistress responded. "But if you do not believe me, I could contact Lena Lenore right now and we could get all this straightened out tonight. It would be easy to give her the condemning proof she is searching for. On the other hand, should having your life completely destroyed not be of interest to you, you could always just do as I say."

I gritted my teeth. "What do you want, Lady Agnue?"

"The very thing that comes least naturally to you, Miss Knight—silence. I shall keep your secret so long as neither you nor your friends speak a word to anyone about what you have learned about the world beyond these walls. But open your mouth even once and I will contact the Godmother Supreme and give her the fate-sealing information about you that she is searching for. Then you and your Pure Magic Disease-ridden self will be on the next transport to Alderon with me happily waving you off."

CHAPTER 27

Dressed to Kill

J flitted back and forth across the room, getting ready for the ball.

She was wearing a fitted, floor-length black satin gown with one strap over her right shoulder. It was a flattering and simple look, which she accessorized with gold, dangling earrings. Her jet-black hair was in a ballet dancer's bun, showing off the earrings. It was wound up tight, opposite to her mood, which seemed unusually loose.

Unlike my friend, I had not yet found the will to reassume our normal princess activities. We'd just returned from a perspective-bending, life-changing, mind-altering mission. The short week we'd been back at school was nowhere near enough time to decompress from it all.

As a result, I was putting off putting on my poofy dress for as long as possible. Spending an evening in a ballroom making small talk with our classmates about hairstyles and homework (and then probably being gossiped about the moment we turned our backs) hardly seemed like a fun time.

"SJ, this is ridiculous," I commented for the fourth time in the last fifteen minutes. "We shouldn't be going to another ball like everything is normal when the truth is anything but."

"I know, Crisa," SJ replied.

"You know," I sighed, "but you're still going."

"As are you," she said, coming over to me. "Yes, it is madness to have to go about business as usual when there is so much malevolence brewing in the world. But for the time being we are at a stalemate in terms of what we can do about it. Since Lady Agnue has leverage on you with regards to your Pure Magic, we have to proceed carefully."

"So what, you're saying we behave ourselves and make believe all is right with the world? We do exactly what our witch of a headmistress wants and don't warn the other protagonists or try to stop Nadia and Arian? We just pretend like nothing is at stake?"

"No, I am saying that we cannot allow our emotions to get the better of us because *everything* is at stake. Just as this is not the time for impetuous, ill-thought-out action, nor is it the time for rebellious protests like locking ourselves in our room like pouting children. We need to be cautiously prudent and put up a front— utilizing it to think about how to best move forward."

I knocked my skull against my headboard. "Ugh. I know you're right. I just hate not doing anything."

"We all do," SJ replied. She fastened the clasps on her fancy shoes. "But with the situation as it stands, that is all we can afford for now."

I twiddled my thumbs and glanced at the floor. "Unless we didn't," I said evenly. "I mean, we could always just disregard Lady Agnue and her stupid leverage over me and tell everyone what we came back to tell them."

"And then one message to Lena Lenore later and you would be sent off to Alderon—delivered to their front porch like a present to the very people who want you dead. Is that what you want?"

"Obviously not. But all the other protagonists . . . we have to think about their safety too. They deserve to know that they're in danger. Isn't it kind of selfish to put my well-being over theirs?"

SJ sighed and sat on the edge of my bed, trying not to wrinkle her dress. "Crisa, I understand where you are coming from. But as difficult a burden as it may be, the best way to keep the other protagonists safe is by keeping you safe. Nadia, Arian, and the people of Alderon want you eliminated because you are the only person supposedly capable of stopping them. So as wrong as it may seem now, it really is in everyone's best interest to bide our time under the thumb of our headmistress until we have a solid plan."

She put her hand on my arm sympathetically, and I sat up to join her at the edge of the comforter. I bumped my shoulder against hers and she responded by giving me a small side hug.

"It will be okay, you know," she said. "We are in this together, which means that we will get through this together."

I nodded in agreement. "I know," I said. "You, me, Blue, Jason, and Daniel—somehow, we'll find a way."

SJ smiled, a glint of mischief in her eye. "So Alderon was not just a fluke then? You are finally recognizing Daniel as a part of our group? My goodness, someone has really grown. I seem to recall you describing him as 'the most obnoxious boy in the history of time' in this very room not so long ago."

"Oh, you're exaggerating."

"You said you wanted to 'smush his face.'"

A small grin escaped my lips. "Yeah, well, just because I like him better now doesn't mean that option's completely off the table."

SJ huffed in amusement then trotted to the other side of the room to collect her purse. As she passed the floor-length mirror, she inadvertently bumped her desk. The slight reverberation caused several glass animal figurines on the desk to tremble, including the glass Pegasus figurine that was perched on the very edge.

"Listen," SJ said, not noticing the precarious state of her collectible. "Get ready in your own time. I am not going to harass you about it. You can meet me, Blue, and the boys in the ballroom when you are done."

"Where is Blue, anyway?" I asked. "Aren't you worried about her not coming to the ball either?"

"No. She went down to the practice fields. She said she wanted to get a workout in and would change in the barn. I think she shoved her dress into a duffle bag. I would wait for both of you, but we are already running late and I want to reassert myself as head of the ball planning committee, which means that before the grand doors open I need to be there to—"

"I know, I know," I interjected. "Go be super-princess. I'll get changed and see you guys there."

SJ made for the door. "I will check you in when I arrive so that you can take your time without getting another lecture from Madame Lisbon about punctuality."

"Having ditched this much school, I think our Damsels in Distress professor might have better topics to talk to me about," I said with a scoff. "But I appreciate your help. Reliable ol' SJ, always looking out for me."

She opened the door to our suite and gave me a wink. "Thank me later," she called back.

It occurred to me then that I had never followed up on her comment. SJ always said "thank me later" whenever she helped me out of a jam, but I couldn't recall ever actually thanking her.

I lay back down on my bed and stared up at the maroon and purple canopy. The tick-tock of the clock on Blue's desk echoed through the empty suite.

I found my mind to be uncharacteristically blank. No thoughts ran through my head. No insecurities or doubts swarmed my subconscious. While everything to do with Lady Agnue and my Pure Magic was bothering me, there was a static nature to this moment. And in it, I drifted off to sleep.

I didn't have many dreams this time. Maybe it was because I hadn't used any magic today. Or maybe I was just too tired.

I caught a glimpse of a black flag with a skull and crossbones insignia fluttering in the night's breeze. An image of Chance Darling in Twenty-Three Skidd armor walking down a corridor. And a flash of Natalie reading in a library. The row of books behind her was labeled "Art History." She sat on the cheap blue carpet with her back against one of the stacks.

The last sight to filter through my dreams was a painting I'd seen at Liza's—the one with the gorge surrounded by a red and orange sky. The image began to flicker until there were no brush strokes or paint and it had become a real setting. My perspective panned over the gorge for about five seconds before it faded to black. When it did, I was in the void.

I heard two voices. First Nadia's. Then mine.

"I guess this comes down to you and me then."

"Didn't it always?"

I woke up.

I thought I'd only been asleep a few minutes, but when I looked at the clock I was amazed to discover it had almost been an hour. The ball was already in full swing and I was probably the only person not in attendance.

While I should have put on my gown, I grabbed a silvery zip-up sweater and slipped out into the hallway instead.

I remembered my routes perfectly. I'd spent too many years roaming these halls to forget them—going to and from classes, trying to evade the guards for some privacy, adventuring with my friends. This place was my home. I could probably navigate through here with my eyes closed. The memory of every twist and turn was ingrained in my mind like a reflex.

I moved with the covertness of a shadow and journeyed down the grand staircase that connected our suites to the main level of the school. The plush fuchsia carpet of the steps squished beneath my boots. The cold, smooth texture of the silver bannister slid under my fingers. Icy winter air flowing through several open windows reddened my cheeks as I descended.

When I reached the ground floor, instead of taking the normal route to the back entrance of the ballroom, I headed in the opposite direction. One of the campus's western towers had a stairwell with a perfect view of the ballroom. I may not have felt like joining the festivities just yet, but part of me wanted to take a look.

On my way there I noticed that the grand columns and tapestries hanging from the walls seemed smaller than they once did. The oil paintings too, seemed less vivid. And the hollow, armored knights that lined the walkway didn't appear threatening in the slightest.

After experiencing so much in the last few weeks, nothing about this school would ever seem larger than life again. I had outgrown feeling small in this setting, just as I had outgrown feeling small around Lady Agnue. The main reason for this being that I had grown.

Eventually I arrived at the tower and climbed the winding stone stairwell until I came to a window. It was supposed to be kept shut, but I knew from experience that you could get it open with a good shove of your elbow.

I did just that, and the wind and music of the ball came floating into the tower. I could see it clearly from this vantage point—the glowing aura of the ballroom's chandeliers poured out of the building like my magic glow had poured out of my hands in Alderon.

I gazed out the window. I had arrived right in time to watch tonight's main event—the senior class waltz, which took place every December.

Good grief, was it already December?

Between all the kingdoms we'd travelled to, the visits to Earth, and all the twists and turns in time, my sense of the day and month had become pretty warped. I mean, it was nearly the end of the semester and my birthday was less than a week away. It had all happened so fast.

The music from the ball picked up and my attention drifted back to it.

Lady Agnue's and Lord Channing's had a ball every month, but the one in December was special. It was at this time that our schools had their annual Ball of the First Frost. This was an important event where the two schools formally presented their senior classes that would be graduating in the spring.

During the fall semester, the seniors from both schools worked with our ballroom dancing professors prior to each of the monthly balls. Paired with a partner chosen at the beginning of the school year, the seniors learned a choreographed waltz that would be performed at the December dance. Nailing this performance was a huge part of our final grade; it fulfilled the mandatory "Ballroom Theory" credit required for all protagonists to graduate.

If you asked me the "performing in front of everybody" aspect added way more pressure than necessary to the test. But holding this presentation ball in the winter meant that seniors could relax during their spring semesters—take some easy classes maybe?

The waltz was just starting as I leaned against the cold stone of the windowsill and watched my older classmates move with the grace of dying autumn leaves caught in a breeze—effortless and beautiful, despite being at the end of this chapter in their lives.

There were a few other traditions associated with the Ball of the First Frost. The seniors didn't enter the ballroom with everyone else. About fifteen minutes after the ball began they were introduced individually. The grand doors at the front of the ballroom were propped ajar and each protagonist descended the staircase. First came the boys; then came the girls.

The outfits for this evening were also unique. While the seniors went through multiple fittings to have the most exquisite, customized ball attire made for their big day, all underclassmen had to rock a more uniformed look.

To contrast the personally designed black tuxedoes of the senior boys, the underclassmen from Lord Channing's wore variations of silver suits. And while the senior girls donned unique and colorful dresses, underclassmen from Lady Agnue's wore pure black gowns that made our graduating protagonists stand out like parrots among a flock of ravens.

As I observed the brilliantly dressed protagonists of Lady Agnue's dance with the sleekly dressed protagonists of Lord Channing's, I found myself thinking how it would soon be my turn to be there. I was a junior, about to turn seventeen.

In one year, I would be graduating. In one year, Nadia's plan would come to fruition. And in one year, I would have to save Natalie—that is, if I decided to go through with my idea to push my Pure Magic and reach her, which Liza had so adamantly advised against.

The sound of applause returned me to the present. The waltz was over, and so was my time here. I made my way back to my room and decided to get ready for the ball.

I went to the bathroom and splashed some water on my face. Then I stared at myself in the mirror. I thought about the night we'd been on the magic train. Sitting in the dining car, I had stared at my reflection in the window and felt so conflicted about the girl staring back at me. Things were different now. The protagonist looking back at me was stronger, more sure of herself, more . . .

I looked down at my right hand and turned it over to examine the palm.

That moment in my headmistress's office had been the last time I would ever feel the magic watering can's liquid metal effect. While it was happening I'd assumed the blurry mark was just acting up again. But when I'd examined it later on, I'd discovered that this time had been the real thing. I'd figured out which of my qualities was my essence—that thing about myself that was my greatest source of internal strength.

I flexed my hand, feeling at peace with the word branded there.

"Self-Acceptance."

I guess Chauncey the talking pig from the Forbidden Forest had been right all that time ago. Accepting myself was what it all came down to.

Makes me wonder why his ex-wife left him.

Maybe it was the kale omelets.

I shook my head and smiled. That was the reason the mark had been acting up periodically over the last few weeks. Every time I accepted a part of myself—being able to see the future, being a leader, being a fighter, being afraid, and so on—the watering can's magic had been triggered because I was getting closer to accepting myself entirely. It wasn't until I accepted who I wanted to be as well that I was able to fully accept myself. And now—as the queen of Adelaide had said—I finally felt whole.

I knew the mark would fade in a matter of weeks—just as Blue's, SJ's, Daniel's, and Jason's had—but for now I was content to see it there. With so many storms brewing, it was a pleasant reminder that through all the bad I could come out the other side with something good and become a better version of myself in the process.

Pushing open the wooden double doors, I stepped inside our walk-in closet. The floor was covered in beige carpet. I kicked off my boots and made my way past SJ's collection of gowns and dresses and Blue's collection of vests, tops, and pants. The floor space of my section held eight different pairs of boots. When I opened the doors to the rest of my wardrobe I found a shimmering princess gown unlike any other.

It hung in front of my normal assortment of leggings, dresses, and jackets. Unlike SJ's black gown, mine was a more traditional princess look that poofed out in the conventional fairytale way. The big skirt was draped in dark, glistening lace that worked its way up to the strapless bodice, climbing it like a maleficent vine.

Usually I would have deemed the thing far too extravagant for my personal taste. But there was something compelling about the dress. I couldn't quite put my finger on this mystifying quality, but I found myself surprisingly enchanted by it. Everything about it seemed perfect, except . . .

Aw, dang it.

The bodice was a corset. I hated corsets. They were super

uncomfortable and getting them on was a challenge in itself because you had to lace them up behind your back like a fancy, reverse shoelace.

I would usually pay a visit to our school's seamstresses a week or two before each ball to specifically request a dress with a zipper instead of a corset. But as we had only returned recently, I'd completely forgotten about the task.

As a result, I garnered it would take me no less than a good twenty minutes to get the dress on without any of my friends to help. I knew from the times SJ had worn a corset gown that getting such a dress laced up properly was a two-person job.

I curtly unlaced the dress's back and stepped into the complex thing. Just as I was making my first attempts to fasten it, I heard a knock on our bedroom door.

"Hello?"

"Uh, who is it?" I called out.

"Crisa," the all-too familiar voice responded. "It is me, Mauvrey. Are SJ or Blue there?"

I scrunched up my nose in confusion. What the heck was she doing here?

"Um, no, they're already downstairs."

"The door is unlocked, may I come in?"

"Uh . . ."

Why would she want to? I may not have seen her for a while, but I was pretty sure we still hated each other.

Then again, I was not in the mood to fight with my old school nemesis. I was so over her it wasn't even funny. I had real enemies now. And as such, our animosity seemed trivial and I felt no qualms about letting her in. Just like with Lady Agnue, the effect of her meanness could no longer touch me. I might as well see what she wanted.

"Yeah, fine. Whatever," I shouted.

I heard the door open then close with a light click as I continued to work the laces of my corset. When Mauvrey didn't say anything after a few seconds, I decided to call out to her. "What are you doing here, Mauvrey? Shouldn't you be at the ball?"

"I was," she responded. "But when I did not see you there I thought I would come looking for you."

"Why?"

There was quiet for a brief pause, and then . . .

"I wanted to apologize," she said.

I recalled the dream I had recently about Mauvrey apologizing in my room. I guess this was that moment.

"Crisa, when you ran away from school a lot of rumors started floating around about why you left," Mauvrey continued. "And after some time had passed, I began to wonder if maybe it was because of me. I wondered if it was my harassment that drove you away. The last time we spoke I more or less sold you out to Lady Agnue for no other reason than satisfying my own spite. So for that, and everything else I have done to you, I am remorseful."

Neither of us spoke for a long beat. I wished I could've gotten a glimpse at her face so I could ascertain whether or not she was being sincere.

Part of me was certain that I shouldn't take her by her word. But another part of me sort of wanted to. I had seen enough of villains in the past few weeks. Mauvrey's apology sounded genuine. Maybe she had changed like I had. Stranger things had happened.

"You understand how sorry I am, right?" Mauvrey asked.

I took a deep breath and resumed struggling to lace up my dress. "Don't be," I responded.

"But I am," Mauvrey said. "Everything that has happened to you . . . I am afraid it all comes back to me."

"Mauvrey," I continued as I pulled on the corset's laces. "I appreciate the apology, but it wasn't your fault I left school." I managed to get one of the laces through a fastening loop then tightened my grip. "You didn't—WHOA!"

I'd given the aforementioned lace such a forceful yank that it knocked me off balance and caused me to topple over.

"Are you okay?" Mauvrey called out in a worried voice.

"Yeah, I'm fine," I replied from the floor of my closet. "It's just this stupid dress I'm supposed to wear to the ball. The bodice is a corset and I can't reach it well enough to fasten myself in."

"Do you want me to lace you up?" Mauvrey offered.

Is she serious? Of course not.

Then I sighed. I was sitting in a giant compression of my dress—squashed pairs of boots beneath me, and clothes I'd knocked off their hangers all over me. Without the assistance of another person I would sooner destroy this closet than get this dress on.

"All right. Yeah," I conceded. "I guess I could use the help." I got up, dusted off my pride, and shuffled into the bedroom with my partially laced-up dress.

Mauvrey stood by SJ's desk wearing her own black gown. It was cut with a high slit in the front and had a plunging neckline. Her long blonde hair was pulled to one side by a sparkling blue clip that matched her eyes. Overall, she looked just as intimidatingly pretty as I remembered.

She gestured to the spot in front of the mirror. "Please," she said.

I came over to meet her and turned to face the mirror as she'd instructed. Looking at my reflection, I admitted to myself once more how stunning the dress was. Although the corset made it much more difficult to get into, I loved how pretty and totally magical I felt in it.

I glanced at Mauvrey in the mirror—she was hard at work behind me, really putting her back into lacing me up. I felt kind of weird about the whole situation, and my face flushed in embarrassment. Despite that, I found the humility to speak to her.

"Thanks," I finally said, ignoring the increasing redness in my cheeks. "I would've been stuck here fiddling with this thing for hours if you hadn't come along."

Mauvrey didn't look up; she kept fastening me in tighter and tighter. "My pleasure," she replied. "I am just glad I can always count on you to be running late, and that SJ and Blue were already downstairs."

"Why's that?"

"Because dyed black or not, there is a decent chance that one of them would have recognized this thing in a second," she said as she threaded the laces through and pulled them tightly.

"There we go, all finished," she said proudly. "Hmm, I think a bow made out of the leftover ends would look quite nice. Thoughts?"

"What do you mean they would've recognized it?" I asked as I tried to turn to face her. But that's when I realized I couldn't turn around. I tried again but still couldn't. I was frozen in place.

My eyes filled with panic as I kept trying to move. Hard as I strained, I was barely able to lift my arms more than a few inches, and when I did my whole body quivered in pain. All I could do was watch Mauvrey make an unnecessarily ornate bow with the remaining laces at the back of my corset.

"Do not bother," Mauvrey said. "The dark magic tied into Snow White's poisoned corset is fast-acting. It has probably already drained you of more than half your life force. And gone with it is the strength to move, let alone fight back."

Snow White's poisoned corset? But that means . . .

I glanced down and that's when I saw them. Peeking out from beneath Mauvrey's dress was a pair of black, glittering pumps with four-inch, silver-sequined heels. I also noticed a purple garment lying on the corner of my bed that hadn't been there when I'd gone into the bathroom. It was a cloak—the same purple cloak I'd seen in my dreams paired with Mauvrey's sparkly shoes.

I gulped down the fear as anger and understanding washed over me.

"How long have you been working for Arian, Mauvrey?" I

asked bluntly, finally realizing that she was the cloaked girl I'd seen talking with him in my dreams.

"Much longer than you might think," Mauvrey responded, not sounding surprised that I'd made the connection. "But I have only been charged with important tasks in the last few months. My first big job was breaking into the Treasure Archives."

I narrowed my eyes. "Care to share how you did it?"

"SJ's special potions book, of course," Mauvrey explained. "I volunteered in the library last spring and found it in the restricted section. I had planned to steal it this semester, but I was dismayed to learn that it had been checked out by one of the teachers. Luckily, I caught a glance of SJ with it in the potions lab, and I knew I could take it from her instead."

"But the only spell in that book that would've silenced the Archives' alarms took weeks to make," I said, thinking back to the potion that SJ had brewed.

There was no way Mauvrey could've used the same tactic. When SJ's special potions book went missing from our room earlier in the semester, it had only been gone a couple of days before the break-in occurred—not enough time for Mauvrey to cook up the same recipe.

So how had she done it? The glass cases of the Archives had been shattered. And even if the alarms had somehow failed, the various security measures in place should've stopped her.

"Do you remember our first day of potions class this semester?" Mauvrey asked. "When she was sucking up to Madame Alexanders, SJ perfectly described the Sleeping Capsule Spell used to enchant my home kingdom when my mother's curse came to fruition all those years ago."

I recalled the spell she was talking about. The Fairy Godmothers had used it when Mauvrey's mother, Sleeping Beauty, had been bewitched. They'd created a complex sleeping potion to keep her kingdom's inhabitants asleep while making time temporarily stand still so that when everyone woke up it was like nothing had happened.

"But that spell required magic," I protested.

"Honestly, do you listen to any of our lectures?" Mauvrey replied. "It is like Madame Alexanders said, the results achieved by spells like those are entirely possible without magic; they are just not as powerful or permanent, and require advanced skill and knowledge to brew. I used the instructions in SJ's book to concoct a potion that put the entire school in a magic-like sleep for an hour. Everything stood still around the campus while I broke into the Archives. It was like a loophole in time. The guards, the students, the staff—even the alarm systems and defense mechanisms—were frozen while I took what I needed. By the time the potion wore off, it was as if not a second had gone by."

"Then what? You planted my pumpkin earring in the wreckage just for kicks so I'd be framed?" I asked, recalling that awful day I'd been summoned to Lady Agnue's office as the lead suspect in the break-in.

"It was not a part of my initial plan," Mauvrey admitted. "But the birds I employed to fly into your room and bring me SJ's book happened to pick it up. They must have thought it was shiny birdseed or something. Anyways, I figured why not? I deserve some fun from time to time in between running Arian's errands."

Fury flashed inside me. Again I tried to take a swing at her but I was only able to twist a couple of inches and move my arms up to my waist before a jolt of pain caused me to stop.

"You're despicable, you know that?" I grimaced. "Do you have any idea what I've had to go through because of you? The magic mirror and genie lamp you gave Arian almost got me killed."

"'Almost' being the operative word," Mauvrey said. "So it is a very good thing that I took this corset from the case as well. Granted I was not one hundred percent sure it would fit you—

Snow White was much thinner. But it looks like I was worried for nothing. Sometimes it is just wonderful how things work out."

I felt so stupid. I thought it was strange how I'd been drawn to this dress, despite my aversion to corseted gowns. But I remembered that SJ said this corset was laced with dark magic and enchanted via potion to attract anyone who got too close to it.

This whole time my face was not flushed from embarrassment at having Mauvrey help me, but from losing oxygen as the poison kicked in. The corset's magical toxins were seeping into me with every passing second.

I tried to harness my own magic in the telepathic way I'd done back in Alderon, but it was no use. Doing that required way more power than I had at the moment. Maybe if I could place my hands on something I could transfer my magic into it that way . . .

"I was supposed to eliminate you after your prologue prophecy appeared," Mauvrey explained as I racked my brain for options. "That is why I stole this corset in addition to the items Arian needed to find and catch Paige Tomkins. My intention was to use it on you at our next ball, but you and your friends fled the campus before I had the chance. You have no idea how furious Arian was. At least now I have a chance to redeem myself."

The poison coursing through my veins was reaching dangerous levels. I felt my heart slowing down. Every breath made my lungs hurt and my core shiver. I couldn't believe that I'd survived antagonists, monsters, and death-defying adventures only to be killed by a dress.

My rage and spite taking a slight back seat, a tinge of confused desperation sunk in. "Are you seriously trying to kill me, Mauvrey?" I gasped, trying to keep a straight face and keep my nemesis from seeing the pain I was in. "I mean, do you really hate me *that* much?"

"Yes and no," Mauvrey chirped. She placed her icy hand on my shoulder. "Do not misunderstand, I do loathe you, Crisa. But you know perfectly well that there are bigger things happening right now than you and me. Although I have to say, after all the trouble you got me into with Arian and Nadia, I am taking great pleasure in this. Do you have any idea how much heat I had to take when they discovered the magic mirror I took from the Treasure Archives was a fake that you and your friends left behind?"

I huffed in amusement. "Oh, I'm sorry. I didn't mean for my escapades to interfere with Nadia's plot to break out of Alderon and murder the realm's protagonists. Why are you even helping her anyways? *You're* a protagonist."

"Correction, Crisa. I *was* a protagonist. A long time ago. My priorities and allegiances have changed. And now I am, shall we say, something quite different."

Her eyes locked with mine in the mirror and for a second their vivid blue color flashed deep, cold black—exactly like the color I'd come to know in Arian's eyes. The dots connected and the last piece of the puzzle became clear.

"You're a Shadow Guardian," I said wearily, thinking back to my visions of Mauvrey in that purple cloak beneath the bunker in the Capitol Building. "That's how you were able to get past the In and Out Spell when you had to meet Arian outside of school."

"Not only that," she confirmed, "it is how I am going to walk out of here now. It is just too bad you can't be there to see me off."

"Cannot."

"Pardon?"

"You used a contraction, Mauvrey;" I replied flatly, calling her on the very stupid grammatical error she'd belittled me for over the years. "A real princess would say 'cannot'—not 'can't.' Your words, not mine. Looks like that Shadow inside you isn't just sucking out your soul, but your good breeding too."

Mauvrey's expression turned sour. The daggers she stared very well could have killed me had the corset not already been doing the job. It felt like my pulse was slowing and an icy sensation was quickly spreading through my nervous system.

"Very good, Crisa," Mauvrey commented, recovering her composure. "Most people in your situation would be groveling. But not you. And that is all right. Actually, it is rather nice to see you retain your irritatingly bold nature even in your last few minutes of life. It makes the situation more meaningful."

I opened my mouth to respond, but it was as dry as the Valley of Strife. I swallowed hard—trying to regain some feeling in my throat, but to no avail.

Mauvrey just laughed.

"Having trouble speaking, are we? Yes, well, that is how this darling corset works. First you lose your ability to move, then your ability to speak, then finally you just lose. Any minute now you will be lying on this floor gasping for air like the homely little fish out of water you always were."

I wanted to say something in retaliation. But I had to conserve whatever energy I had left for a moment when it might be converted into something useful. I just had to figure out what that something was going to be, and fast.

Calling for help would be useless. Even if I could focus the strength to, no one would hear me. The whole school was in the grand ballroom.

Ugh, think. There has to be something.

My eyeballs—the only parts of me still able to move without difficulty—scanned the room. The balcony doors were open. On SJ's perfectly organized desk was her collection of glass figurines . . . including the glass Pegasus.

Memories of the thing flying around my dreams flashed through my head. That was it. I only needed to touch it.

Just as Mauvrey described, my legs gave out and my body fell to the floor. With one last burst of adrenaline and pure will I extended my left arm to grasp the edge of the desk on my way down. This caused it to wobble enough for the Pegasus—already precariously perched on the brink—to topple to the wooden floorboards at the same time I did. The figurine shattered into a dozen tiny pieces.

I could no longer open my mouth to speak, so I lay there motionless and slowed my breathing in an effort to conserve the strength I had left. As I did, my nemesis collected her purple cloak from my bed and moved toward the door. Just before leaving she looked back at my helpless form on the floor.

"Goodbye, Crisa," she said contentedly. "I would say it has been nice knowing you, but princesses are not supposed to lie either, are they?"

She smirked, tossed her hair over her shoulder triumphantly, and left me to die. At least that's what she must've thought. Me, I had a completely different thought. And that thought was: *Sorry Mauvrey, but not today.*

I rallied all my strength, stubbornness, and sense of fight to reach out and touch the broken shards of the Pegasus figurine. When my fingers made contact, I released a breath—concentrating on forcing the magic inside of me to flow through my hands.

Reassemble, I thought desperately. *Then follow Mauvrey. The girl—*

I struggled as the excruciating pain of the corset crushed me.

Follow the girl with the purple cloak. Find out where she's going and don't return to me until you do and can show me the way.

The glow that emanated from my hand was weak. It barely flickered, and for a moment I thought I might not have enough power to bring the figurine to life. But then several brighter wisps of golden light pulsed out of my fingertips. They enveloped the pieces of glass. A few seconds later the shards joined together and reassembled the figurine perfectly. The glass Pegasus flitted to life and took off as I'd ordered—flying through the balcony doors.

My heart was beating as slowly as a rusty clock trying to keep time. But I couldn't give up yet; I had one more play.

I pressed both hands firmly onto the wooden floor and focused so hard I thought my brain might explode. My eyes started to close. I released a final, fading burst of magic from my hands.

Come on, I thought. *Come to life. Rip yourself free and fly.*

Please fly.

The glow was so faint a firefly's funeral would have outshined it. But as my vision hazed over I heard the distinct sound of wood splintering and felt the floor beneath me begin to shake.

Take me to the infirmary, I commanded the wooden floorboard that was beginning to break loose. *It's the third tower from the . . .*

CHAPTER 28

Something New

ou'd think with all the blackouts I'd experienced during this adventure I would've learned to wake from them with a bit more grace.

Ah, wishful thinking.

When I stirred I found my face smooshed into a pillow, a moderate pool of drool beneath me, and my hair matted to my face.

Realizing I was alive, I tried to jump to my feet but serious pain kicked in and I was only able to sit up in bed.

Wait, bed?

I looked around and discovered I was alone in my school's infirmary. It was dark outside. Only one window was open, barely allowing the sound of distant music from the ball to stream in like a melodic whisper.

I was wearing a floor-length, black silk robe. It was the kind that the infirmary reserved solely for people with serious illnesses. The robes were made from rare silk produced by enchanted silkworms in the kingdom of Coventry. I'd had a dream about me wearing one of these. What that dream had failed to illustrate, however, was the searing pain I'd be feeling while wearing it. I doubled over and clutched my ribcage as ache and agony pulsed through my core.

I glanced up and saw the fireplace on the other side of the room was roaring. The infirmary was usually all beige walls, white lace curtains, and unscented wax candles. But the hot orange flames instantly caught my attention. There also seemed to be a bulky object burning inside them.

Gathering all my strength, I forced myself to get up. I staggered like an old woman as I hobbled closer. I made it to the fireplace before the pain became too much and my legs gave way. With an ungraceful stumble, I landed in a seated position right in front of the fire. The flames' warm glow danced on the sheen of my robe.

Sitting on the stone floor, I realized what was burning inside the fire. It was a dress. The black demon gown with Snow White's poisoned corset was roasting in the blaze.

Suddenly the main doors to the infirmary swung open. I turned to see my friends walk in. Well, only SJ and Daniel walked in. Blue and Jason rode in on a flying, jagged plank of wood. I imagined it was the chunk of floorboard that had broken free from our suite in order to bring me here.

I forced myself to my feet. My friends were still in their formal ball attire—SJ in the dress I'd seen earlier, Blue in a black gown with ruffles, and the boys in their handsome silver suits.

"I am so glad you are awake!" SJ gushed. She and Daniel helped me over to the nearest cot, where I sat down.

The enchanted slab of wood didn't have eyes, but somehow it still noticed me. When it did, it started flying around the room in figure-eights that almost tossed Blue and Jason off.

"Whoa there," I said, raising my hands. "Settle down."

Much to my relief, it landed on the ground. Jason and Blue couldn't get off quick enough. Once they'd descended, the flying wooden floorboard abruptly took off back through the infirmary doors.

Hm. I'll have to follow up on that later . . .

Blue dusted off her dress then gave me a mischievous smile. "So who tried to kill you this time?"

"Blue, that is a highly inappropriate and insensitive way to phrase the question," SJ scolded. Then she directed her attention back to me. "But seriously, Crisa, who was it?"

"Was it that Nadia chick?" Blue suggested.

"Or was it that Arian kid again?" Daniel practically growled.

"How did any of those Alderon pains-in-the-neck even get into the school anyhow?" Jason interrupted. "I mean, I get the whole Shadow Guardian concept, but there are guards patrolling the perimeter at all times."

"Guys, it wasn't an Alderon pain-in-the-neck," I said as I sat up straighter. "It was one of our own."

My friends listened as I explained what happened with Mauvrey, from the realization that she had been the girl I'd seen plotting with Arian in my dreams to how I'd harnessed my last bit of strength to give life to the wooden floorboard so that it could bring me to the infirmary.

I also mentioned that I'd sent SJ's glass Pegasus figurine after Mauvrey, hoping that when it eventually returned it would be able to show us where she'd gone. It was extremely important to find out where Arian and his cronies were holding up. They would need a new place to plot and recruit commons for their cause if they could no longer use the bunker beneath the Capitol Building, and I intended to find it.

The others were shocked by the revelation. Not because they were surprised to find out Mauvrey was evil (I guess we all kind of knew that already) but because she was one of *them*. She was with Nadia and Arian. She had a Shadow living inside of her. And she was bent on destroying our realm's protagonists—the very group of people she'd spent her whole life associated with.

Did you see that coming? Cuz I sure didn't.

I wondered how Lady Agnue would take the news. Based on how she'd reacted to our other revelations, I was sure the truth of what happened tonight would never get out. She was probably already plotting with the school nurses about how to cover everything up.

When I finished my tale, SJ explained that my chunk of enchanted wood had dropped off my unconscious body at the infirmary, but the nurse hadn't known what was wrong. She hurried to find my roommates, hoping that they might be able to shed some light on what was happening. It was a good instinct. It only took SJ and Blue a second to recognize the corset and realize the problem. My friends and the nurse unlaced it as quickly as they could. Unfortunately, I had been wearing the corset for so long that simply removing it wasn't enough. They had to burn the thing in order for its dark magic to be disrupted. Doing so in the nick of time saved me.

"That's three, Crisa," Blue commented.

"Three what?"

"Three notable fairytale relics you've obliterated—the magic mirror, Aladdin's genie lamp, and the corset. We might as well go get your mother's glass slipper and chuck it at the wall right now."

"Hey, you destroyed the enchanted pea," I protested.

"And who's fault was it that we were locked in an Alderon prison?" Blue countered.

I sighed and glanced over at SJ. "All right. Remind me to make some time in my calendar to have that talk about my affinity for destruction."

In the aftermath of the corset poisoning I was forced to spend several days in the infirmary recuperating.

My friends periodically checked up on me. Lady Agnue hadn't exactly agreed to let the boys come visit (even after SJ, Blue, and I explained that they could pass through the In and Out Spell like we could). She couldn't risk the other students learning about our new abilities.

Nevertheless, my friends and I had outsmarted villains and monsters of every caliber on our adventure. Daniel and Jason possessed more than enough stealth to come and go from our school without being spotted. Using the forest between Lady Agnue's and Lord Channing's as cover while the other students were in class, they had no problem visiting me during my recovery.

It was a risky endeavor, but they didn't hesitate to do it. Which could be considered both sweet and asking for trouble. I approved on both counts.

On the first day of my recovery I woke to a much different tune than I had the previous night. Instead of ball music, blue birds chirping outside stirred me awake.

It was a pleasant sound, and their merriment helped me shake off the intense nature of the dream flashes I'd been having.

I'd seen the inside of a building collapse and become consumed by fire. A white porcelain teacup with a steaming hot beverage inside. A vision of a compass where the directions—instead of pointing to North, East, South, and West—pointed to the words: Nightmare, Enigma, Sweet Dreams, and Wanderers' Void.

I didn't know what any of those dreams signified, but I immediately reached for the small journal and quill on my bedside table and scribbled everything down. I may not have been a painter like Liza, but I figured it was probably in our best interest to take a page from her playbook and start keeping track of my visions. There was a lot to remember and we might be able to use some of the details in the future.

As I placed the journal back on the table, SJ entered the infirmary carrying a package.

"Good morning," she sang pleasantly.

"Hey, SJ," I said, boosting myself up to a sitting position. "So I guess I owe you a thank you for last night, huh?"

"Please, Crisa. You do not have to. You can simply—"

"Thank you later?" I shook my head. "Nah, that's the old me. The new me knows that I would have died in that dress if it wasn't for you guys, and I probably would have died many more times before that if you weren't always looking out for me. So thank you. It's a million times overdue, but thank you for always being there."

SJ smiled. "You are welcome, Crisa. I am happy to try and keep you out of trouble. But if you could do me a favor and maybe stay out of perilous situations for a couple of weeks, that would be great. I have a lot of homework to catch up on from all the classes we missed."

"I'll do my best." I gestured to the bundle in her hands. "Whatcha got there?"

"You tell me," SJ replied. "One of the guards found it near the practice fields inside a thistle berry bush."

SJ handed me the wrapped bundle and I saw that my name was written on it. Intrigued, I opened the parcel. Inside was a box and a note. Within the box was a small compact mirror with the words "Mark Two" carved into the bronze exterior—just like the compact mirrors I'd been dreaming about.

I unfolded the note.

"*Dear Crisa,*" I read aloud. "*Here's another little bit of fairytale history I bet you didn't know. The magic mirror from your school's Treasure Archives was not always the only one of its kind. Long before* Beauty & the Beast, *these types of mirrors (called Mark Ones) could easily be found and purchased throughout the realm. However, they were later looked on as invasions of privacy since the observed did not know they were being watched. As a result, the Godmothers collected all the Mark Ones and stripped them of their enchantments years ago—all except the mirror that used to be on display in your school.*

"*Although this old era of magic mirrors was eventually forgotten, the Godmothers have been working on a way to repurpose their magic for something more user-friendly. Hence the 'Mark Two.'*

"*This new generation of magic compact mirrors—due to be*

released realm-wide in late spring—will be used as a form of communication. Through the Mark Two you can contact anyone else who has a Mark Two no matter how far away they are.

"I want you to use this Mark Two to keep me up-to-date with what's going on with you. Pure Magic can be as much of a blessing as it is a curse, and I don't want you to have to go through everything on your own like I did.

"All you have to do to operate the Mark Two is open it and say the name of the person you wish to contact. Close the mirror to end the call. And if it starts vibrating, that means someone is calling you.

"Check in with me soon, and do tell me your decision with regards to contacting Natalie Poole. All the best until then.

– Liza

"P.S. Sorry if this package ended up in the river or something. The spell around your school and your Pure Magic make you an easier beacon for me to channel, but aim from the Indexlands to anywhere other than the Forbidden Forest and the Dolohaunty Mountains is still difficult."

I gazed at the small, smooth compact mirror with admiration. "Awesome," I commented.

"Very," SJ agreed. "One thing though, Crisa. I thought Liza said she did not want to help you communicate with Natalie through your dreams; that pushing your magic this way was very dangerous."

"She did," I affirmed. "But she also said that the choice was mine to make and she would support whatever I decide."

"You are not seriously considering it, are you?"

"It would be selfish of me not to. That girl's in trouble, SJ, and if I ignore that then we might all be in trouble."

SJ sat down in the chair of the plain white table across from my cot. "You mean because of the Eternity Gate?"

"Well, yeah. If it's real like our enemies believe and Natalie has the power to open it, then our priority should be her well-being."

"And if that comes at the cost of your own?" SJ asked.

"Then . . ." I glanced at the floor as the thought weighed on me. I swallowed a lump in my throat and sighed. "Then I guess I have to decide if I'm willing to pay it."

"Ha! I take the pot!" Blue announced as she threw down her playing cards and swept all the candy to her side of the table.

"What? Again?" I slammed down my cards in frustration. It was day two of my stay in the infirmary and I was raging with frustration over how many times Blue and Jason had beaten me at cards. We'd been playing for an hour and I hadn't won once.

"Not so fast, Blue," Jason objected. He got up from his chair and walked over to Blue's side of the table, crouching over to look underneath.

"Yup, just as I thought."

I heard the sound of adhesive being ripped, and when Jason rose he was holding three cards that had been taped to the underside of the table.

"You were cheating," he announced. "Ergo, I win."

Jason reached for the candy, but Blue punched him in the arm before he could grab it.

"I don't think so," she said. "You were cheating too."

Moving too fast for him to stop her, Blue swiftly pulled a pair of playing cards out of Jason's sleeve and waved them in his face. Jason was stunned.

"If you knew I was cheating, then why didn't you say something?"

"It was part of my strategy," Blue explained.

"Lulling me into a false sense of security?"

"Yup. How'd you know?"

Reaching over, Jason pulled three additional cards out of

Blue's cloak. "Because I was doing the same thing to you during the hand before that."

Blue affectionately punched Jason in the arm a second time. "Hmm. Not bad, Jas. But that still doesn't decide who gets the pot."

"I do," I interrupted, sweeping all the candy to my side of the table. "You're both cheaters. You hid more cards than were in play! These treats belong to me."

They both shrugged.

"In that case, I need to get more goods from the kitchen," Jason said.

"Be careful," I said. "You know no one at school can see you. Lady Agnue would go ballistic."

"It's fine. Everyone's in class and I'm pretty stealthy."

"Clearly," I said, gesturing to the cards on the table that Blue had pulled from his sleeve.

"Blue, you coming?" he asked as he turned to leave.

"Nah. I've still got some candy in my bag. Plus—unlike you, who can ditch your individual training sessions without anyone being the wiser—the only reason I was able to get out of classes today was because I pretended to be sick and said I needed to stay in the infirmary. Also, while you're gone I have to make sure you didn't plant any more cards around here."

"Fair enough," he said with a grin. "But remember, just because you don't find them, doesn't mean they're not there."

Jason left and I popped a gumdrop in my mouth. "Geez, I thought you guys were supposed to help me relax, not work on your mind games and battle strategy."

Blue lay down on my cot and put her boots up. "For us it's the same thing. Besides, this is way more fun than practicing needlepoint or catching up on homework with SJ."

"You're not wrong about that."

I hopped onto the cot beside her and put my boots up next to hers. Both of us stared at the ceiling. "Hey, Blue. How do you think SJ is doing with the whole 'lack of a protagonist book' thing?" I asked, the thought skimming my mind like a bird on the water.

Blue turned to look at me. "Why? Did she say something?"

"No," I replied. "But when she told us about it I got the feeling that she wanted to vent but didn't know how. She's so composed all the time."

"You make that sound like a bad thing."

"Usually it's not. But take it from someone who's been there. Keeping secrets can slowly eat away at you until you don't even recognize yourself anymore."

"Yeah. I know . . ." Blue sat up. She looked off into the distance, causing me to sit up in concern alongside her.

"What's the matter?"

Blue bit her lip and glanced toward the door. Then she abruptly pivoted to face me. "Crisa, do you remember the last day we were at Ashlyn's house—when I told you that I had a secret too?"

I thought back to the day in question. Blue and I had been on the dock. It was the morning we were going to cross back through the Bermuda wormhole on Earth and face off with Arian on Adelaide.

"Yeah, something about your book," I replied. "You said you'd tell me when I stopped ticking you off."

"Well, lo and behold that day came and went and I still didn't say anything to you or SJ. Which means that she hasn't been the only hypocrite around here afraid of venting. But not anymore." Blue huffed. "I'm going to tell you something, Crisa—the truth about what my prologue prophecy really said and why I was so dead set on changing it."

"I thought it was because of Jason," I asserted. "When your prophecy appeared and I asked you why you were so upset, you said that it was because you were 'supposed to end up with him.'"

"Yeah, well the thing is, those weren't so much the Author's words as they were my own."

"I don't get it."

Blue fidgeted nervously. "Crisa, I think I might have . . . what one might technically call . . . *feelings* for Jason."

I almost fell off the mattress.

"What?"

"Keep it down!"

"Sorry, sorry," I said, whispering so that not even a dust bunny would overhear our conversation.

"Look," Blue went on. "I'm not quite sure how to describe it because I've never had these kinds of girl feelings for a guy before."

"What about Bruce Willis?"

"Bruce is my man and everything, but this is different," she replied. "I mean I'm not saying I *love* Jason or anything. I'm just saying I want to keep my options open—kind of call perpetual dibs on him until I know what I want. But then my prophecy appeared and told me doing so wasn't an option. It said that during the course of our upcoming trials and tribulations he's supposed to 'die twice,' and that both times it's going to be my fault. So of course I freaked out. And I was determined to find the Author because it's not like I can have the guy I'm secretly crushing on go and get killed because of me, you know?"

"Well, that doesn't make any sense," I said, furrowing my eyebrows. "How's a person supposed to die twice?"

"I don't know. Apparently it's an Inherent Fate thing. Based on the phrasing, Liza said the 'dying' thing probably isn't literal and I shouldn't worry about it. All this time my freaking out has likely been for nothing. But, Crisa, big picture. This is major. I just told you I have feelings for an *actual, human boy*."

"Right, sorry. That's . . ." I didn't have the words to describe the situation properly so I made an explosive gesture with my hands, adding a few sound effects for emphasis.

Blue nodded. "Yeah. My thoughts exactly."

"No!" I shouted, jolting upright as I ejected myself from my dreams.

"Are you all right?" SJ—who'd been doing her homework at the infirmary table across from me—scurried over.

"Yeah, yeah," I said hurriedly, swallowing hard afterward. I took a breath and adjusted to the light. "I was dreaming about a fire and that building collapsing again. But this time . . ." I tried to remember. "It was weird. For a second, before the ceiling came down, I thought I saw a flash of my brothers. They were blurred into the image along with the smoke and the ash and when I saw them I felt . . . scared."

"Scared that they were in danger?"

"No," I clarified. "Scared *of them* I think."

I shook my head and tried to will away the headache I felt brewing. "I don't know. It was pretty blurry. I think the dark magic from that corset is still messing with my mind."

"Probably. It is only your third day in the infirmary, Crisa. You must give yourself time to recover. You have been through a lot."

"Yeah." I took a deep breath and shrugged. "Let's change the subject."

"Okay," SJ conceded. "Have you given any more thought to your decision regarding Natalie Poole?"

"Ugh, again with that, SJ? I told you I was thinking about it."

"Yes, but are you thinking it *through*?" she countered.

"What does that mean?

"Crisa," she began slowly. "You are very smart, quick on your feet, clever in a pinch, and naturally skilled at planning big, creative endeavors."

"Why do I feel like there's a 'but' coming?"

SJ crossed her arms. "*But* sometimes you let your impulsive instinct compromise your long game. Like in the case of your prologue prophecy for instance." She gave me a stern look that caught me off guard.

"Wait," I said. "Hold on. Do you think that it was wrong of me not to read it?"

"I am not certain," she responded. "But I do think that you were angry about all the trouble it has caused, overwhelmed with everything Liza told you, and glad to have an opportunity to do whatever you wanted without the Author or anyone else stopping you. So maybe your decision was colored by too much emotion."

"Thanks for the vote of confidence," I replied.

SJ's tone shifted. "I am sorry, I am not trying to upset you. I just want you to think very carefully. What happens in the future might be a frightening thing in more ways than one, and it is best not to carve a path for it on a whim."

"I'm not going to," I assured her. "But I can't make this Natalie decision—or any other decision—on pure logic and reason alone, SJ. It's not a bad way to live life or anything, but it is not a balanced one either. I need to trust my heart just as much as I do my head—the same way I trust Blue as much as I trust you. You're both very different, but if I listen to either one of you alone then stuff doesn't flow as well as it could. We work best when we work together. So I am going to heed your advice and think about this Natalie thing from a logical standpoint, but you've got to appreciate that my gut instinct matters too. Just like it mattered when I decided not to read my prologue prophecy."

"I understand," SJ responded. "And perhaps . . ." Her face fell with sorrow for an instant. "Maybe this time it is you who is thinking clearly while I am letting emotion get the better of my judgment. I shall not nag you about this or your prophecy any longer, Crisa. I do not even have one, so what do I know anyway."

A beat of awkward silence passed.

"I thought you said you were fine with all of that," I said carefully.

"I am. Truly," SJ asserted. "It just takes some getting used to. You spend your whole life thinking you are something and then suddenly find out that it was all a lie. It is a lot to process."

"Yeah," I agreed. "But the question still remains—*are you processing it?*"

SJ put her fingers to her temple and gave a long sigh. "I am trying," she said. "For now, let us leave it at that."

It was night.

The windows were open in the infirmary—not just the ones closest to my cot, but all of them. My friends hadn't been by for some time. Between that and the scent of anti-bacterial soap, I was beginning to feel claustrophobic. The winter breeze was a nice reminder of the outside world that awaited me as soon as I was better. The school's head nurse had told me I only needed to stay in the infirmary for two more days. Then I could go back to my room and regular routine.

One of the nurse's assistants came by and took the cold compress off my head, wringing out the excess water in a silver dish. She had short dark hair that stuck out like a ball of iron wool. Her face was kindly and her nose was pointed like a foxhound.

"Are you hungry?" she asked. "You were asleep during dinner service, but I could go get you something from the kitchens."

"That'd be great, thank you." I smiled.

She nodded, picked up the silver dish, and exited the room. I leaned my head back against the thick white pillow.

There wasn't much light in the room. The infirmary staff must've dimmed all the fixtures when I was asleep so that I might rest better. A half-lit chandelier glowed faintly near the ceiling's rafters and the moon outside provided a ghostly glow, but the main source of light came from candles on the bedside tables.

The flickering flames and white lace curtains fluttering in the silence of the empty, icy room suddenly put me on guard.

Dreamjà vu.

I sat up and reached for my robe pocket. I'd asked Blue to bring me my wandpin from our room. I had left it on a shelf in our closet when I was changing into Mauvrey's death gown before the ball. Having it at my side put my mind at ease.

I touched it in my pocket, hoping to calm my nerves, but I felt something wicked this way coming. As I thought this, a flurry of red sparks zipped through a window.

In a flash, one of my least favorite women appeared.

Lena Lenore was wearing a sleeveless, silvery pink dress just like she had been in my dream of this exact moment when we were back in the Forbidden Forest. Her sleek, dark mane fell behind her shoulders and her eyes sparkled like the stars.

I knew she could pass through the In and Out Spells because Liza had told us she was one of the Fairy Godmothers who'd created them, but it would've been super helpful if she wasn't. I wanted as much distance between Lenore and me as possible.

"Hello, Crisanta," she said as she patted her hair and tucked away a few out-of-place strands. The ruby spiral of her multi-purpose ring glistened in the candlelight.

"Lenore," I said, swinging my legs over the edge of the cot. "I had a feeling you might be checking in on me."

"Is that so?" the Godmother replied.

"Yeah, well, the wicked never rest, do they?"

Lenore stepped closer. Her heels clicked against the stone floor and I rose to meet her.

"You would do well to at least try and mask your contempt, Crisanta. Do you really want me to dislike you more than I already do?"

"Is that even possible?" I asked. "Weren't you just here the other night trying to get my headmistress to give you proof that could condemn me to Alderon?"

Lenore shrugged ever so slightly. "I have an agenda. I am not denying it."

"What about our deal? I thought as long as I kept your despicable Godmother habits a secret you would leave me and my friends alone."

"I said no such thing. Our arrangement was that I would not *harm* you or your friends so long as you keep your mouth shut. But that does not mean I cannot actively try to find another way to get rid of you in the meantime."

"And here I thought you weren't going to make our conflict interesting." I put my hand on my hip defiantly. "You don't scare me, Lenore."

"Well you scare me, Crisanta Knight," Lenore replied coolly. "And you know what I do with the things I fear? I make sure they never see the light of day."

Lenore was four feet away from me and her breathing was even. She reached for her ruby ring and I snatched my wandpin out of my pocket. Both our accessories transformed into wands simultaneously. I instantly morphed mine into a spear.

Our weapons glowed vaguely in the dim light of the infirmary. Lenore raised her wand. "Calm down, Crisanta. I only want to show you something."

She waved her wand and a streak of red sparks flooded from the tip and levitated between us. The sparks formed the holographic shape of a woman. She had braided black hair and a proud face.

"We were finally able to root out the source the antagonists have been using to learn which protagonists pose a threat to them."

"Who is she?" I asked, moving closer to the hologram. The woman seemed about forty. She wore a floor-length silver cape with a hood.

"She was one of the Scribes," Lenore replied. "One of my three most esteemed and elite Fairy Godmothers—trusted to keep all the Author's protagonist books and serve the will of the twenty-six ambassadors, and my own, in terms of protagonist selection."

"*Was?*"

"Now that she has proven to be a traitor, we no longer have use for her services. She was stripped of her Godmother powers yesterday and thrown into Alderon where she belongs." Lenore waved her wand and the hologram shattered like glass. The sparks rained to the floor and disintegrated the moment they touched it.

"Why did you show me that?" I asked. "You offering me the job or something?"

"Hardly," Lenore huffed. "I am offering you a reminder." Lenore took a couple of steps closer. "This woman's name was Tania. She and I have been good friends and close colleagues for many years. I was very fond of her."

"And?"

"And I was there yesterday when she was tossed into Alderon. There were several antagonists and monsters near the border at the time. About sixteen seconds after we threw Tania across the boundary of the In and Out Spell, I watched two ogres rip her apart in front of my eyes and I didn't even blink. That is because I have no tolerance or mercy for people who undermine me and the society I live to serve. So make no mistake, Crisanta Knight—one misstep and imagine what pleasure I'll take in seeing you destroyed."

I transformed my spear back to its wand form and crossed my arms. "I guess it's a good thing I'm known for treading lightly then, isn't it?"

Lenore gave me one of her classic, intimidating smiles, showing off her pearly teeth. Then with another wave of her wand, she evaporated into sparks. Her swarm of energy zipped out the nearest window. The backdraft extinguished all the candles in the room and caused my hair and the hem of my robe to whoosh behind me.

I stood at the window and stared out at the night, watching Lenore's red sparks disappear into the stars.

Dream me was running. Daniel was right behind her. The two were bolting across unfamiliar streets and sidewalks. It was dark, but I knew they were on Earth because of the cars that zoomed by.

He was in a suit and she was in a black dress—not a gown, but more like something you would wear to a nightclub. Dream me was also wearing black combat boots, which was lucky given that she and Daniel were barely able to avoid being hit by cars as they ran. She jumped and slid over the hood of a sleek silver one as it halted beside her.

Flashes of Natalie and Ryan Jackson appeared over this main scene. I saw them dancing in the moonlight. I saw them talking on a picnic blanket. I saw them kissing in a stairwell. But then I heard her scream and it was like all of time stood still.

The sky above Daniel and dream me suddenly started to crackle with thunder. The ground began to shake. Coarse winds howled like a violent warning—lifting fallen leaves and trash into the air.

"Knight!"

I turned to where Daniel's voice had come from, but he was gone. So were the streets and the people and the wind. All that was left was silence and a plaque that read "1890."

Then Natalie screamed a second time and I woke up.

Sunlight was streaming in through the infirmary window. I was alone except for the company of Daniel (the real one this time), who was sitting in a chair by my bedside, reading.

He hadn't noticed me stirring at first, but when I hit my head against the headboard, it got his attention.

"Ow," I yelped.

"Careful there, Knight. Don't you already have enough of a reason to be in here? No need to add concussion to the list."

"Hardy har har." I grabbed my quill and dream journal off the side table and jotted down more notes from my subconscious.

"How long have you been here?" I asked.

"I don't know, a few hours."

"Nothing better to do?"

"Nope."

"Liar."

A beat passed between us. I was glad he was here. At the given moment I also envied him, both him and Jason. While five months of detention awaited SJ, Blue, and myself, Lord Channing had not punished Daniel and Jason for going AWOL.

Protagonists from their school left campus all the time because fighting monsters, going on quests, and surviving in the wilderness were considered important extracurricular activities for heroes. In some cases, I think they even got course credit.

The only thing that Jason and Daniel had gotten in trouble for was losing a couple of Pegasi and a carriage. But they had yet to be officially punished for that either. I speculated that they might avoid it entirely given what they had brought back with them in return.

A dragon.

Lady Agnue forbade me from keeping Lucky on our campus. As such, we had to come to a different arrangement. Lucky would live at Lord Channing's. They had a much bigger campus and were going to utilize Lucky for practicing hero drills.

I was worried about the idea at first, but Jason told me the other day that Lucky was loving it. The boys weren't allowed to hurt him, so my dragon got plenty of exercise and was keeping himself entertained by taking shots at a bunch of heroes while they practiced dodging his fire.

Sigh.

I really missed that dragon. Hopefully we would see each other again soon.

I tucked my hair behind my ears and turned to face Daniel. "It's nice of you to check in on me," I said in all seriousness. "It's my last day here and I'm feeling much better, so you didn't have to."

"Yeah, well, what am I gonna do? We're friends now, right?"

Now it was my turn to shrug. "Looks like." A smile creeped at the corners of my lips. "But let's call it a trial run just to be on the safe side."

"That sounds fair."

My eyes drifted to the table where SJ had been doing her homework the other afternoon. She hadn't come by to see me since our talk about her lack of a protagonist book, and I wondered how she was doing. Then I wondered about the things she'd said about my prologue prophecy in that same conversation.

"Hey, Daniel. You've always been brutally blunt with me. Since we're trial run friends, can I ask you something?"

He looked at me with a raised eyebrow. "I guess."

"In all honesty, do you think it was stupid of me not to look at my prologue prophecy? I mean, with everything that's supposedly coming and the role that I supposedly play in it, SJ thinks it was dumb of me not to look. She thinks that I was acting too much on impulse and emotion when I made the decision."

"I get where she's coming from, Knight," Daniel replied. "But I'm on your side in this case; I don't think it was stupid. I think it was admirable."

"Really?"

"Yeah. If I had thought that refusing to look at my prologue prophecy was an option when mine first popped up, I would have done the same thing. You're taking your fate into your own hands and accepting yourself and your future. That's something to be proud of."

I opened my right fist and stared at my palm. The mark there was very light, but the brand was still perfectly clear. I'd shown SJ, Blue, and Jason already, but this was the first time I'd had a chance to speak with Daniel alone since we'd returned to school.

"You wanna hear something funny?" I said. "That was my inner strength the whole time—the one the magic watering can needed me to figure out. Self-Acceptance." I held my hand out for him to see.

"You're right; that is funny," Daniel said with a wry grin. "But you want to hear something hilarious? That was my mark too."

For about the billionth time since our introduction, Daniel's words caught me off guard. My heart stopped for a second as it processed this precious piece of information.

"Seriously?" I asked.

"'Fraid so," he said opening his own palm and stretching his hand in remembrance. "The mark's been gone a while, but self-acceptance is the inner strength that the witch's watering can took from me."

"Hang on," I interjected. "If you're so 'self-accepting' then why didn't you show me or any of us your mark in the first place?"

"Because I didn't care what you guys thought of me. I've never really put much weight on the judgment of others. I don't mean that to be offensive; it's just the way that I am. I guess it goes along with the whole 'self-acceptance' territory. I'm not really all that concerned with how other people see me because I know how I see me—you know?"

"I do, actually," I admitted. "At least I do now, anyway."

"The only time I didn't feel that secure was in the Forbidden Forest," Daniel continued. "When the witch's watering can took our sources of inner strength, I tried to put more distance between us because I was afraid of the consequences. I told you that I don't blame you for any of the stuff that's in my prologue prophecy, Knight. I've always accepted that it's my problem and that I had to be the one to do something about it, like going with you guys to find the Author. But under the influence of that watering can I blamed you for my problems. So I stayed away from you during our time in Therewolf prison so that I wouldn't lash out at you. But you still managed to overhear what I told Jason the night of our escape anyway. Remember? About me believing that you ruined my life?"

I remembered. And now I understood.

"You didn't mean it," I said.

"No," he replied. "I didn't."

I brought my knees to my chest and hugged them. "You know something, Daniel? Not that you care what I think or anything, but you're a pretty decent guy. And I don't know if it goes without saying after everything we've been through, but I'll say it nonetheless. I was wrong about you and I'm sorry."

"Not surprising," Daniel commented. "You're wrong about a lot of things."

"You certainly seem to think so," I scoffed.

"It's more of a general consensus."

"All right then, Mr. General Consensus," I countered. "Since you're so keen on telling me how wrong I am regardless of my feelings, then tell me whether or not I'm wrong now."

"About what?"

"The other big issue that's hanging over my future. SJ told you guys about the Mark Two that Liza sent me. Our former Author wants to know what I have decided to do in regards to Natalie. So tell me, Daniel Daniels, in all your infamous directness— do you think I have a chance at controlling my Pure Magic enough to send a warning to Natalie but still keep my heart from turning dark like my disease foretells? Or am I wrong about that too?"

Daniel was quiet. He seemed to think on the question heavily. When he finally responded it came across without a hint of doubt. "You're not going to turn dark. You don't have it in you."

Shame passed through me as memories of recent events haunted my thoughts.

"But I think that I do," I responded. "Actually, I know that I do. Helping Nadia and the antagonists succeed wouldn't be one of my Inherent Fates if it wasn't. Besides that, think about all the things I've done. I almost killed Arian in Alderon. I didn't just go back to my step-grandmother's house in the Valley of Strife for closure; I went back for revenge. Even you were surprised by that. And do you remember what happened in Hann. Münden? The Pied Piper's music was only able to fully hypnotize people with pure hearts, like Yunru and those other kids. As you so keenly pointed out, the fact that I wasn't entranced in the same way means that my heart isn't pure."

"So?" he replied with a shrug. "Who cares if you're not pure of heart? Practically no one in the world is, but that doesn't make us bad people. I wasn't fully hypnotized, which means I'm not pure of heart either, and do you think I'm a bad person?"

"No."

"Then there you go. Purity is not a requirement for goodness. It's just another factor. And if it's any consolation, I think it's probably a good thing you're not pure. It makes you more relatable. And it makes you more interesting."

"Um, thanks?"

He nodded. "Plus, all this purity vs. darkness stuff aside, I know that if you set your mind to it and keep your magic in check, you'll be able to fight against your disease."

"What makes you so sure?"

"Because you're stronger than your impulses. Think of it this way: how many times since we first met have you wanted to punch me?"

"Hundreds."

"And how many times have you actually done it?"

"None," I responded. Then I remembered our time in the genie lamp when he pushed me to the brink of my patience. "I did kick you once though."

"Yeah," he admitted. "But I probably deserved it."

"Yeah, you did," I huffed and then smiled. "But hey, if you can promise not to annoy me so much then I can promise to never do it again."

Daniel looked at me like he was sizing up a sparring partner. That smirk I knew so well crossed his face. "You know what they say, Knight. Don't make promises you can't keep."

CHAPTER 29

My New Beginning

arious ends were coming.

It was my last night in the infirmary, fall semester at Lady Agnue's was finishing up, and more than anything it felt like a big chapter in my life was coming to a close. As acceptance of all three settled in, I couldn't help but ponder on the bigger quandaries that had defined my path up 'til now.

My mother had always told me I was going to be a great protagonist. However, the rest of the world had spent years trying to convince me of the opposite, or at the very least attempting to sway my belief about what type of protagonist I could be.

But the question that had been hanging over me since I'd come back from my adventures was what kind of protagonist did I *want* to be?

Protagonist was a weighty word that meant many different things to many different people. I'd spent so much time trying to make my life mean something on those terms—on everyone else's terms—and what had it gotten me? A protagonist journey characterized by regret, confusion, and unresolved fears; and more than anything a protagonist journey defined by everyone else.

But no longer.

Now only I would define my protagonist journey.

When the morning came and I was finally discharged from the

care of the school nurses, I would have to return to the world and brave all that was to come. But that did not scare me. I accepted myself now—who I was and who I wanted to be. Coming to terms with this had given me strength. And if I let it, I knew it would continue to give me strength going forward.

As a calm settled over me, I listened to the light December rain beat against the In and Out Spell surrounding the school.

Our school's force field was weird when it came to weather. While sunshine and breezes could get through just fine, the ordinarily invisible In and Out Spell around Lady Agnue's prevented bad weather from assailing us. Rain, snow, and any other kind of drastic fluctuation in the atmosphere was repelled by the spell's magic. I guess the Godmothers cast it that way so that our shining school would always look perfect.

As I glanced out the window, I saw the normally invisible force field flash with a bright patchwork of multi-colored lights as it worked at maximum capacity to keep the detrimental weather out. I watched the rain pummel the dome and slide down its sides to the tune of a beautiful rhythm.

Soon enough the weeks would change that rain into snow and a new year would begin. Actually, this was already in motion for me. It was my birthday today. I was now seventeen.

I'd asked my friends not to make a big deal about it, but after dinner they'd snuck into the infirmary with a cupcake and a lit candle, insisting on the tradition. They'd even made me a new dartboard for my room as a present, as the old one that Blue, SJ, and I used to have had been confiscated during our absence.

The gift I was more interested in, though, was the book Daniel had brought me this afternoon. I'd told him about this book a few days ago—the one I'd seen in the library at the Capitol Building when Arian's men were chasing us. I had remembered it many times since then, including when I'd discovered the Scribes' protagonist book library and when we'd been in Germany with Yunru and Berto.

I was glad that the memory had been ingrained so well, as I'd only recently recognized the book's importance and was certain that it might help us better understand what we were up against.

I'd asked Daniel to see if one of his friends at the Capitol Building could "borrow" the text and send it to him. He had, and they did. As a result, there was currently a book titled *Shadow Guardians—Origins, Dangers, & Weaknesses* resting on my nightstand.

Of course I would return the copy eventually, but for now I was excited to have it. I smiled at the book and the birthday cupcake wrapper beside it.

It was sweet of my friends to put in the effort, and I appreciated the gesture. I'd always loved celebrating my birthday. The occasion just didn't feel right at the moment because lately I'd been far more focused on someone else's birthday—Natalie's.

According to Liza's prediction the girl would be born very soon, which meant that it was time for me to make my decision. And after days of reflection, I finally knew what I wanted that to be. Because at the end of the day, I knew who I wanted to be.

I picked up the Mark Two from my nightstand and flipped it open. "Liza," I said. The compact flashed a few times before Liza's face appeared in the mirror.

"Crisa," she yawned. "It's late. Are you okay?"

"Yeah," I replied calmly. "I've just been thinking a lot about Natalie and I finally have an answer for you."

Liza rubbed her eyes and tried to blink away her tiredness. "And?"

"I wanna do it. I want to develop my magic—train myself to be strong enough to reach her before time runs out."

Liza was wide awake now. "Are you sure about this, Crisa?" she asked seriously. "You understand what this might mean for you?"

"Yes," I responded firmly. "I know the risks; I know the magic can either burn me out or more likely corrupt me and turn me dark. But I also know what's at stake. Not just for me—for Natalie, her realm, and this one too. Which is why I'm not going to cower behind doubt and lack of belief in myself when I can actually do something about it. That's not the type of person I want to be. So I don't care how hard or painful or dangerous it is, I'm going to learn how to use my magic. I'm going to make myself strong enough to control it. And I am not going to give up until I do."

"All right." Liza nodded. "I'm going to hold you to that."

"So will I," I responded.

"We'll start your training after the new year," Liza continued. "Now it's late and you should be asleep. I'll talk to you in the morning. Get some rest."

I huffed in amusement. "You know that's never really an option for people like us."

I put the Mark Two down, ending the call, and leaned against my headboard.

What does my life mean? And what do I stand for?

I'd once asked myself these questions without any clue of the answers. At last, I finally knew the answers to both.

My life meant what everyone else's did—a chance to live it. A chance to make choices, and forge a path, and work toward whoever you wanted to be in this world.

And what did I stand for? I stood for someone who was confidently, unapologetically, and unwaveringly proud of the person I wanted to be:

A hero.

Not because I desired to be problem-free by means of some impervious physical strength or fearlessness. But because I wanted to take responsibility for those problems, have the conviction of character to accept my challenges and weaknesses, and learn to use my internal strength to never give up and keep fighting on despite them.

And a princess.

Not because I wanted to be swept off my feet at balls or harmonize with the song of woodland creatures. But because, no matter how grave the circumstance or how much the world may try to beat hope and faith out of me, I never wanted my heart to turn hard. I wanted to have the esteem to believe in myself, the compassion to believe in others, and the ability to put aside things like self-interest and pride in order to make graceful and honorable decisions.

That is who I wanted to be—who I stood for. Someone valiant and vulnerable, someone simultaneously strong and soft of heart, and someone who would have the courage and conviction to never stop believing she could be all those things and more.

End of Book Three

ABOUT THE AUTHOR

Geanna Culbertson adores chocolate chip cookies, watching Netflix in pajamas, and the rain. Of course, in her case, the latter is kind of hard to come by. As her dad notes, "In California, we don't have seasons, we have special effects."

On the flip side, she is deeply afraid of ice skating and singing in public. Although she forces herself to do both on occasion because she believes facing your fears can be good for you.

During the week Geanna lives a disciplined, yet preciously ridiculous lifestyle. She gets up before dawn to train and write. Goes to work where she enjoys a double life as a kid undercover in a grown-up world. Then comes home, eats, writes, and watches one of her favorite TV shows.

On weekends, however, Geanna's heart, like her time, is completely off the leash. Usually she'll teach martial arts at her local karate studio, pursue yummy foods, and check out whatever's new at her fav stores. To summarize, she'll wander, play, disregard the clock, and get into as many shenanigans as possible.

Geanna is also passionate about writing books that will speak to young girls and their potential. She is a sponsor and strong proponent of Girls on the Run, Los Angeles, an organization whose vision is "a world where every girl knows and activates her limitless potential and is free to boldly pursue her dreams."